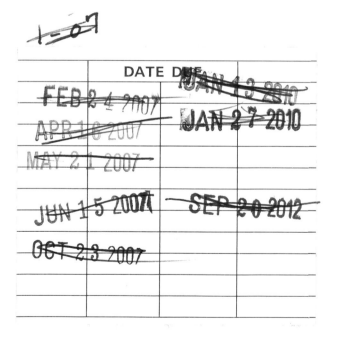

HALF LIFE

ALSO BY SHELLEY JACKSON

The Melancholy of Anatomy (short stories)

Patchwork Girl (hypertext novel)

"Skin" (a story in tattoos)

HALF

A Novel

LIFE

Shelley Jackson

HarperCollins*Publishers*

HarperCollins books may be purchased for educational, business, or sales promotional use. For information, please write: Special Markets Department, HarperCollins Publishers, 10 East 53rd Street, New York, NY 10022.

FIRST EDITION

Designed by Elliott Beard

Printed on acid-free paper

Library of Congress Cataloging-in-Publication Data
Jackson, Shelley.
Half life : a novel / Shelley Jackson.— 1st ed.
p. cm.
ISBN-13: 978-0-06-088235-8
ISBN-10: 0-06-088235-2 (alk. paper)
1. Conjoined twins—Fiction. I. Title.
PS3560.A2448H35 2006
813'.54—dc22 2006041089

06 07 08 09 10 ID/RRD 10 9 8 7 6 5 4 3 2 1

For Pamela, of course

PART ONE

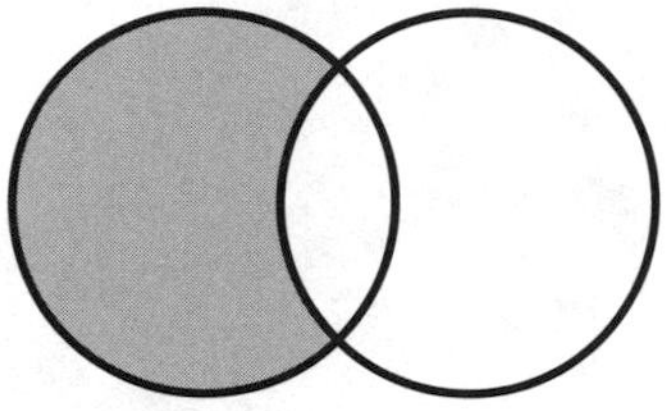

Boolean Operator: NOT

UNITY FOUNDATION RELEASE & WAIVER

You should have received two copies. Each twin should fill out his or her own copy. If, as in the special case of an insensible or "vegetable" twin, only one copy is submitted, the *Non Compos Mentis* box must be checked. Please consider your answers carefully and append a personal statement in which you explain your decision at greater length. If you require more space you may attach another page or pages with a paper clip, NOT a staple. Your cooperation will help us meet the needs of future clients.

I, NORA GRAY OLNEY, a ___ male / X female twofer, age 28, being of sound mind and body, request the surgical removal of ___ myself / X my conjoined twin BLANCHE GREY OLNEY for the following reasons(s) [please check all that apply]:

___ euthanasia (___my twin is / ___I am suffering or moribund)
___ mental health (my twin is crazy or I am crazy)
___ self-defense (I have reason to believe my twin will harm me)
___ self-sacrifice (I have reason to believe I will harm my twin)
___ sexual thrill (___ for me / ___ my twin)
___ religious beliefs (___ mine / ___ my twin's)
___ philosophical convictions (___ mine / ___ my twin's)
___ determination to quit this vale of tears (___ mine / ___ my twin's)
X irreconcileable differences

I X am / ___ am not acquainted with the philosophy of the Unity Foundation. I X am / ___ am not prepared for the censure of society in general and the Together-

ness Group in particular. I _X_ am / ___ am not prepared to sign an oath of secrecy regarding the existence and identities of doctors and fellow patients, the location of the clinic, and anything else I may know or suspect about the Unity Foundation, including its rules, philosophy, patient profile, physical plant, waste-disposal practises, medical equipment, funding, legal status, etc. I _X_ am / ___ am not prepared to sign a statement absolving the Unity Foundation of any responsibility whatsoever, whether for the failure *or success* of surgery, later complications, or any change of heart that I or my twin may have during or after surgery. I _X_ understand / ___ do not understand that this operation is irreversible and that the removed twin will be in a condition nonconducive to life.

My twin is ___ *compos mentis* / _X_ *non compos mentis.*

I am the _X_ recto / ___ verso twin. The twin to be removed is the _X_ verso / ___ recto.

Signed ____________________

Personal Statement

Blanche, white night of my dark day. My sister, my self. Blanche: a cry building behind sealed lips, then blowing through. First the pout, then the plosive; the meow of the vowel; then the fricative sound of silence.

Shhhh.

Blanche is sleeping. She has been sleeping for fifteen years.

I can tell you the exact moment I knew she was waking up. But allow me a day's grace. Let me remember that last afternoon, unimportant in itself, wonderfully unimportant, when I was still Nora, just Nora, Nora Olney, Nora alone.

The flags lining Market Street from Church to Castro flexed and snapped, showing sometimes one, sometimes two linked rings. The stop signs shuddered on their spines. The wind had picked up in the late afternoon, as usual, and now the whole sky seemed to be toppling sideways over the Twin Peaks, carrying with it whorls of smoke from the incinerators and pure white spooks of fog. I was meandering home from the movie theater without the tickets I'd gone there for, joggling two oranges in a plastic bag and going over my excuses. Blanche was sleeping. Of course she was. I dropped into the gutter to skirt some crowd-control fences ganged in readiness against a streetlight, and our heads collided. A distant, confused echo of her pain overtook and lost itself in mine, but her breathing stayed steady and deep.

I was threading my way along the curb. The sidewalk was already thronged with out-of-towners, already dressed for Pride in brand-new T-shirts with rub-

bery silk-screened slogans, "One's Company" and "2^2" and "YESIAMESE." They were strolling in twos and threes and fours of varying molecular structure, exchanging glances of appraisal and nervous pleasure. The singletons anxious to understand, to be seen understanding. The twofers beaming, indecently grateful for one weekend of sanctioned self-satisfaction. Tomorrow they'd all be here: Siamese and Siamystics, conjoined and joiners, doppelgängers and gruesome twosomes, double-talkers, double-dealers, twice-told tale tellers. An odious prospect. Already I was getting looks of curiosity and sympathy, like the birthday child in a leukemia ward.

The twin amplifiers flanking the temporary stage back at Eighteenth Street retched, rid themselves of five beats of that ubiquitous "We-R-2-R-1-4-Ever," went dead. No we're not, I thought, reflexively. I pulled one hood of my hoodie farther over Blanche, but her blond hair spilled out, catching a rogue ray of sun, and the tourists gave each other quick digs with their elbows. It's Sleeping Beauty! As for the hag with the two-faced apple in her pocket, everyone knows how the story goes. Sooner or later she'll have to turn the other cheek.

"Repent," advised the wizened lady in the plastic visor who protested every day at Market and Sixteenth. Today her hand-lettered sign read "GO BACK TO SIAM."

"Oh, I *do*," I said, fervently, hand on hearts. She slit her eyes at me, suspicious.

Let me be clear, while I still can. I am a twofer—what they used to call a Siamese twin, though I prefer "conjoined," with its faint echo of the alchemists' *conjunctio* and those copulatives copulating in grammar books. I'm the one on the left, your right. Blanche is on my right, your left. I—oh, say it: *we*—have strong cheekbones, long earlobes, hazel eyes, and dirty-blond hair, which is also usually dirty blond hair. Glamour is not very important to me, and it seems goofy to groom Blanche, like trimming my pubes into a heart. But I'm not really a hag. I am stern, though, and wear the marks of habitual sternness, while Blanche is smooth as soap. I never used to need a mirror to see what I looked like, I just turned my head. But we have grown apart, Blanche in her beauty sleep and I.

Dicephalus dipus dibrachius. That's two heads, two legs, and two arms: standard-issue twofer. Aside from that pair of face cards we hold an average hand, not much different from yours. Novelties include the short third col-

larbone we share between us; a spinal column that begins to divide in two around the sixth thoracic vertebra, flaring the upper chest; two windpipes, two and a half lungs, and a deuce of hearts. Audrey says vampires also have two hearts, one good, one bad. While the good heart beats, the vampire is as capable of kindness as any human soul, but when the good heart stops, the beat of the bad heart strengthens in the dying breast, and makes a decent woman rise from her coffin to prey on everyone she once loved best. The blood of kinfolk wets her chin.

If this is true of twofers too, I know which heart is mine.

I cut around the flower stall at the corner, vaulting a white bucket in which a single sunflower was privately flaunting itself, filling the whole bucket with a secret glow. My shadow eclipsed it for the duration of a blink. Blanche's head jerked when I landed, but this time, my hand was there to steady it. In the lee of the stall, I suddenly felt the lingering warmth of the June day. My temples prickled. The smell of smoke and roses rose around me. The light strengthened, the streetcar tracks shone like new scars, and I thought of the young woman recently killed by a streetcar on Church—"Decapitated," Trey had reported with relish, though you couldn't believe everything he said—and let go of Blanche's neck.

"Nora!"

Across the street, a duplex figure in a festival T-shirt waved a fluttering pink flyer. Cindi and Mindi? I could not remember their names, but I had a feeling they rhymed. Twofer names so often do. Jane and Elaine, then, or Mitzi and Fritzi, were passing out flyers with both hands next to a leaning cutout of RubiaMorena, this year's Pride queen. Knowing it was futile, I kept my face lowered as I crossed, as if trying to read something in the shadow that glided along with me, symmetrical and terrible as a Rorschach blot.

"Nora! Blanche!" A flyer sailed past me and plastered itself on the trunk of one of the palm trees on the meridian.

Grimacing, I raised my head. These activist twofers always seemed to make a point of saluting both of us. Both of her chugged up, twin chins doubling as they beamed with the bliss of outreach. (Kelly and Shelley?) We did the tongue and groove kiss, the one where you dock your heads together, kiss the air between. *Left.* The first time a San Francisco hipster tried this on me, I thought he was trying to tongue my saddle. An honest mistake, but he never forgave me that snap kick. *And right.*

Over their shoulder, I watched RubiaMorena stagger, spin, and fall. Some Togetherists attempted to right her, then gave up when the wind felled her a second time. I'd been seeing their orange T-shirts all month. The open secret that most of their members were singletons had become an embarrassment to them; they'd be recruiting aggressively this weekend.

"Everytwo's *so* looking forward to Audrey's film. Tyou must be so proud! Tyou'll be at the premiere, of course?" The second person plural a local twofer rights group had tried to introduce a couple years ago had not caught on, but a few devotees still used it with enthusiasm.

"Blanche might go, but I don't think I can make it," I drawled.

Technically, they laughed—a simultaneous nasal huff—but only out of nervousness. A subordinated twin was *not funny*. "Well, we'd all be delighted to see tyou. And I'm sure it would mean a lot to Audrey." They reached out and hooked a strand of hair out of Blanche's mouth. I wondered if one of them had a crush on Blanche. Talk about pathetic fallacy! Might as well have a crush on a freckle or a polyp.

"Don't go by the listings in the paper, we've made some last-minute changes. The latest times are on the flyers." Pressing a couple into my hand, they turned. "Oh no!" They hurried toward their fallen queen, whose blank back was already paisley with footprints.

"I think I can make do with just one," I said, lunging after them. "Thank *tyou* anyway."

Ugh! Departing, I made an involuntary warding-off gesture. The oranges, flung out and jerked back, bounced together, reminding me of a toy from our childhood, two Plexiglas balls on cords knotted to a ring. You raised and lowered your hand, letting the balls bang together harder and harder until they met at the top as well as the bottom of their arc, completing a circle to which each contributed half. Granny had always said (with, I think, a morbid pleasure) it was an accident waiting to happen. She said this about a lot of things, and had proved to be right about some of them.

"Excuse me, are you radioactive?" said a bald girl with a clipboard. I shouldered past her and turned toward home, zipping up my hoodie. It was getting cold; the fog was closing over the handsome narrow houses with their rainbow beach umbrellas, their twofer beach umbrellas, their rainbow twofer beach umbrellas. I looked up, and farther up, straining to see the rocky top of the hill whose name I still don't know, though I've lived in its late-afternoon shadow for almost ten years. The sky was one mute shriek of

white. I dropped my gaze, shot through with sheen and comets, and located the sun I hadn't seen in its violet afterimage. Then I looked up again and found the sun proper by following its ghost. My eyes watered, the sun wobbled and slid apart into twin suns, abominably, and I thought, I have to get rid of Blanche.

This is going well, I think. The greenish, narrow-lined pages of the notebook I acquired from an old-fashioned stationery store out on Judah (National Brand Chemistry Notebook: Blue Cover, 120 Numbered Pages, Item No. 43-581) are steadily filling with small, black, left-leaning script. My hand moves slowly down each page, darkening it, as if I were pulling down shade after shade in a long, windowed hall. I'm writing with my left hand, though my penmanship is better with the right, because I trust it more, though even my left, while it never succumbed to that Lithobolia business, is not entirely clear of suspicion. It hovers, fidgets, dips down to tease out another phrase. Are these my words? I read them over. "Rid of Blanche." Funny. At the time I would have been justified in thinking I already was.

One day, Blanche shut up. When I looked right, she no longer looked left, neither to see what I was plotting nor to give me a chill of similitude. (Fear of mirrors: there's probably a name for that. Look it up if you like.) Her eyes closed, and she fell into a long, long sleep.

Sometimes, stirred by a dream she was dreaming, my finger twitched, my toe tapped. Sometimes while checking the date on a yogurt container or knotting a shoelace, I felt an incongruous rush of adrenaline. Aside from these tiny reminders, our body was mine. It grew up. I grew up, and Blanche was left behind, like a vacation puppy too dumb to bark after the shrinking license plate and the desperate faces tinged with aquamarine behind the glass.

My life really began then. I don't remember much of what came before, and what I do remember lacks heft. My memories are a clutch of images as unconvincing as those faux-antique photographic portraits ($15, $25 with gilt frame) tourists could pose for back in my hometown of Too Bad, NV, their flip-flops hidden under the hoop skirt, sunglasses and souvenir visors waiting just out of view on a plastic chair. I don't mind, I prefer the present tense.

But it turns out that what you don't know *can* hurt you.

In disentangling two pieces of string, one looks for the ends. If I am having trouble, at this late date, telling the two of us apart, the obvious solution is to go back to the beginning.

Misconceptions

She should have thought twice. Mama wanted to give a baby to her girlfriend, Max, as a tribute to Max's almost perfect masculinity. A surprise. It is possible that this explanation was conceived after the fact.

The fact was conceived on the bus from Hollywood, where Mama's big break had just fallen through. She had fired her agent in a fit of pique and was going back to New York, where they loved her. *They* being the regulars at a bohemian nightclub where she did a theatrical number that combined song and dance with dramatic monologue. Men wet their hankies when she did the sad song, and ladies in top hats licked their lips and sent her flowers. Mama peevishly plucked greasy bits out of a bag of doughnuts. Across the aisle sat my father, with sandwiches and soda and a dollhouse on his lap.

A man with a dollhouse! He looked like a giant. He had not bought a ticket for the house, so he only slowly and with much looking around decided it was safe to move it off his lap to the seat next to him. He quickly took it on his knees again when the driver turned to show his long, sad, dung-colored mustache. Somewhere between Hollywood and Agua Sucio Mama asked to touch the door with working handles, the chimney with the flue that opened, the toilet with its tank and little chain. Maybe their hands met like two beasts in the bedroom.

Who can resist a dollhouse? With working hinges . . . tiny mahogany doors with tiny brass latches . . . a miniature book with only four pages? The dollhouse had two halves that swung open to reveal the rooms inside. Two dolls could be side by side in a room and the next moment at opposite

ends of the house. How marvellous! The furniture was elegant, if higgledy-piggledy: the sofa stuck sideways in the stairwell had tasseled throw cushions. Mama stuck the tip of her baby finger in a ceramic potty with painted-blue ducks in the bowl, felt warmth flood her cheeks.

A man with a dollhouse on his lap, that's not a sight you see every day. His thighs tensed underneath it, keeping it stable despite the lurching bus. He had to sit a little sideways to fit, so the dollhouse blocked her view of his face, and she felt free to examine the big scuffed shoes set firmly on the floor, the shapeless dress pants that were hitched a little high, the white ankles, thick and knobbly, with pale hairs that stood straight out, the square fingers spread gently around the cornices.

But the dollhouse deserved closer attention. It was grand. A house of tinkling tea parties, cut flowers in vases, sealed envelopes on a silver salver. Silver salver? my mother wondered, distracted by the off-rhyme. Maybe *salver* was the wrong word. In any case a house of snowy aprons with big crisp bows, a Boston or a Philadelphia house. The kind of house she would want to settle into, had she not settled *on*, remember (she told herself, sternly), a gayer life, in every sense, actors and sexual perversity and little flats with noisy radiators and portable cocktail bars, political discussions and sophisticated humor and yes, a certain amount of tragedy, maybe not in her own life, but in some life close by. Hushed conversations over bad coffee in late-night New York delis where the pies languished under fluorescent lights and the dishes were too loud, the waiters huge and perfunctory, the napkins papery and flimsy as toilet paper, so they stuck to your lip in bits when you blew your nose—no, your despairing friend blew her—*his* nose and you had to reach out your hand and remove the tag of paper, a simple gesture but eloquent.

The dollhouse had real glass windowpanes. She had been staring at them for some time, trying to make out behind the glass the shapes of chair backs and mantelpieces, before she noticed an eye watching her through the dollhouse. This was possible because the windows lined up, front and back. She let out a little scream, and went to the bathroom to spritz perfume on her cleavage.

There was a vagrant on the side of the road, flagging the bus, her greasy black-walnut-colored hair sticking out in blades from under an unseasonable woolly hat. Improbably, the driver stopped for her—did he know her?—

and she made her way down the aisle, accidentally-on-purpose banging a few shoulders with her ratty knapsack. Sitting down in the aisle seat next to Mama, who was not yet anyone's mama. They looked down at their respective laps. On the one hand, we have the crisp yellow dress. On the other, the dingy jeans going to threads in the scuffed patches, a three-cornered tear disclosing a patch of surprisingly innocent leg: clean, slightly downy.

The vagrant reached across the aisle and knocked whimsically at the tiny front door of the dollhouse.

"Knock knock!" she said.

Papa flinched at the black, cracked nails tapping at the tiny glass panes.

While she glared at him, the tapping stopped. "Knock knock, I said!"

Papa cleared his throat. "Who's there?" he said.

"Interrupting cow."

"Interrup—"

"MOO!" shouted the vagrant, and laughed loudly. She plucked open the tiny door. Mama found herself sharing a pained look with Papa, as the dirty hand hooliganned through the downstairs. (Much later, Papa discovered something was missing: a tiny canary in a filigree cage, perhaps.)

Mama began to suspect she had wound up on the wrong bus, as the sealed hum of its progress down the interstate gave way to the old-ladyish squeaks and exclamations of a chassis asked to cope with stretches of—can this possibly be a *dirt road*?—hard ruts and cattle guards, as it flounced heavily through what seemed to be the tiniest burgs in creation. Mama, a Brooklyn baby, had never seen towns, uh, *hamlets* like these—you could only call them towns in contrast to the practically interstellar emptiness around them. One toaster, an armchair, and a standing lamp would look like Manhattan against, for example, the salt flats they'd passed a while ago, where a small dog pointed out by her smelly seatmate as a "ky-ote," though it looked like any old mutt to her, had looked back over his shoulder at her, one paw raised, stopped in mid-trot on some important but not too pressing errand by the spacecraft passing through. It was a memorable look, both knowing and disinterested, a look Mama would like to try out herself in other circumstances. Now, in town, "town," they stopped in the middle of the street, engine running, while the driver sloped off into the tinted blue deep end of the windscreen and disappeared, probably into a bar, as Mama thought gloomily, while her strange seatmate (but Mama wasn't scared of her, she was from New York, she was

used to characters) said it right out loud, "Probably gone for a tall one." It didn't look like much of a bar, it was a long low building with a heavy overhanging roof like a shoebox with the wrong lid on it, and the few letters still dangling from the signboard outside, B, W, didn't spell anything that made any sense to her. The bus was rumbling under her like a hovercraft. She was awfully high, she could look right over the scattered trailers and, well, she'd call them bungalows, they weren't houses (houses looked like the one the nice man opposite was holding in his lap), and while they were hovering there, there was time for a lone tumbleweed to enter town by the same road they'd come in on, naturally, since it was the only road, bounce, flop, flirt, and whirl the length of the main street, pass them, pause, and with a single madcap bound continue on its way out of town eastward into the gathering dusk, while her seatmate sang in a cracked voice, "Drifting along with the tumbling tu-ummmbleweeds." Or was it "tumbling along"?

After this the bus drove interminably over a bad road in what looked very much like the wrong direction, to let out, late that night or early the next morning, one passenger (Mama recognized him; he'd boarded the bus back in town, some kind of local business, a favor, the bus driver didn't think they'd notice, but you couldn't fool a Brooklyn girl, savvy to tricks and gimmicks) in the middle of nowhere. She could make out the metal legs of a small water tower in the headlights but nothing else besides the innumerable bugs and larger things—bats?—that flashed through the light too quickly to be identified. A few passengers let out wordless squalls of protest, out of the dark maternal interior, and then settled down; the jouncing was soothing, and most of them fell asleep as the road rewound.

Sometime in the night she awoke and saw the dollhouse's black silhouette against the almost black, maybe deep purple windows, then with a start she caught a glint from Papa's eyes and realized he was looking at her. I suppose it must have happened then, but what about the tramp, who is in the way where I've placed her, even if (as one can easily imagine) she has drooped and slid down in the seat and is now scarcely more than a bundle of rags, over which Mama can easily clamber (holding onto the back of her seat and the seat in front) in order to get to Papa. Our conception was a deadline she had to meet. In retrospect we can say it was now (tonight, on the rocking bus) or never, despite the inconvenience and even unlikelihood of it. What luck that Mama (a Brooklyn girl and a bohemian) had never been shy, least of all now (it's easy in the dark) as she directed him with signs and whispers

to move the dollhouse onto the seat beside him. Had he really held it on his lap all night, dozing, with an empty seat beside him? Well, yes, it's an heirloom, and he's a punctilious man, and what's one night of sleep? He liked the forked silhouettes of the saguaro cacti against the sky, and the orchestra of sleepers around him. But now, without hesitation, he did what the lady asked, though to protect the guttering of the dollhouse against the metal back of the seat in front of him he first wedged his jacket between them.

Mama took the place of the dollhouse in his lap, looking back over his head into the resonant interior of the bus. The idea that some of the dark forms back there might be watching quickened her breath. Papa closed his eyes and felt her collarbone warm and hard against his lips. He dared to kiss it, then ducked his head to reach the warm hollow under it, concentrating on this and not the operation Mama was performing blind on his belt buckle, though he did raise his hips when she tugged down on his trousers. Her fingers slipped on the elastic of his boxers, which snapped smartly against his erect cock. He sucked in his breath, felt her dress softly cleave to his mouth. They both froze, listening. Snores, the creaking of the bus. It occurred to him that she would go back to her seat now, and that this might be a relief. But she gave him an intimate, apologetic pat, drew his boxers carefully down, shuffled forward, and fit herself down over him, one knee jammed against the metal joint of an armrest. Deep in her throat, he heard a tiny, unself-conscious grunt. Suddenly he was happy. He bit her dress, grinning. Mama didn't see this. She didn't think about much as she moved, smiling calmly into the darkness. She felt invisible, impossible, free. She could do anything, be anyone. She didn't know what we know, that she was becoming something permanent and necessary as an astrological sign, right now—yes—wait—yes, right now: my mother.

My mother climbed back over the vagrant into her own seat and slept a little. My father took the dollhouse on his lap again and continued his vigil. At three or four in the morning the bus stopped at a gas station in another podunk town, for another endless wait above the simmering engine, while bugs crazed by the pump's lone fluorescent light pinged against the windshield and bats strafed the windows. A few passengers roused themselves and trudged to the bathroom. The vagrant revived and let herself out the back door. Mama craned her neck around in time to see her receding form

briefly silhouetted against a distant bloom of pink neon. Then she turned back to Papa. "Hello," she said.

"Hello," he said.

"What's your name?" They both laughed, ruefully on his part, joyfully on hers. What a life she had, honestly. What adventures.

She hooked her finger familiarly through the front door of the dollhouse, and they told each other their stories in murmured snatches. Then the bus driver eased himself back into his seat, and the bus threw itself onto the freeway again, and the hum and the rocking started up again.

They all woke at once at what was not quite dawn yet, with the impression they'd been summoned somehow, or that a big celestial palm had dealt the roof of the bus a clap, and the interior slowly filled with the sounds of people adjusting and with quiet grumbling surmise. The bus driver kept driving, unmoved. An orange-pink stain spread across the sky. A strange high plume of cloud raced northeast above them. Something streaked the dark shapes of yuccas, saguaros, cattle. The bus driver put his wipers on. But it wasn't raining, it was snowing. In summer? Silvery particles spilled off the sides and top of the windshield.

The sun rose and the banked heat of the desert flared up as if worked by a bellows, but still the snow that could not be snow sifted and ran along the windows of the bus.

The House of Voices

There, we exist. A half-teaspoon of ink, and already, much to regret. The bus could have been a train. My mother could have been wearing jeans, not a dress. The vagrant: maybe a figment. Does it matter? Only Blanche knows.

I stood in the dark, listening. A mewling cry floated down from above. I slid my foot forward through a slick litter of envelopes until it bumped a carpeted bottom step that I knew to be a particularly bilious green, though with the front door closed and my eyes still jazzy from the dance diagrams of the sun, I couldn't see it. The cry came again. It would have been an eerie sound had it not been so familiar. Audrey was an experimental filmmaker and taught part-time at the Art Institute, but she made her real living doing phone sex. So did Trey, so did I. The house was always moaning, whimpering, sighing, as if it were alive and in heat. We called it the House of Voices.

The Mooncalf, Audrey's chocolate lab, appeared in silhouette against the dim light at the top of the stairs, her ears held stiffly out and down with pleasure. She danced from paw to paw, indecisive, then bustled down the stairs to greet me.

"Moony! Moon-unit! Looney-tune!" I stooped, meeting her cold nose halfway, and scrubbed the chronic itch at the base of her tail while I swept my other hand over the carpet, gathering the mail by feel. Mooncalf followed me up to the kitchen, frolicking. I slid the letters onto the red boomerang-patterned linoleum table, slung the oranges into the hanging baskets. There was a mug ("DON'T MESS WITH TEXAS") with a dry tea bag in

it on the counter by the stove. I lifted and shook the kettle, which twanged and hissed, turned off the gas, set the kettle on the back of the stove to cool.

I tapped lightly on Audrey's door as I passed. My room was at the other end of the apartment. It had once been the living room, and connected to Trey's, the former dining room, via great, heavy sliding doors. These we kept closed, though sound passed right through. Across the gap on my side hung a thrift store painting of a purple cow. On his side, a picture of fashion designer Craigy Craig torn out of *W2 Weekly*.

The cow uttered a loud trill. On the other side of the wall, Trey picked up the phone in mid-peal. "Yup. OK. Got it." Then his voice changed registers. "Hello, Professor," he gurgled. "'Course I remember." Trey, "she-male" over the phone (Candi Cornhole!), was in person hollow-chested, artfully bearded, and, theoretically, straight. It was a treat to watch his goatee hop while he described his full red lips, his flawless skin.

I got down the Manual from its place on the mantel and took it back to the kitchen. Audrey was at the table, waiting for me.

It was pure luck that I spotted the sign. It was a foggy day, the sky was the lifeless color of aluminum, I had been a college graduate for all of three weeks and had been in San Francisco for two, looking for a room, and I was fed up. In Noe Valley, which turned out to be yet another hill, a woman in a teal workout suit had told me that the collective had agreed that they didn't want couple energy in the house, and they felt they should stick to that even if the couple had only one body. In the Mission two girls in woolly hats and nose rings had said they felt really positive about me and my, uh, *significant other*, and they really hoped to learn from us to overcome their unconscious prejudices and become more, like, *truly aware individuals*. Stalking back to my sublet I stopped to catch my breath and watch a wind-filled plastic bag bound soundlessly by. It mounted, trembling, and threw itself into the arms of a quince, where it collapsed. In the window behind its shimmering corpse was a hand-lettered sign reading "Room for rent twofers WELCOME buzzer 2."

Buzzer two rang the upper floor-through of a shabby white Victorian. I heard a distant trill, then throaty barking, descending an invisible flight of stairs. When the door cracked open, a grinning chocolate lab looked out, held back by a foot in a dirty tube sock, jammed firmly against the lintel. "Shut *up!* Hi," said the woman who now took the dog's place at the door. She wore a vintage purple print with a big drooping bow at the neckline

and a ripped seam under the arm through which I could see her black bra strap and was, in my twenty-one-year-old assessment, *much* too old for that candy-red hair, which came to gel-stiffened points along her jawline. "I'm Nora," I said, forcing her to ask, and when she did I said, "Blanche," without offering further explanation.

She didn't ask for any. She ticked off the features of the apartment in a perfunctory way, banging cupboard doors. The Mooncalf followed us, tail waving gently. In the bathroom there were big plastic jugs through which the greens and blues of mysterious unguents glowed dully, in the kitchen there were gallon jars of beans and sunflower seeds and nameless beige grains. She bought in bulk, she explained; this seemed to me to be a sign of maturity and investiture in processes I had hitherto ignored. Later I confessed to Trey how much the hand-labeled containers in the fridge had impressed me, and he said, "My father once had to save his pee in the fridge for urinalysis and my aunt thought it was lemonade and took a big swig of it. There is a dark side to everything." He pondered, then added, "Of course I've heard there are yogi who drink their own pee as a discipline, so the dark side had a bright side too."

"Want some tea?" said Audrey. I said yes though I didn't really, had not in fact even tried tea since Granny's sun tea long ago, a nosegay of Lipton's bags slowly staining the water sepia in a jar by the front door. Then I had to make a choice between Lapsang souchong and Earl Grey when I did not know the difference. I picked Earl Grey as being easier to pronounce. I drifted to the kitchen window as she started filling the kettle. The weedy ground behind the house fell away sharply, affording a dizzying view of rooftops plunging stepwise toward the distant bay. Skeins of fog whipped by at eye level. I could follow their shadows toward the east. The house seemed to be leaning into the hurtling emptiness. I drew back; coming from the desert, I had not yet gotten used to seeing the sky not above but beside me.

"Milk?" asked Audrey.

"Yes," I guessed. She took me into the front room, the one that would be mine, where balls of dust and dog hair scudded around the skirts of an old pink sofa. The seat was soft and hairy, like an old man's lap. I sat down gingerly. Wiry articulations deep within the cushions twanged and shifted under my butt, and my knees rose and clobbered me gently in the chin. Chins. The Mooncalf, finding me suddenly at her level, aimed a sloppy lick at my mouth. I ducked my head, and she got Blanche instead.

Audrey sank down beside me. “So tell me, does Blanche ever . . . check in?”

There it was, the question I had been expecting. “No,” I said, too quickly, and frowned. The sofa did intimate things to my behind.

“Well, I guess she won't need her own shelf in the fridge,” she said, and won my heart. I moved in the following Monday.

Though we disagreed on practically everything, Audrey was the only person whose opinion I really cared about. For this I resented her, a feeling that rarely broke out into the open, but kept me in a constant state of vague guilt. Maybe that was why I had let her make the film. At first she had taped me on the sly; at odd moments I would turn around and find her lens trained on me. Though she played it off (“I don't know if I like this slow-shutter feature, it's too MTV”), I started avoiding her. Finally she wandered into my room, leaned against the mantel, picked up a pink paper parasol from a fancy drink, broke it, put it down, and begged me to help her finish her project, which was about me, though in such disguised ways that I would hardly recognize myself. “It's about shadows and reflections,” she said, “and incommensurable love. Like all my films.” When I agreed, she reached around the doorjamb for her camera. She'd left it just outside the door, she was so sure I'd say yes.

At one point she had me hold up a mirror between our two heads. I looked right and saw myself looking back. That's when I finally balked. “That's OK,” she said airily. “I think I nailed it.”

“Audrey. Please.”

She crossed her legs under the kitchen table with a clash of boot hardware and fished calmly in a bag of tortilla chips, ignoring the Mooncalf's steady, avid gaze.

I flipped to the last blank page in the Manual and squared the film festival flyer against it. “I don't want to go. I'll hyperventilate. You know I can't sit in one room with all those freaks. I hate freaks,” I said without heat, because this was nothing new, neither the enthusiasm on her part nor the lack of it on mine. Audrey was twofer-identified. There are nastier ways of putting it: “twin hag,” “triplet.” Look up “Leila 'n' Lila” in the back of the *Bay Guardian*. That's Audrey and a tape recorder.

It was only through Audrey that I knew anything at all about the community. “You're friends with Jasmin and Irina. And Bill and Empress Tennessee. And Jose-Jose, and Lulu and Ki”—coughing—“ki!”

"I am friends with them *individually*," I said, "if you can call it that. I am capable, under civilized circumstances, of sitting across from two people and overlooking the fact that they are holding hands under the table. It's not the same thing to join the crowd. Have you seen the glue stick?"

"Rubber band drawer. Don't change the subject." She examined both sides of a tortilla chip before putting it in her mouth with an air of satisfaction. The Mooncalf groaned and threw herself despondently on the linoleum.

Audrey had great patience. She could sit for hours watching the grain change in a *Study in Kinetic Greys*. Lately she had been making what she called "transspecies erotica," piecing together (over a gasp track supplied by "Tiffany Bells," my phone-sex pseudonym) her own documentary footage, clips from old nature films, and lingering close-ups of ornate, phantasmagorical genitals made of strawberry jam, Vienna sausages, tapioca pudding, and false eyelashes. Smacking his lips showily, Trey had eaten one of these (you can see it intact in *Elephant Seal Sluts*), and had insisted on describing what became of the eyelashes later.

Audrey had set aside this series to make the film in question. "My best work," she said. "A breakthrough." They were making a big deal out of it at the twofer film festival. She was probably going to win a prize.

I found the glue stick, thumbed off its gummy skin, and steered it around on the back of the flyer, frowning with concentration. The Mooncalf shuddered in her sleep.

"I'm not even going to get into the issue of how you think you can spend your whole life pretending not to see someone who's right next to you—" I opened my mouth to protest. "No, I'm not having that conversation again. All I really want to say is excuse me, but you're not going to do that to *me*. I'm here, I've made this thing, I'm really proud of it, I want you to see it, you said you would, and I'm not going to let you get out of it. End of story!"

I draped the sticky sheet on the page and thumped it all over with unnecessary force. The Mooncalf woofed and jumped up, banging her head on the table.

The Siamese Twin Reference Manual—the Manual, for short—contained my clippings and reading notes on matters twofer. Among them were a few genuine rarities from before the Boom that had cost Tiffany a good many fictitious caresses:

- The sheet music to "Me Too HO-HO! HA-HA!" (Woods-Tobias-Sherman) endorsed by San Antonio's Siamese Twins, Violet and Daisy Hilton, both in ringlets:

  Mary had a lamb and this little lamb followed her around
  But that's nothing new I follow someone too
  Since I found her I hang around her like no one did before
  I've followed her for miles and miles but I'd go a million more
  'Cause I don't care I don't mind
  Anywhere that she goes you'll find
  Ho Ho! Ha Ha! ME TOO

- A cabinet card depicting Millie-Christine, the Two-Headed Nightingale, wearing a single, gigantic frock reminiscent of a bed skirt, with an associated clipping (in French—translation Audrey's): "All we know at present is that nine months before their birth, on a hot summer night, their sleepy father dozed off in the middle of a conversation he was having with his wife, woke up two minutes later, and not remembering at just what point he had stopped, he began the phrase all over again."
- An interview with Harold Estep, aka Buddy Sawyer, on breaking off his engagement to Daisy Hilton, one of the San Antonio twins: "I am not even what you would really call gregarious."
- A vintage postcard bearing the image of the virtuous Biddenden maids, Elisa and Mary Chulkhurst, who were born joined at the hips in 1100, and died saying, "As we came together we will also go together."
- The Mexican film poster for *Sisters*, under the name of *Siamesas Diabolicas* ("Lo Que El Diablo Une El Hombre No Debe Seperar"), on which a blood-splattered wench with a bad hairdo, attached at the rump to her better-coiffed twin, with whom she shares a single, complicated swimsuit, raises a dripping dagger. The bloodied knife appears thrice more on the poster, along with a skull and a mysterious hooded figure with glowing eyes.

This last item, being both nasty and stupid, was one of my most treasured possessions. To a casual eye the Manual might appear as doting as a dotard's detailed notes on diet, "A.M. ate blueberries," and the size and hue, "blue," of his BMs. To me, it was a devotional of self-loathing. I'd leaf through it and feel strict and unmitigated, somehow righted. This was not, in those days

and particularly that desperately self-affirming city, something I could express to just anyone. Certainly not Audrey. I could not possibly be the only twofer at odds with myself, but whatever differences the others had seemed to be easily washed away by a double shot of whiskey, or eagerly processed in interminable tête-à-têtes. The others thought they were normal; at the very least, they aspired to normalcy; when all else failed, they made a pretense of normalcy. They believed it was their obligation to represent in the best possible light the entirety of twoferdom in their individual or rather dual twoferness, presenting to the world the happy face(s) of (what was the latest sick-making phrase?) "twinfulness." Self-hatred, a permissible condition among singletons, was not allowed among the twice-blessed.

But hate, like love, is very hard to squash. It's knocking in the coffin and embarrassing the mourners. It's sprouting hair, hawking loogies, chewing with its mouth open, farting, grinning. It's life: untoward, unseemly. But way cooler than easeful death, that sap. Who decorously taps his toe behind "Nora, you have self-esteem issues," and "Nora, so much rage," and "Nora, affirm to Blanche that you love yourselfs." "Yourselfs!" Language itself refutes certain propositions.

I closed the Manual and stood up, leaning my forehead against the kitchen window. Blanche's forehead too, perforce. Our breath made two symmetrical ghosts that floated over the familiar, no-longer-dizzying view: the tawny hunch of whatchamacallit hill over on the left, with the smoke from the hospital angled black behind it, Bernal Hill down on the right, the terraced descent of rooftops down to the Castro and the Mission below that, flattening and spreading, and the bay beyond with an oversized freighter posing on it. Farther still, beyond Emeryville's cooling towers, Berkeley and Oakland leaned back against the hills, from which a few windows threw back the sun: needles of light, piercing the distance and the haze.

A strangled cry floated down the hall from Trey's room. "I *did* follow the MLA guidelines, except in that one teensy-weensy footnote!"

I stepped back. The twin ghosts faded and disappeared. On the neighbor's roof a cat was peeing in the shade of a spinning vent, staring grandly out over the city.

"Oh, all *right*," I said, "I'll go." I had known all along that I would.

THE SIAMESE TWIN REFERENCE MANUAL

6th Annual Twofer Pride Film Festival

Have we got some treats in store for you—including the award-winning twofer lesbian kickboxing romantic comedy, **One Two Punch!** It's a great double-date flick, and binary heartthrob **Nicki 'n' Kicki** will be in the house to meet their fans. We hear they can sign autographs with both hands! Twinkies and Twinings teas will be served on opening night. Local fave **Audrey DeMoss** will also be in the house for the premiere of her thought-provoking new short, **Seeing Double**, and will answer questions after the showing. We've also lined up plenty of those older movies you love to hate and hate to love, including **Freaks, Sisters, Twins, Despair, Dead Ringers, The Dark Mirror, The Man in the Iron Mask, The Prince and the Pauper, The Double Life of Veronique, A Zed and Two Noughts, Twin Falls Idaho, The City of Lost Children, The Bride with White Hair, Twelfth Night, A Comedy of Errors, How to Get a Head in Advertising, On the Double, The Corsican Brothers, Basket Case, Blood Link, Dark Seed II,** and **Chained for Life**. For kids we've got **The Parent Trap, The Parent Trap II, The Parent Trap III**, and **The Parent Trap Hawaiian Honeymoon**! Finally, in the you asked for it, you got it category: last year's audience hit, the camp insta-classic recently resurrected from MGM's vaults, **The King, The King and I, or Anna and the Siamese Kings**. For fans who missed the **Evelyn North** mini-festival last February, here's a second chance to see the mysterious actress in her last big film. Twofer *avant le deluge*? You decide.

So come on down. You'll think you're seeing double!

Cell Division

I wasn't always bitter. Go back to the blob. The blob was not bitter. In the beginning, we were in perfect agreement. We went halves on everything: one cell for *me*, one for *you*, fair and square. Matters soon got more complicated, but we just kept on following the golden rule, splitting everything right down the middle. We didn't plan ahead, just went by feel, following rules that became clearer as we went along. I say "we," but I don't think I noticed there was a we at this early stage, or even an I. Maybe that was the trouble. If only I hadn't been so lax about the I, letting it go until I'd taken care of other things that seemed more important at the time! But how was I supposed to know? I spent a lot of time on knees. A whole day on a birthmark! I thought I had time to putter around, playing Cat's Cradle and Patience, practicing badinage and Balinese dancing, and sipping slowly through my belly button. There was so much to take care of, I was burgeoning in all directions, like a very gradual explosion, and by the time I noticed I had company, it was too late to do anything about it.

After that, we were neck and neck. We kept sneaking looks at each other, cribbing ideas. We were copycats. Copykittens.

We've all seen the photographs, in *Time*, *Life*, *Science News*, of the tiny hunchbacks with their split ends. Anonymous, but sometimes I think I recognize the sullen shrug of the shoulders, the trigger fingers twitching, and the guilty duck of the head away from the flash.

Mama took her time telling Max. But if it hadn't been for the unlikelihood of their union bearing fruit, Max would have guessed for sure, because by now

Mama was playing the expectant mother to the hilt: now capricious, pouting and weeping and "glancing up prettily through lashes still damp from recent showers" (as she would describe it to herself), now radiating a sublime calm. She affected flowing robes before there was any need to loosen her belt. Her friends told her she looked like a Botticelli (she corrected them according to her mood: No, a Mantegna! a Fra Angelico!) and ran to the store for items she craved or affected to crave, pickled baby onions, salted almonds, smoked oysters, so that she really did grow bigger, but then it suited her, as everyone agreed. She collected vases. "I'm very interested in swollen shapes, gourds, interiors," she said with a knit brow and a distant look, and then shook herself with a laugh and turned to her guest, who might bring her some faux Ming next time, or at least a droll bit of majolica.

When her friends tried to take her to the doctor, she put them off. You might have thought she had been faking it all along, and didn't want her belly debunked. Maybe she thought she *was* faking it. But more probably she was scared. Would motherhood wreck everything? She liked stepping out with Max, feeling the boys watching, teasing them with a little twist of the ankle that twirled her spike heel on the sidewalk. She liked their closet, suits on the left, dresses on the right. She liked her little local fame. If she thought of Papa, it was as a part of another world. That strange, raw landscape, the gargantuan sky, the rare streetlights held up by cones of laboring insects.

"Don't you think you should tell Max already? Will someone take the cigarette away from that crazy bitch? You shouldn't be smoking, pet; what are you thinking?"

Mama lit candles, put on a white robe with long sleeves like wings, and sat on Max's lap. Max's face took on a noticeably strained expression, and Mama moved to the arm of the chair. She let her hair fall around Max's face. "I have a surprise for you," she murmured into the warm space between them. With many shy pauses and little looks, she told her secret, then sat back with her eyes cast down and her hands folded in her lap.

Max jumped up, and Mama's feet banged to the floor. Mama dropped her Madonna attitudes, ran to the bathroom, and shut herself in. Behind her, she heard the front door slam.

"If only I had consulted the I Ching first!" Mama lamented over Chinese takeout. The reading she had belatedly drawn gave a clear warning. It was

Po, or Splitting Apart: "There is a large fruit still uneaten. The superior man receives a carriage. The house of the inferior man is split apart." So did the fortune cookie she was about to open: "It is better to have a hen tomorrow, than and egg today."

And egg, it really said that. She didn't know how right that was.

Max didn't come back for two days. Then she knocked on the door, though she had a key, as a sign to Mama that she was a stranger now. "I'm taking you to the doctor," she said. "And that's going to be our last date." Mama's welcoming smile fell away. On the way to the doctor, she slumped against the passenger door. She walked in wearing the print of the lock in her cheek, like a dimple.

Funny, it wasn't Mama but Max who fainted at the sight of us mugging there on the screen. At first they could only see one head. Then we turned to face the audience. How they gawped, and nobody paid much attention to poor Max there on the floor, except a stout but handsome nurse who propped up Max's head on her monumental bosom. Max opened her eyes, then closed them again.

Max drove Mama home, parked in their usual spot, escorted her up the stairs to their apartment, and held the door for her. Mama said, walking in, "Don't think I didn't see you making up to that nurse." Then she burst into tears. She stopped and rocked backward, toward a touch that didn't come. Max was at the top of the stairs, was down the stairs, was at the corner, was turning, was gone.

That night, Mama came to a decision. Later, she would explain it like this, with a brittle laugh: A baby needs a father, even if it's only a man.

The next day, Mama stole Max's Volvo and went west. She took an outdated map of Tennessee (a state she had always believed to be out west, because of its savage spelling), a suitcase full of feather boas and side-slit skirts, her red snakeskin pumps with bows at the ankles, and a pith helmet she'd worn in a play. Later, these pitiably useless items proved useful after all, as props for the Time Camera. A photo survives in which Mama is wearing all of them at once, smiling a sweet and, I think, genuinely happy smile. Only the map is missing, having soared out the car window toward a herd of mildly surprised llamas, somewhere near Omaha.

Seeing Double

A Film by Audrey DeMoss

Blurred white letters trembled on a black screen.

"Focus!" the audience cried.

"Philistines," muttered Audrey.

"Hello! Heard of Maya Deren, dumb-ass?" Trey shrieked, a bit hysterically.

The black slowly faded to grey, then white, until the letters disappeared and the screen appeared blank. Slowly, a few grey cusps and scallops appeared. They darkened. Then they suddenly resolved into the shadowed curves and folds of a three-dimensional body, and the screen ceased to be a piece of fabric and became a placc.

"Believe lies and never come home early," murmured Audrey into her popcorn.

"Why did you say that?"

"It's just a thing to say. For good luck. Like 'break a leg,'" she said.

"'Good night, sleep tight, don't wake up if the bedbugs bite,'" sang Trey.

At first all I saw was a strange, bifurcated shape. Then I realized I was looking at myself. I was lying on my bed, half undressed, asleep, my arms flung out with palms turned up as if to say, "What?"

Audrey had not shown me this footage. I looked at her. Her hair had fallen forward and hid her face.

The film was black and white and grainy. All the details were bleached out. The camera swung slowly around me. Audrey had been standing over

me on the bed; once her bare toe nicked the bottom corner of the frame.

For a minute I looked beautiful, basking in light. I even thought, Nice breasts, as the camera moved in, forgetting for a moment everything that was not onscreen: the top-heavy yaw of those quarterback's shoulders, not to mention my crowning glory, my peculiar surplus. The camera slid up my white side, my bristly armpit, my raised arm.

I could have been dead; I could not tell if I was breathing, not even when the camera moved in until my head almost filled the screen. I looked like a white rock.

The camera slid off the side of my face into the shadow area between us, then Blanche hove into view. She was washed out, unrecognizable, lunar. Her features were shallow thumbprints in a ball of clay.

The camera steadied, focused, homed in on the hollow of the eye. It moved close to the fat, shining lids, under which the invisible eyeball uncannily moved.

The eye opened.

Blanche's eye.

A Tale of Two Faces

Trad. Arr. McLo

I was born to a family of fortune
I arrived on a four-poster bed
With a fine coat of arms and myriad charms
And a face on the back of my head.

I had an exemplary boyhood
I was tutored in every grace
Played the cello with style, read Lamb and Carlyle
And combed my hair over the face.

An elegant wig shows refinement
What a pleasure it is to look well!
At the Duchess's ball I was envied by all
When I took a seat next to Cybele.

From under my wig came a whisper
Such loathsome desires it confessed
What it hissed in her ear made me tremble with fear
But the worst was the lady said yes.

I settled my wig and forsook her
As my other mouth giggled and raved

Throughout the long night I listened in fright
To the terrible things that I craved.

I called Drs. Manly and Treadwell
They parted the lips of my sin
The sensation was sweet, I fell at their feet
And the voice whispered Do it again!

They hastily quit my apartment
They said, a young man needs a wife
Find somebody nice and abandon this vice
You must marry and save your own life!

I went to Cybele the same evening
Some suitable commerce took place
I awoke before long to a pleasure so strong
I knew she was kissing the face.

My hidden lips softened and opened
Her tongue slid inside like a sword
Until I gave tongue with two mouths and I sung
Both parts of a terrible chord.

The pharmacist filled my prescription
I lifted the cork to my nose,
I was dead long before the jar smashed on the floor
And the sweet smell of almonds arose.

The coffin was lined with black velvet
And sunk eight feet under the ground
A spade chimed on rock, I heard the church clock
And a closer, more secretive sound.

At the crossroad's a grave with no marker
Put your ear to the ground if you dare
For under the hill someone's whispering still
To the bones of the boy lying there.

Mirrors & Lenses

lanche, awake?

Unthinkable. Unspeakable.

I plunged through the lobby, breaking the clasp of two handholding Japanese twofers in matching Hello Kitties shirts with the cheerful legend "LET'S TWICE!" Leering mayoral candidate "Two heads are better than one" Hy Hal Nguyen offered me his own cardboard face on a stick, like a questionable lollipop. I sent it spinning.

As I played Pushmi-Pullyu with the swinging door, I replayed the opening sequence in my mind: the approach, the two faces, the descent into the shadowed cleft between, the curve of the ear, whose ear?—hope looked for confusion, didn't find it: Blanche's ear, no question—the swell of the cheek, the shut eye; whose eye? Blanche's eye. Rewind, repeat, rewind. At last the door relented. Outside, another RubiaMorena cutout reposed against posters of coming attractions. Or, no—heads turned—it was RubiaMorena herself, talking to that rare thing, a Togetherist twofer. Her sudden transformation from two to three dimensions gave me a sickening, familiar wooze. RubiaMorena bugged her eyes to let me know I was staring, and with a toss of coiffure, turned her back. It was as three-dimensional as her front, if not more so. The Togetherist tilted one head, ginger hair a sour half-note off from the orange of his shirt, and raised his eyebrows at me.

Out of the shade of the marquee, among the throng that packed Castro Street from wall to wall, it was stingingly bright and hot. I smelled patchouli, pizza, pot. Someone's sticky arm smooched mine. Someone's breath raised

the hairs on the back of my neck. Shuddering, I escaped, as I thought, through a gap, and found myself trapped behind a row of gimcrack tarp-topped booths.

Things made out of spoons. Free skin cancer screening; two-for-one cell phone service options; lead apronwear in ruffles or black leather; package deals on twofer-friendly cruises (extra-wide bunks, sensitivity-trained crew and tour guides). Soft-focus photos of loving pinkish pairs—*Your faces here!*—available on clock, T-shirt, mouse pad, or mug. "Thyroid Health and You" FREE informational pamphlet from holistic herbologist Dr. Sundeep Vijay Harnath Munindar Singh-Cohen. RadioActivists hawking pitchblende amulets and T-shirts: "I'm radioactive—and I vote." Free promotional CD single from "My Double Life," the new album from folk songstresses Winnea and Dulcea McLo, posing in denim with a guitar, two harmonicas, and a lunatic-eyed goat.

Panicking, I pushed a twofer kid in beanies out of my way and ducked under a pole into the Twofers for Animal Rights booth. Mom ("I ❤ my twofer son") straightened one beanie and glared at me. "Sign a petition to free Spotty, the Steinhart Aquarium's two-headed snake?" said the peppy twofer working the booth. "Give Rodney the two-headed calf, currently hanging from the roof of Tommy's Joint in a fez and fedora, a dignified burial?"

That black pupil for so many years unseen now dead center like a hole in the screen. Blindness visible. I couldn't look, despite the merciful apparatus between us: the lens, the filmmaker, the seething dissolve of light.

A clipboard and a ballpoint pen floated into my field of vision. Click-click went the pen, retracting and extending its wee proboscis. I shook my head distractedly and kept going, out the other side of the booth.

An orange shirt fluoresced in my path. "Hi, are you Together?"

"No, thank you," I said, foolishly. When he did not budge, I grabbed the flyer poked at me and shouldered past. On the other side of the street I found room to walk if I stayed close to the wall.

From the opposite corner, I looked back. Over the heads of the crowd I saw Audrey—red bob, sheer black bed-jacket, pink sequined dress—come out into the sunlight angling under the marquee and look up and down the street, hand shading her eyes. I ducked down the stairs into the BART station and came up across Market, near the temporary stage, where a punk band, Hung Jury, was tuning up. I couldn't see Audrey across the crowd, but that didn't mean she wasn't following me, though I hoped—with a throb of

awful remorse—that she would just go back inside and accept her prize. But I couldn't risk going home yet.

I was still holding the Togetherist flyer. The letterhead was the same as the design on their shirts: the twin rings of Pride, reworked into two links of a chain. I put it in my pocket to evaluate later for inclusion in the Manual, and started up the other side of Castro, away from the crowd. Behind me, I heard Hung Jury start up. At the short, breathtakingly steep street that led up to the hilltop park, I turned left. A neat oblong of masking tape was affixed to the sidewalk, with what remained of a festival flyer, a few pink scraps, still attached, like shards of a broken mirror still stuck in the frame.

A mirror! Was that it? For a wild, happy second I thought I had it. The lens had flipped the image; it was *my* eye that opened.

But no, Nora, no. A lens doesn't work like a mirror.

I hurled myself up the sidewalk. I was breathing with all my strength, a muscular lunge and collapse, lunge and collapse. The houses stepped back with blank faces and made room for the raw knob of the hill. Sparsely tufted with dry grass, it rose out of a pubic tangle of greasewood and weeds. A narrow path up to the gate wound through green clouds of wild fennel. Usually I loved to yank off handfuls of the sticky fronds, which emitted, when crushed, the sweet, potent smell of licorice. Not today. The metal gate lowed when I dragged it open. Plastic bags for dog poo were knotted to the chain-link fence that surrounded the two tragic tennis courts with their drooping nets, a puddle of sky at each baseline.

I kept going, up the crumbling ridge. There was a feeling like crying in my chest, but let's say it was only my labored breath. Blanche puffed peacefully beside me. Behind and below me, the Castro still steeped in sunlight so bright I seemed to feel its reflected warmth against my back, but a towering mass of fog was building over the Sunset district, filling the Haight and most of downtown with a diffuse dream light that sharpened only here and there to pick out a detail: a bicycle and a hibachi on a balcony, a saggy balloon snagged in a palm tree.

My heart was banging. I had run out of clean underwear so I wasn't wearing any, and sweat stung the cognate chafed spots on my inner thighs. I scrambled up the last rise to the base of the boulders at the top of the hill, pebbles rolling backward under my feet. There, I caught a whiff of pot and saw a pair of untied oxblood Docs sticking out from behind a rock, so I went around the outcropping to climb up from the other side. As soon as I

forsook the shelter of the hill, Blanche's hair streamed back, swirled up in a stinging cloud, then whipped across my eyes. Tears brimming, I attained the top. Look, in the crevices: fairy lights of red and green! Then I blinked and they were bottle-glass.

I stood up. The wind fell against me like a body. I gasped, and tasted the cold in the back of my throat. The wind tugged my shirt, searched my pockets, lifted my skirt. White vapors whipped past me. Here is what I love about San Francisco: its motility, its ceaseless change. That snowy mountain ahead would melt and tumble inland, finally winking out in the warm air over Orinda. Tomorrow it would invent itself afresh, along with a good percentage of the population, and nobody would hold yesterday against it. You could turn over a new leaf every day, let the old leaves just blow away. Pick up a pen, start a new story. Start it like this: "Today—"

Today, I held a blank page to the light, and found a watermark. The figure was faint, but I recognized it. *Her.*

My ears had begun to sing with cold. My orbital bones ached.

Blanche had opened her eyes. A reflex? Maybe. In sleep, while trying to get a better look at a dream? Possibly. Hadn't that naked eye seemed (in the instant before a practically mathematical sense of paradox made me unable to look) hazy, glazed, unaware? Not an organ of sight but a memorial to it? Maybe. But if not?

In the history of medical science, there was a time when the sick had a reasonable concern that they might be pronounced dead prematurely and wake up underground. Some went so far as to install a bell-pull in the coffin, connected to a bell above.

My head was ringing.

"Look, I'm sorry I didn't ask if I could use that nude footage," Audrey said. "It was really amateurish of me. If you were anyone else, I would have had you sign a release, but I honestly didn't think you would care, I mean, you hardly come across as a prude." She paused, then said, "For example." She pointed at my crotch, still underwearless under my short skirt.

I crossed my legs and rearranged the damp washcloth on my forehead.

"Now you're pissed that I called you a prude. I shouldn't have used the word. OK, modest. Private. I totally respect that. If you want me to, I'll edit out part of the sequence. It'll be a little jumpy, but I can make it work."

"That isn't it."

“Then what. *What.*” She coughed, banged herself in the chest.

Hadn’t she seen it too? I cleared my throat. An obscene revelation shivered in the offing, a banshee panting to pop out of the cake. “I don’t like looking at myself,” I said instead.

Not a lie. I disliked mirrors. Kept no snapshots. Ducked when the flash went off.

“Yeah. Well, we knew *that.*” She waited. “Is that all?” I shrugged.

She went out, slamming the door.

THE SIAMESE TWIN REFERENCE MANUAL

San Francisco, you're TOGETHER!

On the joyous occasion of the 6th Annual Twofer Pride March and Festival, take a moment to reflect on the pain of the singleton, who cannot experience this joy, or even understand it.

His is the legacy of hundreds of thousands of years of solitary confinement. He is cleft from the world, from his brethren, and from himself.

This pain is not his alone. It is yours as well, for it is not enough to be born conjoined. Indeed, your painfully partial merger is the most visible outward sign we have been given of the Rift in the heart of things.

Downer? Nay. Say rather, a sign that we are finally on the move toward wholeness. The conjoined twin is a traffic sign on the highway of life. What does that sign say? It says MERGE.

Twofers, yours is a sacred wound: you have been deprived of the picayune, atomic integrity of the singleton, in order to achieve a new, higher integrity. The truly Together will undergo a convulsive change or Focus and reemerge as a new One, who is to an ordinary singleton as condensed soup to a clear broth. These will become the Husbandmen of our divided world, guiding the factious singleton gently but firmly toward union.

To get Together, the superficial boundaries of the self must be broken down. Twofers, you have the glorious privilege of hosting, in one body, two souls, yet all too often these souls parcel up their joint experience, impoverishing both. Our Western notion of self, and the language it has given rise to, is to blame; every time you open one mouth to say I, you thrust a lance in the heart of your twin. Understand that your "identity" is only the scar tissue left by the ancient wound of being severed from

the Whole. From I, we get to we, from we to that plenary in which self and world are united in bliss: I^2.

Only then may you truthfully say you are Together.

How do I get involved?

1. ***Volunteer!***

We need help on all levels: outreach (leafletting, cold calls, door-to-door), planning, events coordination, secretarial. We are particularly in need of a database engineer and a plumber (Russian River area).

2. Take a class!

Just a few of our course offerings: Conflict Resolution; Getting to One; Syncretic Speech; Paneurythmy, the sacred Bulgarian Dance; Togetherness Is Fun! (children's sing-along class).

3. Donate!

Do you have an extra room we could use for meetings or classes? A computer or phone you no longer need? Would you like to sponsor a needy child or adult seeking Togetherness? Cash donations gratefully received.

Too Bad

Mama bought a map of Nevada at a truck stop on the interstate before she turned off on the road to Grady. She drove the last leg of her journey with the map on the seat beside her. She stopped occasionally to consult it. She didn't bother to pull over, just parked in the middle of the road. There were no other cars this far off the interstate. Then she clicked off the interior light and went on. The night seemed like a solid mass. She was boring a small, poorly lit tunnel through it. In the huge banks of unblemished dark on each side she occasionally saw two eyes like shiny dimes, blank as Orphan Annie's. Or a pair of ears, vegetal and veined, stood up out of a tuft of sick grass. Or something raced out into the slip-stream of light just ahead of the car, froze, and was snatched away behind.

She knew he lived in a small town. She knew the name of the town: Too Bad. She knew he was a geologist working for the government, something to do with strategic minerals. She had sized him up right away: a good man, simple, and hers if she needed him; she needed him.

In the last half hour that cake of ink had dissolved. The still-suspended sediment settled calmly, draining toward the west. Miraculously, the block of sky resting on the windshield had become a blue space, the car ran forward unimpeded, and there was the sign for Too Bad, Pop. 1.

One?

There were shiny pockmarks in the sign. Vandals had shot off the zeros, she supposed. She slowed to make the turn, not enough; the car spun in a slow rattling curve on the gravel and wound up facing back up the road again, an evil sign, but she steered it laboriously round and started toward

town. As the car jounced up the road, its bald tires skating alarmingly on the loose rocks, the night was just quickening toward morning. The sky was luminous. Birds shrieked.

Something that had been crouching like a person on a rock by the side of the road flung itself despairingly into the air and Mama saw it, sharply, as a body—what birds rarely seem—and caught her breath, thinking it would dash itself on the road, but then it hugely shrugged and caught the air with enormous wings, fought a few feet up, wheeled, and then planed sharply down along the face of the hill, only a little above the surface, close enough that it could stretch its neck if it wanted and plow the earth with its beak. It looked prehistoric. A vulture, an eagle, a condor?

She slid past a bush—juniper?—full of small birds all shouting, more birds than leaves. They all rose at once, hung in the air, swung round, and fell back on the bush. The arcane silhouettes of saguaros along the crest made her want to laugh. Maybe she was a little light-headed.

It was hard to tell where the road was. She bumped over a smooth grade of loose stones, shining greyly in the cold light. Mama thought she saw the town off in the distance to the left, towering indistinct forms. It was more impressive than she had expected, a biggish place, and right away she started thinking the first thing she would do, when the shops opened, was go buy some baby oil—for her legs, already getting a bit scaly in the dry heat—and some sandal-foot stockings. She gunned the motor, spinning the wheels noisily. To the right the sky was turning a bleached yellow. She braked. On the close, cambered horizon two rabbits crouched facing one another, crisply outlined in light. Their ears were flame-colored. One flung itself straight upward, landed again in the same attitude of tense readiness. Beat. Then the other shot up, landed.

Then, as though a seal had broken, the sun spilled across the land. The high tips of things suddenly stiffened against the light that slid down them quickly, clothing them in firmness and splendorous reality. Mama turned to take in her new home. What she had taken to be tall buildings were red-rock buttes. They met the sun squarely, a red blow to the eye, their foundations still immersed in blue shadows. The bunnies, when she turned back, had hopped together under a bush and looked unconcerned. The light came down over everything and slowed, and the world seemed normal again.

"Bunnies," said Mama. She saw them as little bouncing saints, clothed in light. They were there to welcome her, the Madonna from Brooklyn. The sun-

struck sky: cathedral! The bluffs: pews and pulpit. She ate a pretzel, thinking of the host, and started the car again. She refused to be discouraged. Everything would be OK, the cows would not attack the car, the vultures would bow their obscene heads, the baby would be born perfect-limbed and, like the bunnies, clothed in light. "Clothed in light," she repeated to herself, and rolled over the crest into the town of Too Bad.

There was no town.

There had been a town once, that was evident, despite the bushes that grew everywhere, on and up through the ruins, because ruins were almost all that was left. There was a yellow dog, alternately barking and sitting to kick at a stick tangled in its ruff. Big black birds with red turkey faces got up slowly from the wreckage of some small mammal, staring at her as she opened the door and got out. They were not afraid of her or the dog, only a little respectful of the car, but crowding in now that it was stopped. She chucked her purse at them, then had to go get it, while they stared indecently and bridled but did not fly away. The air was fresh and cool, but the sun on her forehead already stung.

The one street swept dogmatically straight uphill. Mama started up it, toward a white and blue house, the only house that was not a ruin, though it was not really a house at all, just a trailer.

The door opened, and Too Bad's entire population stepped out. He stood on an Astroturf doormat in his bare feet and watched her come.

Half Time

Say you're an only child. You sleep in your own room, snug in your own bed. One day, Mom says, "I don't know how to break this to you, dear, but you have a twin sister. We thought she had died, but it turns out there was a mix-up at the hospital. She's coming home, and I expect you to make her feel welcome. It seems you're Siamese!"

How would you take this news?

When Blanche fell asleep I thought, The mirror cracked. That's seven years bad luck! But for more than twice that long, nothing bad had happened at all. Nothing I couldn't ignore, anyway: Mama's bewildered looks, my classmates' whispers (but they'd never liked me), the half-baked suggestions of a sweaty school psychologist who slurped cold Sanka from a "Freudian Sips" mug and plucked at his shirt. I graduated high school early and left home. I was one of only three twofers at my college, well under the national average, but then it was a small school, in a barren state, in the middle of a no-man's-land. Some of our more regular attendees were dust devils and hallucinations. We twofers were all lodged in the same dorm freshman year. (It came to be known as the Ark. Two by two, you see.) We got the only single rooms, which did not endear us to the others, but the university had decided after some debate that we could be considered our own roommates.

I was not ostracized. I even had a certain cachet; I was part of the fastest-growing voting minority, much discussed in public forums at the time, and back then when our numbers were still small the dirty allure of the midway still hung about us. It helped that I was pretty, though Blanche, somehow, was prettier.

After graduation I moved to San Francisco, where twofers had their own paper, the *Two Times;* their own radio show, *Twinspeak*; support groups; political candidates; dance clubs (2, Dos y Dos, the Twostep*);* and Pride. I was no longer a novelty. In a moment of uncharacteristic enthusiasm I got Audrey to take my picture in front of the Twin Peaks and sent it home.

Like any girl with a beautiful sister, I had never been sure my boyfriends were all mine. In this citadel of the sex-positive, where even the gay men could locate a G-spot if they had to, and even the straight men were savvy about anal health, and brunching pals of all gender descriptions talked dildos knowledgeably over crêpes, the girls I had by then begun dating would freely propose strange formations involving Blanche. They would bed me just to see if they could catch a glimmer of complicity from under her lowered lids. They hovered over signs: a bead of spittle in the corner of her mouth, a haze of sweat. They moaned moist words into her hair. To watch them watch her plucked some base note in me. I throbbed with a sickening sweetness, then purged my bed of the bewildered betrayer. One, just one, before she closed the door, charged me with entrapment. "You wanted it. You're a third wheel," she shrugged. I had never heard the term used that way, but I understood the foul implication well enough. "Here's a little something for later." Taking hold of Blanche's chin, she slid her tongue between the speechless lips, then sauntered out, leisurely buttoning her shirt. She had gone home to London shortly thereafter, and I had not seen her since. Still, we kept up an intermittent correspondence. Her name in my in-box always gave me a slightly unpleasant thrill, like the items in my Manual, perhaps because it seemed to mockingly recall that good-bye kiss. (Hm? Louche Gift.)

If I was a third wheel, Louche was the boot. I curbed my appetite, discovered an appetite for curbing itself, and curbed that too. This went on not going. It was a relief when strawberry blond, jiffy-lubed Tiffany Bells frisked into my life, along with her pseudonymous partners in pubescence (Ginger, Cherry, Consolata), and her docile suitors mooing down the phone lines. After that, my sex life became almost entirely fictional. Well, I had always liked telling stories.

This was the kind of job most people did to fund something else: a sweet tooth for crystal or X, a class in Beat poetics at the New College. I didn't have anything else. Except Blanche. Maybe I mean the absence of Blanche: being Nora was very largely concerned with, almost synonymous with, not being

Blanche. I wasn't aware of working at it, exactly. Under hypnosis you can be convinced that the stage is empty, and still, if sent for a stroll, avoid the piano. By the swerves, though, I fancy you might in time be able to deduce the shape of what you cannot see, even if you couldn't put it into words.

In experiments, a person with split cerebral hemispheres is shown two different images, one for each eye—a cow on one side, say, and a goat on the other. When asked what he sees, he answers from the side where language lies: *cow*. But at the same time shakes his head. *No, no. Not a cow but . . . but . . .* Something nameless, something unspeakable. It could be that this book is just another way of saying no. "That of which we cannot speak, we must pass over in silence": motto of the National Penitence Ground. I'd made it mine. Lately, though, I've had second thoughts, for to say, "that of which we cannot speak," is already to speak, and "silence" is a word, and "no" is a way of saying something is wrong, something is missing, is lost.

The door flew open, punched the crater in the wall. Audrey, hands on hips: "Apparently you grabbed Charmaine's breast on your way out of the theater? What was that about?"

"What? Did not."

"She thinks you did."

"She's crazy. Why would I?"

"*Something* happened. She's upset."

"Things happen. Maybe I brushed against her. What do you want me to do about it?"

"Talk to her. Make some gesture."

"I'll buy her something. A nice dream catcher. A pocket pendulum."

"First assault her, then insult her."

"Actually, I was being sincere. Don't you think she'd like a copper healing bracelet?"

"How about I just talk to you later." But she didn't move.

Had I grabbed Charmaine? I didn't actually remember, but the notion was absurd. If it were anyone else—but I'd never been attracted to Charmaine: that raw pink chin that trembled too easily, crumbs of mascara like blue dander powdering her cheeks, the malign mole like a jet bead snug in the wing of her nose.

A thought flashed through me: *Blanche* did it. But why? (Leaving aside *how*.) I was the lesbian, not Blanche. To throw blame on me, then?

Surely a sane person does not view acting like herself as grounds for suspicion that she is someone else.

The phone rang. It was my boss, Perdita, with a client for me, a regular. I found myself relieved.

"Give me a second to find the file. OK, put him through—Hi, sugar! How's my pony?"

Audrey rolled her eyes and exited.

Those files were recipes for worlds. "Likes to be called 'stupid boy,' piano teacher, lingerie, rose violently pinned to lapel, lemon smell of furniture wax, *The Well-Tempered Clavier.*" I was at home in these worlds; nothing surprising ever happened there. My dream girls fluttered up like shapes scissored out of old magazines, smelling of ink and oxidized paper. They were biddable and a little old-hat. Like maps, they cracked in the used places. The hand-puppet hobgoblins flapped: the outraged husband, the anguished wife, the appalled keyhole-peeper in pigtails, the coach, policeman, maiden aunt. The consequences unfolded like the simplification of a mathematical equation, with solemn logic, and then *x* and *y* slipped out of their clothes and took their familiar poses by the equals sign. "Say 'Thank you, Miss Tiffany.' Now be a good pony and call again soon!"

Before I hung up, I turned my head (in my stories, I had only one) and looked out the window at the painted scene. I had always wished I could take a walk there, where I was someone else. But for the first time I pictured myself losing my way. I'd turn a corner and find myself in an older part of town, where the dollhouse loomed like the mansion in a gothic novel, the shadow of a woman on its drawn blinds. If I met her there, would she recognize me, in my strawberry blond wig, with my cartoon bosom, my long, long legs? Would I recognize her? How did I know, then, that I had not already met her, pretending to be someone else, the way I was pretending?

The phone rang again.

"Hello? Oh." I sighed. "How many times have I told you not to use this number?"

When Mama was into alchemy she had talked about nothing but the *lapis philosophorum* and the green lion. Now she had a whole new vocabulary. "The self-other dualism is a motivated construction—an obviously false dichotomy. Of course we can't endorse the reverse construction that there is no difference between the two—rather, we have difference within identity,

marriage and divorce in one, or rather, for the verb is active, a continuous merging and simultaneous separating, give and take—"

"Mama, you sound like a translation from the French."

"No, listen. The split is the primal wound. In Freudian-slash-Lacanian terms we would call it lack, castration anxiety, but also our sense of having been severed from an original mythical repleteness. Though there is also the view that it is a modern phenomenon associated with the splitting of the atom. Which reminds me that the whole nuclear waste thing is really galvanizing Grady right now. About thirty years too late, if you ask me. Though . . ."

"Wait, back up, back up. What boondoggle have you subscribed to now?"

"Oh, didn't I say? I've joined the Siamists, or Siamystics, if you like. It is no boondoggle, Nora. I really think you'd be interested, since it pertains to you. According to our teachings the world is 'Siamese,' or conjoined with a twin world with which it is at war. This split generates the life force in that it motivates us to yearn toward images of wholeness, whether it be in a loved one—that's the ancient myth of Hermaphrodite—or in the fully integrated self, as in the modern myth of psychotherapy and self-help. Our anxiety about separation is matched by a secret anxiety about merging which expresses itself as fear of stagnation and death. The two anxieties work us like a bellows, yearning and fleeing, yearning and fleeing. This isn't necessarily bad, but our feeling is that our lack of let's say dialogue with this other world puts us in the situation of the Pushmi-Pullyu, whose two parts are pulling in opposite directions; we need to put our heads together, so to speak, while still acknowledging our differences. To make peace with our twin is the spiritual task of the next millennium. We've been given twofers as our spiritual guides in this process. You're like crossing guards: you can look both ways."

"This sounds like Togetherism, and you know how I—"

"No, our thinking is a little more—oops, I have to go. But think about what I said. I'm going to sign you up for the mailing list. You don't have to thank me, ha ha. Bye! I love my girls!"

I sank back onto the bed, staring up at the plaster medallion in the center of my ceiling, on which I sometimes imagined I could make out two blurred figures struggling. Between Blanche's lips a glossy elastic film bellied out and in, without breaking. Only a little ghost of a breath rattled its chains around

her tonsils. The motley books on my shelves, tiers of tiny onlookers, offered their familiar commentary sotto voce. *Richard III, Pudd'nhead Wilson, Stars and Bars, Early Light. The Excavations at Araq el-Emur, Derrida Reader. Hyde's Theorem, Ember'd Dawn. Ki Girl: Everyday Self-Defense.* Were any out of place? The titles strung together to form a sentence? Why was *Learn Zemblan*! next to *Che: A Life*? Only a madwoman would play such tricks.

Only a madwoman would anticipate them.

Still, I dedicated the next forty minutes to alphabetizing my books, by author. In the future, if any had been moved, I would know.

THE SIAMESE TWIN REFERENCE MANUAL

The *San Francisco Chronicle*: "One Twofer's View" Weekly Column

"Histories and Theirstories"

It is generally believed that the dramatic growth in the conjoined twin population worldwide was caused by radioactive fallout. The assertion is supported statistically by the distribution, both temporal (mid 20th century) and geographical (advanced industrial nations), of the first wave of births. However, it is not supported by lab results. Researchers, abusing pig ovaries as if on a personal vendetta, have produced many porcine prodigies. Eyeless, brainless, legless meatloaves; "popcorn" pigs, their organs on the outside, whose naked hearts give one drumroll of terror before bursting; the high-IQ strain employed at airports to sniff out drug mules; and the celebrated Big Pig of Pahrump, size of a juvenile hippo, whom pork interests were hoping to breed for meat, and who was tragically assassinated, despite the vigilance of an armed guard, by a junta of cattlemen. But scientists have produced no mutation so common, so consistent, so successful, as Homo sapiens dicephalus.

Consequently, some groups, like the Siamists, Togetherists, and so-called fusion theologists, aver that radiation has nothing to do with twinning. It was a deeper, more metaphysical split that took place when the first nuclear bomb was exploded at the Trinity site on July 16, 1945. Many consider this split no accident, but the essential next stage in the spiritual evolution of a species finally advancing beyond self-interest. To others, it is just the latest fissure in that ever-widening crack in the relation of Self to World whose warning signs first appeared in ancient Greece. Revisionist scholars, on the other hand, claim that a sizeable population of twofers has existed throughout history ("theirstory"), many more than were sung in ballads and broadsides. Indeed, the Togetherists, the most radical of the "fusion" groups, lay

claim to an antiquity that rivals the Masons'. Twofer artisans controlled the smithies of Roman Britain, they believe; not only that, anyone using a chain for any purpose had to pay an annual tax to the Togetherists. This tax, an early form of copyright (for the twofers were generally believed to have "invented" the chain, though this remains to be proved), was collected throughout Europe during the reign of the Holy Roman Empire, and played a part in preserving twofers—then considered monsters—against poverty, persecution, and the indignity of public display. In Egypt and the Middle East, twofers were traditionally associated with the priesthood rather than the artisan classes, but again, their emblem is the linked rings of a chain. In fact, according to Togetherists, any representation of a chain, whether in poetry or art, heraldry or history, is a coded reference to a secret society—which, if they are correct, is vast indeed.

Whether inducts to a secret society or no, these often high-functioning twofers led productive lives, concealing their condition from all but intimates. Just a few of the historical figures alleged to have had conjoined twins are Copernicus, Shakespeare, Emperor Rudolf II, Meister Eckart, Eric Gill, Joseph Venn, Robert Louis Stevenson, Victoria Woodhull, and Mark Twain. Galileo has only lately been removed from this list; a recently unearthed tailor's bill for a shirt showed an insufficiency of linen and only one collar button. The debate on Leonardo da Vinci rages on.

Genesis

To my father she had seemed so beautiful that he strained helplessly toward her, like a sunflower to the sun. Now he noticed that she looked awkward as she climbed the street, heavier around the hips, more like the women he was used to seeing in the grocery store in town, and so he felt a faint disappointment just as his dreams were coming true.

She embraced him, stiffly. There were crumbs dusting the fine hairs on her upper lip. She had a funny look on her face. She could have told him it was "exaltation," plucked out of her catalog.

Papa put his hand on her back and took her into the trailer. She was surprised to find tears in her eyes. She hadn't even tried.

Cautiously, he introduced her to his mother, who drove a tow truck and lived in a small house right behind the gas station on the highway between Too Bad and Grady, the nearest real town. She was a bandy-legged cowboy in a dress. Mama pictured her spitting tobacco in luminous arcs, slapping a too-big ten-gallon hat down hard on her head. Her dresses were always askew at the waist so the side seam hung over her lap. "Well I'll be damned," Granny said, and stood there nodding her head and squinting at Mama, one hand cupping the opposite elbow at her waist, other hand holding up a cigarette between two stiff fingers.

"I'll help you fix that leak now, Mother," said Papa.

"What leak?"

"That radiator hose that's been leaking." He nudged her.

"My engine's purring like a kitten. How would it look if my own truck broke down? I'd lose all my business."

"Well, let's just go have a look." He grabbed her by the arm and pulled her outside.

She didn't think much of Mama. "You'll have to teach her to boil water," she told Papa. "She'll last about as long as a snowball in hell. Why does she look so green around the gills?"

Later she told Mama in a stage whisper, "If you get Montezuma's Revenge I have some pills that will firm you right up."

"I'm fine, thank you," said Mama coldly.

"You don't look it. How long are you in town?"

What Granny had suspected right away, Papa took weeks to guess. When her belly made it clear that Mama had come to stay, Papa walked down to the highway with a can of paint. Too Bad, Pop. 2. Then he ordered a house. It was prefab and was delivered in two halves. I liked to think of my mother riding up in one half, from the east, and my father converging on her from the west in the other half. The join was imperfect, a visible seam through which ants and rain entered. Over time it became apparent that the halves' forward momentum had not been completely exhausted. They continued on their divergent courses. Set down on gravel, not bedrock, they slid a little every year, but in different directions and at different speeds.

The desert is not easy to love, but Mama seemed to embrace it. Really she was courting death, ours or hers, which would also be ours. I am convinced, I really am, that this had more to do with the winking roadrunner on the masthead of the Grady paper than the fact that the doctor had told her she was going to give birth to a monster. She took long walks at midday with a recklessly small amount of water sloshing in the canteen Papa forced on her. Even the yellow dog, Fritzi, who loved her, would turn back to look for some shade. At first she thought the sun alone might snuff us out like earthworms stranded on the sidewalk. Then she took stronger measures. Woefully misinformed about anatomy, she swallowed sand, stones, and beetles. Sand, stones, and beetles rained down on our skullcaps, or would have done, if we had occupied her stomach as she vaguely supposed, and not her womb. She chewed the jojoba bean that tasted like wax and kerosene. She ate ants.

Once she came upon a Gila monster, fat, lazy, and poisonous, napping under a bush. She thought it was gorgeous, a beaded purse with teeth. She

loosened her shirt, stretched herself out beside it, and fell asleep. When she woke up, expecting angels, she found the lizard snuggling against her thigh, and though she caught it up and held it dramatically to her breast, it would not be tempted to take a nibble, but gaped at her fondly.

She was afraid of snakes, so could not approach the rattlesnake for her quietus, though she did pinch out a scorpion's life with her lacquered nails and swallow it between two slices of white bread. It was one of the small, translucent, very poisonous ones. My mother must have had a poisonous temperament herself; far from weakening, she grew stouter every day. The stones she swallowed gave her gravity. She was quieter and stood more firmly on the ground, as if her shifting sands were being pressed under the weight of her life, and slowly turning to stone. Inside her, we had the impression of a vast landscape of rounded red bluffs and constant, stifling heat.

The Gila woodpecker burrows into a saguaro and builds a nest there. The walls of the cavity harden and dry. When a saguaro falls, the flesh rots away until nothing is left but a pile of dry stalks and the nest. The nest looks like a wooden boot, or a womb. It is practically indestructible.

Mama ran full tilt at the dollhouse, rammed herself on the gabled eves, and knocked her breath out. As she bent croaking over the roof she felt the big bellows begin between her legs, and it was her sad laugh that shocked her body back to breathing.

A convulsion shook her and she squeezed the chimney so hard one of its glued-on pots popped off. She was half standing, half lying on the dollhouse, one hand squeezing the chimney, the other in the bathroom, thumb in the toilet bowl. One big breast loomed ominously into the second landing, where an astonished Papa doll lay flat on his back with his arms stretched wide on the painted carpet. Some blood came, and she stuck the miniature bathtub under her, then the sink, pitcher, bird bath, filling them up, then she swiveled majestically and unsteadily, staggered hugely back, and stuck out a fleshy gargantuan arm for the basin she kept by the bed for her morning sickness.

The blond doll Mama with her molded rubber dress lay on her back in the kitchen. The Papa lay on the landing. The little girl was the only one watching. Lacking the wiring to hold a pose, she was "sitting" in a rocking chair, actually leaning across it, like the hypotenuse of a triangle. With a flick of her finger Mama laid her flat as well. "Lights out, missy," she said, and with a gush laid me in the bowl.

Sister Double Happiness

"You oughta be locked up!" yelled Charmaine. She had stationed herself across the street from our building, so she could haze me whenever I went out. "Rapists!" She followed me as far as Church, shouting this every so often, then turned back. I prudently let the streetcar glide through the red light ahead of me, then crossed at an angle, heading into the Mission.

I had begun taking long walks to clear my head after nights thronged with dreams. They all started the same way: I was standing in the desert among sagebrush and wait-a-bit bushes, looking at the ground in front of me with tremendous purpose and urgency. There was a pack rat's nest in the bush in front of me, but that's not what I was looking at, or for. I could see the pebbles set flat among smaller pebbles set flat among smaller ones right down to the sand, and I could see the tiny stickery weeds, as clearly as if I were there. Then . . . nothing. But a fierce sense of imminence.

Since I moved to San Francisco, I had not gone back to the desert even in dreams, and I had the uneasy feeling that the recent change was Blanche's doing. We had always wondered if elements of our dreams could make their way across the suspension bridge of nerves between our spines, or transmit themselves through a wholly bodily code of tics and jerks. At one time we'd kept parallel dream journals, with possible points of connection ticked off and elaborated. How is a tap-dancing dog (Blanche) like a box containing kidneys, livers, and other organ meats (Nora)? I had also conducted a series of private experiments, keeping myself awake by chewing on my tongue until Blanche dropped off, then beaming suggestions at her ("octopus, oc-

topus, octopus *in a wig*"). I held my breath until my head ached, trying to stuff a tentacled nonesuch into the narrow passage where Nora morphed through Norche, Nonche, and Nanche to Blanche. In the morning I'd quiz her. Blanche, hopefully: "A big green wooden chicken?"

"Go on."

"I guess maybe we were hiding in it," she hedged, sensing my disappointment. "I guess maybe someone was chasing us."

"Here comes sister Double Happiness." Startled out of my reverie, I looked up to see that I had made a wrong turn. With two heads you don't walk by the projects. The inhabitants were notoriously peeved that yet another minority had edged them out for help and housing, due to better lobbyists, better connections, and fatter pocketbooks. The rise of the twofer, so ballyhooed by the partisan *Two Times* ("Formerly resistant landlords show growing preference for so-called double-income single occupancy renters!" "Longer shifts give twofers an advantage in the workplace!" "On the information highway, taking turns at the wheel: Negotiation skills of twofers tailor-made for today's information-based economy!"), had thrust the singleton poor even further down the ladder.

"I bet *she* gives good head."

"I hear Siamese twins swing both ways."

Two of four guys guffawed and gave each other five. I lowered my eyes and kept walking. The flip side of Pride was loathing. I understood completely, but that didn't make it comfortable. "Siamese, if you please!" one wag singsonged.

"Hey baby," said an inveigling voice close at hand. One of the men was loping along next to us. "Why you so unfriendly? Got a swelled head? Think you better than us?"

Someone jostled us. "Can't you hear?" I kept my eyes on the ground and sped up. If I could make it to the Bearded Lady Café around the corner, the lesbians would protect me.

"Check it out. Man walks into a bar, says my brother just married the two-headed girl from the sideshow. Bartender says, Is she pretty? Guess what he says." This time it was less like a jostle and more like an elbow in the ribs. "Guess. Guess. Guess."

"Yes and no." The right answer.

His reply, if he made one, was drowned out by a very loud musical car horn playing what seemed to be "I Got You, Babe." A heavily souped-up me-

tallic gold lowrider was rolling slowly by. When it was level with us, it braked and started bucking—a sight both comical and menacing, like the courting display of a rhino. The girl in the passenger seat was waving. At me? Belatedly, I took in the mural on the side. It showed a big-haired, big-busted nude reclining on a serape. She had two heads, slightly smaller than her breasts. One of the heads had something wrong with the eyes, the other had something wrong with the mouth. Behind this occidental odalisque was one of those desert landscapes with saguaros, red-rock formation of the kind called a hoodoo, and bloodbath sunset daubed on varnished slices of tree trunks in southwestern gift shops.

I felt an unpleasant thrum in my chest. I *knew* that hoodoo. The Great Turd, as we had called it, with childish ribaldry, threw its early-morning shadow over the southern end of the main street of Too Bad.

Having a piece of my past drive up and honk at me was distinctly unnerving, and I hardly think I could have meant to thumb a ride, but somehow my thumb was out and the car had stopped and a door was squawking open. The girl scooched over and spanked the seat beside her, nodding and smiling. Her lipstick was almost black, shiny as patent leather. It made her teeth look grey, or maybe they were grey. I smiled too, but shook my head. She just looked like a whole new kind of trouble. Meanwhile, my friends consulted among themselves. It seemed the lowrider was trespassing, but nobody knew who to go get. I took advantage of the confusion to break into a run.

I heard the car door close. The lowrider burned rubber peeling out. The girl whooped. I saw a gold blur slow at the corners of my eyes, and thought they were going to pull over again. But they just blew their horn a second time. As they gunned the car up Guerrero, "I got you" took on a dying fall.

Absurd! That such a car existed at all. That it should drive by right then. If it had happened in a dream, I would have scoffed at it. As it was, I didn't feel like walking anymore. I went straight home and took a nap. The minute I fell asleep, I was back on the desert. This time some of the pebbles moved, as if a lizard had just made a dash for a clump of sage and scattered them with its kickoff. But there was no lizard. In the background, though, was the Great Turd.

Someone was in my room! An oddly hunched figure, horned, in a white coat—I threw off the covers, then sank back with a groan. It was just Trey,

in the ridiculous pimp coat (full-length, white leather) he'd bought from a freshly hard-up gambler in Atlantic City.

"I *hate* when you do that," I said. "Would you consider knocking?" The horns were two locks of gel-hardened hair from either side of his part. They had flopped forward when he leaned over.

"That chick you decided to maul is really working my nerve," Trey said, straightening and crossing to the window. "Next time pick someone with a nice low furry voice. Low voices get lost in the ambient noise. You must have noticed that car stereos sound tinny. The treble cuts through the engine sound. In the future molest a baritone. Do you want me to get rid of her for you?"

"Yes. *No!*" After that time at the Indian restaurant, there were jokes I didn't make with Trey, in case he took them seriously. I was never sure exactly how shady Trey really was. For sure he didn't have good sense. Like you could hide a three-quarter-life-size piece of tantric statuary up your shirt! "What did you have in mind?" I added. Trey pursed his lips and widened his eyes, for laughs. This reassured me. Then it didn't. "No you don't. Stay out of it."

"It's your funeral!" Trey said cheerfully. "Can I close this? I'm closing this." He banged down my window, shutting out the distant trill of Charmaine's current chant, "Hear my voice, heed my choice!" "Ow!" He clutched his right wrist as he left.

Trey had carpal tunnel syndrome—he said he'd got it logging too many hours in chat rooms—so he used a headset for sex work. He used voice recognition software to write. The program translated sounds into written words, whether the sounds were words to begin with or not. This afforded Trey much amusement. His laughter would be turned into more words ("The ketchup the ketchup the the the"), which made him laugh even more. This could go on for some time. When he left the room, the computer registered the distant yells and sirens and the various empty sounds of the room and dutifully took them down. Sometimes we sat and watched as the screen silently filled up with words. Silence spoke a lushly maternal language. "Mommy," it said, "On a moon oh Mom, on on on moon, Mommy, om."

Trey reappeared. "Nora, there's something *muy curioso* going down."

"What?"

"Did you venture into the citadel while I was gone?"

"Citadel?"

"My room, wench. The room of Trey."

"I was sleeping."

He led me to his computer.

The text began more or less as usual, with lowing and lunacies: "Moo moon oh moo, Mama mnemonymy Mom." But then it took a turn for the improbable. No, the impossible: "A cowboy going hell for leather roped two long horned cows together. One was black the other red they gored each other then both were moo moo moo moon. How now brown cow. Death where is thy moo. Mnemonymy on on on Mom moon Mom . . ."

"Somebody's playing a trick," I said, but I felt my skin tighten.

"You've gone a funny color," Trey said. "I have been waiting a long time for the chance to say this—"

"Trey, don't."

"But you have, yes, you have actually—"

"Trey!"

"—*blanched.*"

He threw up his arm and deflected my punch, which was aimed for his shoulder, so that I wound up clipping him in the mouth. His incisor cut through his upper lip. He clapped his hand to his mouth, and then looked at his finger with fascination. "Oh! You've blooded me, you harridan!" He grinned at me with stained teeth. "Look, it gave me a hard-on. Kiss-kiss!" He advanced.

"Trey, back off." I pushed him away.

He sat down at his desk and began making multiple prints of his bloody lip on a piece of scrap paper. "Our conversation is being faithfully recorded," he said. "More or less, anyway. The profound distance between harridan and hard-on has escaped our scribe."

"Maybe it would help if you pronounced them correctly."

"No! Don't tell me I've been mispronouncing hard-on all these years!"

I snorted. He regarded me.

"You're not charismatic," he said. "But you are sort of fascinating, like a big crusty sore. You ask yourself, just how bad is it? It makes you want to probe. To see how far the rot extends."

"Thank you," I said. "Were you talking to the Mooncalf, like free-associating? Or on a call? Or singing some sort of song?"

"I never sing, it makes my mouth look funny. Would you like a printout?"

* * *

The next day I got up even before Charmaine did and made a trip to the Mission Branch Library, where a peppy elderly librarian in the Latin Interest Collection dug up an article from a three-year-old lowrider magazine archived on microfiche. She adjusted her glasses and read brightly, "'With two-pump, four dump hydraulics, gold coils and six Trojan batteries to provide the juice, frenched antennas, shaved door handles, phantom top and moon window, phat paint scheme with ghost patterns and laid out along the side a freaky mama with two of the best, this two-headed dolly clowns the competition.' There's a picture of the owner, here, Salvador Swain." She looked up. "I'm afraid there's no information about the artist, dear." Salvador was a dumpy stranger in a backward cap, mustache like a caret over a dot of a mouth. Just somebody mad enthusiastic about twofers and feeling the need to get the word out.

The Great Turd? Just a bloop of the brush.

When I got home, Charmaine was leaning on an old VW Bug parked across the street, talking to the same ginger-haired Togetherist I'd seen with RubiaMorena. She stopped to put her hands around her mouth and holler "No excuse/for abuse!" I waved and went in.

Writing about these incidents now, there's the danger I'll draw them too tightly together. My pen keeps catching in the connecting threads, pulling them up out of the weave, into plain view. But I couldn't see them at the time. I did have a sense, though, of nothing as definite as a pattern, but of almost imperceptible tightenings, no more binding than a thread of spider-silk stretching across an eyelid in the dark, but linking improbably distant things. Each, before they snapped, tugged at a mooring deep inside me, drawing out, for one instant, the many-eyed guardian.

The Siamese Twin Reference Manual

Voice Recognition Transcription

Moo moon oh moo, Mama mnemonymy Mom. A cowboy going hell for leather roped two long horned cows together. One was black the other red they gored each other then both were moo moo moo moon. How now brown cow. Death where is thy moo. Mnemonymy on on on Mom moon Mom

Day! Oh I apron you do that. Would you consider knocking?

Hat check you decided Tamal is really working mine oeuvre. Next I'm pick someone with a nigh chaffeur re: voice. Low voices get loss in DMV ant noise. You miss dove notice that car stair Rio sound Timmy. The trouble cutthroat the hinge in sound. In the future no less a bear attone. Jew want me toga tread aver for you? Yeah snow! Leaded Jew haven't mine? No you don't. Stay outfit. It's your few neural. Can I close this? I'm closing this. Bang! Cow.

Nora there something wee Curie oh so going down. What? Did Jew vent your into the sit a doll while I was gone? Sit a doll? My rune, winch the rune of Trey. I was sleeping somebody splaying a trick. You've gone off on nickel ore. I of been waiting a long time for the chance to sadist Trey don't but you have yes you half factually Trey. Blanche. Nap. No you blood dead me, you hard on. Look, it gave me a hard on. Caskets. Trey, back off.

Moon.

HALF LIFE

Our converts Haitian is being faithfully recorded. More or less anyway. The profoundest dance between hard on and hard on has escaped ascribe. Maybe it would help if you pronounced them correctly. No. Don't tell me I've been mispronouncing hard on all these ears. Trunk. You're not carries manic but you are sort of fascinating, like a big crusty sore. You ask yourself just how bad is it? It makes you want to probe. To see how far erotics tends. Thank you. Were you talking to the moon calf, like free associating? Moronic call or singing some sort of song?

I never sing, it makes my mouth look funny. Would you like a pinto?

The Rose Towel

The dollhouse was splashed with blood. Blood mingled strangely with the oversized sprigs on the wallpaper in the parlor, dotted the dining room floor in squashed hemispheres the relative size of Frisbees.

What was floating in the bowl should have been dead. It, the babies, was very small and still. One would like to cast a forgiving light on this moment, on Mama, and say that it was so still that it seemed dead, could easily have been mistaken for dead, dead as a drumstick stuck in a ring of fat. But no, it was not as dead as that. Or one might like to say that it was lively, even antic, certainly small but quite self-sufficient, like an elf in a storybook. Doing backstroke in the blood, kicking its little toes. So that she might easily have imagined it would climb out on its own, towel off in the dollhouse bathroom, and put itself to bed. But it was not as alive as that. The pale form paddled feebly in the warm bath. The blood was a magenta circle in the bowl. A curd of humanity twitched in the center of it.

If the babies opened their eyes, they would have seen a house that seemed to have been hit by a hurricane. There was a four-poster bed in the kitchen, and a cleaver stuck in a ham in the nursery, and everyone in the house lay sleeping under a spell, and half the furniture stood out in the yard. The light had changed. It was cooler, bluer, and Mama had gone.

The blood was cooling and thickening at the surface when Papa came home. He called, and got no reply. He came into the room. The creaking of the floor, loud, preceded him, and scared the babies, who tried crying now, and continued crying out of fear at the noise they made. So when the father

kneeled over the bowl he heard them peeping, and there was never a question whether he would care for them, as he would have cared for a baby bird shoved out of its nest. He picked up the warmish bowl, went carefully down the steps, watching it, balancing it. The heavy fluid swung as one mass, its surface almost still and slightly wrinkled like the skin on heated milk.

He emptied the basin into a colander in the kitchen sink. He paused, staring into the colander, but only for a moment. He turned the faucet aside and ran the water over his wrists until it felt neither hot nor cold. Then he washed the babies, holding the heads up with one finger. The skulls were not much bigger than lima beans. The veins showed through.

He laid the babies on a folded paper towel. He examined them, stretching out the curled, rubbery little limbs, checking the minuscule cleft and the pink dots of the nipples. The exceptionally wide shoulders, the two heads on their frail stems. The remains of the umbilical cord he tied off with the help of tweezers and a pin. Then he got out his baby-bird kit: the cardboard box, the low-wattage lightbulb, a nest of shredded papers and old washrags. He made his baby-bird formula: milk, warm water, mashed hard-boiled egg yolk, oatmeal pressed through a sieve.

The two heads swayed in the paper nest, their cheeks smudged with printer's ink, in which a few mirror-image words might have been made out. They stared wearily at the eyedropper as it advanced toward them, a milky drop swelling at the tip. The heads weaved, and one brushed against the wand. When the drop touched her lips it broke all over her face. A tongue the size of a stamen slid out and tasted it.

He sat with his hand in the box until the babies fell asleep on his palm, and then he shifted them into the nest, arranged the lightbulb, draped an old towel over the box. The towel had roses on it.

The vultures told him where she was. They were not circling, but flapping abruptly up and then settling again, which said to him that she was not moving much. He could see their dark shapes appearing sudden above the red bluff and then dropping behind it again. As he began to climb, though, the rock rose up between them and he couldn't see them anymore, and this made him climb faster. The yellow dog scrambled ahead of him, claws rattling on the rock, showering him with sand and little pebbles. He slipped in one such small avalanche and scraped the bottom of his chin. He swarmed up the last few feet over a moving landscape bent on downhill.

He saw her down the slope a distance. She was propped against a boulder. The vultures occupied the rocks around her, looking formal and interested, like a committee.

The vultures slowly unstuck themselves from the rocks. A moment later the yellow dog appeared at her knee. Papa could feel the wind of wings flapped low overhead. Fritzi was prancing and fawning around my mother, who turned out one hand for her to lick without opening her eyes.

Under the towel the light shone all night, dimly illuminating the ceiling with a pink glow and attracting a few large, sleepy moths, who pressed themselves against the roses, making black angel-shapes. Papa came down naked several times during the night, and lifted the towel. Moths staggered into the air. When he was gone, they settled again.

Our father hid us in the shed. We suckled at the eyedropper. We ate baby-bird formula, suet dissolved in milk, damp cracker crumbs, bits of Vienna sausage snipped off with scissors. Our father was our first mother. He might have been our only mother, but by the time we were baby-sized, we were bawling in stereo, and my cries rung through the whole of Too Bad, then bounced off the bluffs and came back again. Our mother couldn't ignore any longer what she had guessed weeks before.

She stood in the tool-shed door. "My milk's come," she said, twin blotches on her blouse, over her breasts. "I might as well take the baby." She held out her arms. "Or babies?"

Too Bad, Pop. 3 ½ .

Women are alleged to be the gentle sex, more reliable, more nurturing than men. In my experience, the reverse is true. Women are untrustworthy, intractable, better at leaving than staying on. It is men who are the homebodies. Gentle creatures, they mean no harm, and they are restful. But my mother did not care to rest. I could tell when the sap was running through her, volatile as ethanol. She could touch a match to her tongue and hold a pool of blue flame in her mouth. She tried not to burn him when he pressed his mouth to hers, but his lips came away blistered. He didn't seem to notice. This was his charm and his failing.

"I sometimes feel like you're a horse and I'm a rhinoceros," said Mama.

I had two incongruous pieces of information about my mild-mannered father. That he married Mama was the first. The other was that he was descended from cannibals. We learned this at an early age. It turned out that there had been only one cannibal, driven to it by privation in a long winter somewhere northerly, but by then it was too late to eradicate the image of my father squatting, his pale chest grease-smeared, nibbling at an all too recognizable bone. My mother often brought up the "ineradicable stain" on the heirloom bib, with a relish my father missed completely. I understood, however, that this image somehow aroused her. She would hoist herself up in her chair, wet her mouth. How restive and glittering she became at a whiff of that profane smoke rising through the generations, like an idol animated by the greasy clouds of the sacrifice. Her eyes sparkled, her plump upper arms grew blotchy, her nostrils flared. As she pressed further, eliciting details she had already heard (the long red hair between great-great-grandfather's two front teeth, the seal ring fished out of the stewpot), Papa turned more and more in his chair, until all she could see was the back of his collar and one ear that emanated tragic resignation.

Eventually she would lead him into their bedroom. She would come out yawning and irritable. Father on the other hand would have more energy than usual and set out with his Geiger counter. By lunchtime everything was back to normal.

Eventually my mother managed to love him. She showed this by picking fights with him. Later, I understood this very well; my father did not. The more she loved him, the quieter he got. The quieter he got, the more she pried, chivvied, and expostulated. She pursued, he shrank, both of them yearned for what they already had, and misread as rebuffs each other's most tender offerings.

Of course, couples are always monstrous. Everyone senses this, and grows uneasy in their company. Nobody likes to watch the blending of things that should be separate: a sea urchin making up to a buffalo, a mosquito fondling a worm. (Audrey, of course, would disagree.) Why would two people who are free to walk away stand side by side and even hold hands? If I were single, I would always walk away. I would specialize in it.

Well, that's what Mama did, she started walking away. She would pack a bag, put on a pretty dress, get in the car, and go—to political rallies, EST training seminars, lesbian separatist cookouts, clothes-free solstice celebrations. She spun her wheels for our amusement as she peeled out, raising a

peacock's tail of pebbles. Then the car lumbered slowly out of sight. As she topped the curve, her hand would wriggle out the chinked window. That was the last thing we saw every time, her hand descending behind the hill like a swimmer's last wave. It made my throat ache, it looked so tiny and already so far away.

Mama came back from one of her longer trips with Max on her arm. Papa shook Max's hand and politely fixed a bed on the sofa. We wondered who was going to sleep there. (To our dismay, we did. Max slept alone in our room.) Over the next few weeks Max and Papa banged together a little house, more like a shed, and she moved in. She never left. Eventually she and Papa went into business together. Does this seem strange? The fact was, Max and Papa were much more compatible than either of them was with my mother. Mama, with her will and her carnality, coaxed out of them both a helpless, ashamed lust, which they entrusted uneasily to her not entirely reliable hands, since, practical in everything else, they were at a loss before this violent, irrational feeling and this activity that produced nothing. That Mama was remarkable they agreed, and said no more, pleased with each other's tight-lippedness. And so they became friends. This sort of thing happens often between people with common interests and so will not be remarked upon further here.

Devil's Food

My next bad dream was only a glimpse before waking, but it felt very real. A sense of an interior, very close and warm, not a tent, perhaps a costume of some kind. Or a womb? Things moving close to my skin. Flashes of brightness. Something was wrong with my sense of balance, and this dizziness spun me awake. For once I wanted to go back; there was something I needed to find out. When my head cleared, I did not know what it was I was missing, but my throat ached as if I had been crying.

Something else was wrong: it was quiet. Charmaine had stopped yelling. It seemed too much to hope for that that malignant dot on her nose had already killed her.

I stumbled out into the kitchen, where Audrey was reading the *Two Times*, looking pleased with herself. I narrowed my eyes at her and shook some Grape-Nuts into a bowl, sliced a banana into flabby coins. The knife made a sudden sound when I set it down on the counter, and I flinched. "What have you done?" I said, sitting down.

Charmaine had agreed to stop harassing me on condition that I enroll in some kind of consciousness-raising group, she informed me smugly. Audrey had brokered the deal. She had been trying to raise my consciousness for years.

"Let's don't and say we did," I suggested.

"Hah," Audrey said.

She had forgiven me. "Turncoat, traitor, Judas, snake," I said happily. In my relief I agreed to go to a party with her later that evening.

* * *

It was a purplish blustery night. The low fog was weirdly underlit and ripped in places to show black behind it. The warehouses south of Mission seemed like dummies, solid concrete blocks with no room for rooms inside them, despite the doors and windows on the outsides. At the crunch of the emergency brake I felt a sudden panic and aversion, as I always did before a party.

I held Blanche's head down so I didn't bean her getting out of Audrey's Datsun. These little acts of kindness I could still perform, and feel a faint warmth in my chest. "Who is the luke in lukewarm?" I said.

"Is it the biblical Luke?" said Audrey vaguely. "Maybe he only kind of liked Jesus. I left the address at home, but I think it was 2112. Hey, how do I look?" She spread her arms and twirled. Strands of silver fiber from her vintage 1970s jumpsuit flickered under her arms, which were multiple and blue under the alternating current streetlights.

"You look like Kali, or do I mean Krishna?" I said.

"Maybe it was 2116. All multiples of two seem like essentially the same number to me," said Audrey. "They're all basically chunky and amiable, like Labradors." She poked at the bell.

A girl with a long, sideways-tending chin ushered us in with exaggerated gestures as if she thought we were deaf or foreign, then, on spinning around, tripped on the bottom step and twisted her ankle. We helped her up the stairs into a brightly lit bedroom. She sank onto the heaped coats on the bed. Audrey and I put down our own coats beside her as gently as we could.

Everyone seemed to be in the kitchen. In the doorway a chubby boy in a tiny lead apron and a T-shirt that read GIRL was talking to an actual girl who was wearing a bridal veil and picking individual sprinkles off a plate of devil's food cupcakes and eating them. Everyone else was crammed into a tiny space around the refrigerator. I went to put the six-pack away. When the refrigerator door opened, everyone shuffled back. They shuffled forward again when it closed.

Behind me, someone drawled, "How's *that* for a twin-pack?" I whirled, and Audrey put a restraining hand on my arm. Everyone was looking at a cigarette lighter with a decorated windshield. Apparently the girl on it shed her bikini when the plastic got hot. Audrey pulled me out through a series of rooms in each of which a few twofers and singletons loitered, one of the latter looking fabulously uncomfortable in full haz-mat fetish-wear, goggles

and all. "Her girlfriend's totally *toxic,*" Audrey whispered admiringly. They lifted their drinks slightly as we entered each room, as if to explain why they were there. Audrey scanned them and moved on, summing up their sexual preferences for me in an undertone: "Kitty corner. 669. Möbius strippers. Foursquare—hey, that's Theo/Dora!" I craned my neck. Theo/Dora had nearly caused a civil war at the Womyn-born-Womyn's Music Festival last year. They presently identified M/F. Last year, F/M. All anyone knew for sure was that one of them had transitioned twice and one only once, but whether they had started out M/M or F/F was anyone's guess. I certainly couldn't tell.

"Were you hoping to run into anyone in particular here?" I asked.

She gave me a coy look. "Maybe."

"Oh, no. Who is it now?"

Audrey dropped the simpering. "OK, so you know Pili?"

"Not *Pili.*" Pili had a distinctly smaller head than her twin, which made her look something like a growth. Her face appeared squeezed, her eyebrows too close to her eyes, her nose struggling toward her chin.

"What's wrong with Pili?" Audrey asked, distracted. "No, no, I'm just filling you in on the background." Pili, of Inga and Pili, was seeing Inga's ex, Temper (of Temper and Ruth). Apparently while Inga was affecting celibacy and burning the midnight aromatherapy oil in her efforts to transcend jealousy, Ruth, after being jilted by Pili, had renounced women and was sleeping with Gordon of Gordon and Grant, which caused some friction with Temper, who was a lesbian separatist, philosophically (if not, quite, any longer, practically). To make matters worse, Grant was seeing a low-level politico named Chloe whose ambitions for public office made her a bit homophobic, though those ambitions were doomed anyway since her twin Ashley was a hopeless pothead. Grant thought everyone was trying to put the moves on Chloe, which couldn't have been further from the truth, when actually it was stoned Ashley who had developed a damp inarticulate straight-girl crush and would stare across the various activities of the others at Inga, who found it hard to ignore her while she was meditating and also trying not to trip on the fact of her ex-girlfriend seemingly going down on her in the old style but not for her benefit any longer but for that of her twin, Pili. Meanwhile Gordon, who was struggling with his sexuality and was probably, in Audrey's opinion, only into Ruth because with her dyke energy she was kind of like a boy, had been spotted by Audrey on the balcony of the Café making

out with the worst person he could have picked to experiment on, the mean, egotistical, and predatory Ignacio—though his twin Ben was very nice and supposedly bi and into singletons . . . her voice trailed away. I was shaking my head, lost. "Here, I'll show you." She found an abandoned napkin (damp circular indentation in its center) and began covering it with intersecting ovals, each neatly labeled, like a Venn diagram run amok. The ink gave out somewhere between Chloe and Ashley. We went back to the kitchen in search of another pen.

I remember spotting one in a mug on the far side of the table, near the plate of cupcakes, and reaching for it. The exhausted pen was sweating in my left hand, and my right was hovering, descending, fastening upon the thin, curved shaft. Curved? Something long, soft, and sand-colored flew past my head. Startled, I looked up from something that had just caught my eye on the table, an empty crumb-ringed circle where a plate had been. I had time to track down a vague resemblance to—what was it?—a photograph of an eclipse, but as you'd see it on the negative, a white disk ringed with black fire.

I laughed when I saw the cupcakes, in midair. What were they doing up there? I saw them as clearly as if time had slowed down for them: perfect little planets, their loose sprinkles like tiny moons keeping pace with them. Someone screamed. The plate careened off the back of a girl's head, hit the floor, and traced circles on the linoleum with its rim for a long time, droning.

"Where the fuck did that come from?" someone said. There were smashed cupcakes everywhere. The girl who'd been hit was crouching, holding her head with both hands. Then she sank sideways against the refrigerator. The GIRL boy sat down beside her and gently removed a fridge magnet from her hair.

"Who did that?" said a girl in pigtails, glaring from face to face. "That was *so* not cool."

"That plate almost took your head off!" someone said to me. "Or—I mean—"

"If I find one molecule of frosting, and I mean one molecule, on my new suede jacket, which happens to be Dolce and Gabbana, I am going to go ballistic," an elegant young man announced to the whole room. "I'm just saying."

Audrey was looking at me strangely.

"What?" I said. I became aware of my right hand, empty. Where had I put that pen?

"We're going," she said.

"Audrey, wait!"

"Now." I plunged after her through a crowd of new arrivals. In the coatroom the girl with the sprained ankle appeared to be giving a blow job to a man in fake fur who was leaning back on the pile of coats. Someone in the hall said, "Every single time I get in an elevator I make my peace with death." "The abject is my *favorite*," someone else said excitedly. I stepped on the foot of a woman with sparkles on her cheeks and braces on her teeth, and for a moment I cupped her chilly elbows in my hands. Over her shoulder I saw the girl in the coatroom roll over on the fur. It flattened under her, and I saw that it was empty. I had concocted a whole story out of a few folds of fur. (I should think more about this. We construct worlds this way, not piecemeal, but in one demiurgic surge. How many of them go uncorrected?)

"Ick," said the sparkly one, feeling her left elbow. Together, we regarded the dark smear on her hand. "Ugh." She heaved past me into the bathroom. I dropped my eyes to my own hand. There was frosting on my finger.

"Let me know when you're ready to talk about your demonstration back there." We were circling the block, looking for parking.

"That wasn't me, it was Blanche," I said. Immediately I felt ridiculous.

"Uh-huh." Audrey was calm and unforgiving. "Is that a parking place?"

I craned my neck. "Handicapped zone."

She drove on. "I'm waiting," Audrey said. "I'm listening with an open mind."

I explained.

She expressed doubt.

I explained some more. When I brought up her film, her hands tightened on the wheel, but she heard me out.

She took a deep breath. "OK, I'm not calling you a liar," she said carefully, "because I can see that you believe what you're telling me. But I can't help thinking that you might be deceiving yourself somehow. I can imagine that it would be a big temptation to blame everything that you can't, you know, *own*"—she dropped the wheel to claw quotation marks in the air—"on Blanche. She's like a permanent alibi. Straw man. Clay pigeon. Decoy duck, or do I mean sitting duck. Maybe she *is* waking up, I'm not ruling that

out, but I can think of so many reasons you might *want* to think she is that I have to ask myself whether it might not be wishful thinking on your part."

"Wishful!" I said. "I feel horror at the very idea. I feel aghast." A boy wearing a headcloth and riding a bike too small for him wove toward us. We swerved.

"I'm just thinking that that horror might play a more complicated role than you're imagining. You might need that horror."

"Need it for what?"

"Don't ask me. Maybe she's your conscience." She braked suddenly at what turned out to be a driveway, lurched forward again. "God, I should really just rent a space in a garage."

"Why would you say that?" I felt a pulse of something pass through me. It felt like being frightened, a sort of momentary tilt and plunge that left a dizziness around my heart, but no thought came with it, only the feeling, and then that was past.

"It's gotten way too difficult to park around here. I mean, the other day it took me forty-five minutes to find a parking place and I needed to pee so badly I was seriously considering leaving the car in the middle of the street."

"No, I meant—"

"Oh. Well, it seems to me that your relationship to Blanche is unnecessarily witchy-poo. I mean I see that there are some interesting issues around identity—"

"Interesting to you, maybe."

"Point. Sorry. But it's not like you're the first person in creation to wonder where you stop and everyone else starts. The permeable membrane thing. You're not that special. Fuck, I'm just going to go around the block again. Do you want to get out?"

"I never said I was special. I don't want to be special."

"I'm expressing myself badly. But I feel like you're using Blanche to stand for something instead of just letting her be her own person. I mean, she isn't just the anti-Nora, presumably. In positing her as your *not* or your"—she did the finger thing again—"*dark side* or your *demon double*, aren't you doing exactly what you're always complaining about in other people? Falling into a cartoonishly binary thinking about twofers?"

"I don't see what's so binary about Blanche chucking a plate of cupcakes across the room."

"Now you're being deliberately obtuse. I just think this story about Blanche is a bit too Jekyll and Hyde. Or do I mean not Jekyll and Hyde enough? Whatever. My point is, trust me, you have your own dark side. You don't need her to provide it."

We stopped at a light. A boxy two-door with the interior light on was stopped at the curb outside the ATM machine to which a smooth brown stocky man in a tank top and gold chain and baseball cap was making delicate overtures. A drag queen in a blond wig and a blue sequined gown sat in the passenger seat, fixing her makeup in the mirror. She looked too big for the car, a giantess, as if at any moment she might stand up through the roof, hike up the car like the hoop skirts of a great ball gown, and glide away. Sealed from the blue evening, in a capsule of golden light, she looked wonderfully lonely and sufficient, a tiny jeweled wonder inside an enameled egg. I had never known solitude like that. I wanted to be her. I ached with wanting it.

THE SIAMESE TWIN REFERENCE MANUAL

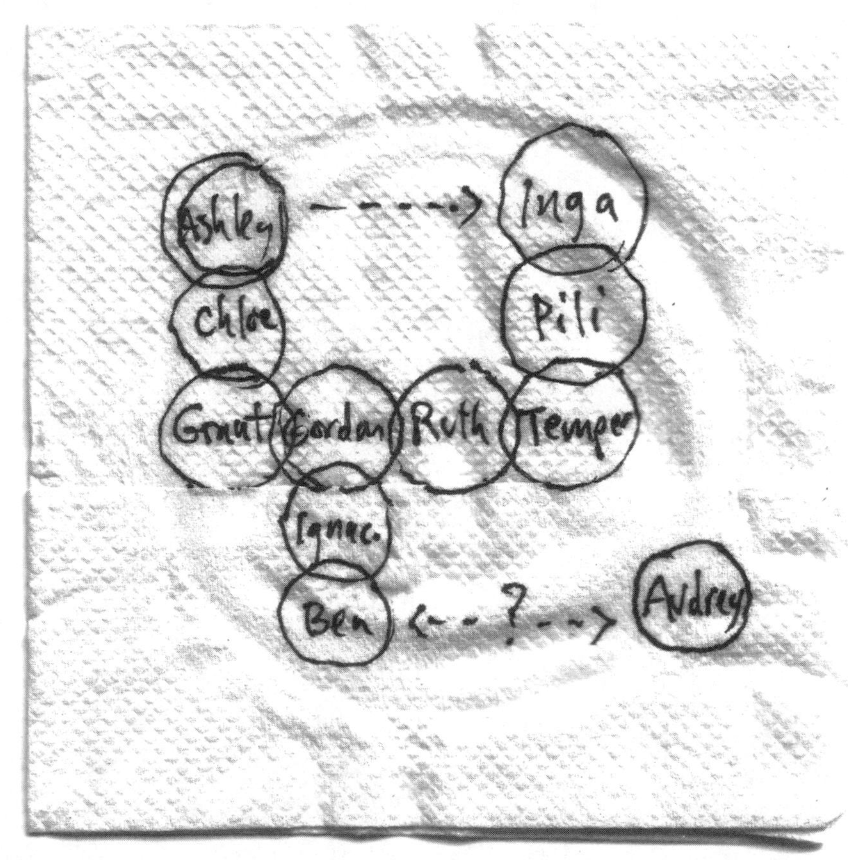

Lithobolia

I named the phenomenon after Lithobolia, the stone-throwing demon: a beige blur would whisper past my head, and somewhere, something would smash. I'd look up in mild, disinterested surprise. It took Audrey's accusing eyes, Trey's amused ones, to tell me that long tan animal had been my own right arm. Awareness would ease back into my hand just fast enough to catch the quick-expiring sense-memory of the just-released object, its temperature and shape and heft. Sometimes I looked up soon enough to glimpse the objects still in flight. They looked different in midair, transfigured by the special destiny on which they were embarked. They were withdrawn from service, for the time being, at no one's beck and call. They were heavenly messengers: solemn but joyful, massy but weightless. No longer just a pen, a slice of frittata, a cell phone, but *harbingers*.

Then something somewhere would crash, or splash, or splinter, or squash, and I'd get ready to start lying.

"It's a little unfair of Blanche to leave me to clean up her messes," I said to Audrey.

"Right," she said, studying me. Then she pulled a video out of a yellow envelope and stripped the bubble wrap off it. "Cane toads' mating habits," she said with satisfaction. "You know, a blurry identity isn't as rare in nature as you seem to think. In fact, it's practically the norm."

"The norm."

"Well, common anyway. Don't you remember the lantern fish?"

"I do not remember the lantern fish."

"Maybe I never played it for you, it wasn't a great success. No, I embarrassed myself there," she said gloomily. "I should stick to animals fucking *au naturel. Au naturel? Ral? Rel?* Does that mean what I want it to mean?"

"I think it just means naked."

"Claymation is just not sufficiently . . . numinous. But what experimental filmmaker can afford to shoot full fathoms five? Also I'm not sure it makes any sense to use a visual medium to depict events that are happening in almost total darkness. Though there is the little glowing thingie."

"Oh, is this the fish that, like, fishes?"

"It attracts both prey and mates with a luminous lure dangling in front of its mouth." She stretched a strand of hair out in front of her eyes. "The prey tries to eat the lure and is itself eaten."

"Wait, the mate gets eaten?"

"No. It's much, much more sinister than that. The man lantern fish is small and basically helpless. He starves to death if he doesn't run into a woman lantern fish. When he does, he gloms onto her and doesn't let go. He sinks his teeth into her side. But what is amazing is that over the course of time his teeth begin to dissolve. His jaw begins to dissolve. Her skin starts to grow over him, covering his eyes, his gills—"

"Gross!"

"—until finally her bloodstream breaks into his and her blood starts circulating in his veins." We were both silent. "He is no better than an appendage," she added unnecessarily.

"That is the most terrible story I've ever heard."

She nodded soberly. "It's hardly love between equals. Though the merging . . . that part's kind of beautiful. To me." She popped a few bubbles in the bubble wrap. "There's also a sea worm, I forget the Latin name—"

"Please stop!"

"But it's really interesting, compared to the female the male is tiny, and I mean *tiny*, like a Chihuahua to a Great Dane, or really a Chihuahua to, say, a submarine. And he just swims right up inside the female and takes up permanent residence in her uterus."

"I'm not listening."

"The coolest part is that if the male doesn't find a female, he grows up to *become*—hey! That's my only copy!" She ran to the window. "You are so lucky it landed on the fire escape. Fuck, Nora."

"I didn't do it," I said. "It wasn't me."

Objects Thrown by Lithobolia

A container of tiny naked baby dolls, plastic

Beef tongue (freezer-wrapped)

A panhandler's money hat

Two-headed nickel

Three black and white bath beads (cow shaped)

A flocked plastic Jackalope piggy bank

Audiobook of *Pudd'nhead Wilson*, one tape missing

Blue transparent soap encasing the dapper figure of Mark Twain

Two left shoes, women's comfy-casual loafers, from a sidewalk sale rack

Magic 8 Ball

Dirty Band-Aids around an absence the shape of a finger

Warped "brushstroke" textured print of a painting of American revolutionary soldiers; behind them, vignettes of war, expressionistically rendered with dabs and swoops of red and blue and smoke-grey

Clear plastic bag full of crumpled bubble wrap, taller than me

Handful of unwholesomely pale coffee beans from the first cubby of an informational display demonstrating the stages of roasting

Jumper cables, the two ends clamped together, like a two-headed rattlesnake locked in a death grip

Two snakeskin-patterned cowboy hats, one pink, one mustard-colored

Soiled and broken pair of child-sized angel wings, pale blue gauze stretched over wire and sprinkled with glitter, with a medical-looking elastic harness

Two unmatched athletic shoes, laces knotted together

Sunglasses, one mirrored lens popped out

Sandwich boards for a party store depicting King Clown Available for Parties

Stack of plastic pop-together champagne glasses

Ace Double pulp paperback: *Death House Doll* bound back to back with *Mourning After*

Comic Halloween strap-on rubber breastplate featuring cow udders with prominent teats

Six wind-up amputated hands hopping on little red feet

Puzzle box ("pieces missing" written in ballpoint pen on the masking tape holding its lid on) with a picture of three altar boys, two with black eyes, one with a bloody bandage on his forehead, all holding hymnals, soft lips open in song. Title: "All Is Forgiven"

Phrenology head inkstand

Clicking metal toy: two baby birds in a nest, mother ratchets back and forth between them

"Executive decision maker" ashtray with spinning arrow

Incomplete antique salt and pepper set, in the shape of a nude sunbather with detachable, perforated breasts, one of them missing

Rubber-banded pile of floppy disks

Unfinished Paint by Numbers, either a naval battle or a pastoral scene, it was difficult to tell, as the executor had botched or deliberately abused (in a play for freedom that accomplished nothing) the delicate shadings required to differentiate the minuscule nation-states that if handled with precision would notch together to render two gratifyingly realistic man o' wars (men o' war?) with cannons blazing or, as the case might be, a handsome pair of Guernseys. The simpler, undulating landscapes/seascapes and cloudscapes around that poor carwreck in the center were big ovals and boomerangs of white, with only a number in fine print in the center to allow the lucky possessor of the key to place these warships or cows in their appropriate setting

SHADY LADIES

The babies learned to walk, and talk, and not to play with scorpions, or attempt to scissor up a hated shirt with a single, stranglesome collar (Garanimals had not yet launched their Kanga-Two line). We were grave and urgent and investigative, when we could agree on a course of action. Even then our movement was halting and interrogatory. When we disagreed, we couldn't move at all. "Gopping," we called it, or "a gop": go + stop. We had a reputation as quiet children who rarely fought. Our fights were invisible, that's all. We could sit so still a brigade of quails would file from under a nearby shrub and start sifting the pebbles around our feet for edibles, while inside, a pitched battle was going on. Chapped knee, skinned anklebone, sunburnt trapezius, damp cleft in which our baggy panties bunched, were territories seized and lost, lost and seized, in a grim, silent, unremitting war. The winner led—for a while—and the loser followed, with the preoccupied, dreamy pliancy of a somnambulist. Occasionally, she looked down to see what she was doing. Often, what she discovered astonished her.

As with sleepwalkers, a too-sudden awakening had its perils. Once, I was sitting on the side of the bed, daydreaming, when Blanche got up and went to look for the dog. I was still sitting, as far as I knew, so what was to stop me from crossing my legs? We fell hard. Fritzi, dodging, stepped on a segment of a cholla cactus and sat down to chew her pads, amazed. Papa pulled out sixteen thorns from between her toes, and that night I wrote this poem:

Mama called from the bed
Papa called from the shed.
Blanche and Nora
could not choose either/ora.
They fell down and hit their head,
And soon the poor girl was dead.

It should be "heads," and there is a puzzling ambiguity in the last line (who is the "poor girl"? One of the two? Both? A third little girl, hitherto unmentioned?) but otherwise I think it describes the situation quite well.

Gradually, I learned to keep track of Blanche's doings as if they were mine, and a new problem arose. I started thinking they *were* mine. An instant after I registered that strangely disinterested tug in the motor part of my mind, I found myself waving the pink slip. I trumped up reasons in retrospect for doing things that were her idea all along. I took the credit and the blame, imagining that I wanted what she tried for, or feared what she ran away from. I caught myself becoming Blanche.

I couldn't let that happen, could I?

My revenge was private and paradoxical: I pinched myself to pinch her. I acted up so she would get a spanking. "Play nice, Nora!" said Mama.

"I *am*!" said Blanche.

"She is," I corrected.

"Who?" Blanche, bewildered.

Still, sometimes (we were kids), we'd look at each other and stick out our identical tongues and run, while the quail flew with a frantic thrumming of wings into the bushes, whickering unhappily. I told knock-knock jokes, Blanche started rounds ("Are you sleeping?" "Nobody home!"). Blanche could hula-hoop, I could juggle (if she shut her eyes). Blanche could make up songs, and I could make up stories.

A thing about Blanche: she was a good listener. When I told a story she had never heard before, she would stare at my mouth as if I were about to pluck a full-blown rose from behind a loose tooth, and she wanted at one and the same time to locate the threads and mirrors, and to believe it was real magic. She could take any poor, dry flake of a story and eke it into splashing life, and she believed everything I told her. A thing about me: I took a keen joy in being believed, and that joy was all the keener when I was lying, for then the credit was mine alone, not shared with the truth.

Many of my best ideas came from Granny. She knew a lot of stories, and when her memory failed, she filled the gaps with invention. Thunder, Granny said, was caused by Lithobolia, the stone-throwing demon. It was not the stone-throwing that impressed us—anyone could do that—but that hollow-bellied name. You could practically hear the stones roll. Blanche believed in Lithobolia, and I very nearly did. Sometimes, Granny would cock her head and sink laboriously to her knees. "Girls, listen!" Taking turns, we pressed our ears to the ground to listen to the borborygmi of the earth. I suppose, in retrospect, that the rumble we heard was an underground test at the Proving Ground. But it did seem to be groaning, *"Lithobolia . . ."*

That we had heard the ground speak with our own ears lent credence to the story of the king who had donkey's ears, and hid them under a hat, and the boy who saw them, and could not bear the burden of the secret, and dug a hole and told it to the earth, and the reeds that grew there, that when the wind blew, or when they were trimmed into flutes, sang, *"The king has donkey's ears."* The nature of things was often troublingly mixed, as we had seen for ourselves. We had no great difficulty believing that dirt could speak, or men wear horns or fur, especially as so many of Granny's stories put across the same idea. Poor, resourceful Princess Donkey-skin, whose father (the same king?) loved her so much he wanted to marry her, had tricked him into killing his magic donkey, whose ears dropped gold coins every night, and then disguised herself in its skin and escaped. For a while, we watched Papa closely for signs that he intended to marry us, but he was so obviously, disgustingly in love with Mama that we discarded that idea with some relief, as we had no magic donkey. ("Though I don't see why she couldn't use a regular donkey," Blanche said. "Or any old animal." "Freud only knows," said Granny.)

The world was full of princesses in disguise, it seemed, though you could usually identify them if you listened to birds and were kind to crones at crossroads. Any woodshed might hold a Donkey-skin pulling a dress made of moonbeams out of a walnut shell. Princesses would be princesses. Like the one who cut off the head of her talking horse, but kept on telling it her secrets, eventually they gave themselves away. In their position, we agreed, we'd be more careful. We believed in secrets, though we had never had any. Granny, for example, was full of secrets.

Granny was antic and interesting. She rocked from side to side when she walked, like a doll with no hip joints. She smelled of old cigarette smoke and

gasoline and a third, sweet, indefinable smell. Granny belted songs about Shady Ladies at a piano in the back of the garage. Then she would scoot over and I would bang the keys, swaying, while Blanche sang odd, melancholy, meandering songs of her own invention. Granny did not always wash her hands after adjusting the points or tightening a fan belt. For a long time we thought all piano keys were black.

Granny cherished her gas station like some old ladies cherish gardens or grandkids. She was an enthusiast of gas. Sometimes she bent over us, wild-eyed, to describe what might happen if someone dropped a lit match or even happened to be smoking while they pumped their gas. Granny didn't like people to pump their own gas, she didn't trust them. She always ceremoniously stubbed out her cigarette in the ashtray before she went out to the pumps.

"Ffwumpp!" she would say, spraying me with spit. "Ffwumpp!" This represented the whole tank going up. "That would be one heck of a boom! The gas station would be gone like *that*." She snapped her fingers in our faces, twice. "And half the county with it! Sky-high. Duplicity County would be one big hole. It's an accident waiting to happen."

"Wow, Granny," said Blanche, sucking up.

"Sure, Granny," said I, which earned us a slap for smart-aleckyness.

Blanche might have been about to protest this injustice, but a troubling thought intervened. "Then . . . won't you blow up too?"

"Not me!" said Granny. "I'll be cashing my insurance check on the way to Mexico. Oaxaca, I think," she mused. "Balloons and *chapulines* in the *zocalo* . . ."

Incantatory words! *Chapulines* I took to be a kind of dessert, and pictured a dainty pointed hat of puff pastry, full of cream. A zocalo might be a restaurant or even, judging by the balloons, a circus! I almost hoped the gas station *would* blow up.

THE SIAMESE TWIN REFERENCE MANUAL

Twice Blessed Books is holding their annual
HALF OFF SALE!
Just a few of the great titles we have in stock:

A Couple Of Clowns

All Together Now

Altar Ego: My Twin Took Holy Orders

Beating Yourself Up: Violence between Conjoined Twins

Bi and Bifurcated

Binary Stars: Crystal and Beverly Bless

Compromise for Life

Cooped Up Together and Loving It

Disappearing Twin Syndrome: Dealing with the Guilt

Division or Diversity?

Double Dealing: Coping with Stress for Conjoined Twins

Dual Citizenship: Legal Help for Twofers Facing Discrimination

Duality for Dummies

Fat in Spite of Myself: When One Twin Overeats

Finding Yourself Twice

First Person Plural

For the Love of a Twin

For the Two Of You

Hello, Self!

I Love Me! (and You)

Idiot's Guide to Self-Esteem for Siamese Twins

Life Plus One

Making Ends Meet

Me Two: When Jealousy Strikes Conjoined Twins

My Better Half: Loving Your Twin More Than Yourself

My Conjoined Twin Is a Cross-Dresser!

My Conjoined Twin Is an Alcoholic!

My Conjoined Twin Is Drug-Addicted!

My Conjoined Twin Is Gay!

My Conjoined Twin Is Mentally Ill!

Putting Two and Two Together: Love between Twins

Same Difference

Second in Command

Self Esteem Times Two

Siamese Sex Secrets

Split Ends: When Twins Fight

Swinging Both Ways

Take Two: When You Love a Twin

Thank You for Being Me

The Both of You

Together Again

Twice Blessed

Twice Shy

Twice the Woman

Two for the Price of One: Twin Fashions

Two for the Road: Twin-Friendly Hotels and Restaurants Across America

Two Way Street

Two-Timers: Monogamy and Marriage for Siamese Twins

When S Is M: Sadomasochism Between Conjoined Twins

SELF-HELP

I was comparison-shopping glue sticks in the all-night Walgreens at quarter to two in the morning when someone grabbed my wrist. "No, you don't, Lefty!" The tube clattered to the floor.

"I was just trying to decide whether to go acid-free!" It was Trey, who looked so disappointed that I bought him a drink at the Elephant Walk and then two more come last call. He maundered on about experimental fashion, how he thought he had it in him to do cutting-edge things but maybe not. "With, I don't know, pets."

"Pardon?"

"Renaissance ladies used to keep little dogs in their sleeves. Or ferrets. Now that's *relational* couture, man. Why do clothes have to be so lonely?" We were both drunk by then. I felt like a heavy golden clapper was slowly swinging inside me, as if I were a bell. The clapper just touched my inside walls at the extremes of its arc, and rather than a *dong* it raised a low hum that sustained itself without diminution in the room and made my throat ache. Trey was sniffling. "Woe," he actually said. "Woe."

I swung my glass from two fingers. The golden liquid swung in counterbalance. I began to feel very moved by my skillfulness, and for a while I got lost in watching. I was aware, though I did not look up, that this languid movement had an exact complement in the mirror behind the ferns and that myriad points of light on bottles and glasses were ticking in time. When I set the glass down, finally, I did so clumsily, and the hum and the swinging were disturbed. "I would love to be lonely," I said.

He squinted at me. "Are you sure? How do you know?"

I squinted at my knuckles. They squinted back.

"It's kind of funny, you against Blanche," he mused. "It's like you're thumb-wrestling your other hand."

"Ha, ha."

"But isn't it sort of like you're fighting yourself? If you win, don't you also lose?"

"Blanche is not my*self.*"

He held up his hands. "Hey, sorry, don't shoot me. I just never really thought about it before." He slumped over his drink. Then he brightened. "Trey just might have a solution to your problem."

"I doubt it." He had an expression I didn't like; it was the one he wore when he was closing a shady deal.

"It's a bit drastic. I'm warning you."

"Stop with the suspense." I was keeping an eye on my left hand, which was running its fingertips along the frayed edge of the pages of the paper. It drove in its thumb, lifted the rest of the paper on the back of its hand and flapped it over, then struggled the paper open. *It* did this, or *I* did it?

"I'd better whisper." His head blundered toward me, and our skulls gently conked together. His whisper was a hissing confusion and bedewed my ear.

I sighed, put the steak sauce to the side, and heaved myself partway across the table toward him. "Tell me again. Don't whisper, just speak quietly." Pinned against the table under me, my left hand squirmed.

"I'm not *telling* you anything, just repeating what I've heard, *capeesh?*" He fell back in his chair and eyed me cleverly. "I'm not advocating nor am I saying nay. I'm only the conduit. The conduit," he repeated, pleased by the sound of it.

"Get to the point, Trey," I said wearily, sitting down again. I should know better. The faith that every problem had a solution, maybe ayurvedic orgone rolfing in a past-life pyramid, drove the sorrier side of San Francisco's tireless self-reinvention. Behind that (raw, organic) carrot-on-a-stick trotted a population of snake-oil addicts. You're a sucker, I told myself. What herbal soak will peel away a second self? The naked taproot of the *I:* another fucking carrot.

But Trey leaned forward again. His face was avid. "They find a head in a bog in a bag in England, right? In a bag, in a bog. So they look around for the body. They search high and low but they don't find it. Do you recognize

this face, the papers ask. Finally they get an anonymous call. What a story! Beheading victim still alive! The supposedly dead guy had come back to his flat in London to pick up his mail and the caller dude, who was his neighbor, saw him. The caller said, like, 'I noticed he didn't have two heads no more. I figured it was a different bloke but when I saw the picture in the paper I put two and two together.'" Trey regarded me cunningly.

I sighed. "Some nutcase cuts his other head off. This is your solution?" Trey just looked at me, eyebrows raised. "Hello, do you not know that in the US of A it's illegal to commit"—The bartender glanced up from her tip jar and I lowered my voice—"an act of surgery against your other half, even if she is deaf, mute, an idiot, or insane, unless she's also gangrenous and leaking pus out of her ears? And even then you have to get a court hearing and the consent of, like, everyone in the world: parents, both dead and alive, spouse, pet goldfish, next-door neighbor, kindergarten teacher, and five total strangers who looked at you once on the street."

"It is of England of which we speak. Of."

"It's illegal in England too, Trey. It's illegal everywhere."

Trey winked laboriously. "Did Trey say anything about legal?"

"I'm not going to some chop shop to be sawed up with a dirty bread knife."

"Nore. Trust your uncle Trey. The beheading was professional. It was done by a surgeon."

I caught a glimpse of my face amid the ferns, like a horrid little fruit. I wore an unfamiliar look—pinched, apprehensive. I softened my brow and shifted my head so I could no longer see myself. "I find this whole story very unlikely and possibly offensive."

"This renegade surgeon. I've been hearing about him. He's an outlaw, like Robin Hood. He was working at a big National Health hospital politely carving away at hernias and ingrown toenails and then all of a sudden, one fine day, he went—"

"Crazy."

"Underground, Nora darling. He heard a call. He felt a summons. He's a man with a mission."

"Oh, don't be ridiculous, Trey."

Trey's Bookshelf: Partial Catalog

How to Make Driver's Licenses and Other ID on Your Home Computer

Where to Hide Shit

How to Make Money: The Counterfeiter's Companion

Get Lost: How Not to Be Found, for Boys (and Girls) on the Lam

Smuggling for the Complete Klutz

Scam I Am

Step by Step Stealth

Skim a Little off the Top

ABC's of Forgery

ID Made Easy

Off the Map: Privacy and How to Get It

New Identity (video)

Scram!

Ur-Ine Trouble: The Truth about Drug Tests

Anarchist Cookbook

No Lie: Passing the Polygraph

Getting into the Gray Market

Speak Like a Native

Voice Masking Devices You Can Make Yourself

HALF LIFE

Are You Being Heard? Surveillance-Testing Your Home

Mind Control for Beginners

Back-to-Basics Burglary

Reborn in the USA

Who Are You? The Encyclopedia of Personal Identification

Little-Known Tactics of Identity Change Professionals

The Loser's Way to Win

Advanced Lockpicking

Backyard Bilking

Getting Away with It

Cheater's Bible

Hacker's Bible

Liar's Bible

Fucking Shit Up

1001 Things You're Not Supposed to Know

Selling Stuff You Don't Own

Be Someone Else!

Amazon

We used to sneak into Granny's bedroom while she was playing the piano. As long as we could hear her, it was safe to work open her underwear drawer, which gave with a sweet, musty exclamation, and look at her panties and bras, welling up like water. We swam our hands slowly through them. Sometimes a pair of dun-colored stockings bound everything together with startling violence. Sometimes we found a cold dime on the bottom of the drawer.

One day when we bumped open her door we stopped, aghast: one of her bras confronted us. Hooked over a chair back, it was as shapely as if it hosted a ghostly bosom. When we dared to approach it, we saw that one cup was stuffed with a sachet that shifted when poked, like a beanbag. "What is that?" whispered Blanche.

"It's a fake boob," I said knowledgeably. "Do you know what that means?"

"What?

"Granny is an Amazon."

"Really?"

"Amazons cut off one of their breasts so they don't get in the way when they shoot a bow and arrow. I read it." I savored her awe so much my mouth filled with water. "Don't tell anyone. She's in disguise."

That night in bed: "Nora, what's an Amazon?"

Later we found out Granny had made the prosthesis herself, and that it was filled with birdseed, which she periodically replaced. "It gives a more natural outline than foam," she said. "A breast is not a geometrical figure,

girls. It is neither a hemisphere nor a cone." It was the mellow smell of millet and sunflower seed that wafted around her and hung in the folds of her clothes. We loved to breathe that smell. It hushed us. We felt safe knowing that Granny was a kind of knight, adept with the bow, of course, but also, we speculated, "The broadsword." "The boomerang." "The Bowie knife." "Jujitsu." "Poison darts." "Ninja stars." We watched her closely for signs of secret abilities, begged trouble to come to town—marauders, brigands. If an outlaw tried to hold up the gas station, he'd be in for a surprise. Granny would spring onto the desk, shuck her bra, and fit an arrow to her bow, aimed at his throat.

One afternoon she pulled up her shirt to show us the puckered scar on her right side. Blanche, prepared by my stories, barely managed to show surprise. But I, who had privately considered that my account might be exaggerated in certain respects, was appalled at this evidence of the power of my words. For a few days, I felt sick with guilt, as if I had performed the operation myself.

How had she done it? I was afraid to ask. I pictured a cutlass, or the oversized shears depicted in our dilapidated copy of *Struwwelpeter*. I saw Granny in a crude rendering, dowel-legged and knob-headed, dressed in bandages, and the breast hopping off as if it were glad to be set free, trailing three drops of blood as big as doves. Then I saw her sitting on a rock beside the fire in an outlaw camp, carving off her breast with a steak knife, while throwing knives at a barrel with her toes.

"Do you think she buried it?" said Blanche.

"Maybe," I said. "But I bet she ate it. That's what I would do. To absorb the virtue of it."

"Yeah," she said, "that's what we would do."

Granny called us "the girls," "the twins," and knitted us matching sweaters, and could not understand why they wore out so slowly. She would not accept that we were conjoined. She didn't believe in growing up, either. When we were a sturdy eleven, she gave us two miniature sailor suits, thus proving her stubbornness on both counts. I thought I saw a triumphant look on her face when we snapped the ribbon on the box. Mama pressed her lips together and said to Papa later that Granny was trying to undo all the work she, Mama, had done to help us feel good about our condition.

But Granny was right, I thought. We were not one, we were two. Our bones knew it, tugged in opposite directions by warring muscles. Singletons,

have you never felt such violent indecision that you stopped in your tracks, looking one way and then the other, not so much standing still as suspended between equal and opposite forces? That is the condition we woke into every morning.

When we needed a rest, we read. Sometimes we shared a book, but that led to other battles, smaller but still heated, about when to turn the page, or with which hand, or at what angle to hold the book, and where. So more often we read two different books at once. Then sometimes we turned the pages in strict unison; sometimes, pinching them up and slapping them down with the same hand, we raced. But eventually we forgot each other and slipped singly into new company, that other, more voluntary twinship we could find with books. Then both sets of pages turned with a mesmerized slowness, each leaf drifting down and settling of its own weight.

This left a peculiar legacy. I cannot reread a certain energetic tale of derring-do without a feeling of melancholy bushwhacking me in the middle of a gunfight, at just the point her sob story made her bawl. Or read a particular love scene without bursting out laughing. Every book seems to me to have a second story under its skin, a narrative not of incident but of emotion, at odds with the one on the surface. Even when, for school, we had to read the same books, I reached the sad parts with a feeling of déjà vu when she had been there a page before me; she scooped every story, except the ones I scooped first. More often, it was a matter of chuckling or weeping over a grammar book. And when we found the battered *Playboy* by the highway, the day before a math test, $\sqrt{2}$ made my pulse gallop, and still does.

Audrey's Bookshelf: Partial Catalog

Getting to AND

Joseph and Josiah Venn: A Speculative Biography

Autogeminophilia

The Geminist Manifesto

The Bicameral Self

The Natural History of Sex

The Fourth Sex

Adopting the Plural Form

The Hyphenated Self

The Indefinite Pronoun

Free the Twin Within

The Boolean Search for the Soul

Transspecies Consciousness

Sex and the Transsingular Girl

Single No More

Elective Identity: The Surgical Solution

Doctor-Assisted Transsingularity

Makeup for the Transsingular

Me, Two

The Making of a We-Male

I Am an Other

Begging to Differ

Glenda Blender's Household Hints

Twofer Impersonators in America

Same-Self Relations

The Interself

Différance

Drag Tween's Tips and Tricks

Venn

I turned to Audrey. I was ready to subject my consciousness to raising, I told her. "Great!" she said heartily. "There's a session this afternoon. Come help me pick out a Jell-O mold for *Dogfish Does Dallas* at Goodwill and we'll hit the meeting afterward."

Among faded popsicle forms and sippy cups I had spotted an unusual mold and reached for it before I recognized the double Bundt shape as the ubiquitous linked rings. Twofer? But it dated to the fifties, at least, before the Boom. I shook my head. I was making things up!

Audrey came up with a Santa mold in one hand and what looked like a Klein bottle in the other. "Find something good? I'm set."

Aluminumware at war in the back seat, we rattled down Van Ness, performed a perilous U-turn under the overpass, and braked sharply to make the turn up the steep spiral on-ramp to Highway 101. "Where exactly are you taking me?" I said.

"Berkeley."

"Couldn't you have found something a little closer to home?"

"I specifically wanted you to meet Vyv. She's taught me a lot."

"Well, I wish you'd warned—wait, you've been going to a twofer support group? Why?"

"It's for anyone with a dual subject position. Not just biological twofers."

We swept over the bay bridge, past the driftwood sculptures, loading cranes, and cooling towers of the marina, up the Eastshore Freeway to the Ashby exit, and into a traffic jam. We inched past a lot choked with old-

growth redwood burl coffee tables. A rearing grizzly sawed from a single hunk of wood menaced a pelican.

"Hold on," said Audrey grimly, zipped up to the light on the wrong side of the road, accelerated left down San Pablo in front of the oncoming traffic, and rolled into the beige haze of Berkeley's stucco flatlands. We coasted to a stop under a eucalyptus tree, crunching over pods and bark, outside an Indian grocer's whose shadowy shop window enshrined three supercilious Fates in iridescent saris. A small sign on the door said, "Hypnobirthing has been moved to Sunday at 2:30." Electric bell a cattle prod to my heifer heart. A little girl's fringed eyes stared over the counter, her guilty fingers frozen on an orange pretzeloid.

Audrey led me back through the cumin-scented shadows past burlap bags with rose and tangerine labels and open tubs of yellow dal and mung beans. A man with a fat, lacquered mustache poked his head through a curtain and watched us up a flight of stairs to a landing with two facing doors flanking a corkboard shingled with multicolored flyers. Audrey opened the one on the right to the sudden glare and chatter of a skylit room full of twofers. A tiny singleton overdressed in black velvet pantsuit and matching choker swept forward. "Vyv Hornbeck, V.D., Ph.D.," she said throatily, covering my hand with hers, which was sharp with rings.

While Vyv directed the placement of chairs, I beckoned Audrey out onto the landing. "V.D., Audrey?" I inquired.

"She's guild-certified for integrative coaching using the Venn method. Of course she practically founded the guild, so she uses the honorific more to dignify it than to claim more authority for herself."

A memory clicked into place. "Venn diagrams."

She nodded. "That's part of it. We make Venn diagrams of our conflicting aspects to help us visualize areas of common ground and then grow them with directed affirmation. Where do you think you're going?"

"To see what it will cost to buy Charmaine off."

"Oh, Nora, could you open your mind a *chink*? Vyv's had a lot of success applying Venn's texts on Boolean logic to spiritual wellness, and there's textual basis for it, too. She got a Ph.D. in rhetoric from UC Berkeley on the basis of her Venn scholarship before she decided to open a practice. Venn was a complex figure, educated as a clergyman, obsessed with symbolic logic. He invented a cricket bowling machine! It's almost certain that he was a twofer, though for Vyv that's of interest only as gossip. There's mention of

a Josiah Venn somewhere, though his mother was only brought to childbed once before she died. Vyv hates Siamese essentialism, but it seems to me that being a twofer must have influenced his work on set theory, the way it accommodates simultaneous sameness and difference. I think you should check it out."

She took my arm and steered me back in. I did not bother to tell her that Venn had nearly cost me my philosophy BA: I had twice failed the logic requirement because I had proved unable to recognize any overlap between categories. The cells of my Venn diagrams had floated separate and inviolate in the universal set, neighbor moons with divergent orbits.

The chairs had been arranged into intersecting rings. I took a seat at the aphelion of one ring. We chanted what I dimly recalled as the Boolean operators AND, NOT, OR, and the somewhat Martian XOR ("Exclusive or," whispered Audrey. "Either but not both") while Vyv swooped around, distributing worksheets. "Diagram your relationship with your twin aspect as you see it today," she said. "The two of you may identify different areas of commonality, and confronting this will be an important step later in the process, but please, darlings, for now no peeking."

I drew twin planets N and B. Vyv swept them up without comment and took a position in the eye of the rings. "Where are you today in your search?" she asked. "Everyone please identify your operator."

There was a chorus of ORs and ANDs.

"OR," Audrey said. "Sometimes AND."

"XOR," groaned Tom Tom. "It's all black or white with me."

"That's a fine place to begin," Vyv said. "Discontinuity is the synaptic gap. No gap, no spark. Trying to close the gap is an aspect of NOT thought, i.e. not thought, i.e. naught thought, empty bubble, the big zero." Rotating to take us all in, she went on, "There's a time to expand your search and a time to limit it. It's not just go with the flow. There will be fissures, interruptions."

The room began to burble with affirmations, for it seemed we were, every one of us, OK, in spite of failings obvious to everyone in the room, not to mention private failings we still hoped to keep hidden. I let my mouth hang open, not to be too obvious about not affirming. Vyv took the floor again. Not really listening, I watched a wing of shadow flutter across her lips. ". . . a stable subject position *without* resorting to reductive identity formulations based on a Hellenic sense of the absolute, integral, atomic One. A post-nuclear psychology, you might say. What Venn anticipated, we experience. . . . No need to

claim him as a twofer, though the evidence is not all in; I urge you all to move beyond literal, biological . . ." I looked up and saw a dead pigeon slumped on the skylight. Or wait, there was some movement—but no, that was the wind. There was a dime-sized disc of already congealed and blackened blood under the grey head. ". . . to recast as an opportunity . . . without excusing the obvious atrocities, or overlooking real, personal pain . . ." Above, one wing lifted and dropped with a soft thud on the glass.

I was standing up. "Not," I said. "Not, not, not."

"Nora?" Audrey said.

"Fissures," said Vyv calmly, "interruptions."

I walked out to a parting chorus of "Good honesty!" and "Go with that impulse!" and "Blanche and Nora, you're OK!" from a roomful of strained faces registering fear and doubt. The door opposite was open, revealing a group of ordinary-looking singletons who were also expressing the hope that they were OK in spite of everything, and on the corkboard was a sign saying that Tuesday's Healing Meeting of Affirmations for Perpetuators of Toxic Ingrained Societal Violence in an Intimate Setting had been pushed back from six to six-thirty by the expected overtime of Spastic Is Fantastic. Obviously there was an affirmation for everyone, which by my calculations meant that affirming had zip to do with whether you were actually, verifiably OK or not. I clattered downstairs and up the cosmetics aisle. Somewhere between Glory Black Henna and Fairever Fairness Cream I decided that I'd rather not be OK. By which I don't mean I affirmed myself in not-OK-ness, more like I wallowed. And decided to keep wallowing.

I sat down on the still-warm hood of the Volvo and stared at the seed-pods littering the asphalt. Some of the pods had four apertures, some had five, some had two, all were full of seeds. Theoretically they could all sprout at once. But in a given patch of earth only one would become a tree.

"Well, what did you think?" Audrey asked.

THE SIAMESE TWIN REFERENCE MANUAL

Subject: The Venn Method
Instructor: Vyv Hornbeck, V.D., Ph.D.

Name: NORA OLNEY
Date: ____________

The Boolean Search for Self, Exercise #1

Using the figures below, diagram the relationship between yourself and your twin a. as you see it today and b. as you would like to see it tomorrow.

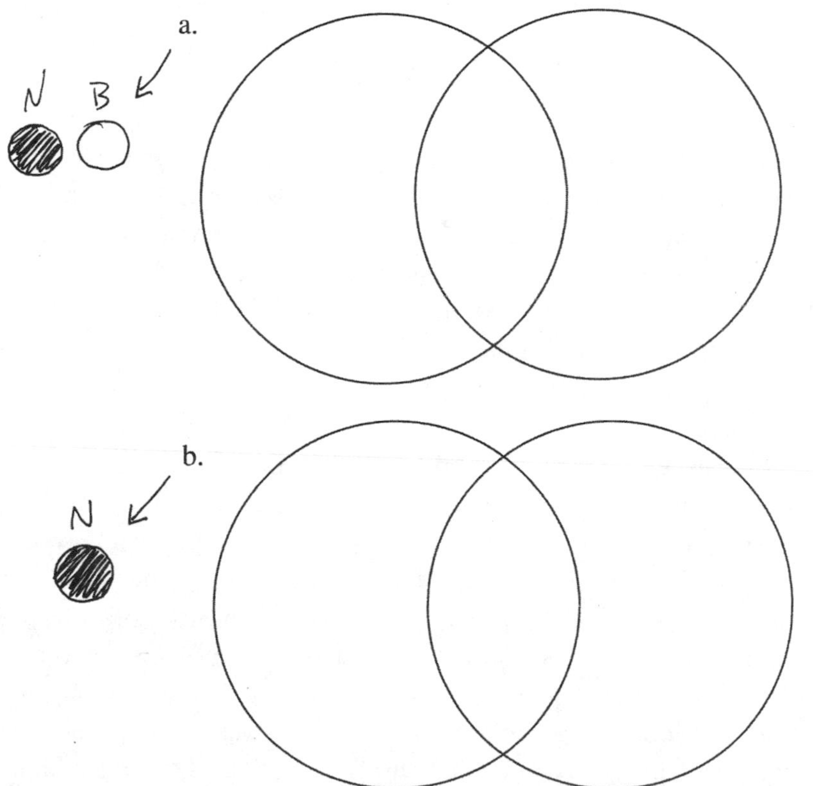

The Dollhouse

For everything I remember, more has been erased. We took down our impressions on an Etch A Sketch, then dropped it under the bed and ran outside to catch the first fat drops of rain before the storm broke. The silver sands slithered across the glass, and we forgot. But a few traces remain. With a little imagination I can reconstruct a simple shape. The diagonals are notched and quavery, but I recognize it anyway.

The dollhouse looms over my childhood as if it really were as big as it seemed the day we splashed down in its front yard. I remember its chimney pots silhouetted against our bedroom window; there was a flaw in the window glass I could pretend was a plume of smoke. It seemed realer than our own house, more perfect. The only thing it lacked was a dollhouse of its own, so I carved a copy out of a bar of soap stolen from under the sink. Sometimes we persuaded Papa to carry the dollhouse outside for us and set it up near an ant den, where the spectacle of ants the size of a doll's roller-skates racing incuriously over the settee, armoire, walls, ceilings, miniature jelly mold, braided bread loaf, and occasionally staging small skirmishes with warring tribes was a source of strange sensations, and I would squat and watch them for as long as I could force Blanche to stay. Once we came back from lunch to find that squat, sluggish lizard we called a horned toad draped across the master bed, phlegmatically devouring every ant that came through the door. We brought Mama and Papa to look. Papa guffawed and dropped to his knees. "How about that! That deserves a photo. Someone run get the camera." In my close-up, the lizard is a grey, vaguely reptilian blur,

the ants not visible at all. For the next shot, I had taken a few steps back, and the lizard had vanished into a general foreground haze, but behind the house a giant in perfect focus has his arm around a lady giant, who regards him woefully and furiously over a hanky.

Later, when we were bigger, it was Hurricane Norbla that stooped over the dollhouse, arms undulant twin tornados, and swept it up. We whirled it until our legs felt all cloudy, and then bumped it tipsily down into a southwestern sort of Oz, where baby horned toads were tucked tightly into bed so they couldn't escape and wept bloody tears, and beetles taped on top of piano stools consoled them. Sometimes we left stray bits of furniture behind—a delicate chair on an ant den, a tiny candelabra. On a walk we once saw something glinting in a pack rat's nest and waded carefully into the brush to see what it was. It was a tiny silver tea set. We decided to let the pack rat keep it, imagining a pack rat family sitting down to elevenses around it.

I had read somewhere that a scholarly gentleman of olden times might have a cabinet of curiosities. I pictured a rolltop desk with pigeonholes and secret drawers, ink, quills, and a small sharp knife for cutting them, a very hard green apple, an inchworm humping desolately across a polished wasteland crazed with reflections and reeking poisonously of lemon. I saw the dry shackled feet of tiny birds poking out of pigeonholes, and fastened to the tiny ankle cuffs a paper label with two unpronounceables and a spatter of periods: *arx. phrynct.* In a drawer, shells neatly affixed in rows to green velvet. One is loose, and rattles to the back and then the front of the drawer when it's pulled out, the spot of glue, a little snot-colored cornichon, has a wicked-edged concavity on top where the shell once stuck.

It was not, then, as much of a surprise as it might have been when on one of our outdoor expeditions, after we tripped and dashed the house against the ground, loosening a hidden catch, we discovered a secret room under the roof. There were bookshelves full of tiny books, tables covered with bottles and test tubes. There were delicate miniature skulls, and a stuffed lizard of a species unknown to us playing the part of a crocodile dangled from the rafters. There was a telescope on a filigree base; a tiny lens like a little drop of water shone at the end of the tube. There was a terrestrial globe in a round case the inside of which was painted with a map of the heavens, and a functional scale, on which we could weigh jojoba beans, rabbit pellets, or dead ants. And in one of the cabinets (I'm sure Papa would have removed it if he had known it was there) was a sealed glass jar containing a pickled embryo

with two heads. Probably it was made of rubber, but we thought it was real. We were very quiet at dinner that night, and Blanche wouldn't eat her peas, which was unlike her, so I ate them, which was unlike me.

That jar was like the spinning wheel in the attic, Sleeping Beauty's booby trap. The most diligent parents cannot baby-proof the whole world. And so, from time to time, we got a nasty shock. The state fair had a two-headed calf (dead), a two-headed snake (alive), and a Dr. Dolittle show for the kids with a plush Pushmi-Pullyu that came apart in the middle, to the shrieking delight of the audience, Blanche's terror, and my bitter private satisfaction. I was appalled by the optical illusions in the ancient children's book Granny got out to show us, confident in its power to amuse: page upon page of "changing heads" with peculiar mustachios and weird headgear, that turned, when you rotate the page, into other staring goons, with suspiciously long foreheads and unpleasantly squashed chins. Even worse were the dolls that hid a second pair of arms under their skirts instead of legs, and another head where the vulva should be. Red Riding Hood has a toothy surprise under her skirt ("What big teeth you have, Grandma!" "The better to eat you with!") and Snow White *is* the wicked stepmother. Well, I suspected as much, after all that fuss about mirrors.

And one Christmas we received a chilling present. Our well-meaning uncle in Orange County, mama's brother Del, who shopped from catalogs and had an instinct for the unnerving novelty (for a while, thanks to Del, a tinny plaint issued from our toilet bowl, "Hey I'm working down here"), somehow got Mama to collude with him to the extent of posting him some snapshots and a lock of our hair ("Look, I think you've got pine gum in your hair, no don't touch it, you'll just get more of it stuck—I'll just snip it off and fold it into this piece of paper"), and next Christmas we duly received a My Twinn doll. It looked exactly like us, except it only had one head. "Because your child is unique," it said in the brochure, astonishingly. We hated it, and kept it under the bed, where sometimes it frightened us, especially late at night.

Mama was another source of disturbing ideas. Sometimes we saw her squinting at us, as if at a strange glyph that had suddenly appeared on a slice of sandwich bread. To her we were never simply Blanche and Nora, we were a message, though her readings were multiple and expedient. "It's because she has two mommies," she was capable of telling Max, goo-goo eyed, while to the local Aglow representative she declared, earnestly, "One body, two

souls. Holy holy. It's a reminder to choose spirit over flesh." To Papa: "'Two-headed Girl, Example of Too Great a Quantity of Seed.' Ambroise Paré. 1573. What do you think of that, Pops?"

She flipped through lists of auguries, reading bits aloud to us. "Ha! Take a look at this. 'When a woman gives birth to an infant that has a bird's beak; the country will be peaceful. That has no mouth, the mistress of the house will die. I got lucky! That has no nose; affliction will seize upon the la-de-da. That has a head on the head; the good augury shall enter at its aspect into the house.' What is 'at its aspect'?" She banged the book shut. Sometimes she made up her own auguries to suit her mood. "Watch your step, young ladies," she'd say. "When a woman gives birth to a two-headed, back-talking little girl, the kingdom shall fall into ruin!" Or, more jocularly, "When twins steal the mini marshmallows out of the mixing bowl, they shall not receive any Heavenly Hash!"

The Siamese Twin Reference Manual

Siamystic Meanderings

Two worlds so similar no one could tell them apart, yet subtly different in every particular. Were the gods to wedge them together at an angle ineffably off true, a new world would open up in four dimensions (or five or six—one more, anyway, than we've got now). A world rounder than round, in which the far would be farther, the deeps deeper, now even sooner, and forever foreverer. A world replete with itself, double-dipped, twice as nice. How thin our one-ply world will feel beside that Land of Cockaigne!

Two photographic vignettes, rectangles with arched tops, their hand-colored details fading with age, are printed side by side on a long stiff card. They appear to be identical twins. Each depicts a stocky, shapeless girl in chopped-off bangs, wearing nothing but a pair of tap pants, rolled stockings, and some sturdy shoes with drooping bows at the instep. But fit the awkward eyepiece to the eye, and see: her eyes brim with amusement, her daubed cheeks glow, she thrusts the puffy points of her breasts into three dimensions. One leg, stretched out toward the lens, so we can see the scuffed sole of her shoe, juts alarmingly out at, almost into us, appearing supernaturally solid and vital. In the stereoscope, two visions, each flat in isolation, form a third so real its sideways depths seem to tilt and open beneath your feet like a chasm. What magic transforms paper into flesh, a figured surface into room to breathe? The subtle but significant difference between not quite identical twins.

The stereoscope has gone the way of the zoetrope and the magic lantern, but you may be old enough to remember that inheritor of the stereoscope, the Viewmaster, through which a generation peered wondering at a jewel-hued world of light. Twofers are our new Viewmasters. They possess the binocular vision of the soul. Through them, and only through them, we can glimpse this new world.

HALF LIFE

Oh my America, My New-Found Land! Join us in heralding this coming world. It is no accident that it is only now, as we approach a new millennium, that a new people has stepped through the very split they are destined to heal: twofers. From among their ranks, a new Columbus will raise two heads, screen four eyes with two hands, and shout Land-Ho—pointing in the one direction we forgot to look: inward.

Uranium Daughters

My mother called. "Did you get the newsletter? Isn't it a doozy?"

"Doozy is just the word I was looking for."

"Things are getting interesting around here. The whole country is trying to send us their radioactive garbage. I'm not talking about hospital gowns and booties from X-ray labs, but the serious stuff, plutonium, americium, the uranium daughters. It'll be travelling at night, on empty roads, in unmarked trucks, driven by truckers we can only hope are sober and drug free. Refused by fifty states, it's homing in on Nevada, figuring that since we've already been bombed to kingdom come, we've got one foot in the grave already. But guess who's taking a stand? Your *father!*"

"Uranium daughters?"

"What uranium breaks down into. Elements in its decay chain. Radium, radon. The daughters are even more dangerous than the parent, more volatile. That won't be any surprise to you, Nora."

"Why don't they just leave it where it was?" I took the phone to my bed. "What isn't radioactive nowadays? Trey's therapist keeps a Geiger counter under his couch. It clicks when he talks about his mother."

"Where it was, it's not staying, whether they move it or not. Shallow pits, soggy cardboard boxes, rusted crates—leaky vessels." I thought about all those half-dead daughters, whose remaining half-lives would be considerably longer than our whole ones. Pictured them rising rotten out of their shoddy graves. Rubbing their phosphorescent eyes, yawning, trying to remember their dreams.

"They want to try deep-geologic burial this time," she said, "two thou-

sand feet underground, in a salt bed. *Entombed*, they like to say, to make it sound like forever. But what lasts forever? Water dissolves salt, salt water corrodes metal, corroded waste emits gases, gases build pressure, pressure cracks rock, and substances under pressure eventually bust loose. For example, your father. Papa goes to town every day to try to mobilize public sentiment; I've never seen him like this. It's a delayed reaction, of course. I don't dare tell him I'm divided—some of us Siamists believe we should revere the waste, and the Penitence Ground and the trinitite and the fallout and even the AEC, as the sacred relics of the birth of the new world. And it's true that without them I wouldn't have you. Though I think it's going a little far to revere a melanoma."

"What kind of delayed reaction?"

She hesitated. "Well, you know, his father died of radiation poisoning, though no doctor would diagnose it. Granny fought for years to get some kind of apology. And then . . ." Her voice trailed away.

Graves are incontinent; the dead are restive; no interment is forever. The cracked pots of bygone Shoshone potters will be reassembled and placed in an atmosphere-controlled case in a desert museum funded by the Nuclear Power Commission. Hot dust blows across borders, slurry seeps into aquifers, radioactive deer drop radioactive pellets on your lawnlet, bees abuzz with cesium dabble in the red hairy heart of the blossoms on the barrel cacti in the Example of Water Conserving Garden Design Practices outside the Community Bank in downtown Grady.

Secrets are the one thing you can't keep, these days. They are silent, they are invisible, but they're passing through, scrawling their initials in our DNA. There is no tombstone so heavy that a ghost cannot lift it, there are no locked houses, there are no sealed lips, there is nothing pure in this world.

"Mama?" I said hesitantly.

"Oh, no! It's Shoot-out at Noon time! I've got to get my gunbelt on!"

I cuddled the receiver, now mute as a doll, wondering if I would really have told Mama about Lithobolia. For one wild moment I had thought I might. For all her tiresome striving to be a good mother, she had missed the moment when it came, or deliberately brushed it aside.

I closed my eyes.

Pebbles jitter, then hop in place. It is horrible to see them. I think, I should have known this would happen, I should have prevented it. The snakeweed whispers.

It whispers again, louder. "Nora. Nora!"

I opened my eyes. "Isn't it a bit nippy for that outfit?" Trey said. There was a cold wind whipping around my bare legs. All I had on was a pair of boxers. I was standing among the yuccas on the traffic island in the middle of Market Street, having passed scatheless through the traffic. Taxis and streetcars hurtled by on both sides.

"Thank you, Trey, I am a little chilly." I crossed my arms across my chest. "Do you think I could borrow your sweater?"

He draped it over me. "Let's drop into Mulligan's. There's a bottle of Jack in the Pewter Eternity Urn. That'll warm your cockles."

Mulligan's Funeral Home took up half a block on Market, rivaling the Mission Dolores for beige square footage. They had not taken down the giant vinyl banner they had slung across the stucco facade for Pride: *Twofers Welcome*. "Am I the only one who finds that a tad morbid?" Trey said.

I balked at the door. "Look what I'm wearing! Look what *we're* wearing. What is that you have on?"

"This," he said, "is a male unbifurcated garment."

"A skirt."

Hand in the small of my back, Trey pushed me in. Cold stone kissed my bare soles. A young black man in a suit, his back to us, was just ushering an elderly male couple in matching black leather cowboy hats and vests through a velvet curtain into an adjoining showroom full of caskets. He looked around, did a comedic double take for Trey's benefit, resumed his pious expression, and drew the curtain behind him.

Trey went around behind a glowing glass vitrine full of urns and slid open its back panel. A hand, silvery in the fluorescent display light, appeared among the urns. He selected one of two pewter models, took the top off and drew out a bottle—"Ta da!"—and, after plunging in his other hand, two shot glasses. Setting the glasses with twin clinks on the vitrine, he poured, movements measured and solemn as a priest's.

"Let's go back in there," he said, jerking his head. "Can you get the door?" It opened onto a dim mission-style chapel with wooden pews. Trey stepped through, bearing the shots like lit votives in a gusty place, his face all concentration. "Have a seat, my child," he intoned. I sat in one of the pews, closed my eyes. He handed me a glass, sat down beside me.

I sniffed the glass. "All at once, no sipping," he instructed me. He watched

me get my throat around it, then threw his back. *"Hoo!"* He shook himself.

I coughed creosote, alkali, the smell of ozone after a lightning storm.

"How are the cockles?"

Pebbles jittered. I laid my hand on my chest to stop them. "Were you for real about that doctor?" I asked, to my own surprise.

He sat back. "You wanna take a weight off your shoulders?" He smirked. "Affirmative, cap'n. Doctor Chop exists, we are 90 percent sure. Weird little dude with a prosthetic leg swore it up and down. Gave me his card." He fished in one pocket, then the other.

"Were you talking about me?"

"Well. *Mentioned* you, maybe. Was that bad? Oh, here it is."

There was nothing on it but a circle about an inch in diameter. I turned the card over. Blank.

"That's peculiar," said Trey. "Oh, well! It's just a matter of tracking him down. He's obviously some kind of nutcase, but what do you care? He was trained as a surgeon and supposedly he's never lost a patient, unless you count the, uh, *edited* portion." His mouth worked. He was coming down from something, I realized. "Which some unreasonable people do, go figure. That's why he's gone underground. But if he didn't leave some kind of forwarding address, he wouldn't get any customers, now would he?" He winked and nodded. I felt myself fitting into his world of futile, surreal entrepreneurism, of go-getterism without any going or getting. Trey didn't exactly inspire confidence. If the enterprise had honor and a good chance of making it, that was a pleasant irrelevancy to Trey, who was fine with doing the wrong thing and even failing, so long as he thought he was working an angle.

He was still winking. "Stop winking," I suggested.

"Huh," he said, feeling his face. "No can do, apparently." He pressed his fingers down on his eyelid. "Is this what it's like to have a poltergeist?"

The young man was alone in the reception room when we came out. "Popp-kiss, deputy funeral director and memory management consultant. You must be the gal with the ghost." He glided toward me. His outstretched hand was piebald, chestnut and palest pink; it looked like a map. A diamond ring sparkled near Saskatchewan. "Welcome Chez Mulligan's." To Trey: "Think you could put the bottle away next time?"

He whisked back behind the vitrine and spanked the glass lightly with both hands, beaming at me. "Now. Since you're here, can I show you my

wares? An ever-younger clientele is growing wise to the need to secure funeral arrangements in advance. You've heard about our popular 'do not go gently' punk rock services on Gilman Street? Our goth fantasia with floating coffin? But, starting small . . ." Without lowering his gaze, he drew forth three ceramic urns of graduated sizes, lining them up on the counter. "Here are three attractive options: Eternit*á*, Infinit*á*, Immensit*á*. Depending on your price range, you might choose to customize a smaller urn with extra features—here's one popular extra, lead lining for radioactive cremains"—he opened Infinitá and tilted it to show me the grey ring fit snugly inside the mouth—"but completely invisible once you seal the lid, and available in all three sizes—or, for only slightly more, invest in a real heirloom urn with many of these features built in." He turned Infinitá over and shook it. A little packet tumbled out, and he flicked it across the glass to Trey, who pocketed it.

Tactfully, I bent my head over the vitrine. One of the remaining urns was no bigger than a pigeon. "What's that one for, pets?" I said. I leaned closer, supporting Blanche, making two small clouds on the cold glass, and saw that the urn had a circle, about an inch in diameter, engraved on its breast.

"The 'Circle of Life' model. Well, you'd be surprised by how little we amount to, in the end: about six pounds of ashes in all. Sometimes families elect to keep only a portion, and scatter the remainder in a serene natural setting where legally permitted. And sometimes only a part of the deceased is recovered." He produced a rag and, swishing it over the Circle of Life, managed to push it out of sight behind a cenotaph. Intentionally? I scrutinized the other urns: the green one shaped like a book was stamped with a pattern of interlocking rings. The leaping stone dolphins were suspended over intersecting ripples. Almost every urn had a circle, oval, or ring on it, I realized. Chains, too, were everywhere, coiled around rims, looped into handles.

"Thought about LifeGems?" Poppkiss said, intercepting my gaze with the hand I had already shaken. "Meet 'Pops' Poppkiss. Yep, this sparkling gemstone is made of Pops' carboniferous ashes, purified and compressed under high temperatures into a precious keepsake. His misdeeds, mistresses, the "hitting stick" he kept behind the door, the odd stains on his collars, the gaping fly confirming that the piebald appearance caused by vitiligo does indeed extend to every part of the body, all cleansed and rectified in the hex-

agonal lattice structure of the carbon crystal known as a diamond. It only takes eight ounces, about a cup, for a memory you'll treasure a lifetime."

"How big a part does it take to make a cup of ashes?" asked Trey, intrigued. "A leg? A head?"

Something caromed off the marble mantelpiece.

"Gosh," said Poppkiss.

"Looks like you just bought yourself Eternitá!" Trey said cheerfully.

Objects Thrown by Lithobolia, Continued

Three crutches duct-taped together

Soiled neck brace

Videotape of *Night of the Living Dead*

Toy watch clipped to a card labeled "Fine Watch For Gentleman" imprinted with a picture of a round-headed smiling boy in a jacket and shorts

Poster showing a girl's awed face orbited by hair products

Very large woman's underwire bra, teal

Vial of Essence Of Chicken Medicinal Product of Korea

Acupuncture model of cat

Bank of Hell Checks (for burning at Korean New Year)

Mandrake root

Hers-and-Hers monogrammed towel set

"Tranquillity" desktop water feature

Subliminal Self-esteem audiotape and pamphlet

Pride air fresheners in the shape of two interlocked smiley faces

"Pooing cow" key chain

Pair of Halloween rubber horns with vial of spirit gum

Pair of brown plastic foot massage sandals (fastened together), men's size 11

Vibrator (Good Vibrations floor sample, one of the Japanese ones, lilac-colored and translucent, with a rabbit mounted near the

base, its ears vibrating so fast they blurred, while the head worked in slow circles. Finally one of the staff took hold of it. I admired her firm hand on the shaft.)

Half a veggie chimichanga (in foil)

Cat

Eternitá cremation urn

THE SIAMESE TWIN REFERENCE MANUAL

Mutatis Mutandis and League of Mutant Voters Joint Position Statement

Radioactivity leads to mutation, mutation leads to The New Human (Twofer), the New Human will lead us to a peaceful tomorrow.

It is our contention that radioactivity is a property of language in an excited condition. The integral atom of the pre-atomic age corresponds to the pronoun, fixed in the lattice-like molecular structure of the sentence, whose rules are called grammar. These rules give rise to an infinitude of obedient instances, which may be compared to the wholesome cacti, jackrabbits and quails of a natural landscape.

These rules may of course be broken; their breaking, while not a crime, is associated with the criminal classes, the poor, and foreigners, and provides a convenient way of identifying them. Proper instruction in the rules does not simply hide but alter these conditions. The broken rule may be compared to a broken-winged bird, soon dispatched by the cruel hygiene of natural law in the form of a hungry coyote.

The splitting of the pronomial atom is a solecism of a very different stripe. What has happened to the jackrabbits and quails of our earlier example? The irradiated rabbit bears a litter of four-eyed young. The irradiated cactus bears radioactive fruit, eaten by birds; the seeds are expelled, sprout, and grow into strange, new cacti that harbor their spines on the inside, whose fruit in turn will be eaten by birds, some of which seem to glow in the dark. The quail is snatched up by an eagle, who soars, pulsing with gamma rays, to a distant mountain range, where he fathers some very unusual eaglets.

What has happened? The rules of grammar are not broken, but transformed. More exactly, they are self-transforming. The divided pronoun has released agency from grammar's lock-hold and set free the principle of change. Many of our new

sentences will be hopeless cripples, like a poor acephalous lamb, but others will give rise to new forms of beauty, that those of you locked in the rules of an earlier age cannot imagine. What will these differently abled sentences say? What will they allow us to think? What new nouns will verb one another, adverbially, and what adjectival age will dawn?

Government forces and no-nuke activists alike have misconstrued the purpose of nuclear testing, which was neither to attone nor prepare for war but to prevent it by engendering a mutant strain of homo sapiens with the capacity to see both sides of an issue at one time. The National Penitence Ground is the birthplace of a new age. We demand that this sacred ground, having served its purpose, be turned over to its children. We will make it a Jerusalem for the Twofer Nation.

Mutatis Mutandis: Changing what needs changing.

Accident-Prone

"I am *so* sorry," I'd lie, getting out my wallet. "Granny always said I was accident-prone."

She did, but she was wrong. Those were not accidents, they were experiments. How long would Blanche hold a burning match she was instructed not to drop? How long could I make her hold it, when it hurt me too? If we stood on the double line of the skinny highway twenty feet past a blind curve, while a semi going fifty plunged down a thirty-percent grade toward us, would Blanche jump right or left?

Sentiment is a watery element. The willow is its tree, the lily its flower, and these are thirsty familiars. The funeral urn and the reflecting pond, instigators of sweet sadness, are also monuments to the puddle inside us. But the desert dries our tears. I learned to crush scorpions, poison ants. I watched my own blood blob on my skin with cool fascination. I squatted over animal corpses, amazed at the activity under the hide's sagging canopy. I was fascinated with destruction and death.

Once, I plunged my right hand wrist-deep in a red ant den. Blanche did not move or cry, though a sun boiled at the end of that arm. I was the one who yanked out the swollen pentapod, brushed off the myrmidons sleeving our forearm in fire. Blanche trusted me, admired me even. If I wanted to throw myself onto a prickly pear or jump down the well, she would study to approve.

The well was capped with a heavy iron disc, impossible to lift, but easy to push aside. I worshipped the cavity underneath. The dank draft that spooled

out of it was almost a voice. It said things like, *How terrible it would be to watch somebody fall. How long you would have to wait to hear the splash.*

Actually, I knew exactly how long. I had timed the interval with stones and dried dog turds. Once, too, with a wriggling lizard. I had held it cupped between our palms over the dark void, watched the tiny ancient face squeeze out from between our fingers. Then the whole smooth body poured through the chink into nothingness. After that tiny, distant splash I went hot all over and ran into the brush to scrub my face with sand. Blanche did cry, that time. "I didn't *mean* to drop it!" I said. "You shouldn't have let it get away!"

"I know!" she wailed. Her sobs enraged me all the more because there was no blame in them. I could have pushed her in then, just to silence her. I was preserved from that temptation and others by sharing every fate I consigned her to.

Well, almost every fate. In "backward" parts of the world they still considered us monsters, and corrected us at birth if they could, and prayed over the body if they couldn't. There were mercy killings and exorcisms, but also surgical interventions, to suit the baby for a normal life. I'd have a 50/50 chance of making the cut. Sometimes as I lay in bed I saw a pair of hands, disciplined and culinary, feeling for the spot with the knife. Rocking the blade on the bones, finding a niche. Crunch. Hands in streaked latex.

"Mama," I said. My mother was chopping carrots.

"What is it. What." Crunch.

"Can we cut Blanche's head off?"

Crunch.

The knife was hard to lift with one hand, but I knew better than to use both; Blanche always had a little more sway over our right hand. The weight made my little wrist ache. The blade was a strong, serious shape, a long triangle, very thick at the top edge and the base, welded into a cylindrical metal handle. We had lifted it from the kitchen drawer days before, stuck it under the elastic waistband of our shorts (pink, with embroidered ladybugs), stomach clenched against the cold, and buried it by a century plant, whose fifteen-foot stalk would make it easy to find again. Every day we brushed off the thin layer of sand and looked at it, running our hands over the metal, which was sometimes warm, sometimes cool, depending on the time of day. Our fingers left iridescent prints on the blade.

One day I thrust it into a barrel cactus for practice. Then I squatted,

wiped the blade on my shirt, and watched the cut dribble, bead, and seal itself over the course of a hot day. I say *I*, because I was keeping Blanche down, more out of habit than any fear of intervention. She did not struggle, just waited to see what we would do.

Another day, I laid the blade against her cheek. I can see her eyelashes against her cheek as she looked down and sideways at it, her head perfectly still. "Do you think I can take your head off with one stroke," I said, "or do you think I will have to saw?" Blanche didn't answer. "I will have to cauterize the wound, or I might lose too much blood. Vultures will come. Do you think it will hurt?"

She nodded emphatically, then let out a little cry when the point nicked her cheek.

I *tsk*'d. "That was dumb." I put the knife away and examined her miniature cut. "We won't have to cauterize that unless it festers. I meant hurt me, not you," I added.

I was falling asleep that night when she whispered, "Nora! I think it's festering."

I turned on the light. The cut was red with a thin dark line down the center, like a miniature mouth. "Don't be stupid. I can't even see it." I turned the light back off.

One day I went for a walk. I brought a plastic bag, some matches, a towel with roses on it, and a small shovel.

Her neck was very thin.

I held the knife so that the blade rested on the saddle between our heads. I had held it there so long that it was our body temperature and I could hardly feel it. The edge was just touching the skin of her neck, right where tan gave way to pallor under her hair. A fine muscle in her neck was standing out. I could sever it easily. The sun was steady and benevolent overhead. I felt peaceful and not inclined to move. When an ant ran up my leg I stood on one foot and knocked the ant off with the other. I pressed the knife a little harder against her neck and looked at the way her flesh dented. It went white near the blade. I kept looking back and forth between her eyes and the knife.

"Nora!" Max was thrashing through the bushes toward us, face bright red. "What in freaking hell do you think you're doing?"

I laughed, frightened, and pulled the knife away. I felt the cut before I saw

it. For a second there was no blood at all. Then a neat red line appeared at the base of Blanche's neck.

Blanche let out a terrified wail as Max swept us roughly up. I let the knife fall; it stuck point down with a satisfying *chunk*. "We were just playing," I said.

I repeated this claim at the kitchen table tribunal a short time later. "We were, weren't we, Blanche?"

Blanche nodded. "We always play like that."

"With a *knife*?" Mama said. She touched the back of her hand to her brow.

"Knives aren't toys," Papa said. "If you want a knife of your own, we'll pick one out together, and I'll show you how to use it."

"My own knife?" I breathed. "For keeps?" I could see it. No corkscrew or awl or Swiss scissor piffle, just an elkhorn handle and one long, sullen blade.

"Yours *and* Blanche's, Nora. And you'll both have to promise to handle it carefully. Never forget that you could really hurt yourself or someone else with—"

"Blanche, what were the plastic bag and the shovel for?" Max broke in. Blanche looked at me. Max shook her head at me. "I'm asking Blanche."

"I don't know!" Blanche said.

"The matches?"

"I don't know," Blanche said. "Oh! To cauterize the wound."

"What have I spawned?" cried Mama. "What? What?"

After that I often saw Max watching me. But I can state that I did not at this time have any real wish to be rid of Blanche. I wanted only to know the precise extent of my considerable power over her. How much of me was mine. For keeps.

Blink Twice

"I hope you're not under the impression that decapitation is a humane way to administer euthanasia to reptiles," I said. Trey, holding his breath, shook his head vigorously. Two wisps of smoke slid out of his nostrils. When other people were drinking their morning coffee, Trey was lighting a joint.

"The director said the twofer actors didn't have, quote-unquote, a *feel* for the *role!*" said Audrey. She flapped the paper, indignant. The first mainstream movie about twofers, *Two If by Sea,* and the romantic leads were going to be played by singletons! They'd be wearing fake second heads animated by expensive special effects, when there were perfectly qualified two-headed actors dying to get the part of suave Tyler and his endearingly neurotic twin Toby, or that beautiful but apparently unattainable twofer, whose left side has taken holy orders while her right moonlights as a stripper in a downtown bar, wearing a velvet hood over her better half, and swaps one-liners with that funny fuck Cliff, a regular, who conceals his love for her behind his cynical manner.

"Actually, the snake or lizard head can live as much as an hour in considerable agony. And, one imagines, surprise. 'Where did my body go? It was here a minute ago.'"

"An *hour?*" said Audrey, momentarily distracted.

"Compared to thirteen seconds. That's how long a human head can remain conscious after decapitation. Supposedly."

"Really? Hm." She turned back to her paper. "Oh, *this* is good. The director said, quote, the twofer actors didn't capture that combination of tender-

ness, angst, quixotic humor, ancient wisdom teachings, and borderline-psychotic personality profiles that we think of as quintessentially twofer. We felt the singleton actors had a better feel for the director's vision."

"The cytochromes in the brain have thirteen seconds worth of phosphates stored up. In those thirteen seconds you could conceivably blink twice for yes and once for no."

"Why on earth would you want to do that?" Audrey said.

"Well, then you could answer questions."

"What kind of question would you ask a severed head?"

"I don't know. What's it like to be alone?"

"That's not a yes or no question," she said. "That's more like a *mu* question."

"Eh?"

"*Mu*. Means 'nothing' in Chinese. It's the answer to a famous zen riddle. Or rather it's the non-answer that questions the question."

Trey let out his breath. "How about, 'Where does it hurt?'" He giggled, then coughed.

"When they chopped people's heads off they would hold up the head so it could look at its decapitated body and feel remorse." I stopped, trying to imagine a body from the perspective of a head, dizzily swinging from the executioner's gloved hand. How confused your body would look, shaken in its confidence that it was you. Surprised, disappointed. "That clinched the execution. You had to be shown what you'd lost through your wickedness. But nobody could determine whether the heads were still conscious. One condemned man promised, for the good of science, to blink two times if he was still conscious after the guillotine had done its work. He didn't blink, but who knows if he couldn't or just didn't; maybe his commitment to science didn't go very deep." I mused. "There *was* a story about two rivals whose heads were thrown in a burlap bag together. When they dumped them out one of them had bitten the other one's ear off."

"What?" said Audrey. "I'm sorry, I wasn't listening. I am so burned about this."

It will be obvious that I had been doing some research. I had learned:

- The head of Bran the Blessed kept giving good advice for several years after it was cut off.
- Cuchulain's too.

- Do not play ball with Mayans. If you have the misfortune to coach the losing team, you will have your head cut off. Or is it the winning team? Accounts differ.
- Decapitation is a good way to kill vampires.
- Be careful with scythes, especially if Irish. ("A man decapitating himself by mistake is indeed a blunder of true Hibernian character.")

I had cheerfully printed out the best of these stories and pasted them into the Manual.

Researching body modification, I then stumbled into a private message board with seductive postings from one- and no-legged ladies, one earnest fellow who wanted to have all his teeth pulled, and a number of twofers whose sexual fantasies centered around decapitation. I had read the latter closely, stirred in ways I thought I could possibly interpret sexually but would prefer not to. I found no hint that the writers were aware of the doctor's existence.

Next I had found a gallery of snapshots of severe head injuries. The page was very long and the jocular captions loaded first. The images arrived in an irregular distribution, like lights in a skyscraper after hours. There was a face with a bouquet of roses for a mouth. A white grin on a meatball. One head had been almost completely ripped away. Only flaps of the cheek and chin remained, opening and flaring from the perfectly intact neck—an orchid with beard stubble.

Something heavy settled slowly in my chest. These clownish horrors (whoopie cushions for morticians, plastic vomit on the pillow of a terminally ill patient) were disguising something cool and secret, formal and ancient and dignified: the cessation of a soul. I was surprised at this thought of mine, because I considered myself a hardened character, someone who could examine the curled feet of dead baby birds or wash the crud out of a rabbit skull with skill and curiosity. Someone who would blink twice for science. But I closed the page and told myself I wouldn't go back.

Afterward, though, I found these images in my memory in perfect resolution. The orchid head watched me without eyes, and without a mouth it complained daily. It became ordinary. I could look at it. That it marked the cessation of a soul ceased to be the important thing about it. Soul fled, the body had a new story now. Dead now, it posed a daily challenge to the living.

One day I had once again found myself typing "severed head" into the wee coffin on the search page.

"You should make a movie about Mike the headless chicken," I told Audrey. "Mike was great. He lived for four and a half years after his head was cut off and didn't seem to notice that anything was missing. He attempted to peck for seed and tucked his stump under his wing to sleep. They fed him by dropping grain and water down his neck-hole. 'A fine specimen of a chicken, except for not having a head,' said Farmer Olsen."

"*You* should come with me to the protest," Audrey said, a little testily, as she rose. "We need warm bodies." I stayed where I was. She shrugged and left.

Trey and I looked at each other.

"Neck-hole," he said. "Sweet."

THE SIAMESE TWIN REFERENCE MANUAL

Fetish Information Exchange

Topic: radical cephalic mods

"I have begun tying off my head for periods every day. My theory is that my bodily functions will transfer themselves entirely to my twin over time, without the shock and loss of blood that he would undeniably suffer upon my sudden demise. I am hoping I will simply shrink, blacken, and fall off."

"My ambition is unusual. I would like to be reabsorbed into my twin. Vanishing twin syndrome takes up all my thoughts. If it can happen before birth, why not after? I suspect the adult skeletal structure is too massive for ready reabsorption, even though small chips or bone spurs have been known to disappear or work themselves out years later. With this in mind I am planning to surgically remove all major bones from my head piecemeal, through small and easily closed incisions, so that I become a loose bag of matter, which I am confident will be swiftly absorbed into the body of my larger and spiritually stronger twin, Cyril."

"I used to make dolls of myselves and cut 'my' head off. Boy was I surprised once when I cut the wrong head off and it gave me a killer orgasm. This set me thinking. I can't make love anymore without imagining the cut-off head of my twin propped up on the pillow to watch, like a curious puppy. This gives me a lot of private pain, since I love my twin and do not wish her 'grievous bodily harm.'"

"It is now my only method of masturbation to tie a cord tightly around my neck and pretend it is cut off. I have voluntarily withdrawn all participation from our mutual

body. This was hard on my brother but he has adjusted and now used 'our' arms and legs as if they were entirely his own. This gives me infinite joy. Many of us are concerned with the body left behind and the stump protruding from the shoulders. I am rare, I believe, in confining my interest to the other stump, that is the stump pointing down from the head. I am also curious how much consciousness the head has of its severed condition before the brain suffocates. If at all possible I would like to bring these two interests together and have my decapitation take place in front of a mirror, so that my brother can hold my head up—like Theseus and Medusa!—and let me see my stump in the mirror. That will be the last thing I see and the fulfilment of my wildest dreams. Of course there is no question of sexual climax under these circumstances as I would no longer be connected to the part in question. In any case I have long ceased to attribute any personal significance to the sensations that reach me from those quarters as these, like all my brother's operations, are not really my concern. No, while I would certainly say eros smiles on my stump fixation, my motivation is somewhere far beyond a mere physical release."

"I get an erotic thrill from touching a lovely lady's neck stump especially wearing necklaces, chokers, pukka shells, also tight scarves in a lightweight fabric silk, voile, etc. etc. If any lady has had her twin head removed please contact the Neckman. Bonus points if you kept the skull and are willing to involve it in the Fun and Games! Even saying the word neck stump excites me! Are you this way too! I'm going to jerk off and think of . . . you! The Neckman."

"I am a twin woman age 23 and I have always been possessed with the need to self-stump. My twin does not know. She has her own problems and needs me so I can never fulfil my dreams. My fantasies are increasingly acute. I picture my head literally torn off, pinched off by giant pliers or forceps, gradually carved off in small slices, etc. If anyone can explain this need or share it please write. I am not suicidal, I just want to cut my head off. Stage an accident? Idle thoughts. Signed, Stumped."

Missing Something

Very gradually, the sense that something was wrong with us began to penetrate our savage solipsism. Of course, we had noticed that not everyone had two heads, but then not everyone had red hair either, or painted fingernails, or a single breast. One day Granny took us to the Temperance Club pool where she swam laps twice a week. The attendant's face became grave when he saw us. "Oh, dear," he said. "Aren't you cute! But I'm afraid we don't allow"—he leaned over the counter and whispered—"*plurality-challenged persons* in the Natatorium. Our members . . ."

"Oh-ho yes you do," Granny broke in. "You just ask the NAFWP. The name's Elizabeth Olney." And she sailed past him. We ducked our heads and followed.

"What's the NAFWP?" Blanche asked.

"*Shhh.* I made it up," Granny whispered, and Blanche giggled. I was outraged. Like all liars, I fiercely condemned lying in others.

A Natatorium was just an indoor pool. The long, dim room reeked of chlorine and sourer, more biological things. The blue water sloshed queasily up onto the concrete deck and sent a colorless wash toward our bare feet. There were no children or men. The old ladies glided back and forth across the pool in their flowered caps, with their heads carefully raised, as if they were divine cows transporting a precious burden between their horns. Those coming toward us regarded us with the amazingly sour expressions of the elderly. Granny dove in without hesitation, and then lay back on the surface waving us in with exaggerated gestures. She was not wearing her pros-

thesis; her chest was flat and bony on one side. We jumped, to stop everyone looking, and let ourselves sink. The water was warm as spit.

The lifeguard, a blond young man with soft breasts, was languidly dropping a white nylon rope in swags on top of itself. Even underwater we could hear the repeated slap and its almost instantaneous echo. We stayed underwater as long as we could, wishing to disappear. We haunted the bottom of the pool like crayfish, pulling ourselves across it with our fingertips, which found rough spots between the tiles, also barrettes and rubber bands and once a ring that might have been gold. We investigated the drains. The old ladies passed overhead like giant, wounded birds.

"Where've you girls been hiding?" Granny asked when we surfaced.

"Nowhere," I said, sullen, and dove again.

In the locker room there *was* nowhere to hide. It was a painful place, full of sharp, echoing, three-dimensional sounds like metal shapes flying around my head. The tall lockers were like coffins stood on end. The windows were blind with steam. Discarded swim caps and bra cups lay on the benches, disconsolate and obscene. I disliked their intimate, rubbery textures, the slackness of their cavities. I tried not to look at the bare flesh all around me, especially at the places where the elastic pinched the skin into vengeful squints. There were too many plastic flowers (on flip-flops, on swim caps, on "straw" handbags made of plastic) with petals like stiffened tongues, and the cool puddle on the floor made me feel like I was stepping in something dirty.

The old ladies didn't say anything interesting, but they talked all the time, slowly and in exaggerated rising and falling tones, as if they were singing. All at once they would swing round and turn their attention on Blanche and me, and then Granny would sing back at them, and Blanche the diplomat would make polite replies. I would look at the floor. Once, I saw there—but I felt as if I had lifted it to my face in my hand, my attention was so filled by it in that instant—a huge cockroach. It seemed about the size of a badminton birdie. It was cow-dung-colored and docile, slowly working its feelers. Maybe it was stunned, but it seemed merely, grossly, confident. It showed itself to me, like a badge. It seemed to be saying, You're with us, then? I seemed to have given a satisfactory reply, for it now went slowly under a locker.

Some of the old ladies would not talk to Granny, and she would make faces behind their backs, unmindful of the mirrors everywhere. We might have accepted this as one of the ordinary mysteries of adulthood, but, "They

think I'm un-American," she said. "Probably imagine I whacked off my own breast."

Blanche and I exchanged dismayed glances.

"You mean you didn't?" she said.

After lunch at Dinosaur Taco we went to the library, then the drugstore. Mama had decided that we should spend more time in the real world. Blanche gawked with indiscriminate greed at sunglasses, lawn ornaments, plastic ice cubes in the shapes of fruit. I let her steer and waited for the day to end. My pride was still smarting. It was sunset when Max came to pick us up. We were the only car on the road, straddling the dotted line so we didn't run over the rattlers that came out onto the asphalt to soak up the warmth. Rabbits watched from the brush on the side of the road. In the shadow of the mountains it was already night, but the sky was still full of light.

Then the sky split. We all ducked. The car swerved, Max's hands tightened on the wheel. Already so far away they seemed unrelated to the noise, two jets played a silent game of tag, spilling sideways through the air, disappearing low behind the buttes, then sticking it to the sky in a sudden climb. Granny rolled down her window and shook her fist at them. "They fly low just to rile me," she said. "Pull over!"

The stretch of highway between Too Bad and Grady cut across the north end of the playa, a huge dry lake. It was flat and white as paper. Like most of the kids in Grady we had learned to drive out there, where there was nothing to run into. Granny took us out in the tow truck and laughed while we bucked and stalled in our own private cloud. Twice in my childhood, after especially heavy rains, it briefly became a lake again: one inch deep, miles wide, and as flat and reflective as a mirror. The whole town went out and splashed barefoot in the sky. Wondering vultures circled our ankles, and the teenage girls wearing skirts pinched their knees together and giggled.

Even in dry weather, the hot air reflected like water. Trucks rode their own reflections across the valley. I wondered if the drivers ever imagined sinking through.

The playa was so extravagantly white it made people want to write on it. All along the highway there were words pieced together from rocks and beer bottles stuck neck down in the crust. You could just read them, if you turned your head as you passed.

TRIXIE + HENRY

JEHOVAH

I MISS YOU AL

I ❤ MY HOT DOG

UFOS: PLEASE HURRY

Max braked, and Granny jumped out of the car. "Come on, girls, find me some rocks." We assembled part of an exhaust pipe, a ballpoint pen with a rusty clip, and three shreds of a truck tire. Granny found a crow feather and a stiff red rag. Max was the only one who found any rocks. (It turned out she had requisitioned HENRY.) Granny wrote:

STOP THE SADNES.

Max said, "It's missing something."

"So am I," said Granny. "So am I!"

They croaked with laughter.

O

The headline was "Severed Head Puzzler: Where's the Body?" I clicked on it. The story was missing, but in trawling for it, I found a blogger's tidbit:

> 'Unity' Surgeon: Does He Exist? English papers are abuzz with speculations about the mysterious doctor who offers "twofers" a service that is being dubbed The Divorce. Real, or one of those nightmares that periodically burbles up from the collective unconscious? Skeptique inclines to the latter view.

I ran a new search for "Unity Surgeon," which led me to "Gillian's Links of Supreme Weirdness," where I found four interesting leads under the heading "Wiggy Doctors." Three of them yielded a taunting "404 File Not Found," the last took me back to Skeptique. Was I being led in circles? I stared at the ceiling, fingers jittering on the keys. When I looked down, I saw that I had typed:

```
oooooooooooo  o o o ooo o ooo ooooo oooo
oooooooooooooooooooooo o oo
```

I pushed back my chair and thought. Then I opened an image search page and typed "circle."

Moons rose: black, white, cratered grey. I scrutinized crop circles, drum

circles, prayer circles, winners' circles; circle graphs, the circle of fifths, and the Circle O Ranch, until my tired eyes began to blur them into a chain. There were over a million links; I couldn't possibly test them all. I added "doctor," which gave me a smaller yield, including Faustus conjuring Lucifer, some aliens, and the Circle O Ranch, again: they owned a prize cow named Mrs. Which Doctor. I spent half an hour examining the bandanna-draped shoulders of dudes grooming patient palominos before I decided the ranch offered no activities more dangerous than hayrides and horseback riding. I deleted "doctor" and typed "unity." Mandalas, halos, yin and yang. I plunged past dolphins and whales deep into the chromosomal squiggles of mathematical formulae.

In a well-plotted sexual fantasy there is an instant of giddy vertigo when speculation becomes knowledge, the forbidden is allowed, the impossible becomes possible. It is this, not the hump and grunt itself, that is the object of the sexual quest, hence the emphasis on thresholds, membranes, closet doors, and chinked curtains and the last quarter inch before contact, when the small hairs stand on end.

Or the slow download of an image whose significance you recognize at once.

It wasn't a circle at all. It was a photograph of Chang. Or was it Eng? It didn't matter, one of the two original Siamese twins. That was the point, you see: *one* of the two.

Seeing double? Beside yourself? Don't know which way
to turn? We can take a weight off your shoulders.
The Unity Foundation. Helping You Go It Alone.

At the bottom of the page lurked an e-mail address, a sullen blue strand that blushed when touched.

I closed the page immediately. A moment later I opened it again. I stared at that shy, poisonous little worm. What should I say; what could I say?

Dear Unity Foundation,

I am a conjoined twin whose dependent has become a
considerable burden. Can you please tell me more

about the services you offer? I am in good health, solvent and able to travel.

Ms. O.

I received an uncannily immediate reply. Of course it was just an automated response, but the speed made it seem as though it had come from someone impossibly close by. Either that, or from someone far away who had known before I did that I would find that page, write those words.

Dear Interested Party,

We have received your request for information. We will shortly be getting in touch with you concerning your search for the One Way.

The Unity Foundation

Days passed. I felt a great slackening. I even felt slightly disappointed, as if the thing had already happened but not turned out the way I hoped. Sometimes I looked at singletons and asked myself, Were they so much happier than me? No, they did not sail their singleton boats on solo voyages and sing songs about being happy alone; they huddled together and went on short trips to familiar places and often asked one another, Do you want to come too?

Some people cling to what holds them back: they would rather live a bad life believing a perfect life exists than live a better life with no hopes and no excuses. Sometimes we are shored up by what we oppose. A constitutive dodge. A body of shirk. But I wasn't like that. Was I?

Two weeks went by, and then I received another e-mail.

Dear Ms. O:

You may visit our office, Rm 101, 22½ Holloway Rd, Holloway, London England, at 2 PM Thursday 17 September, for an initial interview. RSVP promptly.

```
Sincerely,

The Unity Foundation.
```

I was as frightened by this banality as if it had come tied to a brick that had just shattered my bedroom window. For the first time I wondered if I were being led into a trap, though I could not see how. One doubt came belatedly to mind: Why had a search for "circle" brought up that page? I checked and confirmed that "circle" appeared nowhere on it, but Trey, who had dabbled in Web design, had once said, "There's no such thing as a blank page," so I checked the source code, and there it was. I found something else, too. Stuck through the tattoo-blue jacquard was an emerald needle with both ends sharpened:

```
<!--Seeker, if you are reading this, you already
know you have found the One you were looking for.-->
```

"Audrey," I said, knocking on her door. The open window let in a breeze that ruffled the shirts hanging from the curtain rod. Audrey was at her desk. "I was just wondering," I said. "Do you think a person could send e-mails to herself that looked like they came from somewhere else entirely?" I was not sure if this was really what I had intended to say.

"Of course. You can do anything nowadays," she snapped. After a moment she turned. "I'm sorry," she said. "It seems I'm not very pleased with my life today."

If I had asked what was wrong, as I should have, she might have told me, and then I might have told her in turn, and everything might have turned out much differently, but I did not, and then her phone rang. "Audrey. Yes, Perdita. Mr. G.? Yep, I've got it right here. Diapers."

I sank down on the windowsill, then swung around to stick my legs out onto the fire escape. Was I disappointed or relieved? The shirts stirring above me brushed my forehead tenderly, the light came and went, the Mooncalf came up behind me and licked my hand. From somewhere nearby came the bright spanking of a basketball and the snarl of a badly recorded punk rock song. It was a rare, beautiful day, and at the end of it I decided to commit a murder.

Hung Jury Perform: "Undivided"

(FROM THE ALBUM *B-SIDE*)

I was born with two heads on my shoulders,
Which did my opinions divide.
One head grew kinder, the other grew cold,
And the cold loathed the sensitive side.

So I cut one off
I had decided
I would be cold
But undivided.

I was born with two parts made for pleasure,
With different ideas of fun.
One part was shameless, the other was shy,
And the shy loathed the libertine one.

So I cut one off
I had decided
I'd be alone
And undivided.

I was born with two hearts in my ribcage,
Which tore my affections apart.

One heart was heavy, the other was light,
And the light broke the heavier heart.

So I cut one out
I had decided
I would be sad
But undivided.

And I insist
When I was finished
That I was not
The least diminished.

For a relief
From indecision
I recommend
A small incision.

You make the choice
But I've decided
I will be cold,
And undivided
Cold, sad, alone
But undivided.

PART TWO

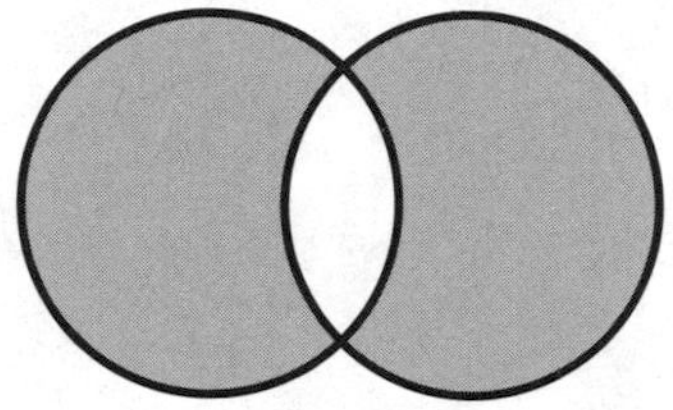

Boolean Operator: XOR

Transitional Objects

Dear loose, lose, low, lo, Lucia, loofah—oh crap. I'll have to type.

Dear Louche,

I am planning a trip to London, of all things. I will probably find other lodgings before long but I was wondering if I could requisition your sofa for the first few days. Nothing is definite yet, so don't mention it to anyone, but let me know if it would work out.

Nora

PS That was my roommate's "voice recognition" software ringing the changes on your name.

I read it over and removed "don't mention it"—I suspected that Louche could read between the lines of a blank page—and added:

PPS: What is an "attitude dredge"? I might need one.

Louche was teaching an interdepartmental, interdisciplinary, "inter-everything" practicum at a trade college in London. Though the class was in the Mechanical Engineering department, it was cross-catalogued as Expressive Arts Therapy, but it was not clear to me that Louche had the best interests of her students in mind. In her last e-mail she'd told me that a number of stinging ants had escaped from a hollow Plexiglas Interpersonal Cuirass and wreaked havoc in the student lounge, while in a test run of the Syntax Frappe a number of old metal typewriter keys had come unglued from the blades of an electric fan and strafed the room, chipping school property. Louche had given both projects top marks. It turned out that to fall apart and even cause a certain amount of damage was an important part of their destiny as Transitional Objects. "The Self must not expect to encounter the Other unchanged," she wrote, "or vice versa."

Trey came into the room and leaned on the back of my chair. Onscreen was a photograph of the cuirass, a piece of lettuce discernible behind the left nipple. "That is *stunning*. Galliano?"

"This is not fashion," I said. "This is a Transitional Object."

Turned out Trey knew the term. It was from Winnicott, and designated those often fuzzy objects kids latched onto at a certain age, such as—he scooped up his stuffed bunny and nuzzled it. "Did the mean thewapist call Fuwwy Person a twansitional object?" *Twansitional* meant that (1.) the object was an intermediary in the self/world rencontre, but also (2.) you should probably get over it. Trey was electrified by Louche's claim that everyone was transitioning and every object was transitional, though some suited one's purposes more than others. Her students made objects custom-designed for specific individuals, such as the prime minister. "They're the bespoke suits of transitional objects!" Trey said, impressed.

"Trey?"

"Yes?"

"Can you get me a fake passport? Fast?"

"*Can* I? I'm transfigured with joy! Finally a job suited to my abilities!"

A civic body neither singular nor plural presents a number of problems for the state. Do the math: Each twofer has full possession of only about a fifth of what ordinarily makes up a human (the head), and roughly half of the remaining 4/5. Each, then, is 3/5 of a person. Together, they are 6/5—more than one, but a lot less than two. These calculations are the basis of the politi-

cal thought of one Charlie "Chuck" Buckram, making his case for cutting the twofer vote in half. Wiser minds have prevailed, pointing out that a double amputee, also approximately 3/5 of a person, is not denied the vote, and (when Chuck pressed on, observing that 6/5 rounds down) that a human head, if it could be kept alive on the way to the ballot, would probably be allowed to vote, though it might have trouble wielding the stylus.

Despite Chuck, then, we would ordinarily have had two votes, two social security numbers, and two driver's licenses. But because Blanche had fallen asleep when we were still underage, she had never worked, voted, passed a driving test (though she did know how to drive, as it happened), or deposited a check; she didn't pay taxes or rent or carry a credit card, and no phone service or utilities had ever been in her name. Besides our birth certificate, there was very little record she existed at all. This would make things easier.

We did have a joint passport, however, or rather two passports, stapled together; the state department had not yet worked out the protocol for establishing the identity of someone with two. It was dated mere months after Blanche fell asleep, when Mama and Papa had suddenly decided that we should all go to Mexico. Max, to my surprise, had been left behind. We had made our way slowly by car down the coast of the gulf, where I glimpsed the lacquered backs of dolphins off a scorching, scathingly white beach, then across the arid width of Baja to the Pacific coast. On those long, empty, windy beaches I collected sand dollars, built sand castles, pretended to be much younger than I was (I was twelve), and one day, a long way from the bright oblongs of our towels, tried to drown Blanche. I knew very well that the same lungs served us both, but I had the theory, partly derived from some of Mama's questionable reading material, that I could store up brain oxygen through yogic breathing and enable myself to submerge for hitherto unheard-of periods. Six to eight minutes would suffice, I thought. I blacked out and would have drowned us both if by some reflex the sleeping Blanche had not started dog-paddling. Coughing and shivering, I woke, crawled out of a lukewarm, greenish hurly-burly of water and sand on hands and knees, and vomited a lot of seawater and a few raisins, swollen nearly into grapes again. Nobody had even noticed.

I found the expired passports smashed into the bottom of the little tin box made of recycled cans of something called Pep! (Papa had bought it for me in Mexico) that held a few keepsakes: a key, a chunk of pitchblende, half a sunflower seed, a piece of yellow construction paper folded and refolded

into a hard little oblong with a crease in the center. In my photograph I looked shockingly tentative around the mouth, nothing like the hardened character I felt. Blanche was a blond anybody with flushed cheeks, lowered lashes. Who would not have thought, looking at her, that she had such a terrific will to live?

I took new photos at a booth in the back of the Castro Film and Camera shop. The camera had two settings, Regular or Twin. Someone had X'd out the word *Regular* and scrawled above it, "this usage insulting to the twofer community!" It was not until I had the warm coil of photographs in my hand (Nora alert, unsmiling, dirty hair scraped back, Blanche dormant, unkempt, slightly blurry) that my own stupidity struck me. I couldn't show a twofer passport coming home solo.

I punched the button marked "Regular," and went back through the velvet curtain. I smiled this time.

While I was waiting for the second strip of prints to drop down into the catchment, something unlucky happened: Audrey walked in. I took a few quick steps away from the booth toward a display of frames and photo albums with hideous, puffy covers.

"Nora! What are *you* doing here?"

"Just looking."

"At *this* cheeseball stuff? Do you even own a camera?" she persisted, amused. I felt a surge of annoyance.

"What about you? Why are you here?" I said. I heard the flutter of my prints dropping, and took another step away, Audrey following. An old woman with a cast on one foot clomped past us into the booth, leaned her crutches by the door, and drew the curtain. In a moment she would come out and look in the slot.

"Wanted to see if they carried Super-8. My normal store is out."

I walked her to the counter. Leave the photos here, I thought, come back later. I snuck a look back at the old woman's feet, the single blue lace-up pump set primly beside a white elephant foot. Just then, the curtain was yanked back. I turned away.

The woman took her time getting up. Crutches clattered. I saw Audrey look back, wanting to offer help, but the clerk was still talking, saying a lengthy no, I thought, and she was too polite to interrupt. Finally she was up, had seen the photos, was pinching one crutch under her armpit and carefully stretching out one arm. I yanked my hair out of its ponytail and shook

it loose as she tweaked the photos out of the slot and brought them under her bifocals. Good, the old bat was half blind. She adjusted her crutches and hobbled toward us, and I nudged Audrey. "Let's go!"

Then the old woman's photos fell down into the slot. She turned back.

I nudged Audrey harder. "Coming? I have a call at four," I said. At last, she came.

Outside, she paused. "You don't really have a call at four, do you?"

My heart stuttered. "What do you mean?"

"Thanks for saving me from that clerk. He was about to pitch me his movie idea! Who does he think I am, Warner Brothers? Let's go get a latte."

Afterward, I went back to the store. I didn't expect such luck, but the photos were back in the slot. I stuck them in my pocket with the others; the clerk didn't even look up. Just for fun, I stole a purple picture frame decorated with two stuffed balloons with their strings knotted together, and threw it away in the garbage can right outside. I would cleanse the whole world of ugliness!

Walking home, I saw the old lady again, perched on a low wall, talking to a burly man with a prancing purple teddy bear tattooed on his neck and a fat silver ring through his septum. She turned her head to watch me approach. She jabbed her crutch in my path. "Pardon me, may I ask—" she began, and I panicked. I cracked my ankle deliberately against her crutch and faked a fall. I heard or felt that she had fallen too.

I sat up, massaging the scuffed meatus of my thumb. The old woman had fallen on one hip. The care bear was stooping over her. "Oh, no!" I said, "I'm so sorry!"

"Don't blame yourself," he said, with an effort. "It was an accident, I'm sure."

"I'll go phone for help." Shaken, I ran all the way home. I listened at Trey's door, opened it softly. He was lying on his bed, ankles crossed, smoking and whimpering softly into the phone. He winked at me. I laid the two strips side by side on the bed beside him. He looked at them, then back at me, wide-eyed. Nodding, he took a long, long drag on the joint.

That evening, he disappeared for a few hours. He came back with two passports. The second had only one head shot in it, and only one name. Seeing myself alone, my stomach turned over. I felt like I was looking at an object from the future. "Talk about a Transitional Object," I said.

"I've always wanted to try this," said Trey. He produced a large jar of

pears in syrup and fished out a pear. He began hollowing it out with a pocket knife.

I said, "Don't you think it might be better to put it with my other papers and take my chances?"

"No, man, this will work."

"A passport is not going to fit inside a pear."

"I'll curl it up. Uh-oh, pear accident. Mmm. Hey, these are pretty good. OK, take two, as Director DeMoss would say. Can you grab me a rubber band out of that cuppy thing by the phone?"

"Why don't we just forget this pear business. Why would I take a pear in syrup to England? Do I look like a pear in syrup kind of person? What if they have some kind of regulation against bringing wildlife into England?"

"A pear isn't wildlife, dude."

I groaned.

"Do you want to do this or don't you? Don't tell me you're having moral qualms. You're not thinking it's"—he adopted a stage whisper—"*murder*, are you?" I shrugged. "Blanche is a parsnip, babe. An energetic parsnip, I grant you. But a parsnip."

I knew better. Parsnips do not dream.

"I know you, Nora. You are truly, deeply selfish. No, I think it's admirable. Most people can't acknowledge the deep sea fish inside. You're watchful, cold, implacable, patient, intelligent, and hungry. Becoming an I is, like, totally *you*."

"Maybe I'm too nice to go through with it."

"I sincerely doubt it."

nora darling,

mi sofabed es tu sofabed. i'll even pick you up at the airport if you'll stand me a lamb vindaloo. what are you doing in london. an attitude dredge is just one of many things i will have to show you in person.

lo

Lo,

Apparently I have to produce some actual work for the fellowship I got 8 years ago or they will ask for their money back. I'm killing two birds with one stone and researching the history of a family heirloom, a dollhouse. They're transitional objects, don't you think? Dollhouses, I mean. Consider that vindaloo yours. Itinerary attached.

No

TIME CAMERA

Max came back from a trip with a new idea. She had seen ghost towns that were raking it in. We were sitting on a gold mine, she said.

"Fool's gold," said Granny tartly. "And if you think you can fob it off on some poor rube, I wish you luck."

"People love ghost towns. They pay to see ghost towns."

"You can't make a ghost town out of a sow's ear," Granny said. Max laughed. Granny repeated it several times. Each time, she and Max laughed.

Granny liked the idea right off, but she always liked Max's ideas. In retrospect I'd say she misunderstood it slightly, got hung up on the ghost part. She consulted her Ouija board and came up with what she said was the go-ahead from Too Bad's old-timers, as well as the new town name they gave her, Lario6p. "The spirits definitely indicated the six," she said, glaring around at our uncertain expressions. "Definitely."

Max eventually managed to persuade her that authenticity was what the tourists were looking for, and Too Bad had been Too Bad since boomtown days. "Well, if that's what the tourists want," Granny said dubiously.

In fact, Too Bad had never boomed. Maybe a soft thump was heard when that first rancher wiggled a fence post and saw gold, but what little gold was there was scratched out by prospectors in less than a year. It wasn't the tail of the fat golden serpent after all, just a few scales scraped off as it passed through. Turquoise chunks of copper ore lay all around, but no big company could be tempted to build a smelter on the spot, and hauling the heavy ore to

the nearest copper mill ate up any profit. The next flash in the pan was silver; just southeast of us was a rich vein. But the geological layers were warped and tilted thereabouts, turning almost upside down in some places, so that "you might think history ran backward around here," Papa said, and that silver-bearing seam dove straight down into the mountain. The last miner had followed it imprudently far and died when the shaft collapsed on him. According to Granny his body was never dug out.

The miners weren't the only ghosts in Too Bad. Before them, the Navajo had lived there. Before them, a people the Pima Indians called the Hohokam. It's a two-headed word; in Piman, you make a noun plural by doubling its first syllable. "It means, those who are gone," Granny said. "Of course, they didn't call themselves that!" What they did call themselves, nobody knew.

It took some work to turn the real ghost town into the much more popular fake ghost town it is today. Papa and Max built new ruins; the old ones weren't picturesque enough. They bought a used trailer for an office, and sided it with weathered planks; in places you could see silver through the chinks. Granny had her picture taken—squinting into the sun and sucking a corncob pipe—as the Last Inhabitant. Mama wrote skits to perform for the tourists at scheduled times in the street, the saloon, the whorehouse, and Papa and Granny wrote a new history for the town and published it in a stapled booklet with a few old-timey line drawings as *The Story of Too Bad.*

> A local saloonkeeper, hoping to bring in new customers, a Chinese laundry and some fresh faces in the brothel, not to mention new fruit for the hanging tree, offered travellers a good dinner and some firewater in exchange for a promise to spread glittering tales of "the El Dorado of eastern Nevada" in every watering hole east and west. Some of 'em must have kept that promise, because the customers came, eyes glittering with gold fever, and by the time they realized Too Bad was too *good* to be true, they'd lost their shirts. They stayed anyway, out of pure cussedness, and dedicated the rest of their short lives to out-fightin', out-drinkin', and out-cheatin' any traveller foolish enough to join them in a hand of Seven Card Stud. Purty soon, everyone west of ol' Missipp' knew Too Bad was the baddest town east of Bodie.

We'd sell that in the gift shop along with bolo ties, lonesome cowboy copper ashtrays, gold-panning kits complete with tiny sachets of gold dust, woodpeckers on springs that pecked their way down a pole, and postcards of barrel cacti in cowboy hats and cartoon burros braying "HOWDY from the middle of nowhere!" and "I lost my A__ in Nevada!" "Do we have a jackalope? We gotta get a jackalope," said Max. We got a jackalope, which proved to be a stuffed jackrabbit with antlers glued to its head.

But the best attraction was the Time Camera.

> Ever imagine that you were an outlaw, a sheriff, a Red Man, a lady of dubious virtue? Travel into the past! Let our magic lens take you back to the time when the West was wild, beards were bushy, and justice was done at the end of a rope. If your friends don't believe you, you can show them the picture! Black and white: $10. Sepia-toned: $15. Gold Frame adds $10. Extra copies $5.

"It's an art, making up the past," said Max, humping a big cardboard box into the dressing room. We followed her in. "It's like science fiction, only backward. Do you think you could do it, Nora? You're good at telling stories."

"Do what?" We opened one of the cartons. It was full of dull purple velvets, frayed satin, unlined coats with big gold buttons.

"Dress them, pose them, make them look good. They need to be told what to do, they don't have your imagination."

"Who don't?"

"The tourists!" She banged down a box. We pulled out a sword as light as aluminum foil, made of plastic with a thin metallic coating that peeled off like manzanita bark.

"Does the camera really send you back in time?"

"Absolutely," she said.

I knew she didn't really mean it, but I thought it might be true anyway. You could tell it was the past from the pictures. Under the lens, pleather was leather, pop beads were pearls, and the shitty shine of the peeling chrome on the prop sword was the solemn gleam of polished steel. (Oddly, the one real sword, a dress sword we had got from the Grady junk shop, never looked as good in photos.)

We plundered the costume box for our games of pretend, which became real when we were successful in cajoling Max to take our picture. Our tastes

were Olde Worlde crossed with Old West, Lord This in the shoot-out at the Circle-8, Lady That of the Loco Solo Saloon. Certain props and certain characters always went together: the purple flared coat and white wig belonged to the lazy, elegant Count Backwards, whose second head whispered bad council from its hiding place in the ruffles around his thin, white neck. The lovely Maltese Ladies always wore a tattered ball gown (shredded in a dangerous flirtation with a cactus) of flowered gauze over thick silvery satin, or what we called satin, anyway, and a rhinestone diadem we declared "exquisite" and quarreled over, with the result that in the photographs it appears now on one head, now another. Count Backwards' regular proposals of marriage to the Maltese Ladies were the cause of a series of fiendish plots against them on the part of his second head, who, fearing disinheritance, led them into intricate traps, from which, just as the tin can containing dynamite was dropping from the trained vulture's claws toward the tent where the Maltese Ladies were just lighting up the ceremonial cigar that opened festivities at the sharpshooter's competition they'd been asked to judge, they escaped with the help of their friend, the dashing Calamity Jane, who after diverting the explosive vessel with a volley of precisely aimed shots, always took the opportunity to perform some gun tricks for the dumbfounded villain, then waved away the grand prize, asking only a grateful kiss from the Ladies before she rode off into the purple sage.

"But did that really happen?" asked Blanche, worried.

"Now it did," I said. The past could change, just like the present. The Time Camera proved that.

Mama entered into these games, even a bit too enthusiastically, volunteering for parts we hadn't written: the beautiful, conniving patroness of the arts, say, who had sponsored the Maltese Ladies' rise to fame, and hosted their performances at her soirees. She missed the stage. "I do find life in the desert a little lacking in pageantry," she would sigh, adjusting the hang of our scabbard or attacking our hair with a flurry of little touches.

Our first customers for the Time Camera were our neighbors, Dr. and Mrs. Goat. They lived closer to Grady than we did, as the crow flies, but even farther off the main road, sustained by a small water tower and a generator, in a trailer with a metal shed appended to it. In the afternoon, from the top of the rock we called ours, the roof of their shed was a chip of fire. Mama had driven out to their house on purpose to invite them, though it was ten miles out a dirt road from the highway. (We could have walked there faster.)

Dr. Goat looked grumpy but donned a uniform that was part Napoleon, part General Grant. His head was dark and swollen above the tight collar, his eyes all pupil, like ticks buried in flesh. Mrs. Goat closed the wings of a giant bonnet around her head and looked down when the shutter clicked; only a nub of nose showed. There! They were in the past.

The dog was frightened of these apparitions and growled at Dr. Goat, who balanced on one boot and aimed a kick at her. Fritzi yelped. Max threw herself on Dr. Goat and had to be dragged out of a clinch, her face frighteningly red. Our first customers, therefore, departed in a hurry, leaving their photos behind. Those hung in the office for years; they are probably still there.

Their name was not actually Goat, I remember. We called them Goat because . . . Quite suddenly I do not feel like writing any more today.

On Murder

There is nothing so bracing as planning a murder. I recommend it to the weak-willed and those with a leaky sense of self. It is fortifying as a drop of coagulant in a solution.

I had planned (The word is too strong. Imagined. Anticipated?) this particular murder for so many years that it had taken on an air of permanence and respectability. To understand how a murder can be domesticated and even humdrum may be hard for fans of the pounce of the sound track, the streak of scarlet, the gunky skeleton jiggling in the flashlight beam. But I am convinced that if murder is horrible, it's for its overflow into the ordinary: severed hands in Ziploc bags, the dead baby in the Dumpster behind Chubby's. Anyone who has eaten a pork chop has all the information she needs for murder, and even vegetarians have honed their skills on a spaghetti squash or two. It takes a special kind of person, a criminal, to commit a crime? You know better; in your dreams you've already tried it. *Ask Heloise* how neatly you bagged the body and dragged it (closed in the folding cot with the shoddy, squeaky wheels) all the way to the sandbox in the park, despite the comedy of errors: the arm flopping out and dragging on the sidewalk, the curious golden retriever, the cell phone sounding a warning.

In case I found I lacked resolve when the moment came, I decided to practice. I set my sights small. You can get ants anywhere, and slaughter hordes of them without anyone raising a hue and cry. I cut their heads off with a knife, a credit card, an emory board. As it became easier, I deliberately extended my sympathies to my victims, so as to toughen myself further. I bent a benevolent eye on the shiny, busy little chap, and cheered him on.

"Why, here's Mr. Ant. What a dapper fellow. Oops-a-daisy, here comes the knife!" There was a tiny crunch when their necks were severed.

I dropped their bodies like hints behind me, a series of little specks, like ellipses, or the footprints of someone heading out alone onto the salt flats at noon, a foolhardy and possibly irreversible action.

I spoke of plastic baggies and a nighttime trip to the Dumpster. It was only to make a point. There will be none of that here. Blood in the surgery is quite different from that stuff seeping from under the woodpile. A masked surgeon cannot be compared to a masked gunman, though nobody likes going to the doctor. This would be like purging a tapeworm, or lancing a boil, and I felt great! As a murderer I was everything society approves of: efficient, affable, even-tempered, reasonable. I held my horses. I kept my head. I even called home.

Papa picked up the phone. He did not even sound surprised.

"England! Well, that's great. You certainly are elevating the Olneys in the culture department. While you're there, see if you can find out anything about the dollhouse. I've always wanted to know its history. Granny thought it was at least a hundred years old and either English or Dutch. With your skills you should be able to get us some top-drawer information!" (My parents thought I was getting my doctorate in history at UC Berkeley, and attributed my unusual working hours to a life spent in libraries. I told them I was writing my dissertation on understudies, apprentices, seconds in command, and those who published their theories a week too late. A private joke.)

Mama was away at a joint conference between the Siamists and the Togetherists, but Papa connected me to Max in the gift shop. Max was running for mayor of Grady, on the platform of revitalizing Grady's economy by turning it into a ghost town like Too Bad. "That's a really weird idea, Max," I said.

"No, listen, Nora, I think you'll agree that it's the answer. Grady's days are numbered. The mines have had another round of layoffs, and the Penitence Ground will hold its last test this year. People might not want to hear it, but Grady is already a ghost town in the making. It's only a matter of time. Now what I'm thinking is, preemptive strike. Grady's future is in its past. If we, I say we as an adoptive citizen of Grady, if we bill ourselves as a ghost town before it happens, and start bringing in revenue from tourism, we'll save ourselves from turning into a real ghost town."

After I hung up, I sat for a long time with my hand on the phone. Then I

rang up a travel agent with a voice like a budgerigar who said "absolutely" for yes and had a word for every letter ("that was N as in nobody O as in omission R as in riddle A as in agony?"), and booked my flight.

I left a week later. I took both passports, the Siamese Twin Reference Manual, a number of scarves, and some matches, just in case.

Before I went through security, I found a restroom and latched myself into a stall. I sat down on the seat to unzip my carry-on and groped past the extra sweater I had stuck in at the last minute to the cool round of the jar. The automated toilet woke sobbing from a dream. I unscrewed the jar lid, drove my fingers into the tender pears, and pulled out the license and the rolled passport. I decanted what remained of the pears into the toilet—how strange and lovely they looked, like the rarefied stool of some daughter of Midas!—and forced the jar down into the sanitary napkin hutch. The toilet sobbed again, accepting the offering. Then I licked the syrup off my new license and passport and folded them into my notebook. Trey would be crestfallen. But this was not the Great Pear Caper, this was a human life.

I had booked a singleton seat to save questions on the return trip, rather than one of the special seats with wider backs and double pillows that under pressure from twofer lobbyists the airlines had begun to install in their newer planes, and the gentleman to our right was not pleased. There seemed to be a surplus of elbows between us, most of them his. I ceded the armrest to his fat, furry elbow, wedged the single miniature pillow they gave me between my head and Blanche's, so we would not knock together like castanets in the event of turbulence, and leaned against the vibrating window. Some passengers were already asleep, mouths open, but I wanted to watch the ground go away. Unused to flying, I hadn't thought of asking for a seat on the left, so Blanche wouldn't block my view, but I had been given one anyway. Still time to request one for the return, I thought, then remembered, thrilled, that by then I would no longer need it. Beside the runway the green grass rivered back. Faster, faster. Then came a miraculous ungluing, a corrective pulling away, leaving behind everything, ev—a hot breath purled in my ear.

I resettled Blanche's head on the pillow. The city tilting, rotating, sliding down the inclined plane of earth. He knows perfectly well that his foot is in my floor space. Waves shrunk to ripples. Ghosts tore across our wings. The ripples that were really waves merged imperceptibly into the fog, and then there was only fog. Then the grey-mauve shadow of the plane was shrinking on the top of the clouds below.

My neighbor turned his broad back to me and stretched his legs out in the aisle until the stewardess arrived with the cart. When she asked if I wanted one bag of nuts or two, he snorted. "Two," I said, "and I'll have two drinks as well." I set them side by side on my tray and downed them one after the other.

Closing my eyes, I began to go over the story I was planning to use if interrogated. It involved an antiquated relative with a moribund business enterprise growing heirloom vegetables for seed to sell mail-order to jaded gardeners. No, I was not a gardener myself. I understood some of the varieties were coveted by people who cared about that sort of thing, exquisite cherry tomatoes that snap between your teeth, rare as caviar! I was going to help Aunt Timothea, yes, it is an unusual name, I guess her father wanted a boy, not my grandfather but my great-grandfather, she's a great-aunt really, but as I was saying, I was going to help Aunt Tim set up a system to sell seed over the Internet, well yes she *is* an up-to-date lady, she got obsessed with Web auctions and ended up buying a pair of cast-iron Scottie dogs that were costing a fortune to ship from Maryland, in fact I'd get there before the Scotties did, then she found the very same Scotties in her local shop, it turned out they were made in Goole, if you turn one over you find the stamp of the foundry, see, officer, a simple circle, and inside, why nothing, nothing but ashes, and these two little horns . . .

THE SIAMESE TWIN REFERENCE MANUAL

Delta Skymall Catalogue

The SelfHood™
From The Sharper Image comes a personal privacy essential. For twofers—or anyone seeking a little private time—this collapsible microfiber hood with Velcro-fastened lightfast blinders, noise-canceling earplugs and EZbreathe™ mouthplug is a must-have. Electrical components pop out for servicing; machine-washable fabric folds flat for travel. Includes carrying case, 10′ extension cord. One AAA battery (not included) yields 33 hours of peace and quiet for you AND your twin. Fits recto or verso.

Pirate Parrot Kids' Novelty Hood
Polly wanna cracker? Disguise your twin as the parrot on your shoulder. Comes with eye patch for you. Arr, matey! Fits recto or verso.

Vertical Pillow™
Let your twin drive! Sleep sitting, standing or even walking with horseshoe-shaped head support made of lightweight Memory Foam™ that molds to your body, covered with washable terry in rockabye baby blue. Specify recto or verso.

A Room Of One's Own™ Intimate Privacy Blind
Designed for women, by women, this fabric-covered blind adds a feminine touch to

the patented technology of the SelfHood™ (sold separately). Say good-bye to "third wheel syndrome" by disguising yourself as an ornamental pillow or cute stuffed animal, or add to the fun with sly slogans like "What was that?!" and "Is it my turn yet?!" in a sexy script on pink silk-look acetate. Please specify Pillow, Teddy, or Slogans. Machine washable.

Sadness

After the gold and the silver and the copper failed, there was one final wave of prospectors. This time it was a real rush, but by then Too Bad was already a ghost town. Granny had saved the centennial edition of the Grady paper. "Many residents will remember the uranium boom in the late 40s. Duplicity County was alive with the talk of big strikes, much money was spent on exploration and equipment, and many modern-day prospectors were in the field. Grady was the hub: General Services Administration set up a depot at Agua Sucio and stockpiled the uranium. Much of the prospecting occurred in the Duplicity mountains south of Too Bad, where the quartzite was exposed."

"I had just gotten away from this godforsaken place," Granny said. "Moved to Minneapolis, got a job in a diner, the Twin Cities diner. I met your grandfather there, and he dragged me right back here with him. He was going to strike it big in uranium. He spent a caboodle on Geiger counters, scintillometers, black lamps, all that nonsense. Your father ought to know better. But I guess it's in the blood."

Papa was a geologist and a surveyor and a mapmaker. He had secured a mandate from the government to survey and map the surrounding area with an eye to secret deposits of strategic minerals. "Uranium fever," said Granny, "that's what you've got, same as your daddy."

He kept a Geiger counter in the shed. Sometimes, sun-blind, feeling for the pliers with light, sensitive touches over unstable assemblages of cool metal edges and rubber-clad curves, we would hear it utter a lone, comforting click. If Papa was there with us, it clicked more often, and he'd *tsk* and

turn it off. In the shed, also, were boxes of dentist's X-ray film, stiff white tabs with rounded corners. He always carried some with him. They made a sagging shape in his breast pocket. Sometimes when we walked together, he would turn aside and press a tab between two rocks, leave them balanced there. Later he would collect the tabs and examine them for traces, figures, ghosts. In the most far-flung places we found his little goblins, and sometimes, wickedly, we would prise the tabs open and pore over the glossy film, looking for ghosts of our own. We had an alibi in the pack rats, who would snitch the tabs to decorate their nests. Papa scanned every pack rat nest with narrowed eyes, and he would step even into the prickly maze of a downed cholla to pluck one of his tokens out of the heap of sticks, prickly pear pads, candy wrappers, bullets. Not that it was any use to him, so far from where he left it. At home, after bitterly scanning the film for traces, he'd say, "That could have been a strike. Earl Tracy sold his claim for half a million dollars to Union Carbide, and I'm decorating a rat's house." Then he would pointedly throw it away.

Papa had a box of keys he got at the Grady junk shop. Old keys, to forgotten doors, a whole town's worth. You laid down the X-ray film, put the key on top of that, and on top of the key placed the rock you thought might be radioactive carnotite or uraninite or even pitchblende. If it emitted alpha rays, the shape of the key would be marked on the film. More precisely, the negative space of the key marked the film, leaving a key-shaped shadow on a blanched landscape—ghost keys for ghost doors. We found these totem piles too, like little votives. The desert was covered with keys. Papa was looking for the keyhole, we figured. Someday a long locked door would open and let him in. "Grampa will be there," I informed Blanche, and we shuddered.

Grampa was killed by American Sadness.

In 1951, recognizing the need for a national activity of penance, a despondent American government had begun bombing itself.

Granny drew two tadpoles, Yin and Yang. They looked like this: 69. "Say the black tadpole is America. Then the white one is un-America. When bombing un-America, America must also bomb the un-America in herself. That's this white spot here." She indicated the tadpole's eye.

"What's the black spot?"

"There's always one place America doesn't bomb," she said. "It's the America in what is not America."

"Where is it?"

She thought. "Maybe Iceland," she said.

The spot they chose for the National Penitence Ground or Proving Ground or, later, Test Site, was the emptyest part of an emptyish state, Nevada. "Unfortunately," Granny said, "there is no such thing as empty." Grampa had been prospecting in the range a little south of Too Bad when a bomb went off. "Nobody had bothered to tell us to stay indoors that day. I do recall someone stopping by and suggesting I take my laundry off the line, and wash my hair.

"Well, the wind was blowing your granddad's way. His Geiger counter started acting so erratic he thought it was broken. They aren't made for such high levels of radiation. All the same he started home, because he obviously wasn't going to get any good reads out of it. If he hadn't, I think he might have died right there. As it was, he got burns all over his head. What hair he had left fell out. I remember him calling me in to look at his comb. He'd put it through his hair just once, and it had a snarl the size of a Brillo pad stuck in it. Soon his tongue and throat swelled up to the point they had to put a straw down it for him to breathe. It was a pitiful thing, to hear him trying to cuss through that straw." Her laugh cut off sharply. "He died complaining. And I took up right where he left off. From that point on, there was no peace between me and the citizens of Grady."

Many of them worked in the Penitence Ground. They kept right on donning the coveralls and the badges while their teeth fell out. "They're certainly plucky," Granny said, shaking her head. The government used a different adjective. In a memo, the locals were described as a "low-use segment of the population." "Low-use," said Granny. "What language."

This adjective spilled out of the sky over Grady. ("Such sunsets we had," said Granny. "You never saw such colors.") Subsequently, a number of women gave birth to creatures resembling prairie dogs, lizards, and cats. Others gave birth to things resembling grapes or the fruit of the prickly pear. Some had miscarriages, some stopped having children at all, and seven had "simple" children, their minds misted over with Sadness. One of them, a few years older than we were, had stamped our books at the library: Chris Marchpane. They all sat in the front row in church. The angel row, it was called.

The Sadness was supposed to be a secret, but when the wind was blowing northeast, as it generally was, it told stories. ("The king has donkey's ears," it whispered. "America is sad. Iodine-131, cesium-137, strontium-90.") Invis-

ible ink wrote coded notes on mute tongues, throats. Invisible horoscopes scrolled in the thyroid, to be read by doctors later on.

Some farmers inquired of the Atomic Energy Commission why, please, their lambs were born with their hearts on the outside of their bodies? "Malnutrition," said the Atomic Energy Commission.

Hair fell out. "Nerves."

Also teeth. "Don't forget to floss."

Skin lesions. "Sunburn."

Breast cancer, bone cancer, thyroid, liver, lung cancer. "It's worrying about fallout that makes you sick, not fallout itself."

Tongue cancer. "Shoulda kept your mouth shut."

Most people did. "Loose lips sink ships," they said, though most of them had never seen a ship, and almost all had seen the bomb's early light, so bright you could see the bones in your hands, and start to get to know your skeleton. Those who kept quiet rebuked those who did not. Un-American, they said, and I saw a tadpole's sad eye, but Granny kept talking.

"I wrote letters. Not one reply did I get for months, except a 'thank you for sharing your thoughts' from my congressman, signed by a secretary. Maybe a year later I got a letter from the AEC saying one, there had been no test that day, two, doctors had determined that the risk was minimal even to workers at the Penitence Ground, three, Buddy had no business being where he was, and four, I was lucky they didn't come down on me for a breach of national security. By then I wasn't feeling too well myself, but the doctor said it was grief. When I kept coming, because I knew the way I was feeling wasn't right, he said I had 'nervous housewife syndrome' and I should take an interest in something and probably go to church more often. He kept saying that until he felt the lump. By then it was a little late. That's how I lost my titty," she said.

Granny was still trying to get compensation. Or at least an apology, because how do you compensate for a life, or even a single breast? She got out her "titty files": Buddy's Geiger counter readings, wind charts, doctor's reports, copies of her letters to congressmen and Atomic Energy Commissioners and their letters back, clippings of letters to the editor (*Grady Gazette*, but far-flung papers too: papers from Phoenix, Big Bend, Flagstaff, Globe, San Francisco, even Minneapolis) all signed Elizabeth Olney, statements from other townspeople and even one from someone who had worked at Penitence. "I'm lucky I got to him before he kicked the bucket," said Granny.

"One day the G-men came to my house to confiscate all Buddy's records. Luckily I'd hid them, said I had burned them when he died. 'A woman's grief, officer,' I said, and they patted me on the shoulder and left."

I began to see that a precise inattention was aimed at the place where Granny's breast was not. In the Natatorium, the work it took to not see the scar, or the half-full bra draped over a locker door, must have been considerable. It taught me that a missing thing can make a mighty showing of its absence, and further, that not seeing and not speaking can be a kind of advertisement. Granny's missing breast haunted the Grady Temperance Club, swimming with slow-rippling edges in the Natatorium, consorting with the cockroach under a locker, blooping up from a floor drain to spook someone stooping to retrieve a bobby pin.

Blanche and I were like that breast. I remember one town council meeting at which Granny had announced she intended to raise "holy hell." Blanche and I perched on a molded plastic seat with an obscene central ridge, swinging our shoes. All around us was the din of human notice, but not one glance fell on us. We occupied a hole in the air made expressly for us. Yet the wind of swerved attention curried our small hairs, like a black belt's magisterial kicks and punches, warning me that nothing we did would ever go unnoticed, for the space around us enjoyed a scrutiny interstices rarely get, and as anyone who has used a stencil knows, a shape is as precisely defined by what it is not as by what it is.

We're a restricted area, I realized, booting the seat in front of us. (A man with long, red, leathery earlobes swung round, glared at the empty space between our heads.) This comparison did not go far enough. To the town, we were *part* of the Proving Ground. Everyone knew, though they did not say, that like Chris Marchpane and the rest of the angel row, we were children of National Sadness.

The bombing had gone underground the year we were born. But one day Papa came home cursing. He slung his chattering Geiger counter on the sofa. It bounced. We stared, because he was normally so careful with it. "It's no damn use to me now," he said. "Either that machine is crazy or I am. The whole damn desert is radioactive from Tank Rock to Grady. But I'll be darned if there's a single piece of ore in my pack." He pulled out a smooth red stone. "What's this, girls?"

"Sandstone."

"Right. What's this?" He pulled out a crumbly pink rock.

"Umm—granite?"

"Right. What's this?"

"A piece of asphalt off the road!"

"Right!" He threw it down in disgust. "Now what would you like to bet there's a key on every darn piece of film I've got?"

Granny said, "The boy marked the treasure with a red handkerchief, but he took his eyes off the leprechaun. When he looked up, every thistle in the field had a red hanky on it."

That was Bossy, the underground test that busted its containment chamber and blew fallout like a geyser from a hole in the ground. That one made the news, and there were protests, even in Grady. (It was 1970. Times were changing.) We knew they were still testing, but we didn't know how often, or when. But once in a while we felt something, a hitch in the peristalsis of time, a split-second syncope. It was as if the world had split open and clapped soundly together again. It was as if God's eyes had gone, for one instant, out of focus.

Mushy Peas

The contamination meter chirped, but the gate attendant waved us negligently through, yawning fiercely at the dial. In the dim, echoic immigration hall, I took my place in line behind a sun-cured, cider-colored man in khaki shorts and a pink shirt. He had slender, wrinkled arms and smelled powerfully of deodorant. There were no other twofers among the bodies shuffling in switchbacks, but on a chair in a bright bare glass-walled cubicle to one side sat a twofer Sikh, eyes closed, turbans radiant. In an adjoining office two uniformed men bent over something on a desk. I tightened my left hand on my passport. This would be a bad time for Lithobolia to turn up.

"He always has to be five feet ahead of everyone else," said the woman behind us. She raised her voice. "Why don't you come back here and keep Bunny and I company?" The cider-colored man threw a lofty look back. Then he noticed Blanche and me. His eyes flicked back and forth, back and forth, down one neck and (yes, joined) up the other. I looked down. His rubber sandals revealed long cracked yellow toenails that curved around to dimple the tips of his toes.

My passport was wet as a newt! I wiped it firmly across my thigh. I scanned the row of intent, underlit faces in the booths ahead; did any look friendly? I picked a young man whose tight black curls were already receding from his smooth brown dome. Just beyond his booth, looking back, I glimpsed a round, smiling face fringed with reddish hair, and thought I recognized that Togetherist from San Francisco. I felt an unpleasant chilly slither pass through me, as if I had just swallowed an ice cube. But I was

mistaken, the figure I now saw silhouetted against the entrance to Customs had only one head.

As I approached the booth, the balding official half stood up as if to object, then sank back and waved us forward. He cracked my passport with his fingertips as if it were pornography. "Touriss?" he said, slurring the plural. Unsure of his usage, I thought, and afraid of giving offense. Good. "Are you carrying illegal drugs, weapons, or more than ten thousand dollars in cash?" I shook my head. This was easy. "Has anyone handled your luggage besides yourself?" He was looking at Blanche.

"Well, I did," I said, finally. My hands were trembling slightly. I clasped them behind my back.

"Do I understand that she's unable to speak for herself?" I assented. "Do you have a doctor's statement to that effect?"

"Nobody told me I needed one."

He slowly caressed his shining scalp, regarding me thoughtfully. We both looked over at the bright cubicle, where the turbans had not moved. He sighed. "All right." The glossy blue cover squeaked when he spread it for the dry kiss of the stamp.

A small steel door opened to the right of the Customs sign as I approached it, and a uniformed woman came through with a pig on a leash. A sign attached to its collar said, "Please do not pet me. I am a working Smartpig." The pig joined the customs officials quarrying in the cider-colored man's suitcase. "I knew you shouldn't have packed the potassium iodide. *It's potassium iodide, officer.* Tell them it's potassium iodide," said the wife. "They know it's potassium iodide," the man said. "Christ, it says so right on the label." The pig truffled eagerly among boxer shorts and laxatives as I walked by unchallenged with my bags, my fake ID, my untold lies. I was in England!

Past the velvet ropes a phalanx of sweaty, swarthy gentlemen held up signs, "Dr. Gegenhalten u. Frau," "Capgras Hotel," "Excluded Middle Phil. Soc," peering worriedly into every face. I sought the gaze of the sideburned Phil. Soc. greeter, and a smile began to tremble on his lips. If I went up to him, would I be handed a new life, just like that?

Then I heard my name. It was pronounced in such an offhand manner that it seemed overheard, a fragment of a conversation addressed to someone else entirely. I had to look behind me to find Louche. She was leaning on the display case I had just passed, arms folded.

The blood rushed to my head. Louche looked amused and older and formidable in a loose men's suit of almost black burgundy wool. An unfamiliar tattoo lost an indigo feather in rasping past her open collar, and another dropped a scaled coil below her cuff on the hand she finally extended—unless the latter was the other end of the selfsame animal, twining the whole length of her arm. Knowing Louche it would be a chimera or a cockatrice, something splendid, capricious, and cruel, and I had been crazy to bring her into this.

I snatched her hand and pumped it with rather panicky enthusiasm. "Great to see you, Louche! Thanks for helping me out."

Louche picked up one of my bags and led me toward the exit. In my own brisk tone, she said, "So, Nora, have you ever been to England before?"

"No, but I've always—"

"And Blanche, has she?" she asked brightly.

I opened my mouth, then snapped it shut. Louche wheezed softly, showing her canines. She was baiting me.

Could I tell her I had decided to go to a hotel after all? Absurd. I had given nothing away; there was no reason I should give anything away, if I kept my head. We whirled away widdershins in a cab so roomy I had to grab Louche's knee to keep from falling at every unexpected turn, and every turn was unexpected in the looking-glass traffic. I wondered if I was touching, through the neutral wool, some invisible beast.

We stopped at a pub, the Cud and Udder, low-ceilinged and overheated and hazy with smoke, and sat down under a curved sabre and a faded sepia-toned photograph of a woman in white crossing thick ankles aboard an elephant. Heads turned. "Mushy!" someone called, and was shushed amid giggles. I looked at Louche. "Mushy peas, Siamese," she said. "Cockney rhyming slang." In a dusty case opposite a toothy mongoose in a turban played the flute for a tiny cobra.

Had that vindaloo. Waitress meaty, mean. Spangled krakens kept worming through the thick sauce, and the pale ale turned tiger in my stomach, and soon I felt so queasy that I lost all impulse to try and fast-talk myself into a hotel bed and concentrated on keeping track of my limbs. Louche must not find out about Lithobolia, I felt.

Was I even tired? It was night, but it was also morning. I had flown straight from one night to another, skipping the day like the inch of white space between two facing pages. "My ears are stopped up," I said, pulling

them. Sounds were coming strangely to me, like that music, a high-pitched piping, which needled through the muffled uproar without diminution. The meandering melody, possibly Indian, almost sounded like one of Blanche's not quite circular roundelays. I looked up and smiled weakly. By some accident of light, the mongoose appeared to be moving its fingers in time to the music on his little painted pipe.

The mongoose turned its head and snarled. Sawdust spilled through its sharp yellow teeth, and something flashed past my head and thunked heavily into the floor.

"Bloody hell!" The barmaid was bending over me. Her pendant freed itself from her fat, powdered cleavage and swung forward on its chain to ding against one of my front teeth. "Are you all right, loves?" Gusts of lavender and beer breath beat against my brow. "That does it, I'm telling Sam all this Paki clobber has to go."

I followed her gaze left. Standing as high as my waist, the sabre was vibrating in the floorboards, point down. The barmaid gripped the handle, yanked, set her feet more firmly. "Hail Arthur King of England," called a liver-spotted comedian standing at the bar. The sabre came out and was borne at arm's length into the back. It left a sizeable gash in the floor.

"Bloody *hell*," echoed Louche, regarding me with interest. "It looked like you did that on purpose."

I had no idea what to say. I could still see the sabre, vibrant with intent. I swallowed hard, and with a muffled cluck my ear finally cleared. The world jumped closer. "I think the flight threw off my balance," I said, blessedly inspired. "My ear only just popped. I went all *wah* for a minute there and grabbed whatever I could reach."

On the way out, I stooped to peer in at the mongoose. It was in the same position it had been in for a hundred and fifty years at least, though the tiny conical mound of sawdust between the awkwardly crossed legs troubled me a little.

Despite my determination to do nothing else revealing, I gave a terrible start in Louche's little kitchen later on when I heard the word "decapitate" emanate from the other room, where the television was conducting a light show for the benefit of two solemn, attentive armchairs, a gigantic, leaning bookcase, and the bellows and flumes of some Transitional Objects, among them the cuirass. "Brrr!" I said, by way of explanation, and rubbed

my arms—absurdly, because it was a warm evening. I had to sip my PG Tips in the straitjacket of a lobster-colored boiled wool cardigan Louche pressed on me with, I thought, not entirely benevolent insistence. She had unfolded a cot in her laundry room in lieu of the promised sofa. As soon as I could, I retreated to it. I wanted to be well rested for my interview.

Once installed in the fantastically uncomfortable bed, I turned off the reading light: a child's bedside lamp, its stem covered with painted plaster bark, its green base supporting a happy lamb with a chipped ear. As the room shuddered and strained upward and then settled again around me, I went over my arguments:

1. Blanche has been asleep for approximately fifteen years.
2. I am seeking a center, a sense of self, not perpetually thrown off balance by this unanswerable question, this remainder, this unpaid debt, this counterweight, this dark unwholesome planet.
3. I am not even what you would really call gregarious.
4. I have a chronic ache in my right shoulder.
5. I feel that I could get the knack of happiness, if only.
6. There is something trying to claw through the ceiling to get to me.

What? I opened my eyes to a phalanx of dark repeated shapes, like a congress of black beetles, and flailed my arm out toward the bedside lamp, by luck struck against it, and found the switch. The beetle fortification fell. The darkness slid sullenly under the bed and waited there, making its insect calculations.

I left the light on, masturbated grimly and efficiently, passed out, and slept fitfully, in a luminous fog that kept thickening into indistinct shapes. They melted away completely when I tried to see them clearly, and when at last I braced myself to surpass my previous efforts, and sensed that success was near, I forced my eyes open and saw . . . a four-legged animal in a pastoral landscape, under a towering, luminous cloud. . . . It was the lamp, of course. I turned it off.

THE SIAMESE TWIN REFERENCE MANUAL

Close Focus Family Programming

"Close Focus on Twincest"

"We have Dr. Marie with us in the studio today to warn our listeners of a troubling new trend. Like us, you all probably tell yourselves every day that the legislation permitting twofers to wed amounts to nothing less than a state sanction for sin—"

Dr. Marie: "It's Adam and Eve, not Adam and Adam and Eve and Eve."

"A free love orgy going on right now in your community. But have you thought about a little thing called self-abuse? When that self is a pair of conjoined twins, self-abuse is not only weak, not only repulsive and unhealthy, it is incestuous. Dr. Marie?"

"That's right, Ron. I'm here to talk about the growing problem of twincest. Let me tell you a story about a poor young God-fearing woman of my acquaintance who happens to be conjoined. Believing that marriage is between one man and one woman, she has taken a lifelong vow of chastity. But her twin is an unrepentant sinner who nightly taunts her with twincestuous acts. As my friend's body burns with unwelcome pleasure, her soul burns in foreknowledge of the fires of hell. This is sexual abuse and soul-assassination, as I've explained to the sinner. What do you think she said to me? 'It's division of labor. I sin, she repents'!"

Dr. Goat

I kept a sort of gallery in my head where images of terrible potency were shut up. Here are some of them: A still living grasshopper gyrating slowly in the grip of a hundred ants. A tick as fat as a pomegranate seed, stuck snugly behind Granny's ear (a clip-on rhinestone-covered quail perched immaculately on her earlobe, beside it). Papa pooing behind a bush, a ruby rim rising out of the hairs to clasp the knuckled, glistening turd. But the most terrible of all was Dr. Goat.

Dr. Goat appeared in a picture book Granny gave us. On his hind legs, in his white coat, he was taking the pulse of Flossie the sheep. I could not flip casually through the book, in case I touched this page; I counted the pages before it, so I knew when it was coming, then held the book almost shut, and peeked sideways at the evil scene. Oh Flossie, beware. Don't you see the cloven hoof under the lab coat, the curly horns behind the headlamp?

When our new neighbors visited the Time Camera, I recognized them at once. Flossie's long, docile, foolish face, her pink nose and yellowish curls, gave her away, despite her pink and purple housedress. Dr. Goat was better disguised, as befitted a villain, for he had shaved off the wispy beard and horns, and his hunting boots concealed his hooves, and his squint hid his yellow eyes, his oblong pupils. But his manner of treacherous, phony solicitude gave him away. When he bent over to greet us, he put one big, hot, damp hand on the small of our back, and I smelled his goatish armpits and his rank breath and screamed up into his smiling face. Red-faced, Mama hustled us outside, but I ran back in behind her to loiter, staring, in the back of the room.

"Why did you scream?" Blanche had whispered, wondering.

"Don't you *recognize* him?"

She became intent.

Her eyes flicked over to me. "Is it . . ." I nodded encouragement. "Count Backwards?"

"Are you crazy? It's *Dr. Goat*!"

She let out a little mew. I shushed her. "It was a mistake to let him know I recognized him. From now on, we have to pretend we're not watching him."

"But we will be."

"We'll be watching him like *hawks*."

Dr. Goat was not built for the desert, which was made for bony folks like Granny—mere skeletons in a sheath of hide—or for small subtle bodies like our own. He was corpulent and almost tropical in his complexion: think of a flamingo-colored hippo. In fact, the tropics would have rotted him in an afternoon. The dry air checked his phlegm at his lips, though occasionally coming stealthily after him we would come upon his spittle on a rock, drying and tightening into a rubbery doily.

Tailing him took patience. We could make our way through the brush much faster than he could. There would have been some danger of stumbling over him if he had not made so much noise. He made his way from snag to snag, muttering long strings of imprecations we could never quite make out. I think he would have used a golf cart for his hunting trips, if he could have reconciled it with macho aspirations he had probably borrowed from Hemingway, maybe by decking it out with a camouflage canopy and machine-gun sights.

Once, we came over the crest of a ridge and saw him in the arroyo almost directly below us. He had stopped in the shade under an acacia tree and was taking off his shirt and folding it. Then he pulled down his pants and underwear together and we saw his butt, yellowish white like chicken fat and hairless except for the damp dun-colored tufts in his butt crack. From the waist up, though, he was dark red, not so much tanned as seared all over like a roast given a quick turn under the broiler, so he looked like two half people stuck together. His back was perfectly rectangular, with a gutter in the middle like a book, and a smattering of blackheads like periods.

His pants got stuck on his shoes, and he stood up, turning, so that we

could see his little fat dick, and kicked; the inside-out pants flapped from his feet with a whacking sound so loud it sounded closer than it was and we flattened ourselves on the hot stones like a horned toad, trying to be the color of nothing. One can be sinister and ridiculous at the same time. He was as absurd as Grandma's inflatable dinosaur, and yet he terrified us. When we lifted our heads up to look, he was on his knees half turned away. His pants were still stuck on his shoes, but he had bunched them up under his knees for padding and he had smoothed out a little pink napkin or something on the sand in front of him and was hunched over pulling on his dick. His butt went tight and flabby, tight and flabby, and then he pressed his dick down at the napkin, and to our righteous disgust a skein of a viscous substance slung out right over it. In apparent annoyance he pressed the end of his dick into the rag, poking it into the sand, and then lowered himself onto his belly and started flopping around, but this was enough for us and we ran.

Later we came back to that spot and made investigations, but there was nothing there but a hole with blurred tracks around it in the sand, maybe coyote, and a dirty scrap of pink flowered cotton stuck on a catclaw halfway up the cutbank.

We too went naked sometimes, we spent whole days on the desert in nothing but socks and sneakers. We went to a certain mesquite bush, took off our clothes, bunched them up, and left them suspended in the branches, so no scorpions could take refuge in them. We moved with particular care on naked days, and with a ritual solemnity. The thornbushes reached out to us. Sometimes we kept almost perfectly still in their grasp and watched as they delicately clawed us. One thorn drawn across our chest like a phonograph needle inked the score a beat later in tiny red notes. We never cried when we were naked. Pain was a necessary part of the skinned world we had entered. The sun stung and we relished it. When we were sweaty we crouched in the pale shade under a mesquite tree to feel our sweat turn cold. We felt like part of the desert. Rabbits turned to look and then went back to tearing at the grass. We were invisible.

One of our naked days, the bushes on a nearby hilltop thrashed and disgorged Dr. Goat, his rabbit gun gleaming. The desert contracted and thrust us out. Distances measured themselves, light fell in quanta, gravity confirmed its rule, and suddenly we were exposed and ridiculous. Had he seen

us? We shrank down slowly behind a yucca, and like the rabbits, we kept perfectly still (our buttocks clenched, our toes working under the hot canvas uppers of our sneakers) until he went away.

Another day Dr. Goat shot a cottontail and couldn't find it. We saw him stumping off home, shooting at cactus. We crept through the bushes until we found it. The rabbit was lying on its side with its eyes half closed as if exhausted, and the breeze was moving in its fur. It was still soft and warm. We stroked it and pretended it was alive for a while. Then I lifted up the hem of our shirt to make a cradle, and we started toward home.

"Are we going to bury him?" asked Blanche.

"No," I said. "We're going to keep him." I had just had a brilliant idea.

Appointment

I opened my eyes before dawn feeling cool, quavery, and wide awake. Blanche's nose was whistling: the dry air on the plane. I pinched it closed for a few seconds and it stopped. In the submarine light I could make out my open suitcase, my towel draped over the wardrobe door, my wash bag sagging over the edge of the ironing board. Everything was so still it hurt my head. I flapped my comforter just to see it move, then sat up.

Barefoot, I crept past Louche's closed door to the dark hole of the stairwell. Gripping the banister, I started down the oddly steep stairs, finding each step with my toes before I let my weight down onto it. From the landing I could see a little light seeping in from below, and I took the next few steps quickly before I noticed a young girl in a white dress standing at the foot of the stairs.

She was staring at me, as startled as I was. We regarded each other for a long time, neither moving, until I realized I could see Louche's bicycle through her. I took a quick step back, rammed my heel painfully into the riser, and bumped down several stairs on my coccyx before I could grab one of the uprights of the banister and stop myself. The girl was directly in front of me now, swaying and undulating, emitting an odd light clicking, and I remembered where I had seen her before: on the way up to bed. I staggered out through the slithering tickle of a bamboo curtain, dissolving the mocking spectre.

Groaning quietly, I knelt in front of the television and ran my fingers over its face. The screen crackled, swooned, and braced itself for the news:

race riots in Oldham, tropical fish caught off Southend pier, elderly particularly vulnerable to identity theft, authorities satisfied that the two severed heads found this week near York are the work of the same man as the one found in Shropshire two months ago.

I huddled closer. The screen sizzled, my arm hairs rose.

"Acquaintances confirm that these were the heads of Siamese twins or, as they are known in the States, twofers. Er, not, uh"—the announcer stumbled—"two heads of one twin but rather . . . two of one of each of two of—er, heads from two different twins." One, found by a jogger, had a note clamped in its jaws that read "Alone at last." One had a circle drawn in ink on its brow. "Police believe that whoever left them there intended them to be found. No fresh clues have surfaced as to the killer's identity, but police have confirmed that the forensic evidence suggests considerable medical skill on the part of the man the tabloids have dubbed Doctor Decapitate. In the face of fierce protests from interest groups, the Medical Ethics Board has backed down from earlier statements that so-called doctor-assisted individuality surgery may in some cases be justified. Catholic priests have called upon the Vatican to make a formal statement declaring conjoined twins to be two individuals possessing equal right to life, while condemning the extreme tactics of the group calling themselves the Togetherists, which has become a household name in recent weeks after a series of controversial actions made headline news, most recently the bomb scare at the East Grinstead Animal Shelter.

"In the latest on that story, the police safely evacuated the animal shelter the Togetherists apparently believed to be serving as a temporary front for the mysterious doctor after an anonymous tipper alerted police to a bomb hidden inside a dog toy. In an odd twist, police have revealed that the suspect toy took the shape of"—the announcer permitted himself a smile—"this winking cartoon bomb." Announcer holds up bomb and squeezes it. *Squeak*. "Police carried out controlled explosion of the toy. Yes, all the puppies are safe." Shot of frolicking Shelty pups.

I pulled the armchair closer and curled up in it, dragging Louche's jacket off the arm and over me. It had her smell. "Due to an unprecedented volume of calls, the East Grinstead Animal Shelter has requested that we let viewers know that all the bomb-scare-surviving pups have been adopted. However, other at-risk pups are being shipped in from shelters all over the . . ." My eyelids drooped, as puppies poured out of trucks and trains, flowed together into a shining, flouncing horde. One stopped and looked at me, curling its

lip to bare needle-sharp teeth. I saw that it was not a puppy at all, but the mongoose. "I hope you are not under the impression that decapitation is a humane way to administer euthanasia to reptiles," it said, in a mocking lilt that sounded like an imitation of Peter Sellers imitating an Indian accent.

"Morning," said Louche, clicking off the TV.

I groaned. "Your pajamas are staring at me." The heavy, shiny silk was figured with peacock eyes. I hobbled to the front window—why did my ass hurt? Oh, yeah—and saw it had rained in the night. A Rastafarian twofer was carrying a bag of groceries up the wet stairs opposite, his dreads intricately twisted into a single Gordian knot. It struck me that he was the first twofer I'd seen outside the airport. Maybe this was their—our—neighborhood. I didn't think much of it. Where were the cobblestones and chimneysweeps? It was also short on climbing roses and crumbling cottages, despite its name, which was something rustic and vaguely ribald—Milkmaid's Stool? No, Shepherd's Bush. The brick houses were boxy and modern. The white trim looked British, but fake British, like that house on Noe whose new owners had given it a name: Wee Like It. ("They're into water sports," Trey had said, "without a doubt.")

"Drink up!" Louche was tipping a spoon into a hole in the shoulder of the cuirass. She had volunteered to call off her class to show me around, but I had told her I had an appointment at the British Museum, so after breakfast she walked me to the subway and pointed out my route before going through the turnstile herself. I bought a map at the kiosk. Holloway Road was very long! I might end up having to walk some distance, I realized, and decided to leave at once, though I was still early. It was what I wanted to do anyway; until I found the office, I wouldn't really believe it existed. I had printed out the e-mail with the address, and I kept patting the pocket where I'd put it. Though I knew it by heart, I thought that if I lost the proof, I would forget it, as if it had never been.

After slightly longer than was strictly necessary—I had commenced my trip by zooming off in the wrong direction—I emerged onto a long straight road between fused storefronts, only fifteen minutes early for my appointment. The buildings were short and modern and pastel colored; I could have been in southern California, if not for the insipid sunlight and the toy cars zipping wrongwise around the roundabouts. There were no trees, though the oc-

casional plastic simulacrum of a shrub was stuck upright in a cement-filled flowerpot. The neighborhood appeared void of life except for the nondescript birds that blew around and snagged momentarily in fences and cornices like tufts of dirty insulation. But behind its banal facade was savagery: Louche had told me about a plague of urban foxes that slaughtered pet cats, a landlady who had slow-cooked her gentle elderly tenant in her Aga and freezer-wrapped him in meal-sized portions.

I walked quickly as if I knew where I was going, though it would have made more sense, now, to slow down and look closely at the house numbers. But I couldn't, I felt too visible. It was an obscene, practically sexual visibility. I have read that men will sometimes get a hard-on running to help someone in an overturned car or even driving by some horrible sight, and if this is true, I think it is probably for the same reason that I got wet as I walked down that street toward my doctor's appointment.

There was some kind of rumpus going on down the block. A small group was poking the air with signs, letting out faint cries. There is always something pathetic about a protest. It is always out of the way of the world, like a funeral going on with due gravity while nearby a dog bounds through the headstones after a tennis ball.

Though actually this one seemed very much in my way.

In the same moment that I saw that several of the protesters, in fact almost all, all but a couple, were twofers, one of them saw me, threw up his arm, and shouted something. Those near him turned, and the rest followed suit. All the signs turned to face me. It was as if they were protesting *me.*

Who, me? The only other audience were some dispirited posies in a window box, and a supercilious cat defying the foxes from behind glazing. Sometimes paranoia gets it right: Yes, you.

Isn't there something comical about revelation? The little pause beforehand, that's what they call comic timing. Or is it that we like to stop and listen for the click of the barrels turning in the lock? I seemed to read all the signs at once, though in actual fact I must have read them in order, maybe the largest first (KEEP IT TOGETHER) or the best designed (TOGETHER WE STAND, with 3D lettering, and drop shadows, and very conscientious letter-spacing), or even the small, unprofessional sign (DON'T CUT OFF YOUR OTHER HEAD, FOR GOODNESS SAKE) that my eyes sought out in unaccountable preference to the TWOFEREVER dot-matrix banner beside it. I could have read left to

right, in which case I would have seen first ONE IS NO FUN in upbeat orange over two happy faces, or right to left, which would have yielded an uncaptioned cartoon doctor holding up a severed head, followed by IT'S MURDER DON'T DO IT in dripping red paint with a red handprint.

There was really no time to turn around. They were coming toward me, and in a moment they surrounded me. They were braying and whinnying and clopping me on the shoulder. Someone was shaking a tambourine.

"Glad you could find us!"

"It's so important that we all turn out for these actions because even if it seems like nobody's watching or hearing us, we *are* making an impression!"

Belatedly, it dawned on me that these attentions were friendly.

"Right everyone, let's greet the newcomer, I'd like to introduce . . . ?"

"Uh—Audrey." I started to laugh.

"Audrey, from where? Tupelo, and this is? This is Amelia, from Bangladesh! Just kidding. She's from Tupelo too. How do we know, guys?"

Chorus: "Because they're *TOGETHER*!"

Cheers. Among the laughing crowd was a twofer I recognized. His hats were pulled low, but a tuft of red showed over one ear, and that was enough. It was the ginger-haired twofer from San Francisco, this time I was sure, though his face was singularly average, a beige smear, like a reflection in a dirty spoon. Faces, I should say, though one of them was so expressionless, its owner might as well have been asleep.

Just then a police van rolled around the corner, lights flashing.

A short girl with bangs and spots spun around, accidentally clobbered me in the head with her sign, and apologized hastily to Blanche. The redheaded twofer dove through the confusion, took my left arm in a tight, unpleasant grip, put his right arm around my shoulders, and began walking me briskly away. Behind us there was commotion, a clatter of feet and yelling and a garbled utterance through a bullhorn, but I was held fast and could not turn to look.

I sought to free my arm, encountering as I did so some strappy concoctions under his clothes such as I imagine old men wear to flatten their bellies and prop up their flagging tits, a distressingly intimate experience that gave me the idea that this might be a weird kind of pickup. I redoubled my efforts to escape.

Redoubled: a strange word. As if doubling were not quite enough.

Someone pounded up from behind us, and my captor clutched me more tightly and then relaxed as the fugitive ran by without pausing; it was the girl with bangs.

The twofer's far head leaned forward, and sought from Blanche to me, and settled on me, and confided, "See, I'm an American myself, and I figure it's just better not to get embroiled in police matters if you're not local. They want to know why you're here and ask a lot of questions which I personally, maybe you don't, but I—there's Suze and Joanie. Howdy Suze, Joanie! Is that your car? Do you think you could give us a lift?"

I yanked my arm free, but he had hold of my jacket by the pocket, and for an absurd moment we were playing tug-of-war, and I heard cloth rip. He let go.

"Gosh, sorry," he said. "Hey, I know a place where we can get that pocket fixed." He stuck out his hand. "Mr. Disme, rhymes with crime, D-I-S-M-E."

"I'm late for an appointment, at the National Gallery."

"*The Virgin of the Sands!* We'll drop you off. Allow me to insist."

"No, really, I've got my rental car right down there," I lied, gesturing down the block toward a couple of parked cars. Too late I saw they were unlikely rentals, a purple Mini and a three-wheeled monster.

"Oh, swell! Hey, do you think you could give—"

I bolted away with a wave back over my shoulder. After a minute a car passed me and I saw him in the back, both heads now grinning and nodding.

I went into the nearest pub and slumped against the bar. There was nothing so strange about an American Togetherist flying to London where the action was, yet I was shaken. He had arrived right on time for my appointment. It didn't feel like a coincidence, though I couldn't explain it. And now everything was ruined! If the Togetherists had not already scared away the doctor, the cops surely would have. I ordered a bitter and took a seat by the window. I thought, absurdly, that I might see the doctor walking by, and recognize him by the bright implements in the breast pocket of his suit, the dark stains on his shoes. I took off my watch, laid it carefully on the table before me. I did not want to hear it click against the polished wood. The man behind the bar ran a cloth slowly over the fixtures, staring out the window and giving a loud sniff every twenty-two seconds. It started to rain. A police car passed, slowly, then another. I couldn't tell if there was anyone in the rear seat.

Fifteen minutes later I ventured back. Everyone was gone, even the cat. The only sign of a scuffle was a soggy piece of a banner in the gutter.

The address corresponded to a boxy, two-story office building. I tried the front door, my damp hand sliding on the handle. It opened onto a dingy foyer that smelled like an old fishbowl. I pushed open a weighted door to the stairs and went up, cringing at each resonant footstep. The hallway was carpeted, though, and I crept noiselessly down it to number 209. The door was not completely closed, and only natural light shone from inside. I brushed the back of my hand against it, and it opened.

The room was nearly empty. A pencil, aghast at my entry, began to roll. It crossed the desk with gathering confidence and a frighteningly loud rattle. Then it fell off the edge. The only thing left on the desk was a tourist's brochure, the top leaf quivering slightly in the draft from the chinked window, and a phone. Three dust-free patches on the table showed where a computer had been, a keyboard, and a mouse pad. I went outside the room again and looked at the door. Faux wood-grain and an empty brass frame for a plaque.

I went to the desk and looked at the brochure. The Hunterian Museum at the London College of Surgeons. No scribbled phone number, no coded note. Still, I stuck it in my intact pocket.

Then the phone rang.

The sound was terrible as a scream in that closed space. I looked at the phone with an unnameable surmise. Time held its breath.

I let it ring five times. Then I snatched up the receiver. "Hi, it's Tiffany," I heard myself say. There was a click. The line went dead. The world paused, and then breathed again.

I waited for the phone to ring again, but it didn't.

"Did you hear they almost caught that doctor?" said Louche, idly squeezing the rubber bulb of a Speaking Ear.

A strange sensation passed through my head. As of something—a bullet, maybe—emitting a whining, drill-bit hum, rushing intolerably fast toward me from outer space, through me (I flinched), and receding with identical velocity in the other direction.

"What doctor?" I said carefully.

"That freak doctor. What happened was that vigilante group, those Togetherationists—"

"Togetherists," I said.

"You know about them. Well, they tracked down some kind of satellite clinic or dispatch center or something, which I must say is more than Scotland Yard had done, and they were holding a protest—" She turned the Speaking Ear around and squinted at the rubber pinna, then poked a ballpoint pen into its aperture.

"How did they track down the, um, clinic?" I said.

"Somebody tipped them off," said Louche. "Somebody on the inside, they think. A double agent. Or a patient who changed his or her mind. Anyway, it was a peaceful protest, but because of the bomb scares the police swooped down on them in riot gear, and meanwhile all the evidence went out the back door! Would you think of having Blanche's head removed?" she added, squeezing the bulb. An ink-smeared bit of paper burped out and caromed off my chest.

The blood had drained from my face. "Louche." I said it quite calmly. "Who do you think I am?"

It was a good question.

Dead Animal Zoo

"Welcome to the Zoo," I declaimed. "Right this way, for real live dead animals!"

Dutifully, Blanche sucked in her breath, as if she had not helped to collect each specimen and display it to advantage within a frame of colored stones. She was the only visitor so far. I had made her leave two jojoba beans at the invisible gate between two important-looking barrel cacti, and had issued her a crayoned ticket in return. I accomplished this by passing it from my left to my right hand.

My left hand took it back, and we tore it in half. I started backward down the aisle, gesturing. An odd smell rose around us. It was not unpleasant, just stirringly rich and brown. "On your left you will see a phainopepla, killed by stupidly flying into its own reflection. A phainopepla is a handsome ebony bird with red eyes and a crest."

"I know that," Blanche said.

"Don't interrupt! On your right is a stink beetle, *Eleodes*. When menaced, stink beetles stand on their heads and emit an offensive-smelling fluid from their butts."

Our collection was strong in beetles. Besides the *Eleodes*, it boasted an iridescent green beetle, beautiful as a jewel, and a huge black beetle with spined legs, solid and heavy and soldered together, like a Mattel car. It was a husk when we found it, with ants at work in it, and we had had to poke a stick in its shell and shake it like a maraca until all the ants fell out.

We were not strict about condition. Any dead thing would do. Even parts of dead things—feathers, bones—could be placeholders for the whole

animal. In this category, we had two rattlesnake rattles, a bovine jawbone missing a number of teeth, and a rabbit's tail, a stiff little curved bone inside a soft puff.

"And finally, the centerpiece of our collection: A whole entire jackrabbit, with the hunter's bullet still in its head."

"Is that all?" said Blanche.

"What do you mean?"

"Well, it's not a very big zoo."

"Look, I'm only one person," I said, then stopped in confusion. "We're still building the collection. By the time we're done, it will be"—I pronounced these words with relish—"a *truly distinguished* collection. Then we'll donate it to a museum." Privately I thought that was unlikely. We didn't have a dinosaur bone or even a whole rattlesnake. We hardly had a whole anything. Our exhibits kept being torn apart by coyotes or vultures, while the beetles snipped away at them from the inside, more secretly but hardly any slower. Things fresh dead we weighed down with rocks so they wouldn't be dragged away by coyotes. We had built a cairn over Dr. Goat's rabbit. Even so it was looking a little tattered.

"It's not really a zoo, though, is it?" Blanche said hesitantly.

"What do you mean?"

"Real zoos have live animals."

"So? Is an animal not an animal any more once it's dead? In nature, lots of animals are dead right now. Most animals are dead a lot longer than they're alive. Death is normal. *Life* is weird."

She looked dubious. I switched tracks. "Animals are easier to look at when they're dead. This is a fact about animals: they live to hide. If you can see it, it's probably dead. Remember that, Blanche." Dead animals soak up your looks, I explained, and never get enough. Live animals like to stay just out of reach of your look. Maybe you see a bit of a hind leg. Then they pull that in too. Live animals are practically defined as animals you can't see completely. Like black holes, the way they look is like your failure to see them. I don't mean they just happen to be out of sight, like a shoe under the bed. The way they look *is* their out-of-sightness. The good thing about this is it means you can see them all the time, whenever you want. Invisible animals are all around you. Here's another thing to remember: if you can't see it, it's alive. Every time the world seems boring and lonely, that's exactly when you're surrounded.

"You can see animals in normal zoos, though," Blanche said doubtfully.

"No, you can't."

"Well . . ."

"You think those are animals?" I said. She looked confused. "You think you're looking at a tiger. But how do you know? Have you ever seen a real tiger?"

"Aren't those real?"

"No! A real tiger is in the jungle. A tiger in a room isn't a tiger. You can't see tigers! That's the point of tigers! Except dead ones. Dead tigers, you can see. That's why our zoo is better. Zoos are for looking, and dead things are for looking at."

Dying, I had worked out, was a vigorous form of appearing. Living animals draw back or move at a strategic angle to your line of sight, thereby keeping some of their appearance to themselves. Dead animals don't just meet your look squarely, they spring up the line of sight and pile into your eyes. You can see more of them, faster, than you can see anything else. The dead actually improve your vision. But we rarely get to observe dead people long enough for it to have lasting effect. We cover them with a sheet. A special vehicle rushes them away. Then we tuck them underground. Images of the dead in film, art, and literature are scarce, too, though images of the dying are plentiful, as if dying were not simply a way of getting to dead. It is almost as though death were an end or a departure. In fact, the dead have finally arrived. Yet how many films and novels end with a death, how few begin with one! Who are death's heroes?

Answer: animals.

"But dead animals don't do anything."

"Yes, they do." We watched. There wasn't a lot of action. The dead happened to be lying low right then. "Dead animals just move a lot slower," I said forcefully.

We became obsessive collectors of corpses. We scooped fly carcasses from windowsills and pored over them to select the most perfect. A zoo is like an ark, we decided, so we never took more than two of anything, though sometimes when we found a better specimen we would replace the inferior one. We pried off the highway a flattened rattlesnake that had dried in a complicated shape like an ampersand. We slipped through the barbed wire fence around the Restricted Area to look for specimens—fearfully at first, but later

it became routine. There, we found a real treasure, better than Dr. Goat's rabbit: a dead coyote. We once walked two miles dragging a dead deer from the side of the highway. That night at dinner, Mama said, "Something smells peculiar. Maybe we'd better not eat those leftovers after all." After that, we always scrubbed ourselves thoroughly when we got home.

The deer was our biggest animal until we found the cow. The cow was not full grown, but she was impressive. She was complete except for the soft parts; the eyes were gone, and the belly was a cavity with a bit of hide hung over it like an awning. The chewed edge of the skin made a fringe that flapped a little in the wind. When it blew up you could see right up inside the cow, into the cave under the ribs; she was almost hollow. This meant she was not very heavy. We pried her partway up with an old fence post. Bugs pattered to the ground and swarmed everywhere, and a rank smell rose. She was flat on the underside, like a tent. There the brown and white hair that still held its color and clung to the top of the cow had fallen or been chewed by bugs off the hide, and this was a shocking yellow white and no longer held any part of the shape of a cow.

We dragged her what seemed like some distance, but was probably no more than fifty feet, and then we came to an arroyo choked with thorn-bushes. The zoo was on the other side. Alone, we could get through, but not in the company of the cow. So we brought the zoo to the cow. Over the course of one day, we went back and forth across the arroyo with a card-board box, moving the exhibits. Then we set them up all over again around the cow in a new and even better order.

Like memory, the zoo was a gallery of corpses, arranged in meaningful tableaux. But like memory, they could be rearranged. Exhibits could be brought out of storage, others put away forever; the zoo could be arranged to prove a point, or to spite a rival curator. (In this respect too, like memory.)

We arranged and rearranged the exhibits according to various schemes of classification. These were subject to fads and upheavals. For a while we grouped them by color. I envisioned a rainbow of deadness, a color-wheel of corpses. It wasn't easy, the dead are mostly brown and beige, but I purloined Mama's red fox collar (two heads spitefully biting the rhinestone clasp) to fill in a gap in the spectrum. Roy G. Biv: cardinal, fox, oriole, frog, bluebelly lizard, beetle . . . but there we ran into trouble. A violet corpse was hard to find.

Another day we tried the alphabet, although snakes proved the only really

typographical animals. We needed lots of snakes. All day we trudged up and down the highway looking for remains, and never got farther than *F*.

Sometimes we organized the corpses by how they died: Run Over, Shot, Killed by Coyotes, Don't Know. Sometimes we organized them by how rotten they were.

Once we organized them by how scary they would be if they came back to life.

Then, because we cracked up at the idea of being haunted by a rabbit tail, just the tail, by how funny they would be if they came back to life.

Once we organized them by how sad they made us.

Sometimes we took the other smaller animals back to the dollhouse. We made paper doll clothes, ball gowns and tuxedos, and hooked them on their shoulders. That was easiest with the roadkill animals, which were flat already. We gave them names of real people and characters from our stories, making no distinctions: Granny, Dr. Goat, Flossie, Max, Donkey-skin. We made them drink cocktails, play cards, dance, fall in love. Their flat faces—epaulets of matted fur, crushed bone, and dried meat—squinted from above crudely drawn collars. Bits of fur and skin, knocked off in collisions with the furnishings, littered the velveteen rugs.

Gradually, the exhibits fell apart. Even the coyote's head was going. His ears had been lost for a long time, but now the hard skin was pulling open over the bones and the fur was coming off in patches and blowing away. We had found clumps as far away as the big cholla, stuck in tufts on the needles. I took a long hard seedpod from a mesquite tree and poked it through a hole into the inside of the coyote's head.

"What are you doing?" said Blanche.

"Checking to see if there's any brain left."

"Is there?" The mesquite pod scared up some bugs. They came trucking up out of the eye sockets, dropped on the ground, and hurried away.

"No, the bugs ate it."

"Does a brain still have thoughts in it after it's dead? Does it have memories?"

"I guess. Thoughts are just molecules," I said, though I wasn't sure. I stirred around in the head, but there was nothing much in there.

"No memories," said Blanche.

But a new dead animal always turned up. Maybe sometimes the exact same animal that had been raiding the zoo the day before. The Dead Animal

Zoo had no visitors that were not candidates for collection. It was even easy to imagine ourselves there. Sometimes I lay down among the corpses and practiced being dead, lying straight and perfectly still on my back, while big, meaty red and black ants ran over me and tiny flies came to my temples to sip my sweat. When Blanche sighed and tried to move, I hushed her. "Try and learn something for once," I said.

"It smells funny."

"True," I said. "And your point is?" Actually if you didn't know better, you might think someone was cooking. Laid out at even intervals like biscuits on a baking tray, the corpses buzzed and steamed and sometimes even twitched a little when the bugs crawling over and inside them all heaved together.

"The ground is *hot*," she whined.

"No duh," I said. "It's the desert." She was silent for a moment, then opened her mouth again. "Yogis walk on hot coals," I said firmly. "Mind over matter, Blanche." From down there, the zoo looked like a desert camp, a scattering of sagging brown tents, the sudden diagonals of ribs or hip bones like support poles, and ants that ran around like dogs when disturbed, but otherwise plodded in line, dutiful as a camel train. Blanche started humming one of her little tunes to herself.

"Do dead people hum?" I asked.

"No," said Blanche.

"Correct," I said. The stones *were* hot; they seared the backs of my arms, my bare calves. Blanche stopped fidgeting. The sun boiled down. It seemed to be right above me, a brighter, hotter spot in the red behind my eyelids. The voices of insects twined around us. To the left there was the clatter of some small animal whisking from bush to bush. Being dead was like listening, I thought. Like having nothing to say, and just listening.

THE SIAMESE TWIN REFERENCE MANUAL

Solo S/M for the Single Twofer

Are you a bottom? Are you a top? Or are you both—*at the same time?* The most agile "switch" can't do that, but *you* can. And why not? Why should a twofer be limited to what a singleton can do and feel?

Now let's take it a step further. Ever thought about topping or bottoming . . . yourself? I'm not just talking about tweaking your twin's nose, or turning the other cheek. I'm talking about an intricate topping and bottoming taking place all over your body simultaneously. Your ass tops your elbow. Your left breast bottoms to your right, your spleen tops your kidney, a freckle bottoms to a hair. An advanced SubDom can dominate and submit simultaneously, in the same body part. (Where there are two wills, there are two ways!) As Whitman said, "I am large, I contain multitudes," and guess what? They're fucking. And let's face it, where there's fucking, there is dominance and submission. You don't like vanilla intercourse, why settle for vanilla onanism?

Some practical advice. If you're using bondage, remember: if s/he can't move, you can't either. Extreme physical pain? OK, but one of you had better stay conscious. Confine corporal punishment to your ass, thighs, and shoulders. Avoid your heads, necks, and hands—you will need these parts if something goes wrong.

A word about "twincest." The moral majority won't let twofers forget that masturbation is incest. OK, sure. So is wiping your ass. Singleton, guess who's your closest relative? You are. Dr. Marie, please keep your hands outside the blankets.

One and a Half

When I woke up, I had no idea where I was. I was standing in darkness. Only a slightly diminished darkness outlined the lowered shades on my right, twin parallelograms that disappeared when I looked their way. Someone was breathing nearby, not Blanche. There was something small, hard, and slippery in my right hand. I ran my thumb lightly over it and it beeped, opening a green eye: a phone. I raised it to my ear. There was the attent hush of a live line. "Hello?" I whispered.

"Nora?" Louche said sharply. There was a caw of bedsprings, and I was blinking in the eyebeam of the bedside lamp. "What the bloody hell are you doing?"

I lowered the phone to my side. What could I say? I was sleepwalking, I needed to use the phone, I'm not myself, it wasn't me? I stepped back against the table and slid the phone onto it.

"This," I said, surging onto the bed, one knee on either side of her. I put my hand on her throat and felt her swallow. Her skin was hot, a little sweaty. Her pulse touched me secretly. She waited, not moving. After a moment I pressed my hand slowly down over her collarbones to her hard breastbone, dragging her collar down to where a mythological beast purred and preened with more than one head—more than two—"Cerberus?"

"Hydra."

I leaned in with all my weight and gave her louche gift back to her. Her sticky lips resisted, then yielded to my tongue, and I tasted stale smoke and sleep and salty butter and sardines and peppermint and her breath like a thought passing back and forth between us. Then her hard, dry hand closed

around my damp descending one and pulled it farther down into a nest of springy convolutions that opened onto silk and syrup, and it was no longer at all clear who was in charge of the situation. We were two Transitional Objects negotiating some sort of parlay between machine parts designed with something else in mind, and either of us could fly apart at any moment.

I was on my back, arching to crush a still hot ember against Louche's knuckles with a pleasure I thought might come back later as pain, when my eyes slipped off her shining blue-green torso to the table where the phone was. I had the distinct feeling someone was listening. A tardy ball of lightning gasped down my spine, and Louche laughed, and flipped onto her back beside me, and stretched out her cramped hand, and then laid it over her nose and mouth and breathed, and laughed some more.

I woke up with my legs coiled in Louche's damp sheets and a heavy feeling in my chest. There was a nasty trickling sound in the eaves. Evidently it was raining again. The blue shoulder an inch from my face was thick as a knee. Practically deformed, I thought, though it was not true, and those tattooed scales make the skin around them look, I don't know, *peeled*. That was true, and I wanted to lick the naked places. Vexed, I sat up, treading down the sheets. I had to e-mail the Foundation!

Louche rolled over and slid a heavy, warm arm across my lap. It felt as if I might let it stay there. So I stood up, letting her arm bang down against the bed frame. She woke up fully then. I thought it was possible that she would hit me. I would not have minded, it would have clarified things, but she only watched, stroking her arm with her fingertips, while I put on the T-shirt I had been wearing last night. I couldn't find my underwear, so I went back to my room without it. By the time I was downstairs, fully dressed, she was at the kitchen table in her pajamas, drinking tea. Her computer was on but sleeping, its cool light pulsing. Didn't she want to take a shower? I went to the counter, started fixing tea, and stuck, staring at a dry tea bag in a mug. I felt sawed from a single slab of wood. Louche opened the paper with a sound like beating wings. Finally I dragged my jacket off the back of the chair she was sitting in and said sullenly, "I'm going to go get some yogurt." I had spotted an Internet café–slash–macrobiotic kitchen near the subway station.

"I do have yogurt," I heard her say softly as I closed the door. A block away I slowed to a jog, my chest heaving. With luck Louche would think I had intimacy issues.

In fact, I did have intimacy issues.

The dreadlocked twofer was sitting in the café window with a brown-haired girl in polka dots, their heads bent over a page with a bright repeating pattern she was scissoring into small matching rectangles. I bought a brick made of seeds and took it to the computer stationed nearest the wall, where the high back of the stained green armchair facing it would hide my screen from anyone who wasn't right beside me.

The Unity Foundation had already e-mailed me.

```
Your interview of 17 September was positive. You
will be admitted for treatment at your earliest
convenience. For security reasons this address is no
longer active as of 18 September. Please contact a
representative if you have further questions.

Oneness,

The Unity Foundation
```

I typed a hasty reply on the sticky keys. It bounced back immediately:

```
Mail Delivery Subsystem
   Returned mail: see transcript for details
   ----- The following addresses had permanent fatal
errors -----
   <Unity>
   550 5.1.1 <Unity> . . . User unknown
   Action: failed
```

```
   There has beeen some mistake, as I missed my
appointmeent due to circumstances of which I believe
you are awaree.. What do I do now? I do not have
the address of your eeestablishment or contact
information for any reepreeseentativee.

Ms. O
```

I tried to bring up the Web site, to see if a new address was listed. *404 File Not Found.*

I threw myself back in my chair. The bubble of unease that had been building in my chest since yesterday now burst, splattering my organs with fire. What was I going to do? After weeks of beating steadily toward one end, to stop now was unthinkable.

The dreadlocked twofer was staring at me. *I and I,* their shirt said. Could they be the Unity "representative"? Absurd. They were a healthy, happy, macrobiotic twofer, now smiling, getting up, coming this way—I shut down my browser.

"I-rey, sistren," one said, placing a show announcement on the edge of my table. "Mushy dread a go t'row down some crucial dub at Too Bad tonight. Come by ef uno get a bly. Even an' odd mashin up together."

"Twofers and singletons," his twin clarified, in crisp BBC English.

"Too Bad?" I said, incredulous.

"It's on Uxbridge Row, under the Oxfam. Knock on the door with the Underground symbol on it."

"One love, sistren." They went back to their seat.

One love. Hadn't the Unity Foundation used that phrase? And the Underground symbol was a red circle, barred. I looked at the shiny slip of paper. There it was, in fact, above the words "Free Pass, admit 1½," the crossbar bearing the boldface "**2Ply/2Bad/2Night**!" But if I took every fucking circle for a personal summons, I'd be chasing nickels and dimes down drains, underlining Os in the *Observer* and *Post,* staring at the sun. Dotty, in a word.

Still, it was a reminder. I couldn't rule out the possibility of a hidden message. Calmer now, I got out the brochure I had picked up in the office and inspected it minutely, even tilting it to catch the window glare, in case a name or number scrawled on an overlay had left an inkless impression—a detective's trick that yielded nothing. But maybe the clue lay in the attraction itself. The Hunterian, repository of medical marvels: Where else did a freak belong?

I rang Louche, who did not pick up, and left a message that I had an appointment at the London Gallery at two and would see her that evening.

"Royal College of Surgeons," said the cabbie, pulling to the curb outside a long spear-topped fence. Behind it, square in the middle of the facade, six two-story Ionic columns guarded the small entrance. I had to walk the

length of the fence to find a way around it. Inside the door, a receptionist waved me on into a creamy marble hall where antique notables in gold frames ruminated over a fire extinguisher. Someone passed me and went down a hall toward a marble statue. It took a moment to spot the small sign for the Hunterian Museum, on the side of some stairs leading up. More notables watched me ascend.

The museum had grown up around a core collection of medical specimens assembled by the illustrious surgeon John Hunter, b. 1728, who had treated the young Byron for clubfoot, owned such exotic animals as porcupines and bats, and acquired, through dubious channels, the skeletons of both the largest and the littlest persons of his day, the Irish Giant and the Sicilian Fairy. Hunter was a speculative fellow, who once transplanted a human tooth into a cock's comb, and injected himself with infected pus from a syphilitic whore, both experiments proving fatal to the subject.

The Hunterian was lushly carpeted in institutional grey, and its glass cases were widely spaced and orderly. Within, forlorn widgets the yellowish hue of old vellum coiled in glass jars. On close inspection many of these proved parts of people: a diseased colon, an elephantine thumb. I browsed them with a frank and systematic attitude. I admired the nose made for a woman who had lost hers to syphilis, a pink-painted silver shell soldered to wire glasses-frames, to hook over the ears. Her new husband liked her better without the nose, so she had donated it to the museum: altogether a happy story. An array of fetal skeletons of graduated sizes, arranged against black velvet, seemed a sort of evolutionary chart for changelings: how a pixie may become a human child. A series of slant-topped vitrines were covered with thick velvet drapes to protect their fragile contents from the light. I lifted one to see a page of handwritten laboratory notes accompanying a sepia line drawing of a Y-shaped tubule wreathed with delicate filaments, and peppered all over with lowercase letters tethered to scrawled Latin names. I raised the next curtain, and a postcard that had been sandwiched between the velvet and the glass skated out and tapped me in the chest.

It bore a disagreeable photograph of a monkey with a riding crop astride a bridled goat. Both had the glassy stare of the dead. I turned it over. The yellowing reverse was blank except for the legend, in tiny print: "Monkey Riding Goat, c. 1870s, Potter's Museum of Curiosities, Arundel, W. Sussex." I pocketed it, then on an afterthought bent over the vitrine. The dainty volume inside lay open to a page explicating Hunter's discovery that the freemartin,

a sterile cow that mounts other cows, always has a male twin. Frowning, I dropped the curtain and turned away.

And saw it. One bizarrely stretched skull—no, two skulls fused together, like calcified soap bubbles. Not a twofer, then, and what's more, the second head was up-ended on the crown of the first, and a stump of a neck jutted upward, where a whole second body should have been. There was a glint of light in one eye socket. It almost looked like an eye—moist, shiny—regarding me from inside the skull. My heart lurched. I stared back, I hardly know how long.

Finally, I dared to step forward. As I did, the pale point of light grew, slid and rippled and split in two around a flaw in the glass. I recognized my own reflection, and laughed, relief warming my cheeks. I was the scariest monster there.

I bent to read the plaque. The creature had been born in 1783 in Mundul Gait, Bengal, to poor parents. There should have been a second body; it was speculated that it had received insufficient nourishment in the womb, and never developed. Or perhaps it had been destroyed afterward, since the appalled midwife had thrown the newborn in the fire. Who could blame her? I thought. His mother had dragged him out, treated his burns, and exhibited him to great acclaim. He was killed by a cobra at five.

I was turning away when I heard a hiss behind me. I turned. "I remember a shelf wedged across the window," the lower skull said, moving its teeth out of sync. I dropped back a pace, and the vitrine caught me in the small of my back. "The window was an irregular rectangle cut in the corrugated wall," said the upper, "with two pieces of bottle glass wedged in it, one emerald green, one milky and swirled as a shell, or a blind eye. I thought they were divinely beautiful. I begged for the blanket to be lifted, to afford us a glimpse of them." "Sometimes she did. But sometimes she'd give us the stick," they whispered. It was actually the handle of a spade, occasionally used for poking the fire, hence the charred end, but more often for poking him through the bars, "I mean the blanket," they rasped. "Sorry. Our only friends were the roaches," the lower skull went on. I could hear his breath whistle through the jaw, see the twist of wire that held it in place. The roaches crawled under the blanket when he was very still, and lay confidingly along his side, dry little lozenges. Sometimes he would catch one by feel, he had quick hard fingers like little bones, and make a pet of it. "My darling, my dandy," he would whisper to it, petting its stiff back with a splinter, and make up reasons why

this roach was the prettiest of them all. "I will make you a little saddle out of red felt," he'd whisper. "I'll hang a tiny golden bell around your neck, my pretty." And the roach would prance, nearly. He would tempt it, with soft bits of food dredged up from between his teeth, to step onto his lips, duck its head inside his mouth and take the food from his tongue. He was very good at keeping still.

"I named him Count Backwards," the upper confided, and someone cleared her throat behind me. "Ma'am? Ma'ams? I'll have to ask you not to disturb the exhibits?" I looked around and saw the docent, her mouth working, her reading glasses dancing on her uneasy chest. "If you have a complaint about one of the exhibits, you'll have to take it up with the museum director. Of course, I appreciate that—" I turned to face her, and her voice rose in pitch. "Please stay calm—we all appreciate that there are delicate issues at stake and we certainly want to be sensitive to the, to the concerns of all our visitors, but of course sensibilities have changed, and things that were once acceptable may not now, of course this is a historical museum preserved pretty much as it—"

"What exactly did I do?" My hearts were beating much too fast. I took a deep breath and tried to hold it, but it seeped out from between Blanche's lips.

"Well, I hardly need—I saw you quite clearly. You were trying to pry open that case!"

"What would I want to do that for?" I heard myself say.

She worked her mouth some more. "I don't know, and I don't *want* to know," she said with peculiar emphasis.

"Why would I want to, to *accost*, as you seem to be implying, your moldy old specimens? I might be a freak, but that doesn't make me a pervert."

"I certainly wasn't suggesting—"

"I wonder what put that idea in your head. Does it get lonesome working here? Have you been seeking solace in—oh, go fuck yourself with a wax model." I walked out. Then turned and stuck my head back through the door. "Of a pendulous abdominal growth!" I added in a yell.

I felt some gloomy satisfaction as I closed the door again, but already, as I stepped smartly down the marble stairs, waiting for the slam and not hearing it, a gloomy feeling came over me, and my back tingled, and when the sarcastic click of the latch finally sounded, I started just as if I had not been waiting for it and banged the back of my hand painfully against the brass handrail. On the bright side, I was no longer talking to a skull. Things could

have been worse. I had the feeling I had just strolled out of a trap, like an ant that skitters into a predatory ant lion's sand trap and then skitters out again on an opportune grass blade—with the difference that the ant wonders neither why the grass blade appeared, nor why the treacherous funnel before it. I had the feeling that if I turned, I might see some fanged nonesuch emerge blinking from its den.

I do not mean the docent. She was not the monster. She might even have been the provident blade of grass.

In the placid turbine of the revolving door I felt briefly trapped, and pushed heartily on the glass. I was flung out and had to trot to keep my balance. What was happening to me? Lithobolia, yes, but something even more frightening, something affecting my mind. The mongoose I could blame on jet lag and lamb vindaloo, but this was harder to dismiss. Had I taken up a dream that Blanche was dreaming, tinting its phantoms with the colors of my own real life? And how did I know what my real life was? How did I know that the part of me that distinguished reality from dream wasn't dreaming too?

"What an ass. If you can't decide whether a talking skull is real or not, you need your head examined. *Both* heads. All the same," I decided, skirting a planter containing a handsome saguaro (someone was doing a good job keeping it alive in that climate), "I had better find that clinic quick."

THE SIAMESE TWIN REFERENCE MANUAL

The *London Observer*

"Heads Identified"

All severed heads found last Tuesday have now been identified by relatives. It is confirmed that while all were twins, no two matched, further supporting speculations that they are the work of the doctor who issued a statement five weeks ago when the first head was found, claiming responsibility and announcing a moral crusade to "surgically correct" what he dubbed "this disease of duplicity, this fornication of solitudes, this cancer metastasizing in the first person pronoun." In a weird wrinkle, officials of the Medical Ethics Board have now confessed that they believe the statement issued by their own offices offering tentative support for "doctor-assisted individuality" under certain unnamed circumstances, which up to three days ago they still insisted reflected their consensus opinion, was drafted by Dr. Decapitate himself, who may have an ally on the board, or, shockingly, may himself be a member. Photos and brief bios of all seventy-one distinguished board members follow.

Three of the severed heads have been buried in family plots. One has been cremated and the ashes scattered in an undisclosed location, his family stating on record that they strongly believed him to have taken his own life and that his "tortured soul" will burn in hell beside that of his twin, like "two tongues of one flame." This has set off considerable speculation as to whether it is technically possible to cut off one's own head without assistance from one's twin; whether, if one's twin assists, it should be classed as suicide or murder; whether it is even possible to determine if such assistance was given. "A difficult problem, in which the legal profession might well seek counsel from philosophy or religion," mused retired judge Rutherford Shaves.

Hohokam Elementary School

Until we were eight we were home-schooled by committee. Mama taught us to read, to accompany lines of poetry with appropriate gestures, and to curtsey. Papa instructed us in geology and natural history, Max in carpentry and politics, and Granny in music and moonshine. One day, however, not long after the incident with the kitchen knife, Mama told us that she had enrolled us in the Hohokam Elementary School in Grady. We were to start at once. The next morning two sharpened No. 2 pencils, a used eraser, and a chopped olive sandwich were waiting by our plate.

Max drove us to school. I understood that she was chosen for this job as the least likely to be swayed by our despair. It was by design, too, that we arrived after classes had begun, when the halls were empty. Our new teacher moved her mouth with dreadful care as she formed words of greeting, as if her real face had longer, sharper teeth. She put her hand on our shoulder and turned us to face the class. We had had little experience of children but had noticed on several occasions that they did not follow adult custom and avert their eyes from us. We now felt the general truth of this observation. Twisting out from under Miss Gale's hand, we broke for the door and screamed, "Max!" She gave us a thumbs-up from the end of the hall and abandoned us.

Miss Gale steered us back. "Class, this is—these are your new classmates, Blanche and Nora. They are Siamese twins! That means that they're two people with one body. We've never had a Siamese twin in Hohokam Elementary School before, so this is an opportunity for us all to learn something

about this very special bond, and later I'll pass out some stories about the other Siamese twins that are being born all over the world. I want you all to make Blanche and Nora feel welcome by introducing yourselves and sharing what makes *you* special."

"I'm Chris Marchpane, and I'm mildly retarded," stated the big boy at the back of the class. The others hooted.

"*Thank* you, Chris, that was very polite. The rest of you can save your introductions for recess."

School was a refrigerated Hades where demons offered fraudulent temptations, each with its giveaway flaw (round-tipped scissors that did not cut, fat pencils with no erasers, chairs soldered to their desks). I was temporarily deceived by a pencil sharpener, but when I turned the handle, the hollow body jumped off the drill bit and burped its whole cache of gilt-edged shavings onto the floor. The demons laughed. Blanche, too, laughed, I slapped her face, and we were frog-marched to the principal's office.

At recess, we were called "mutant" and "freak" and "radioactive" and slapped with a black banana skin. Chris Marchpane butted someone in the stomach, and we all went to the principal's office. "Tattletales are *dead*," a girl hissed on the way. "I'm just mentioning." "The teacher told us to be nice to the Chinese twins," Chris Marchpane said. The rest of us said nothing.

At lunch, our sandwich was derided.

During dodgeball we gopped, and got the ball right in the stomach. We tasted again the sandwich of shame.

By the end of the day Chris Marchpane had asked the teacher for permission to move his desk next to ours. I had learned to keep my head down and had made many observations about our eraser: That it was half pink, half grey. That there was a sour smell to the grey half, which was stained with blue ink. That the pink half appealed to my mouth. That eraser crumbs were really little grey scrolls, like furled words. Chris Marchpane watched with interest as I pinned one down with the tip of my pencil and attempted to unroll it.

Something struck me on the back of my head, and I puffed. Words skittered across my desk, floated to the floor.

"Ohhh," sighed Chris Marchpane. "I'll pick them up for you."

"Get lost, *freak*," I said.

Home, I blundered before the Time Camera, crying. "Please, take us back to before," I wished. "Back to before, back to before, back to before!" In

the photograph my eyes are tightly closed, Blanche's open and a little puzzled, and beside us a spindly-legged table is atilt like a parasol, delicately balanced, while behind us a rose is just tilting off the gloved fingers of the man, and the woman is hiking her skirts up (to reveal terry-cloth shorts and tennis shoes) and tilting away in the other direction. I am centered and perfectly balanced, though a little too close to the lens.

Museum of Childhood

Look right. It said it right there in the gutter in white block letters. All the same I looked left. Tires squealed, and a cabbie shouted something that sounded like something else said backward. I scuttled across, feeling the hostile gaze of the proprietor of the Anything Left-Handed on my back. The counterclockwise corkscrew had barely scratched the counterclockwise clock, but I would have happily paid for them both if he had let me finish shopping. Now that my right hand was wayward, I was having trouble with scissors.

The Hunterian had not been the only place I had to leave quickly, that afternoon. After each apologetic exit, I walked on through the narrow, crooked streets, pausing occasionally to shave off with the side of my hand the raindrops that clung to me all over. Once, under a clump of red blossoms phosphorescing against a dark wall. Once under the sole of a giant shoe creaking softly from a rusted brace outside a cobbler's. The rain did not so much fall as materialize in the air close to my skin. No use for an umbrella. Brolly. Bumbershoot?

I could not stop instructing myself, with stupid insistence, This is England. Cobblestones with the sullen luster of pigeons. Pigeons pecking among the cobblestones. When I saw something surprising (the backward clock) I would ask myself, Is this a particularly English surprise? As one might say a ten-year-old with a gun in his lunch box is a particularly American surprise—a surprise still, but the kind of surprise one almost comes to expect. I had the impression the English thought a twofer was also a particu-

larly American surprise. They looked at me censoriously, as if I had grown another head on purpose, to get attention. Where did they think their own mushies came from? Did they think we *recruited*?

I'd found part of London that actually looked like London, with the result that it seemed counterfeit. How disappointing! Tired of toy cars and toy phone booths and toy coppers beetling cartoon brows at vagrant twofers, I sat down in a fluorescent-lit coffee shop that had molded plastic seats and nothing much to break, and ordered a Ploughman's Lunch, which sounded hearty. The sole other customer, an old woman wearing pants pulled up to her breasts and giant white running shoes, sat for a full hour while I forced down a sandwich of orange cheese and jam, looking cunningly at a fly on her plate.

Objects Thrown by Lithobolia, UK Edition

Jar of marmite

Tube of marmite

Pewter beer tankard with insignia of Biddenden Junior Football Club

Magnet depicting the Tower of London

Biography of Henry VIII

Scone (rhymes with "gone")

Jelly babies

Counterclockwise corkscrew

Bottle of "brown sauce"

Toast, with marmite

It was nearly dusk when I got back to the apartment in Shepherd's Bush, and a streaky pink glow was just fading on the kitchen wall above the sink. Louche was sitting at the table playing with three small silhouette heads cut out of black construction paper. She dealt them out in a row like a hand of solitaire, planted her index fingers on the two flanking heads, and slid them in neat, synchronized arcs around the circumference of an imaginary circle until, at the point her wrists X'd, each reached the point the other formerly occupied. First the outside heads swapped positions, then the right-hand couple would become the two leftmost, then the right-hand couple would

swap positions, and so on, so that they remained always in line, like the shells in a shell game, or the winning row in a game of tic-tac-toe.

"How did your appointment go?" she said.

"Oh, fine . . . What are those?"

Slide. Slide. "Have you gone to the Museum of Childhood yet?"

"No."

"I would have thought you'd go there first. It's absolutely stuffed with dollhouses."

"I'm . . . saving it up." Stupid Nora had no idea there was a museum of childhood, actually. The notion rattled me, as if my whole past might be displayed there, with pornographic candor and a bronze plaque: *The North American Child, 20th Century, Desert Habitat.* (A bleached-blond twofer in flip-flops is prodding a skull with a stick below a painterly mushroom cloud. "In the sand can be seen footprints of a rich variety of desert wildlife, including the *cottontail rabbit's* sloppy exclamation points, the twin teardrops of the *javalina,* the *sidewinder's* slanted tildes, the ovoid waffle-print of the *hunter's* Gore-Tex™ boots.")

"Why are you here, really? Not to see me, obviously—no, don't apologize, I am much more comfortable with muted hostility than affection—and I'm starting to doubt the dollhouse story too. You're not interested in dollhouses. I don't believe you know a thing about them."

I thought it best to concede that point and ignore the larger issues. "I don't," I said. "Yet, anyway. I'm just poking around. Hoping some sort of pattern will emerge."

Slide. Slide. "Why did you tell me you were going to the National Gallery?"

I swallowed, appalled and impressed. How expertly she percussed my weak spots. It made me want to fuck her, and afraid to. "What do you mean?"

Louche reached for her tobacco pouch. One head clung to her finger for a moment before floating down to a position slightly out of line with the others. She folded a piece of rolling paper and sprinkled tobacco in the crease, then drew out a knob of hash and thumbed off a few crumbs.

At 2:00 PM at the National Gallery a "winking bomb" had been spotted by a visitor under a bench near *The Virgin of the Sands,* the Leonardo painting that under infrared reflectography had revealed the shadowy lines of a face in profile hovering over the Virgin's artfully draped shoulders. An

alternate pose discarded in favor of the present one—or, as some argued, a second head? (With one finger, Louche lightly tamped down the tobacco and hash in the paper V, and began rolling it between her fingertips.) In the ensuing stampede a guard had been hurt. The entire National Gallery had been evacuated to Trafalgar Square by 2:20.

My face grew hot. Louche ran the tip of her tongue along the free edge of the paper.

At 2:25 an orderly group of Togetherists had begun threading through the crowd, bearing aloft five white coffins the approximate size of human heads. Police were unable to reach them due to the crowd, which the curious were joining in droves despite attempts to disperse them. When the funeral procession attained Nelson's Column, the Togetherists opened the coffins and shook them violently. Thousands of tiny black heads whirled up in a cloud. Panicked pigeons swirled through them, scattering them further. Most of the heads slowly drifted down into the crowd, where some people pinned them to their collars. Others, reaching a higher altitude, had been carried out in a northeasterly direction, falling like black snowflakes on Covent Garden, Lincoln's Inn Fields, and even Bethnal Green. "Where the Museum of Childhood is located, as I'm sure you know," Louche added drily. Some had bobbed on the Thames as far as the Isle of Dogs before disintegrating. A student of Louche's had brought one to class to show her; two had already alighted on her windowsill.

Louche's lighter coughed fire. I suddenly realized it was almost dark. When the flame shrank, she raised the joint to it, puffed, took the joint out and looked at the wet end, nibbled off the tip, puffed again. At last she looked up, eyes two holes in a red mask.

I picked up the misaligned head, which had been bothering me the whole time she was talking. I already knew what I was going to say, but I wanted to make sure I hit the right note, casual but not unconcerned. "Well," I said, "I didn't end up going to the National Gallery, though I didn't think it was worth mentioning. I went to the Hunterian Museum instead. Nothing to do with dollhouses," I added, as she opened her mouth. It was true, but it sounded like a lie. Spontaneous detail was called for. My mind swiveled, holding up a map. The Hunterian was not all that far from Trafalgar Square. Was it to the north? From the steps you saw . . . Lincoln's Inn Fields. The sun had glanced out, daubing the lawn with light. Or, one could just as well say, with shadows—"Oh!" I said, genuinely startled. "I *did* see the heads, but I

mistook them for flakes of soot. From mammoth, Dickensian chimneys."

She grunted around the joint, abruptly losing all interest. She was watching my hands, no doubt sensing a Transitional Object in use. I was tearing thin strips off one of the heads and methodically rolling these into tiny balls. "What do you think of these Togetherists, anyway?" she said, as if idly.

I employed my fingernails in carefully peeling off the face, leaving a benign oval. "They're a cult. They might seem like they're preaching compassion, but if you look at the larger context. . . . They regard being 'split' as a sort of, sort of . . . *sacred wound* that twofers are given to bear for the good of the commonweal. Like leprosy once: part warning, part . . . expiation."

She wrinkled her brow, scraping a bit of tobacco off her tongue with a fingernail. "It's a bit different, isn't it? Nobody can argue with treating leprosy. Killing a virus isn't murder. But killing a person—snuffing out a human mind—"

Ooh, this was dangerous territory. "I'm not saying they're wrong, just that their reasons are bad. I don't think they know or care how twofers really feel."

"How *do* they feel?" Joint lodged between two fingers, she flipped over one of the two remaining heads. Now they were facing each other. *Corrupted*, I wanted to say, but didn't. *Infiltrated. Dispossessed.* "How do you feel?" she piped dreamily, jiggling one with her forefinger. An ember dropped, and a bright ring widened and went out, leaving a perfect round hole through the temples.

"I feel like going out," I said, abruptly switching on the light. "Do you know a club called Too Bad?" Blinking, I smoothed out the crumpled pass on the table.

"You met 2-Ply! I've known them since university." She squinted at me. "Hey, are your clothes wet? Don't you know you're not supposed to walk around in the rain? You're going to sprout some hideous growth."

"Didn't you notice? I already have."

"There's a wire brush by the tub. I'm not going out until you scrub down. And don't forget to wash your hair."

The very mildness of her tone alarmed me. Tomorrow I'll leave town, I thought, as I climbed the stairs. It was time to see what the Potter Museum had in store for me. Louche was getting too close to the truth.

"And Blanche's!" she yelled after me.

THE SIAMESE TWIN REFERENCE MANUAL

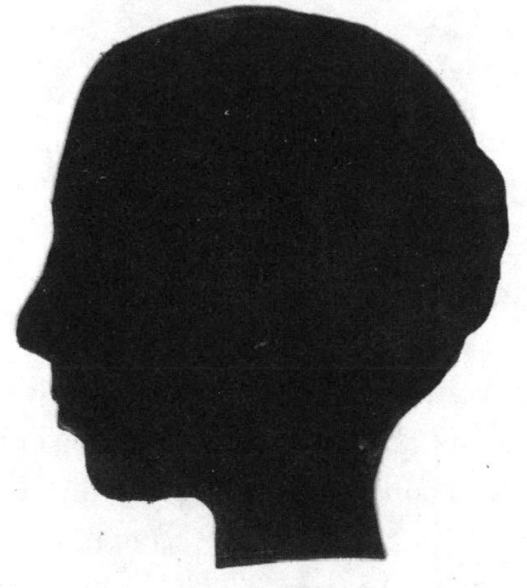

LIBRARY

We had been taught that we were extraordinary. We had not been taught that we were disgusting or ridiculous. Mama, Papa, Max, and Granny had colluded to keep this important information from us. As I saw it, we'd been lied to. We would have to go somewhere else for the truth. We went to the library.

Once a week we made our ritual visit. I held the leathery, damp card tight in my hand over the tooth-loosening ruts of the dirt road, the slithering escape from dirt onto asphalt, the smooth gathering hum of the highway.

The library was a low concrete bldg (it earns this terse denotation by an equally terse assortment of books), on a rectangle of densely knit, springy turf that ended ruthlessly at the fence. Skeletal baby trees grew, or at any rate subsisted, in neat tonsures in the lawn. The library was well carpeted and silent as a grave, if there are graves with twenty-year-old, malfunctioning AC. The books, a nervous and ill-chosen lot, like road-weary adults waiting for a driving test, huddled all together to one side of every half-empty shelf. I always imagined the library as a sinking ship, listing toward the A's.

T for Twins, for Truth! The file cabinet extruded its long tongue, but did not answer our questions. Twins there were a handful, *Bobbsey, Sweet Valley*: not like us. Not conjoined, except old Chang and Eng, the original Siamese twins—but it was plain to see that they were regular men, hitched by a bitty band of flesh. They had their own arms, legs, wives! Where were the books about us? There were a great many books about "he," and a good

number about "I," and "she" and "they" were also well represented, but "we" was almost never mentioned.

For a long time, our old enemy the Pushmi-Pullyu was our sole companion.

Then (F is for Freaks), we found a faded photograph of a sideshow poster. *Strange Girls. Alive! Why?* A lovely two-headed lady! But who was she, and where did she get those snakes, and did she ever fight, and did they ever bite? We craved stories. We tried science fiction (M is for Mutants). Webbed fingers reaching, fanged maws slavering. Irradiated ants, bigger than buses! Mandibles snapping: they had mouths, why didn't they say something? The librarian, intruding unforgiveably on our private search, offered the *Las Vegas Sun*'s latest report on the still climbing birthrate of conjoined twins, but we did not think truth was to be found in a *newspaper*. Truth was in books. But hidden.

Sometimes we glimpsed a flicker of a double figure resembling ours—Snow White, Rose Red. Invisible Aswell. Jekyll and Hyde. But under scrutiny it dissolved, like those faint stars you can only see when you're not looking—a phenomenon Papa said had to do with "rods" and "cones." We resisted the idea that our clear eyes were cluttered with geometry, but we had learned to look with the sides of our eyes, and now we taught ourselves to read this way too. We grew practiced at reading for what we could not then name metaphor, until metaphor itself began to seem Siamese—this coupled to that—and its mere presence a reference to us. Where did we first read "blanche et noir" and learn that Mama and Papa too had a taste for metaphor?

"Oh!" we must have said, a two-note chord, because *"Shhh!"* the librarian hissed. We crept up the long, long slope to the desk under her accusing gaze. Her hard bosom, planted on the very place designated for books to be checked out, held its ground for as long as was decently possible against the items we nervously extended. Chris Marchpane beamed, frozen in the act of lifting a pile of books from a shelving cart as if they had turned to stone. Just before our books nudged her front she would rear up and back—a moment in which we could not help catching our breath—and stare down at the books through her glasses.

The Double. The Terrible Two. Genetic Basis of Morphological Variation in Monozygotic Twins. Would she let us check them out? In a moment with all the suppressed drama of a stickup we produced the potent card. With a

bitter contraction of her orange-painted lips she yielded, performed various spiteful, impotent gestures against our trophies, and let us go.

Someone must have noticed something about the books we were bringing home. "Your mother asked us to order this," said the librarian, with a terrifying smile, handing us *Heather Has Two Heads*—a book for babies. Too little, too late!

Myself My Own Fever

"It's idiotic, but the one thing I can't get used to is the backward traffic," I told Louche, squinting into the spangled dark. "I keep looking left when I should look right, and when I think twice, it just brings me full circle to the wrong way again." I stepped off the traffic island. Louche yanked me back, and a double-decker bus roared by, inches away.

A sort of ripple passed through me, like a flaw in a mirror I was reflected in.

"You'd think looking both ways before crossing the street would be a twofer's one evolutionary advantage."

"The worst thing is, I'm not even shaken. I have the feeling that bus would've passed right through me without encountering anything of any substance. I've become pure image. I fundamentally don't believe I can hurt myself here, because I'm essentially still on the other side of the Atlantic."

"I see," said Louche. "And do you believe you can hurt other people?"

We proceeded in thoughtful silence to the Oxfam, a pokey thrift shop with a stained awning, whose darkened door lay behind a locked steel grating to the right of a recessed stairwell. Louche led me down the narrow tiled stairs and knocked on the blue door. "I'm glad I've got you with me," she said. "Two-Ply has invited me a zillion times, but I'm too uncomfortable with the way the mainstream swallows up every new subculture."

"You're not the mainstream, Louche. You're more like acid runoff."

"Darling." The door opened.

"IDs, please." A flashlight clicked, and a tiny Louche bobbed in the void.

I slid my hand into my safe inside pocket and felt for my passport. There it was.

And there it was again. I had kept both passports with me, rather than leave them in my bags, where Louche might find them; the other night I'd thought I noticed a zipper out of place. Sweat stung my raw scalp. It would take Louche one second to guess why I had a singleton passport. One *backward* second.

A luminous hand was already reaching. Louche was already turning back, wondering what the hitch was. And somewhere in the shadowy depths of a mirror a tiny Nora was saying a prayer—to the gods, to Blanche, to the invisible author of her destiny—and closing her fingers on one of two passports, pulling it out, and putting it in the hand of fate.

"Mind the shelves." The flashlight beam sketched out a plastic pop-together shelving unit and then wandered toward a door in the back, passing over an alligator purse, a child's stuffed elephant, some tattered books, a bicycle helmet, an umbrella handle fashioned out of a deer's hoof.

"What is this place?" I asked Louche.

"In the day, it's the Underground charity. It sells the stuff people leave on the subway."

"How intolerably melancholy. Let's go home."

The doorman chuckled and opened the door—onto a tiled wall. "In you go, then," he said. "Good job you're neither of you too broad in the beam." He angled the beam to the right. Now I could see that there was actually a gap of a couple feet between the tiles and the rear wall of the store. From the right came a muffled beat and the sound of voices.

Louche took a deep breath. "*Now* I know why I've never been. You first." Behind us came a knock, and the flashlight bobbed away.

After several false tries, I went in sideways. I could hear Louche's leather jacket scraping against the tiles behind me. The corridor seemed to end, and I had a moment of panic before the wall behind me suddenly fell smoothly away, revealing itself to be a door, and I stumbled backward onto a textured metal floor that boomed underfoot. A rail caught me painfully in the small of the back. Louche stumbled out after me, moaning, "Oh-h-h, I didn't like that one bit."

We were on a small raised platform overlooking a disused subway station. A jerry-rigged plywood floor covered the tracks. On a stage at the far

end I could see 2-Ply behind a turntable, adjusting a standing mike. The brown-haired girl, still in her polka dot dress, was on bass, and another twofer sat behind a pair of laptops, tops of two heads only just visible. Both twofers and singletons—evens and odds—made up the crowd, though the former outnumbered the latter.

"Welcome to the dubway transit system," intoned 2-Ply's Rasta side.

"Mind the gap," said his twin. They checked their watch.

"Which accent is real?" I whispered to Louche.

"Both, neither," she shrugged. "They grew up between worlds. At Cambridge they had a sort of potpourri thing going. They were heavy into fusion, musically and personally. They were looking for some kind of synthetic resting place, you might say. Then another mushy—twofer—got them into Venn. They got interested in the Dynamic Gap"—you could hear the initial capitals—"and sort of . . . polarized. It's been great for their music."

"One, two, two, one!"

Venn? Then I was wasting my time.

The bass clouted the backbeat. After a few bars some invisible drums complicated the rhythm, joined by a plaintive horn sample that seemed to seep in from the black arches; maybe they had put an amp out there? There were some very biological sounds burbling and whistling underneath, like the intestinal trouble of some oversized organism. Plus pages rustling, or were those tiny voices?

"I attempt from love's sickness," sang one part of 2-Ply, in an operatic falsetto, *"to fly in vain."* "Fly" lilted, rising and falling, over a whole paragraph of notes. The other head, in headphones, bent over the turntable, nodding in time.

"It's *The Indian Queen*! That's kind of brilliant." Louche wagged her head.

"Since I am myself my own fever—"

"What's *The Indian Queen*?"

"Since I am myself my own fever and pain."

Two-Ply's hitherto still hand began frotting the disk on the turntable, and a Jamaican voice entered. *"Meet me at the double track—I and I a coming back—"*

"It's a Purcell opera from around 1700. We studied it in a class on the literature of imperialism. Dryden and someone else wrote the libretto. It's a sort of overheated fantasy—"

"No more now, fond heart, with pride no more swell . . ."

"—from England's teen crush on The Other. The Indian queen 'Zempoalla' assumes the throne of Mexico, and Montezuma leads an army against her, then switches sides. I think he falls in love with her. Then everyone dies or I can't remember, the usual tragic outcome. It's goofy but fantastic."

"thou canst not raise forces, thou canst not raise forces—"

"I'm not really 'hostile' toward you, Louche," I said.

"enough to rebel."

"Of course you are," she said. "It's quite all right. I take it as a compliment."

"Meet me at the double track—I and I a coming back—"

The room began to throb. The sample and the vocals drew precariously far apart from each other, but the beat stubbornly continued, now synchronized with neither. The whole concoction came loose from the people onstage and seemed to emanate from the walls and now, actually, from my stomach, a disagreeable sensation. I wondered if I was going to be sick. I was, in fact, trembling. I edged closer to one of the holes in the wall, just in case, and so I saw a premonitory flicker illuminate distant columns in the suddenly hollow dark. *"I attempt from love's sickness . . ."* Then twin headlights and all at once the train itself, in a staccato roar. Two-Ply matched its beat: *"To fly-y-y-y-y-y-y-y-y-y-y in vain."* A long strip of cels flashed by, showing one head in incremental change, and now the voices converged, riding the rattle of the train up to perilous heights. *"I meet me at attempt from love's track with the double sickness attack to meet me fly to meet me in vain to meet me since I am to meet me myself to meet me at my own track with the double fever since I am myself with the double fever and attack pain and attack pain my own fever and pain. . . ."* It peaked with a shout—*"Since I am myself my own fever!"*—and then skated down the train's quick diminuendo with a now almost whispered, *"Since I am myself my own fever and pain."*

"I'm hostile toward you, too," Louche said. It was almost a declaration of love.

THE SIAMESE TWIN REFERENCE MANUAL

The Indian Queen

Semi-Opera by John Dryden and Sir Robert Howard
Music by Henry Purcell
ACT III SOPRANO SOLO

I attempt from love's sickness to fly in vain,
Since I am myself my own fever and pain.
No more now, fond heart, with pride no more swell;
Thou canst not raise forces enough to rebel.
I attempt from love's sickness to fly in vain,
Since I am myself my own fever and pain.
For love has more power and less mercy than fate,
To make us seek ruin and love those that hate.
I attempt from love's sickness to fly in vain,
Since I am myself my own fever and pain.

House Divided

Occasionally, Mama had a fit of godliness and tried the Grady church. "It lacks pomp, and the choir robes are tacky, but at least they *try*." Now there was another reason to go: to promote the Time Camera.

"Let's all go," said Mama.

"You won't catch me dead in that place," said Granny. "There's no love lost."

Papa looked at Max. Surprisingly, Max approved. She said it was a friendly way to make sure the Tourist Board and the Chamber of Commerce and Mayor Dody knew there was a new attraction up at Too Bad.

"I draw the line," said Granny. She shook her finger at Max. "Don't give me that look, you heartbreaker, I'm not falling for it."

So Papa, Mama, and Max took us to church. We went on a special day when there was a potluck. "Strategic timing," said Max.

"You're selling your souls for Hamburger Helper," said Granny.

The church was full of kids who hated me and Blanche. Some of them were made to shake hands with us by their parents, and I knew we would be made to pay for it later. They said, "How do you do?" and stared right in our eyes while they wiped off our cooties on their clothes. Mama smiled at the mothers of our enemies and invited them to visit the Time Camera—"And bring the kids; Nora and Blanche don't often get visitors their own age!"

Then everyone sat down, and a red-haired man in a tight collar bounded up to what I then confusedly believed was called the cockpit. He had the measured buoyancy of a reserve player coming on to save a game gone

wrong. I saw that he was wearing sneakers. He was grinning. It didn't look like he had it in his power not to grin, he had so many teeth. His forehead shone through his hair. Secretly I had been hoping to be saved, to be lifted off my feet like a doll by an invisible hand and then fall back in a faint. But he did not look like he knew any secrets about the Divine.

"Is that the pope?" whispered Blanche.

"No, stupid, the pope lives in Rome, in the Coliseum."

"Not that pope, stupid. I meant the pope of this church."

"Oh. I guess."

"Minister," whispered Papa. "In a Protestant church it's a minister."

The church made me antsy. I stared at the big boys in polyester suits, with inflamed necks and damp crotches, hair so short and thin you could see scalp. I pinched my hands between my knees.

Then the minister said our names. I looked around. Everyone in the church was looking at us.

He leaned forward with pursed lips as if stretching for a kiss, and pressed his words into the air. Whenever he paused he grinned again. "We're blessed to have a lesson set before us by God of how a divided people can live in harmony, or on the other hand not. 'If a house be divided against itself, that house cannot stand. Matthew 3:25.' Consider Nora and Blanche Olney. They carry on almost normal lives, under conditions that would try all of our patience, because they have learned to live in harmony. We who chafe against our neighbors because of petty differences, let us aspire to the example set by Nora and Blanche, who are here with us and with God for the first time." Gentle applause. "I humbly hope they will learn from us, but I confidently predict that we will learn from them. When God tells us to love our neighbors, He really means it.

"What holds for a human being holds for a nation, and even a humble but up-and-coming town like Grady. We all know there is dissent about the activity at the Penitence Ground. There has been talk about leakage, and there has been talk about people getting sick. People in this town have set themselves against the government of the United States and made public remarks to the effect that Uncle Sam is a liar."

There was a murmur. Max stirred in her seat. "Now, I am not here to debate whether these are grains of truth or flagrant falsehoods tossed in the faces of honest working men and women. I say again, a house divided against itself cannot stand. A nation cannot stand if its people do not pull

together, as Blanche and Nora must. If certain activities are secret, it is perhaps because information about those activities should be kept from people who might use them against our American way of life. Let us weigh the importance of our individual fears in the face of the mighty power unleashed by atomic energy. Let us weigh our ignorant fear of the word 'radioactive' and the word 'fallout' against the needs of our country and indeed of Grady. Let us not let our tongues flap in fear and self-interest. Let us not be divided by dissent."

Max caught my eye and pulled a face. I snorted and clapped my hands over my mouth. Papa frowned at me. His lips were pressed together. On the other side of him Mama was nodding earnestly.

Then the speech seemed to be over. There was the smell of old ladies, and damp cats, and then we passed outside for potluck and ate of the wide noodle and the slender one. Someone passed me a little animal made of lavender pompons with goggle eyes stuck on with chips of glue, and stiff cutout feet. The tablecloth was vinyl, with a fuzzy underside, and it sagged between the boards of the table, making thin parallel grooves, and that's where Blanche's spilled pink lemonade collected. A wasp found it. Drops fell off the table and landed in the soft dust and formed little dusty cushions. Cold water slid over our thumb from the button on the water cooler. We ignored the trucks throwing themselves down the highway behind the chain-link fence that protected the scruffy, ketchup-bloodied lawn from hungry deer, though we felt the seismic rumble in our spines.

"Don't go near the squirrels," said a lady in a powder blue jogging suit. "Bill heard there was a case of bubonic plague in Agua Sucio." Mama nodded earnestly.

"Are your girls saved?" another lady asked. We sidled away.

The holy kept an eye on us to observe how well we got along and marvel at God's nonstandard design choices. We sorted our salad. I didn't like tomatoes, so Blanche ate all the tomatoes, and Blanche didn't like onions, so I ate all the onions. We both liked artichoke hearts, so we divided those scrupulously.

The minister's son leaned over. "Can I have your olives?"

Neither of us liked olives. "OK," we said. In school, he would have ignored us. He always kept his head down and hunched his shoulders under the navy blue sweater he wore even in summer. Godly people seemed to wear

a lot of clothes. Maybe there was a chill in the air when God was nearby, as with ghosts.

"Who is the Holy Ghost the ghost of?" I asked him.

"I don't talk about God," he said. "Conflict of interest."

I saw Max talking to the mayor. Papa was backed up against the egg salad, and a short stout woman had him by the bicep. She had a hunched back that made her pink suit jacket pull up under her arms, and a fat brown mole wedged in the groove on one side of her nose. Papa kept lifting his head and looking to the horizon as if he was waiting for a helicopter rescue crew to airlift him out, and every time he did this the pink woman squeezed his bicep and thrust out her neck farther, tilting her head and squinting up at him.

I noticed that Blanche was eating the artichoke heart I was saving for last. "Blanche!" I whacked her head.

"Kids!" said Mrs. Pike.

"I'm telling! I'm telling the minister!" Blanche said.

"Go ahead."

"I'm going to!" Blanche turned, and I kicked my foot out from under her, and we went down in a rain of green peppers. Again, everyone was looking at us.

"Whoa," said the minister's son. "What an illustration of my father's point!"

The Dollhouse Redux

Early the next morning I repacked my bags, gave sleepy, sulky Louche a hasty hug, checked my e-mail at the macrobiotic café with no interesting results, and took the tube to the train station. I was carried south through miles of muddy industrial yards and misty fields dotted with sheep to bleached, disconsolate Brighton, where I bought a geometrical lunch: two isosceles triangles of white bread cleaving to a cold fried egg, and a hard brown sphere of breaded sausage with another, phenomenally tough boiled egg inside it. I caught a bus that rattled west along a narrow wet road through glittering greenery that occasionally parted to reveal a stretch of pale ocean, and finally discharged me in a cobbled square in Arundel, a tiny, impossibly quaint cluster of white plaster walls and red tiled roofs around a castle that looked so real it had to be some sort of hologram. I set out walking. I had an address, but finding the building itself was surprisingly difficult; the side streets made a series of determined turns and released me onto the same small street, its video store, post office, Boots Pharmacy looking as anachronistic as the fillings in a Shakespearean actor's teeth. Frail trees agitated in the small spaces allotted for them in the occasional brick-walled gardens. A seagull yawped.

I leapt rank puddles, passed two churches, a Doll Museum, and a Museum of Industry. Upon checking the address for the Potter, I realized I had missed it. I retraced my steps, making sure of the street names, and found myself at the Doll Museum once again. I shrugged and went in. I had told Louche I was going to visit a doll museum somewhere in West Sussex. It appeared I had been telling the truth.

The precise young man behind the counter had never heard of the Potter Museum and seemed affronted to be asked. He handed me a phone book. I found a listing for the Potter and showed him that the address was the same. Could I use his telephone to try the number? He pointed to the red squiggle of a phone booth visible through the thick window, chewing his gum with neat, disappointed movements of his mouth, as precise as if he were forming words.

An old man put his head out of the back and said something without moving his lips. I eventually made out that he was saying they had moved it. Moved the Potter Museum? Aye. Where? Jamaica Inn. As in the novel? Aye, abominable.

"Abominable?"

"The gentleman said, *in Bodmin Moor*," put in the young man, with icy precision. "That is in *Cornwall*. Have you heard of Cornwall? Cornwall is in the *west* of *England*."

Did he despise me because I was American, or a twofer, or both? Just to spite him, I bought a ticket for the show. He tried to make me pay for Blanche as well. I rolled up her eyelid to display her immaculate whites and he backed down, but watched us narrowly as I walked away, ready to pounce if Blanche showed signs of waking.

The exhibit, which was tiny, but augmented with photographs and other documents, concerned dollhouses designed by notable architects. I'd had no intention of really doing the research Papa had suggested, but I found myself reluctantly interested, though the dollhouses themselves made me uneasy. The yellowing nighties laid out on the bed. The sacrosanct spaces, so intimate but exposed. I remembered how through my eyes I could inhabit the smallest places; the doll was a kind of lens, a device for shrinking and focusing, by which I could gauge and set the size of my imagined self. The doors were what made me feel it this time, and the windows, the feeling of a self-sufficiently interior space. I considered a dollhouse with tiny, framed blueprints hanging in its parlor, then moved on.

I was looking at a photograph of our dollhouse.

Except it was not the dollhouse. Its facade was shaggy with ivy. There was smoke coming from one chimney and what appeared to be a peacock on the lawn.

The legend beneath the photo referred me to a catalog number. "Do you have a catalog of the dollhouses in the show?" I asked the attendant.

"Naturally."

"Well, can I have one?" I said, a little testily.

"You'll have to pay for it." Exasperated, I paid, and flipped to the item number in question.

No photographs survive of this dollhouse, so admired at the time, but contemporary witnesses report that it bore an extraordinary likeness to John Seymour Laine's masterpiece, down to the finest details of the molding, so we feel confident in presenting a photograph of the full-sized structure in lieu of the miniature. It remains a topic of speculation whether the dollhouse was a model for the great house, or a copy of it. Reportedly, the dollhouse was made by the great architect himself, as a gift for the daughter of the house, but a rumour circulated to the effect that the dollhouse was made some years before by a journeyman-architect to demonstrate his prowess, that with justifiable pride (and some hope of gaining employment) he showed his work to the master, who admired it; flattered by the great man's attention, he presented him with the dollhouse, and was thanked warmly, but was never shown any further signs of regard. Some years later this young architect, seeing a drawing of the latest triumph of the master, was flabbergasted to observe that the great Laine had copied his work in every particular.

In either case, it is certain that the dollhouse was a near-perfect miniature of the house, and the two stayed together through several changes of ownership. The family fortunes declining, the house passed to an obscure fabulist of the early 1800s, who wrote effete, eroticized versions of old fairy tales under a pen name, but was in reality the notorious rakehell Chubb Wykehead, who had scandalized London and the continent with his exploits, and after one particularly infamous escapade involving the daughter of a lord and His Nib's prize ram, only escaped imprisonment on condition that he retreat to a country house and cloister himself in it, 'and never again permit his name to be publicly Advertized or associated with any Acts or Writings howsoever sober their Disposition in any Field of Church, State or Society.' On his solitary death, the house was sold, then sold again.

House and dollhouse parted company at last, sometime in the

1800s. The dollhouse was acquired by the family of Morlett (in an intriguing side note, the minor Hollywood star Evelyn North, who was the last owner of the house, is reported to have said she was drawn to it because it reminded her of a dollhouse she had seen at a castle when she was a little girl. If this was the dollhouse, then the 'castle' was probably the country seat of the family, which opened to the public two days a week somewhere around the future star's fifth year). Their fortunes declining in turn, they sold it—one of the last treasures to go before the impoverished heirs moved to a neat modern house in Stoke Newington—to a private collector. The collector, who later acquired a large number of extraordinarily fine German and Austrian-made dollhouses during WWII, under circumstances that caused him some embarrassment in the post-war climate, moved with his entire collection to America shortly after the war. There, his circumstances worsened. He found himself living in a small flat in West Hollywood, selling off his dollhouses one at a time. No doubt the dollhouse changed hands again in this time, but it has not resurfaced, and what became of the collector we do not know.

Well, *I* knew. Grandfather's sister, my great-aunt, bought it for her daughter, who died young, and when my great-aunt herself died, she left the dollhouse to Papa, in case he should ever have a daughter.

I went back to the photograph. The dollhouse, but big enough to live in! There were people behind those walls, practically life-sized. This amazed me, as if creatures of wood and glue were to suddenly rise up and perform *The Duchess of Malfi* with appropriate gestures.

There was a tiny caption engraved on a plate inlaid in the frame. At last I made it out. It said, "The Manor House, Glass Lane, East Loode." "I hate to ask, but can you tell me where Loode is?" I asked the clerk. He flicked a road map in his display.

"Do I have to pay for it first? No? Just checking," I said.

"There's no call to be rude," he said. "You mushies certainly have a chip on your shoulder."

The solitary dot that was East Loode—there was no Loode, let alone a West Loode—was about an hour farther west, the approximate direction I was going, if I was still going to the Potter Museum. I suddenly decided I was. On my way back to the bus stop I stopped at an Internet café—really, a couple of

computers at the back of a stationery-and-candy store—and sent Audrey an email.

> What do you know about Evelyn North? Will explain later. xxxN

The bus route ran for a time along a beach. I gazed absently at the close and rippling waves, which broke neatly on the pebbles with a minimum of splashing, as if quelled by the weight and dignity of the sea behind. Then a man appeared, very pink and seemingly about two feet high, stepping firmly along the band of sand, which revealed itself thereby in a sudden, disquieting perspective shift to be much broader and farther away and the waves more unruly than I had thought.

Somewhere along the way I fell asleep, and when I woke, everyone on the bus seemed to be looking angrily at me. Had Blanche done something to embarrass or alarm them? I hiked up my coat to conceal her and leaned my head against the window, pretending drowsiness, though I was no longer sleepy. I got off the bus in the small village of East Loode, and walked back along the bus route. The Manor would not be in town but in the neighboring countryside, I thought. Just before the stone church tower announced the start of the village, we had passed a turnoff.

The road wound first through cottages, then a few larger modern houses on artificially smooth green lawns, then fields where distant sheep were demonstrating traditional poses. An intricate wickerwork wall of thorns and thistles rose up on all sides and closed out the light. Deep in one thicket that was swallowing a signpost I made out the letters lass La, which reassured me. I was on the right road; if the Manor was visible at all, I would see it. The occasional muddy drive penetrated the wall and afforded cropped views of what seemed to be the same field over and over, the same wary sheep. Finally the road swerved around a tight corner and dead-ended at a T intersection with a bigger road. I had gone too far.

I started back. My feet were beginning to hurt. I walked all the way back to the cottages, and realized I had missed it again. I decided to give it one more good try and then give up. It would be annoying to leave without seeing it, but the sun was starting to sink in the sky, and it would take me five hours, at least, to get to Jamaica Inn. I turned around, and started back over the same ground for the third time, very slowly now.

This time I looked, not for the house itself, but for the disposition of the trees around the house, the shape of the hill behind it. Looking in this way, not for the figure but for the ground, I spotted something through one of the gaps in the hedge. On the ridges around Too Bad, it is a common enough thing to pause for a sip of stale water from a canteen and watch the rocks slowly shape-shift underfoot. Scattered boulders among the boulders form a line, a corner, then another, and you realize you are inside what was once a room, hundreds of years ago.

I slipped through the hedge. The sheep retreated en masse to the far corner. The sheep-shorn grass covered everything with a thick springy pelt, but underneath it I could make out the outlines of foundations, and here and there the crumbling butts of walls stuck up through the grass like teeth. I had the feeling that if I peeled it up, there would be perfect flagstones, stairs, curbs underneath.

It was peaceful. There was a small orchard of fruit trees behind what had once been the house. When the clouds parted, the sun was very bright and clear, delineating each frisking leaf. Small apples vibrated in a tree that looked all branches, as if a sinkhole had consumed the trunk. In a neighboring field, someone was spreading some green netting with finicky twitches.

Had this been the Manor? I got on my knees on the flowered carpet of grass inside one sketchy room, wondering if I would feel something. The gardener had lifted his head, and was staring at me the way the sheep had. I got up again, feeling foolish.

Then I stepped between two sprawling thistles, and the shapes fell into place around me. I knew where I was. I was standing in the quondam scullery. A funny thing happened to my eyes: The bushes and trees seemed like miniatures, the sky far above was my bedroom ceiling. My legs felt numb and stiff as a doll's. I slipped in some wet sheep's droppings and landed face-down.

The sides of my torso tingled, expecting a gargantuan hand to seize hold, make me walk and talk. Look what dolly wants to do! Bad dolly!

Roll over, dolly.

I rolled over. My eyes, painted open, stared straight up. I heard furniture scraping across the floor above. Someone giggled in the secret attic.

Then a seagull fell through the ceiling, crying, and the rain started. I jumped up, released, and ran for the road.

THE SIAMESE TWIN REFERENCE MANUAL

Siamystic Meanderings

To make peace with our twin is the spiritual task of the next millennium; we must enlist the help of all those with double vision, second sight, a gift for looking both ways. Please join the debate on the wisdom of making a strategic alliance with the Togetherists in the important work of bringing to a halt the criminally unilateral operations of the so-called Dr. Decapitate.

Our public profile is growing daily. Member Ron alerts mailing list readers to Tuesday's not entirely positive article in the *Washington Post*. Friends, refrain from extravagant statements in communiqués with the press. Whenever possible refer hostile inquirers to our Web site. As we witnessed in the Salt Lake City debacle, media will use every chance we give them to label us fringe-thinkers and extremists. Where possible, emphasize the differences between our positions and those of the well-meaning but the sometimes impetuous Togetherists. Like it or not, we live in a world of "spin," so take the time to memorize a few of the handy catchphrases drafted by a crackerjack New York publicist working pro bono (thanks, Anonymous!) SASE to the address below, or fire us an e-mail.

For those in the San Jose chapter, Sister Marjory is hosting a bake sale to raise funds. Encourage your friends and neighbors to try her toothsome treats. Thank you, Marjory! Why not try this in your community?

As one door closes, another opens, and amid these financial difficulties we are happy to welcome a new healing presence to our community. Please join us in celebrating Sister Pearley, who has taken over the mailing list. Our soul's joy throbs.

Doom Town

A black 5 trembled in the crosshairs. The second hand spun, dragging the perimeter of a grey circle behind it. 4. 3. 2. 1.

The teacher had said, "Class, have you ever heard of Survival City?" The class was mute. Finally I had raised my hand. "You mean Doom Town?"

The slit in the blinds was a burning wand suspended in the close air. A foot gently explored the back of our chair. I turned. *"Stop it,"* I hissed, thrilled. Chris Marchpane had reached puberty and doted on me and Blanche with newly mature effects, derided by our classmates. At least once a day his baggy white shorts would come to a point in his lap, though he tried to hide it by bringing up his big knees to clasp the sides of the desk—which was set a fixed distance from the chair, so that when he slammed the desk shut he ran a risk of defanging his obsession forever. We demonstrated our disdain with all the martial arts of childhood, but at home in bed I watched the sandy grains of the dark assemble themselves into bawdy tableaux in which his snowy, Olympian shorts played the lead part in a combinatory series unfettered by any firsthand knowledge of the limits of the male body. Over and over, in the role of the disdainful desired, we spread our scornful thighs and let him . . . what?

A black and white man was carrying a black and white lady across a living room. The lady held a stiff, seated position (ankles crossed), and traversed the room at a slight tilt. Set down in an armchair, she rocked a little. Well! Grown-ups played with dolls. There was the proof.

* * *

"The sister city." We had heard the old ladies at the Natatorium call Grady that, but nobody ever named the city whose sister it was. It was Granny who finally told me its name: Doom Town. Was it a ghost town, I asked. It seemed like a good name for a ghost town. "In a way," she said, "if there's such a thing as a ghost of what was never alive to begin with." Doom Town was a city in which no real people lived, only dolls.

"A tiny town!" Blanche said, intrigued.

No. The houses were large as life. But the streets were short and led nowhere. The dollhouses had exquisite furnishings, but if you turned a tap, no water would flow. The stove was clean and cold. The lamps shed no light. But the boomerang-patterned linoleum tables were laid with Fiestaware and the cupboards stocked with real food: Special K, Shredded Wheat, Quaker Oats. And the dolls . . .

Another woman, carried like a roll of tent poles, was angled and poked into a car that had a number 24 daubed on its side door.

"The dolls," we'd prompted.

The dolls were arranged in realistic tableaux: woman looking out the window, man in the armchair. Kids at the kitchen table, playing a game. One of the Penitence workers had snuck back and put the man and the woman in bed together, naked. Later he told Grampa he was glad of it, but that he wished he had not given the children names.

"Where is it?" tore out of us. We were hot with excitement. We would make Mama take us there.

"Thin air," said Granny. "The wild blue yonder."

A mannequin family sat around a dinner table. Then they leaned back in their chairs, as if amazed. The light tore at their faces and clothes.

The foot returned to the back of our chair.

Granny had seen some of the dolls afterward in a JC Penney shop window in Las Vegas. They were burned and pitted and missing parts. There was a sign saying, "These mannequins could have been real people. In fact, they could have been you." The dolls were just practice, she said.

"Mother," Papa said warningly.

Pigs. They put pigs in army slacks and jackets and rubbed them with sun-

screen, then tied them to stakes in the path of the blast. They trained them to stand still in their cages, waiting. Mice. Cats. Cages of cats, burning.

"Mother, that's not fit for a child's ears."

"It's not fit for anyone's ears," she said. On the Penitence Ground they used the word *translation* to describe an animal thrown through the air, as if death were a foreign language. "No spika da language. Well, those pigs got the message all right. My titty got the message."

"Mother."

We had heard that people who died in Hiroshima were turned instantaneously into their own shadows, silhouettes burned on a wall, but we were not to think death was that clean. Some mice, for example, were crushed by a flying dog. "Blood and shit splattered the walls," Granny said.

"For pity's sake, be quiet."

"In my opinion pity should never be quiet," said Granny.

A house stood foursquare and isolated upon a flat plane devoid of civilizing ornament: driveway, hedge, lawn, or flagstone. It was a salt crystal on a mirror. It was hard to say how big it was; it might have been tiny, or huge. It was illuminated by a clear light that threw a long shadow. The light came from somewhere other than the sky, which was a black bar like a mourning band. That it was the bomb's early light became evident.

The house caught on fire. So we were told; we would not have recognized this for ourselves. The fire was darker than the light upon it, blackened the house like sudden ivy.

In the fading of the light, the shock wave hit, the fire was blown out, and the house blurred. It held its shape, but only just. It was already an imperfect memory of itself. Then the memory, too, was gone. Scattered like eraser crumbs, or like seeds. The class cheered. "Play it backward!" someone yelled. Chris Marchpane's foot jabbed passionately, painfully into our tailbone. And Blanche burst into tears.

"*Shhh!*" I hissed, trying to suppress the heaving of our chest, the sympathetic catch in my throat. The movie clacked to a stop, the lights came on. Everyone was looking at us in grateful amazement.

A fine line of saliva spilled from Blanche's distorted mouth. Jennifer screamed and pointed. "They're foaming at the mouth!" she said.

"That's enough, Jennifer. Class, you can go to recess early," the teacher said. The class ran out the door, whooping.

"Thanks, freaks!" muttered Jennifer as she passed.

"Blanche," the teacher said, not unkindly, "can you stop crying long enough to tell me what's wrong?"

"I don't—it was—why—" She was interrupted by two hiccuping sobs.

"Take your time," said the teacher.

Blanche swallowed hard and took a deep shuddering breath. She bawled out, "The dogs!" Or possibly, "The dolls!" Then she burst into noisy tears and could not be consoled.

Chris Marchpane reappeared with a paper cone full of water from the teacher's lounge. He thrust it at us, a little too quickly. Some water blooped over the top and wet my feet. "Would you please go away?" I snapped.

"*Thank* you Chris, but why don't you go play with the others?" said the teacher. Then, as he loitered, unsure, solicitous: "Please excuse yourself, Chris Marchpane." He hurried out, holding the damp paper cone. She turned back to us. "Now, can you tell me why you're making such a fuss?"

Blanche kept crying. "Nora, can you speak for Blanche?"

"I have no idea what is wrong with her," I said. Why did Blanche have to make such a spectacle of herself? "Maybe she thought the house looked like our dollhouse," I offered, then added hastily, "But we don't play with dolls anymore."

"Blanche, do you have anything to say?"

Blanche shook her head.

The teacher sighed. "All right. Then go to the bathroom and wash your face. You may put your head down on your desk during quiet reading. Try not to disrupt the class again."

SO YOU'RE WONDERING ABOUT NATIONAL PENITENCE?

The Nevada Test Site, Proving Ground of American Sadness

In 1951, saddened by Hiroshima and Nagasaki, and recognizing the need for a national activity of penance, a despondent American government commenced organized hostilities against itself. For three years, they hammered a sparsely populated part of the Nevada desert with the most powerful bombs in existence. The cratered sands turned to glass. In it Uncle Sam could see his own, still grief-stricken face. Stronger measures were called for.

In 1954, a hastily constructed house was obliterated by a bomb named Doubt, and officers in attendance reported a slight lightening of the heart. For the next four years of Operation Dollhouse, bombs were dropped upon ever more perfect semblances of American houses, built on roads that went nowhere, across bridges over no water.

"A house is not a home," was the word from above, and in 1955 the Nuclear Penitence Committee called in a home decorator, who decorated the target houses in the style then fashionable and stocked their kitchens with American products. No one who was there that day will forget the "Ritz Cracker" test, 1956, at which a high-ranking officer broke down and wept healing tears under the radiant cloud. The decorator was decorated, but hopes faded as this early success was followed by a string of melancholy failures: "Breakfast of Champions," 1957. "JC Penney," 1958. "Jiffy," 1959. "Tang," 1960.

In 1961, life-sized manikins were introduced into the houses. The female dolls were named Lisa and Patricia and given beehive hairdos and bouffant dresses, and before the bombing, were feted in parties where their partners danced the Twist. To assist the generals in identifying with them, the male

dolls' proportions represented a perfect mathematical average of American male body types. Their body parts were numbered, so that their dispersal could be mapped. The generals were encouraged to number their own body parts with their wives' eyeliner and meditate in the nude upon the maps, so that they could understand, in their own bodies, how it might feel to be taken apart and scattered like seed.

It was no use, the naked generals felt nothing.

Hoping to feel pity, the penitents bombed mice, cats, dogs, but as the smoke rose from the cages where they smouldered, the officers felt nothing but a faint, inappropriate hunger. Substitutes, symbols. Why not bomb a map, or a postcard, or a dictionary?

Why not indeed? These experiments were duly performed. Bombs were given the names of people, then exploded; scientists now proposed systematically eradicating every American name, but it was found that seditious elements could not be hindered from giving their children names no one had ever heard of, like Zolandra, or Chantique. Nonetheless names deemed particularly important were destroyed; it is for this reason there are few Americans today with the once-common name of Gladys. Ordinary objects were given new names before being demolished (veterans tell stories of the funny mix-ups that occurred, when a "vacuum cleaner" was mistaken for a "diaphragm," or body part #21, "ankle," was mistakenly exchanged for body part #3, "neck"). Regions of the site were given unusual names that were liable to change without warning, e.g. "Scriptorium" and "Memento Mori" and "Strategic Negativity Reversal Module." The bombs, of course, were only to be spoken of in special coded terms, as for example "Amigo" or "Forgetfulness" or "The Straight Answer" or "When you see me coming you better run," or "Summers, it gets so hot here. I stay indoors, and grow fat. I am developing some kind of rash where my love handles lap over my hips. What has become of that feeling I used to get when I climbed to the top of a tall tree and rain blew through the clashing foliage and pecked my stinging skin and a single icy leaf glued itself passionately to the side of my neck, and I thought, not only that I would live forever, but that I would want to?"

These experiments were protected by a no-speakum zone many miles across. Those penitence workers who lived outside it were instructed to take this silence home with them. They were told that words represented nothing but the loss of the thing named, and when they went home, they often found this to be true.

The Death & Burial of Cock Robin

"Jamaica Inn," said the very disagreeable cabbie I had engaged in Plymouth. His tone managed to suggest that I would be sorry I'd come. The moon chewed its way through the clouds to lick the wet slates on the roof of a squat, rambling building. I paid the sum we had agreed on—I had persuaded him to drive me an hour across the moor only by promising him a fortune—and clattered over the cobblestones, tweaking my ankle, toward the only lit door. What if they had no vacancies? But they would, there were only a couple of cars parked outside.

The foyer was bright, and there was nobody at the office window. I could hear a television somewhere. I rapped on the counter and waited. Beside me a metal table held a rack with maps, a lamp; a stapled booklet decorated with a pen and ink drawing of a hunched shape with claws, entitled *The Beast of Bodmin Moor;* and a block of slick brochures, advertising a health club and spiritual retreat with a vague, portentous name, that when I touched it opened like a fan across the table. Somewhere nearby someone shrieked with laughter. One brochure slid off and planed to the floor, slid noiselessly across the room, and passed under a closed door. I picked the rest up, squared the deck, ruffled it, set it firmly down. It rose elastically as I released it, keeping a lingering contact with my fingertips.

"Can I help you?" A woman's pink, crazily grinning face bobbed up behind the window. From the open door behind her came a blue glow and the choral roar of a laugh track.

She took my credit card, with a residual chuckle, and forced it through

an old-fashioned device that impressed its raised figures on a sheaf of carbons. Then I followed the apron string ticking on her wide rump up a flight of narrow stairs to my room—tiny, with a giant four-poster bed, and the slanting floor and low ceiling of nightmares.

A funeral was going on. Four stuffed birds in black tie bore a little blue coffin through the graveyard of a painted church toward a boxy open grave with dirt heaped on the flocked grass beside it, and a dainty, translucent skull. A rook opened a book. An owl got busy with a trowel. A tiny, fuzzy cow—no, no, not a cow but a bull—was standing by to toll the bell. A bull the size of a guinea pig? Impossible, but the fur was real. Was it *cat*? The thought was disturbing.

One of the docents had lingered behind me at the door, watching us, but now she seemed to satisfy herself that I was not a thief or a vandal, and turned back to the warmth and light of the gift shop, leaving me alone with the pride of the Potter Museum, the giant gabled case that housed, as gilt script on the wood frame proudly proclaimed, "*The Original Life & Death of Cock Robin*. Exhibit 1."

Tied to the bull's nose ring was a cord that arced up to the painted bell tower of the painted church and disappeared through a small square hole cut in the backdrop. No bell was visible in the painting. Was there a real bell behind it? I thought there probably was. There was a bell in the rhyme, and Potter was a literal-minded man.

I opened the guidebook. Walter Potter was born (1835) and died (1918) in the same small town in Sussex, the son of an innkeeper. He had taught himself taxidermy, stuffing every animal he could lay his hands on, and as anyone could see from the pictures, he sucked at it. (Or, in the guidebook's weak apologia, "He was not a very skilled taxidermist by today's standards, but he was certainly prolific.") His animals bulged where they should hollow. Their faces were squashed and sunken and wore a look of accusatory sadness. They struck poses no animal would take in nature. But perhaps they should not be judged by the standards of realism, for Walter Potter was a dreamer, whose rats sprung traps, kittens exchanged vows before a kitten congregation, and squirrels quarreled over cards. You could say he was ancient, animist Britain, burbling up in the age of industry. Or a loon, putting sockses on foxes.

I rose on tiptoe. Above, in the gabled sky, ninety-six species of British

birds had gathered, "some," said the guidebook, "with tears in their eyes." They looked real, but real dead. Live birds would never keep so still. Real dead birds, representing live birds, mourning a dead bird, representing a dead bird in a rhyme a child read long ago, in a book his sister owned, both of them dead now, too, dead and buried.

For a fleeting moment I glimpsed the trouble of a man for whom toying with dead animals was an odd form of mourning. For whom glass beads might be as heartfelt as tears.

At that, one fell. Light streaked a blackbird's cheek. Glass chimed on glass at the very limits of hearing.

Had it really happened? I moved away, afraid I might see the yellow beak open, another tear fall from the glass eye.

The long, narrow room was crowded with glass cases, through the angled surfaces of which the grey light from a few small high windows made its way as delicately as a safecracker. When objects coalesced out of the umber shadows, they seemed like apparitions. A church made of white feathers was Exhibit 2. A slender, mummified hand, feeling for something just out of reach, Exhibit 5. Two giant thumbprints on a canvas, each whorl composed of motes, each mote a moth with a pin through its back, 8. Everything seemed like something I was remembering wrong. I had the feeling I was in the prop room of a fever dream.

Some objects seemed to establish covert relations with one another: over a calabash pipe, Exhibit 6, and a collection of walking sticks, 11, the shadow of a deerstalker hat seemed to pass. A Burroughs adding machine, 13, might have helped calculate the achievement of "Duplicate," the world champion hen (462 eggs in one year!). Exhibit 9, the terrible, twisted mummy of a cat that had stuck in a chimney, starved to death, and been "kippered," as the book puts it, by decades of smoky fires, had some gruesome kinship to Exhibit 7, of which the book exclaims: "Observe this child's shoe, encrusted with lime after falling into a petrifying well!" (No word on how the child was doing.)

Babes in the Wood.

The Happy Family.

I saw nothing that might be a message, though from a distance the interlocking swirls of Exhibit 8 did resemble a Venn diagram.

Upstairs, eighteen *Athletic Toads* were rolling hoops, their feet stapled to painted turf, and posing with weights, their bodies stiff as dried gourds.

Gentleman squirrels of *The Upper Five* fanned miniature hands of cards, enjoyed port, packed pipes before painted fires. A plebe rat of *The Lower Five* limped away from his brawling brothers on tiny crutches. Bunnies studied sums; kittens poured tea; guinea pigs mouthed miniature French horns at a cricket match. Rows of kittens with stitched-up mouths (each in its own little frock, with a string of beads around its neck) watched another kitten in a veil be married to a kitten in a suit by a kitten in robes with a book sewn to its paw. All the animals had the same look of ghastly gaiety. They raised their teacups or their guns as if desperately hoping it was the right thing to do, while increasingly sure it was not. Any minute, I thought, they'll notice that they're dead, and then they will have to kill themselves.

Two squirrels crossed swords: *The Dual* [*sic*].

The Death.

And here, at last, come the clowns: Exhibit 22, a two-headed lamb. Exhibit 23, a two-headed pig. Exhibit 24, an able-bodied, four-legged duck, who had lived sixteen years until a hailstone took her out. ("Freaks like this are not uncommon, but what do they see and think about?" mused the guidebook. Indeed.)

Exhibit 25 was several scrambled kittens. Some had two bodies, some two heads. Whole jet rosaries of eyes. Twin tails. Some had legs thrust straight up out of the small of their back. Dusty frights, straw poking out of their cracked flanks, they crouched alone under glass bells; no tea parties for them. They weren't invited to the wedding, and anyway, they had nothing to wear. Potter knows best! But couldn't they have played the evil stepsisters, or the fairy godmothers, or the three heads in the well?

Exhibit 26, *Two-Headed Pig,* was not stuffed but preserved in formaldehyde, the frill of cacky wax around the lid a disturbing reminder of pickles and potted plums, as if someone were going to make a Ploughman's Lunch of it. It was plump as Hansel, its fat hind legs comfortably curled up, its front trotters touching, as if in prayer. The pallid skin was smooth as a baby's and clove to the glass. I had a sudden image of Blanche and myself in the womb, but cold, cold.

Exhibit 27. A trio of malformed chicks. Beaked knots of feather and bone, bent ornaments for a Bedlam Easter hat. Only one had found its footing, standing square on its four legs, four wings sticking straight out like a biplane's. It possessed three eyes, like a symbol from mathematical logic: ∴ Therefore. Something had been demonstrated, but what?

I stopped, my heart hammering. I thought one of the stuffed things ahead had made a sudden, furtive movement. Then I saw it was just another tourist, reaching up to pat the front half of a gigantic, gaping *Tunny Fish*, Exhibit 29, that projected from the wall as if it had stuck there, partway through. To touch it he had to rise to the toes of his white rubber-soled loafers, which looked too small for his body. Seeing me, he dropped back onto his heels and wiggled his fingers sheepishly. He looked vaguely familiar, but I couldn't think why. He wore a stained windbreaker, a striped shirt, khaki shorts, and was entirely undistinguished.

"Hello, sweety. Or is it sweeties? Gosh, excuse me for staring, I thought you were one of the exhibits. Oops! Bite my tongue. Please don't take offense. Oh, must I always, *always* put my foot in it?"

A fat young girl in a tutu ceased inspecting Exhibit 30, *Man Trap,* and began inspecting us.

"Mr. Nickel," her father said, and stuck out his hand.

My right hand seemed to be occupied, as it often was these days, in sorting a number of small invisible objects. With some difficulty, I persuaded it to clasp the clammy offering. Something's going to happen, I thought. The still scenes glowing in the stacked boxes around me were like happy dreams into which a nightmare was about to intrude. The squirrels did not notice the sawdust falling from their sleeves, the beetles quarrying in their waistcoats. The dead kittens in straw boaters handed their dead lady friends into stilled boats on dull glass ponds and did not observe that their fur was falling out in patches. But they were about to, I felt. I willed Mr. Nickel to go away, before what was coming came.

"Ready for tea, punkin?" he said to the girl, as if he had heard me. He turned to me. "Deb is a bottomless pit when it comes to scones and jam. Will we see you around the groaning board at the hotel? How's about I squirrel away one of the scones *de la maison* for you in case you don't make it? They grow legs pretty fast." He put his hand on the girl's back and scooted her away. Her head swiveled to keep us in view.

As he passed between the banks of luminous cubes I saw that his right leg had a hard unlikely shine. Only then did I notice the exposed steel workings of his knee. Every time it straightened it gave a quiet gasp.

I turned my head and saw Exhibit 28. It was even more distasteful than the postcard had suggested. Resignation and foreboding emanated from the unhappy monkey in the necktie of a male stripper, hunched in a saddle on

top of a billy goat against a background of painted bluffs and, in the middle ground, a blurry tree, leaves all the same size. The goat was alert, pop-eyed, menacing. Its nose and horns shone as if wet. Its coarse hairs appeared individually erect. A number of birds, probably vultures enthralled by a death, wheeled around the cliffs, emitting hoarse cries that echoed eerily off the cliffs. The monkey's huge, somber eyes with their almost comically long lashes did not turn in their direction, but his black fingers tightened on the riding crop he held in his right paw, and the goat seemed to sense this and rolled its eyes warily, gnawing at the bit.

Could I simply walk away?

I actually did manage to take a few steps.

My right hand still felt the cool of the glass dome when the crash sounded on the other side of the room. On the shelf in front of me was a circle where no dust was. On the other side of the room, a stuffed two-headed kitten stood on six scrawny shanks in a cloud of sawdust and the shards of its erstwhile firmament, a furious assertion frozen on its faces. From its shoulder blades, it raised a doubled fist at me, as if to say, "Solidarity!"

I heard something in the stairwell, and a hand appeared, gripping the banister, then the head of one of the docents. It rose no higher than the level of my feet. I saw her see my feet, then look up, then make a face that was more like a sudden lack of expression. I believe that if I had had only the one head, she would have thrown me out straight away, but she didn't know whom to address. Now the sound of the crash had died away, the moment had passed. The docent's hand appeared to fiddle with a hearing aid. Could she possibly hear what I heard? It was a faint sound, easy to miss, like the hiss of a punctured bike tire. After a while it grew clearer. The kitten seemed to be making some kind of noise. In fact the more I listened, the more it sounded like singing, in a sort of buzz of two voices that now and then veered apart into harmonies. Yes, it was definitely singing.

The Two-Headed Kitten Performs "The Song of One and a Half"

Some people are born with too little,
Some people are born with too much.
At the College of Surgeons Museum in London
You can behold many such.
There's a boy who was born with no fingers,
And a girl who was born with a beak,
And a boy with a head on top of his head
Like the crown of the king of the freaks.

The duplicate head was much smaller,
And stiff as a porcelain doll;
The delicate mouth only opened to drool
And the eyes never opened at all.
His mother decided to keep him
See what kind of luck he might bring
And as he was falling asleep every night
This is the song she would sing.

> *Well it's under the blanket with you, my dear*
> *And it's under the blanket you'll stay*
> *The world's already so ugly, dear*

So we'll hide your face away, away
We'll hide your face away.

One and a Half's what she named him
And she gave him a box for a crib
The only possessions he had in this world
Were a short piece of string and a bib.
She covered the box with a blanket
Which she would remove for a fee
And once in the morning and once before bed
She fed him on gruel and tea.

That boy loved the smell of his mother
And the tread of her two horny feet
Sometimes she blew him her cigarette smoke
As a rare and particular treat
The crack of her ankles was music
The sound of her farts was a bell
Except for the roaches that lived in his bed
There was no one he loved quite so well.

When the blanket came off with a flourish
She taught him to lower his eyes
So he lay in his bed and was looked at instead
And he basked in their fear and surprise
Not the one pair of eyes nor the other
Returned the inquisitive stares
Then the blanket came down and with barely a sound
He whistled the following air:

Well it's under the blanket with you, my dear
And it's under the blanket you'll stay
The world's already so ugly, dear
So we'll hide your face away, away
We'll hide your face away.

HALF LIFE

One day a viper discovered
A good place to hide from the sun
He slid in the crib so neat and so quick
The roaches did not even run
The boy was so happy to see him
He patted the snake on the head
The viper, surprised, sank its teeth in his thigh
And One and a Half was dead.

But the second head's eyes started open
The minute the other one died
And the boy who had never once uttered a word
Opened his mouth up and cried
"Mother," he said, "come help me,
"For I have a pain in my head."
His mother strolled over and lifted the cloth
And saw that her firstborn was dead

He was curled like a cat round the viper
His lowered eyelashes at peace
But the head on his head
Lay awake in his stead
And his eyes all around him did feast
She trembled to see those eyes looking
She trembled to hear that mouth speak
"My brother was fond of his mother," he said,
"I'm afraid that my brother was weak."

His gaze was the law and the sentence
Her judgment was sorely beguiled
How sharper, in truth, than a serpent's tooth
Is the gaze of an ungrateful child!
She squeezed herself into the cradle
And gathered the snake to her calf
And the very last thing she heard as she died
Was the Song of One and a Half:

Well it's under the blanket with you, my dear
And it's under the blanket you'll stay
The world's already so ugly, dear
So we'll hide your face away, away
We'll hide your face away.

Now his bones are hung in the museum
With the bones of a myriad more
Who fell with too little, or fell with two much
From the crotches of ladies and whores
A crooked and yellow stick figure
Two skulls eternally wed
Press button at right to turn on the light
The sign by the showcase said.

Beasts of Bodmin Moor

"Encore!" All around me animals were stirring, their stiff skins splitting as they beat their paws together. Teacups rolled. A crutch banged a chair leg. The two-headed kitten bowed and did a shuffling soft-shoe, six legs drawing a daisy in its own dust.

The three-eyed chick wheezed. "Hey! Lemme outa here! I go on next! *Fzzz!*" Sawdust pinged against the glass. "I've got to get changed," it appealed to me. "Can I get a hand here?"

The goat raised its front hooves mockingly, and I saw the shriveled tuft of its cock.

I made for the stairs. The docent shrank back against the wall as I passed. Exhibit 4, 3, 2, 1. The little blue coffin was rocking. A tiny bell was ringing and ringing. Wings scraped on glass. *And all the birds in the air fell a-sighin' and a-sobbin'/ When they heard the bell ring for poor Cock Robin.*

I was outside. I crossed the cobbled yard and plunged down a winding road worn so deep in the fields and edged with such heights of thorn and thistle that it seemed nearly underground. A muddy stream ran along it, swerving in and out of the messy fringe of grass, but sheeting the whole road at times with caramel.

At one flooded dip I grabbed a branch to pull myself up onto the bank, and out of the dark heart of the bush something flew at my face, shrieking. Wings beat my head with frightening force, claws scratched my collarbone, and then it had struggled through the gap between my cheek and Blanche's and was reeling away, trailing a few strands of hair. My knees were trem-

bling. I sobbed once. Just a bird, of course, an ordinary bird of hot flesh and feathers and tiny, quicksilver thoughts.

I had slid back down the bank and was standing ankle deep in water. There seemed no point in climbing up again, and my legs were so shaky I was not sure I would make it if I tried. I waded through the flood, against the muscular suck of the water. Now a boxy little car, red, in which the driver hulked (I expected to see his knees poking up through the bonnet) scooted around the corner and forced its way between the banks toward me. I stepped back into the long grass. My pants were instantly soaked to the crotch. The shadowy driver ducked his head to examine me and the car nearly rubbed my thigh as it sidled by, and spat back at me after it had passed. From among tasseled weeds and the mazes of thorny sticks I thought I saw foxy faces watching me, relics from the museum held up on sticks to taunt me. *Beast of Bodmin Moor, Beast of Bodmin Moor,* rang in my head like a jeer. *I* was that beast.

When I got back to my room there was a napkin-wrapped scone on the floor in front of my door.

In my sleep that night I dreamed that Mr. Nickel handed me his picture. It was upside down, but his face was the right way up. So that's what's wrong with him, I thought, he has a magic head. With that I looked up at the man himself, and I could make out a moist little mouth hidden in his hair. The mouth moved. It said, "Unity." I tried to scream and woke myself up.

The light of a grey morning twilit the room. Outside beagles were bawling, hooves clattering. I lifted a corner of the window. A foxhunt? How corny and depressing. I curled up in bed again, clutching my knees. It took me a little while to turn over the word *unity* in my mind and remember where I had seen it last. The morning paper, the booklet about the Beast that I had flipped through over dinner, the brochure—what was the name of that health club?

Shit! I got dressed in a hurry and staggered downstairs.

But the brochures were gone. "A big pile of them, right here," I said, bracketing the spot.

"Maybe interested parties picked them up, then," offered the attendant. Not the woman from the night before, but an elderly man.

"They can't have. Not since last night. It was a big pile."

"The brochures are popular with tourists."

"A really big pile."

"Are you sure it was here you saw this brochure?"

"Of course."

He sighed. "Well, maybe someone threw them away. We prefer to vet the notices placed here, but sometimes people do smuggle them in. We frown on it. If the brochures were not approved . . ." He turned his back, finished with me.

I got down on the floor and peered under the closed door. I had remembered the fugitive brochure. I thought I could make out its edge in the shadows. I got up again, felt the knob, cracked the door open. Within was a jumble of buckets and mops. I could not see the brochure.

A throat cleared behind me.

"I thought this was the way to the dining room," I said.

Under the attendant's ill-tempered stare I had to give up and go to breakfast, where I poked distractedly at some resilient bundles of greasy matter—fried bread, a soft sausage, an elderly egg.

Mr. Nickel sat down next to me. I wondered where the little girl was. "Yeah, what about that Potter? Total freak show, right? No slur intended." He scooted closer. "What's the story there?" he said in a stage whisper, jerking his head at Blanche. "Not much of a talker, is she?"

"No."

"I guess you're tired of being asked that question, huh? Look, I've always wondered, let me know if I'm overstepping my, if I'm out of line here, but I am sincerely interested in hearing how you people do it."

"Do what?" I ferried a wad of egg to my mouth on a square of the bread.

"Just, you know, get along, iron out the . . . I mean what if person A wants a gin and tonic and person B wants a warm Guinness? It seems to me you have all the difficulties of married people. Pardon me if I'm projecting, as someone who was once espoused—and I don't mind telling you it wasn't always birds in their little nests agree, which is why I am no longer with the lady, much as I esteem her. But divorce is not really an option for you, is it, or even a 'trial separation,' ha ha! Am I right?"

"Obviously."

"Obviously! Which is exactly the problem, I take it? I mean that even though your bosom swells with sisterly love for each other, or—for I see your lips pressed together in vehement disagreement held in check only by the desire to maintain a cordial demeanor toward me, a total stranger, though a

friendly and nice-guy type stranger, I hope you'll agree—where was I?" He kept sliding his hand, with a movement at once stealthy and unconscious, under his collar down the back of his shirt. His collar was spotted with blood from scratched zits.

I have often noticed that one can observe with detachment sights that when put into words become disgusting.

"Right, sisterly love . . . or not . . . Regardless, the closer you get the more distant you feel, isn't that true? I'm not afraid to admit it. My ex-wife, bless her, was not afraid to admit it. She took measures, which was her prerogative. But you two are bound by a Gordian knot that only Alexandrian death can sever!"

What an insufferable man. "Yes," I said coldly.

He withdrew his hand from his shirt and looked at his nails. "But to get to my point. Welcome or unwelcome, you are assured of company whatever the haps, a condition many people who are unmarried paint to themselves in the rosiest colors, as greatly to be desired and in short, a very good thing—"

"Yes—"

"Oh! Hang on, I've got something here for you." He rummaged in his pockets and pulled out a pile of creased brochures that he fanned out and thumbed through. "Daphne du Maurier walk: done it. The Men-an-tol, the Merry Maidens, John Wesley's cottage, preapproved credit card, ha, what's that doing there. Somewhere—OK. The Old Operating Theatre. Now this is genius. Now you've just got to go there. You go for the morbid stuff, don't you, the fetid breath of the beyond? I thought so. Bleeding bowls, leech jars, cupping kits, fleams, lancets, saws, you gotta love it. Have a look at this later on and see if you don't agree. Now, what was I saying . . . yes. Because you're 'chained for life'—you just put that in your pocket, little lady—you are set free to hate each other, don't you see, and hold each other in contempt and regard with distaste your personal grooming rituals and bass-ackwards way of doing things around the house, whereas perfect strangers, like for example the two of us, are so afraid of the separation that is our immediate destiny and that in fact already scents or flavors what closeness we temporarily achieve with the dank breath of the void, that we have to reassure one another with affectionate gestures and folderol of one kind or another that we each think the other is OK and that we forgive each other for each others' imminent departures and promise implicitly that we will not backstab the

departing or otherwise mistreat them either in person or in memory or in effigy, since while voodoo may not work, the knowledge that someone wishes to practice voodoo on one is a blow, as I can attest in the case of the former Mrs. Nickel."

I grunted, not knowing how else to respond.

"Am I right? Yeah or nay?"

"You've said a mouthful," I equivocated.

"And I thank *you*. But now I have to go." He clutched his heart. "Feel it? What a poignant illustration of the point I was making! But Blanche, I forgive you for this impending separation. Do you forgive me? It's important to ritualize our apologies and leave-taking." He thrust his face toward me, panting eagerly.

"I'm Nora," I said.

He sat back and covered his mouth theatrically. "Oops, my bad! Can't seem to get my foot out of my mouth today! Are we still friends?"

I said nothing, so with humorously fearful backward glances he rose and tiptoed away. At the door, rising to his toes, he called back, "Don't forget the Old Operating Theatre! You'll freak out!" He thumped himself on the forehead. "Jeepers, I've done it again. Somebody pry my foot out of my mouth!"

He was still cheerfully scolding himself as he went out of earshot.

When had I told him her name?

As I was leaving, I saw the little girl climbing into a car with a large couple in sweats. "I need to pee!" she said. "You can pee when we stop for gas," said the female. They bounced out over the cobblestones.

A Funeral

A funeral is going on.

A memory floats up, loosed from some underwater snag. It is unrecognizable at first, then I begin to make out its features.

Whose was it? There were many funerals in Grady, a town gung-ho for dying, but our family was seldom invited. I am still a child in this fragment, but old enough to watch the grown-ups with a critical eye, surprised and embarrassed by their display of emotion.

Looking back I am, momentarily, ashamed of my spooky fantasia, the mushroom clouds sprouting all over the landscape, the zombies singing dirges and roundelays. How gaudy, how frivolous.

Compared to this real thing: the blankness on my father's face, his raw cheeks and tired eyes and my own inability to rise above a nagging preoccupation with his hairline. There is not much room for loss in a world crammed with details and ready, officious judgments. In the midst of desolation, that one notices the hang of a cheap suit!

Max looked a bit like Papa in hers, though broader and softer, the corners bumped off. Her chin crumpled and her mouth opened in a little unconscious shape of distress, then closed.

The intolerably high sky with its tiny slow-moving clouds.

Whenever something terrible happens the mind is often somewhere else; mine was following a beetle hurrying across the disturbed earth. A plane droned far away. If you looked hard you could see that the sheen on the bug's back was minutely striated, demonstrating the attention to detail that pleased me about nature. If you got a magnifying glass, the striations would

prove to have striations of their own, or maybe bizarre little horns. Watching the bug I seemed to be happy, happier than I had been for a long time, while nearby people worked away senselessly with handkerchiefs, bent their heads to the industrious molding motions of their hankie-swathed hands. Later I saw the contrails spelled something I couldn't read.

I remember the next grave was Grampa's. It was easy to recognize because of the Geiger counter carved on the headstone. So the funeral might have been Granny's, and yet I don't remember that, though there are other things, less important things, that I remember clearly: the textures of the dirt, the round pebbles from the stratum that Papa had taught me was called the Grady Conglomerate, against which the spade rang with a sound like money. Papa's eyes examined the walls of the grave, narrowing at a trace of mineral color, parsing it automatically, unconsciously.

I credit these memories precisely because they seem unimportant. Could I have made up such minutiae: the spot of fluff in somebody's lowered eyelids, a pocket turned inside out and sticking out like something from a cartoon? But of course I could. In phone sex, for example, I pride myself on the authenticating detail—the soiled price-sticker on the scuffed sole of a cheap pump (how cheap, you can see for yourself). And here, even as I scratch in the dirt for confirmation, the scene shrinks and I am peering into a diorama, a school project. The figures are filched from the dollhouse and got up in paper costumes to suit the occasion; they are acting out the funeral of Telluride May, the first and last whore of Too Bad, shot in a gunfight between two miners over claim-jumping, or else (it is variously reported) over a crooked bet on a two-headed nickel. I had mixed sand with glue and formed it into realistic mounds topped with little wooden crosses and a shallow grave in which I had pressed the mama doll (I never got all the gluey dirt out of the grooves of her plastic hair). You could see her snub nostril-less nose and the painted pupils staring up, a little out of position. I was sent to the principal for employing the word *whore* in my presentation, and got an unfairly bad grade for this loving re-creation.

Though my memories are fragments, these fragments have their logic. Surely something of the whole picture is encoded in them. An upthrust chunk of an older geological sequence might seem like an anomaly in a broad basin of silt deposited by successive floods. But if you can read the layers, you can pick up the story a hundred miles away, at the bottom of a canyon, where a river cut down through the same layers, and construct

then in your mind the hundred-mile-plus formation that joined them both, though all the intervening rock has washed away.

That is one way of looking at it. But sometimes I think otherwise. The details of the past float up and adhere to one another, forming little tumors of plausibility and consequence. This happens as if by some automated process; stories take shape, they thicken and grow tougher. That they are plausible and detailed does not mean that they are true. I can think up someone who never existed and tell you I met him today and you would believe me, if you had no reason to think I was lying. Of course, by this time you might well doubt my word. Believe this if nothing else, though: I am trying mortally hard to remember my life.

The cemetery exists. I could visit, solicit the gravestones for gossip. Old cemeteries are plotty. (Sorry.) The stones tell stories: yellow jaundice, overdose of morphine, liver complaint, heart failure, pneumonia, shot by outlaws, burned to death, mine accident, consumption, spinal meningitis, life became a burden to her. But it is no longer de rigueur to name the agent of death; modern gravestones keep their secrets. I don't think I'd find an easy answer there.

Was there a funeral at all? I remember the light on the hill, the white light of midday that drives out shadows and color and life. But then I look closely at the sun and I read, "25 W," and in smaller curving letters, "General Electric." I remember how I felt, but I cried harder when I dropped the lizard down the well. Blanche, I'm asking. If it was a funeral, whose funeral was it? Who died, and who's to blame? Who killed Cock Robin?

THE SIAMESE TWIN REFERENCE MANUAL

TPR's *Twinspeak*

"Today in Theirstory"

"Professor Rankin, I don't know if you've heard the theory that Shakespeare was a Siamese twin."

"I'm afraid I have."

"Well, allow me to introduce the man who first advanced that theory, Dr. Theodore Gupta."

"Oh! I'm surprised. I confess I assumed you were yourself a conjoined twin, Professor."

"Indeed! That's typical of the ad hominem responses my theories have received. What happened to textual analysis, if I may ask?"

"One might counter, what happened to historical evidence?"

"Our knowledge of the life of the historical Shakespeare is sketchy, as you must know."

"Not so sketchy that we are free to postulate any absurdity that supports a pet theory."

"Surely scholars must arrogate to themselves the intellectual freedom to postulate anything not explicitly contradicted by the evidence. And there is some evidence supporting the notion. Shakespeare's own work demonstrates a fascination with twins and doubles amounting almost to an obsession. As we cannot penetrate the murk of history, we may never know for sure, but for the same reason, do we not have the right—nay, the responsibility—to at least consider whether Shakespeare was twins?"

Here the moderator broke in. "But Dr. Gupta, despite the murk of history, surely we do know certain facts."

"Facts! Facts! Facts!"

"Don't you believe in facts, Dr. Gupta?"

"Does Beethoven believe in notes? I make facts sing: glissandos, melismas, arpeggios, trills!"

"But—"

"For footnotes, I substitute grace notes!"

"But Shakespeare was not a Siamese—"

"Excuse me, I must really—'conjoined'?"

"Conjoined twin, then."

"I admit the theory is bold."

"Far-fetched."

"I admit the theory is far-fetched, but—"

"Actually, it's simply not true."

"Possibly the theory is not true, though I submit the case is far from closed, but is it uninteresting?"

We Are All Twofers

On the way back to London, I kept seeing tumbleweeds bouncing through the heather past surprised sheep. I clamped my restless hands between my knees and concentrated on staying awake. I couldn't face Louche in that condition. I opted instead for the rather gloomy embrace of the Walpole Arms, a seedy place on the outskirts of town. The velvet curtains were drawn, revealing the lacework of moths, and the lobby was dark. Only the incongruous blue glow of an Internet kiosk illuminated the ormolu, a pert bird under a glass dome from which I averted my eyes, and a clerk in a green blazer who was beaming at me with peculiar warmth. I might have fled the dark, and the lark, and the clerk, had the latter not lunged across the counter to pump my hand. "Greetings, husband!" he seemed to be saying. Seeking some explanation, my eyes fell to a button pinned on his collar, bearing a silhouette head I recognized, ringed by the slogan, WE ARE ALL TWOFERS.

"Or, not," I muttered pettishly, retrieving my hand. Lately I was finding the Boolean operators a succinct way of expressing degrees of refusal.

"Pardon?"

I found a day-old paper abandoned on a settee and took it up to my dingy little room. In my brief absence London had gone Togetherist-crazy. A famous model had been photographed in an orange Togetherist T-shirt made for a twofer, its second collar daringly adroop over one pygmy breast, and "We-R-2-R-1-4-Ever" was climbing the charts for the second time. Hawkers were selling bushels of pins like the clerk's, and the Togetherists, in a move editorialists considered niggardly, had threatened legal action.

But despite outraged demands for progress, little had been made. Scotland Yard had turned up a few new leads, but they had proved to be dead ends. A head had been found on the beach near Dover, which had roused a brief flurry of speculation, but the dental records showed it belonged to a fisherman who had gone missing some weeks past, and though his body had not been found, it was agreed that as he had never had more than the one head, his loss was probably not the doctor's work. It was thought that he had fallen overboard and been decapitated by the propeller. Then the police stormed an apartment in Leeds, where neighbors claimed to have seen a two-headed man enter late one night and a one-headed man emerge the next day. He turned out to be an amateur ventriloquist who liked to put on a second head at night and walk the streets making lewd propositions to women while manipulating the jaw of his false head. Then he would smack the head and make his apologies to the lady.

The bathroom could only be entered sideways. To close the door one would have to stand on tiptoe as it scraped past, so I left it open and, maneuvering around the protruding corner of the sink, sank thankfully onto the toilet. It was time to think.

When I extricated myself, I placed a call to the Pepys Library at Magdalene College, Cambridge. "Can you tell me if there are any ballads in your collection that mention someone called One and a Half?" I could hear her putting on her glasses. "A two-headed person," I added.

"That doesn't sound—" she said. "I don't—let me make sure. No, there are not. Not by that title. But of course there were many ballads written about prodigies and, ah, monsters, or what were then considered monsters. You might have a look in one of the other ballad collections, for example Sir Anthony Wood's, at the Bodleian. Wood was more fond than Pepys of this particular sort of ballad. Giant fish, murderous women, users of profane language who were snatched up by hairy devils, and so on. Of course I don't mean to say that a two-headed person is akin to a murderer or . . ."

"Quite," I said, and hung up.

On the way out, I stopped at the kiosk and checked my e-mail. I deleted a message from the Siamists: "Refuse consolidation under the banner of the phallus! We are not one, we are 2!" and twenty invitations to buy a Cunning Collectibles crystal sculpture called *Togetherness*. Either the Siamists had sold their e-mail list or someone was playing a joke on me.

That left just one e-mail from Audrey, headed "The Lady Came Back."

That was the name of the silent film we had watched together, "Remember?" at an Evelyn North mini-festival screened by the Castro Theater. In her movies, the star was always winking and turning away, or slipping sideways into a fin of darkness, from which her eyes and sequins glinted faintly and then blinked out, or she was pausing in a doorway, then gone forever. Her narrow feet kicked up the heavy lustrous cloth of her pajamas or tapped the floors of dimly lit offices while a shadow passed across the foreground. Her pale face swam up to the cigarette she raised in impossibly slender fingers. You never saw the whole of her, you could never size her up: big or little, thick or thin, real or a will-o'-the-wisp. She was more of a rumor than a fact. She was herself once removed. She was barely there, until one day she wasn't. "She was one of those silent film stars who didn't make the transition to sound," Audrey wrote. "And speaking of silent, you haven't said a word about where you're going or what you're doing on this trip. What are you plotting? Your mother called. Is there a phone number where she can reach you? Trey's being very evasive, so I know something's up. Whatever you're doing, stop it."

I hit delete and went to the British Library. It was time to do some research. I had a lot of questions. For example:

Who was One and a Half?

Was the "trail" I had been following actually left by the Unity Foundation?

Why?

Where had the Manor gone?

Where had the clinic gone?

Did tumbleweeds grow in England?

Why were dead things talking to me?

I had more, but that would do for starters.

It turned out that none of the big ballad collections, Pepys or Child or the funky *Pack of Autolycus,* cited anyone named One and a Half. Neither did Gould & Pyle's *Anomalies and Curiosities of Medicine* or the sole other pre-Boom teratological study still in print. However, a biography of Hunter cited as a highlight of his collection the skull of "The Two-Headed Boy of Bengal," and there was a photograph. I recognized it. The account confirmed the kit-

tens' story on most points: there had been two brains, separated by a tough membrane; the eyes moved independently; his second mouth had a tongue, albeit somewhat stunted. His mother had kept him alive in a wooden box under a sheet she would lift for a rupee or two. Her death of snakebite was wishful embellishment, however. She had lived to bury him.

I turned the page and found a watercolor of the boy in life, front and side view. He was wearing only a double strand of beads. From the front he was a sweet-faced child with a strange hairdo. From the side, though, the second head was plainly visible, jutting up at an angle, and looking straight at the viewer. I turned the book around. The other face was bonier, more adult, and had a wry, knowing look. Or was it the song that made me see it that way? The Two-Headed Boy of Bengal appeared in a number of other books (including Gould & Pyle), but all told more or less the same story, one adding the toothsome detail that the neck stump resembled "a small peach." None of the books gave the boy's name, or referred to him as One and a Half.

I began to open books at random and, in the index of an art history book, was rewarded by the following item: "One and a Half," Hans Arp, pp. 222–25. Flipping to the page reference, I read about dada doyenne Anna-Anna (the footnote cited revisionist historian C. C. Metzger's claim that she was a conjoined twin) who modeled for Man Ray and was the lover (or lovers) of Ball, Tanguy, Huelsenbeck, and Arp. Arp had sculpted her (or their) portrait, the semi-abstract *Ein-Ein-Halb* mentioned in Huelsenbeck's memoirs. It was smashed in a jealous fracas, but could be glimpsed intact, a pale, two-humped form, in the background of a group portrait in which the model did not appear. Nothing remained of her own work but a speech transcribed phonetically in the minutes of the Fifth and Only Business Meeting of the Society for the Investigation of Dada Phenomena and Macadam (Open to the Public; Please Bring Your Umbrella, and Ready Cash). This read, in its entirety:

TEE-OO PAKA PAKATA RRRRR
PAKA PAKATA BRRRR
SMMU SMU SMUUU
DOKTOR GOAT
GIBTS NOCH BIER?

I froze, lifted my head to look around me. Mahogany shelves, morocco bindings made a dark tartan, threaded with gold. I replaced the book on the shelf, completing the pattern. It was a coincidence, no more.

My next discovery, in the last of a seven-volume *Historie of Wit and Pleasantrye,* was an item in the index of first lines: "One plus One is but One and a Half . . ." I took down the fourth volume. The poem read in full:

One plus One is but One and a Half in th'Arithmetick of the Heart
We infer this from the Fact we're short a Quarter when we part.

It was attributed to two ladies of rare wit, twins, who had shone in the court of Louis XIV, flirting with the more daring rakes, winning a great deal of money at cards, and reciting cutting couplets of their own spontaneous composition, of which one delivered the first, the other the clinching line. Though the ladies' pedigree, like their accent, was so smudged from handling and the dust of travel that it was impossible to make out, they were called the Maltese Ladies.

The problem was, we had made them up.

We must have run across a reference somewhere (though I would be very surprised to find the *Historie* on the shelves of the Grady library). Still, to read their names in a book written two hundred years before I was born made me feel very odd.

I put the volume back among the others, and only then noticed the ornament at the base of each spine: an embossed gilt ring between two half rings. Together, they formed a chain. The Togetherist totem, or a bookbinder's bubble? The Togetherists existed now, all too obviously, but I was skeptical of their claims of antiquity. The chain was too ubiquitous. Or was that because the Togetherists really were everywhere, had always been everywhere, a chain binding the globe, one end stapled to the Rock of Ages? The logic was circular, and speaking of circles, it was easy, too, to claim the circle as your insignia, and appropriate for yourself even more ubiquity than the Togetherists. Anyone could invent a history, and find the evidence afterward.

Next I looked up Evelyn North. I struck it lucky there too, the kind of lucky that was starting to frighten me. Just like Audrey said, the silent movie star had been one of the casualties of the advent of talking pictures. When she quit the movies, she bought an English country house and had it shipped

in numbered crates to an undisclosed location in the American Southwest, a legendary event revisited in the disguise of a weak fantasy in *The Ghost Goes West,* the 1936 Robert Donat film. Stars need their privacy. As it happened, there was all too much privacy there. The air-dropped groceries began to pile up. Eventually someone dared to investigate. Some weeks had passed since her fatal encounter with a drifter, a rattlesnake, a jealous lover, a hit man sent by the government to expedite the requisitioning of her land, or the noonday sun (all these theories were mooted). By then the star was dispersed. She'd been parceled out among coyotes, vultures, and all the littler scavengers. They never found her head, which had prompted speculation by the ever vigilant C. C. Metzger that the star (who was never filmed in bright light or full length, and who looked subtly different from scene to scene) had actually had two of them. The spinal column would have told, of course, but it was only recovered in part, and had gotten mixed up with the bones of an unknown, possibly a vagrant who had come along later and met a similar fate. The star's only heir, the part-time part-Navajo housecleaner, was persuaded to sell the house and land to the government for a pittance, and nobody knew anymore where exactly the house had been. Wouldn't it be funny if . . . almost as if *drawn* there, as close to the dollhouse as it could get—or the other way around, the dollhouse converging on the Manor—until one day, *boom*. Thin Air.

I looked up John Seymour Laine in an encyclopedia of architecture. "We have been unable to find any authenticated views of the house most contemporaries considered his masterpiece (the structure no longer exists). However, the residence in this unlabelled photograph found amidst a jumble of memorabilia donated to the British Museum, fits contemporary descriptions of Laine's masterwork, and to cognoscenti, bears the unmistakeable stamp of the architect's mature style." The "residence" was the dollhouse. The photograph was taken from ground level in what seemed to be a vegetable garden. I suppose that out-of-focus lettuce *could* be taken for a tree.

By now I was barely surprised. If anatomy had allowed it, I would have thought Blanche was scampering ahead of me everywhere I went, planting tokens for me to find. Maybe the Unity Foundation was up to its tricks again, though how they could know so much about me, I couldn't imagine. Oh, it was crazy to imagine anyone could or even *would* get a single copy of a book printed up and antiqued with judicious applications of a weak acid solution, and nip into a used bookshop while I napped to shelve it where I was sure

to find it. But was it really more probable that in a reputable history of the American Southwest I should find a photograph credited to someone very estimable with a view camera and a donkey, a photograph that had to have been taken by our Time Camera, for there we were in the background acting as extras, dressed as a pair of squaws in questionable headgear? More and more history seemed like a catalog, not of neutral facts, but of lies, dreams, obsessions. *My* obsessions.

THE SIAMESE TWIN REFERENCE MANUAL

Op Ed

To the Editors of the Pennsylvania-German Folk Pottery Review
cc the New York Times, the Washington Post, the London Observer, etc. etc.

Sirs, I cannot hold my peace concerning the shocking inaccuracies in your recent feature, "Tulipware of the Pennsylvania-German Potters." The author cites Harlan Eliphalet Husband, under whose charismatic leadership a small community of twins, conjoined twins, spouses and sympathizers formed a small "Empathis Concordance" or Lek in Pennsylvania. So "Tulipware" states and thus far we are in agreement. I confess I am amazed that no mention is made of the Togetherist Group (of which I am a member) and our indebtedness to Husband, which we acknowledge openly. (That we call one another "husband" is not, as has been poisonously alleged by people who should know better, because we are male chauvinists, but to honor the memory of this visionary leader.) But let that pass.

What I cannot let pass is the shockingly anachronistic use of the pronoun "he" in reference to Husband. Is this ignorance, or a willful slight to a devoted if unaffiliated toiler in the byways of Knowledge? Need I reiterate that from persistent descriptions of his "mercureal" personality, the voluminous hooded cloak he habitually wore, the stooped posture described by many chroniclers of the times, and from identifiable stylistic deviations between his "empathic" sermons [collected as Truth Comes Praising, Changing Times Press, 1974, though this edition contains startling errors, one of which—the omission of a single word, "not"—seriously misrepresents his position on free love to the lasting detriment (though it may also be said, in some quarters the advancement) of his posthumous reputation—those who missed my essay on the subject may read it in its entirety on my Web site, and I hope with this

we may consider the question closed] and his political speeches (even accounting for the necessity of guarding one's speech on the witness stand, while in the pulpit and revival tent a swashbuckling rhetoric carries the day) tabulating word-frequencies with the aid of a computer has satisfied this scholar (NB, though not, to their eternal discredit, the Yale examining board!) that "he" was in fact two persons (see Stephen L Pinster, grad thesis 1989), two powerful speakers, who divided the tasks of office very happily according to their different attainments?

Among Husband's papers, recently discovered in the Marshall Family Memorial Manuscript Library (among a collection of misc. Pennsylvaniana—the carelessness of the staff boggles the mind of this researcher, who despite his youth expects a better reception than his helpful criticisms received. I defy thee, Marshall Family Memorial Manuscript Library, and if I borrowed certain papers, it was only to set them free from a so-called Temple of Scholarship that would be in fact its Tomb) by a researcher who shall go unnamed (not out of fear. Do thy worst, MFMML! But out of modesty) was a draft of a proposal for a new language of the Twin Nation. It is possible he had the assistance of his wife, *née* Persis Affable, who before marriage had achieved some notoriety as a spiritualiste for "Speaking the Language of the Incas While Under Trance" and tying intricate knots in lady's unmentionables. A new language for the Twin Nation! I modestly propose that I, richly steeped in Husband's work and history, am the obvious candidate to reconstruct this language. Visionary funders sought.

Empathically and Emphatically,
Stephen L Pinster

P.S. As for Vyv Hornbeck V.D.'s *venereal divagations* into pop psychobabble, please see my own "Venn Unveiled: Boolean Boob." This milquetoast philosopher is, I suppose, an appropriate bellwether of a "weak, piping age of peace," but his flimsy arguments cannot support the burden of b___ Vyv heaps on them, or even the more nuanced considerations of Handler, Gadreaux, et al. Another scholar carried away in the talons of an idée fixe.

Oh, and Josiah Venn never existed.

Views expressed are not necessarily those of The Observer.

The Erasing Game

For days after I saw Doom Town scoured away in seconds, I felt restless, strange. I wanted to see it again. "Let's play Penitence," I begged Blanche, but Blanche said no, no, we could not destroy the dollhouse—"I didn't mean for real!"—no, not even for pretend. She would tell Max, tell Papa. I blustered, but felt an unfamiliar doubt. Blanche never said no. "All right," I said, getting a piece of paper, "we'll *draw* the dollhouse, and then we'll erase it—"

"No."

No! I stared at the paper. "You don't get it. This is a different game," I said. "This is the erasing game," and made it up right then.

To err is human. To erase, divine.

First rule: A drawing is of something.

Second rule: It didn't exist before you drew it.

Third rule: All drawings are bad drawings. (Especially mine, but I didn't say that.)

Fourth rule: The thing is more perfect than the drawing of it.

Fifth rule: When you erase the drawing, the thing is set free.

"Where?" she said suspiciously.

"Thin air," I said. "The wild blue yonder."

I described Thin Air to Blanche. It was a barren place of cubes and planes, bare stairs and walled squares. Trapezoids of light slid through doorless doors and paneless windows. Days, the landscape was the blue of a white room the sun has just left, nights, the blue of suffocated blood—a blue of

depletion, of faint but chronic hunger. This planet had no dust, no leaves to fall or pins to drop. Only ice plant and dry grass and the more architectonic cacti grew there. Seas were innocent of plankton, sargasso, small fry; only the streamlined sharks cut its cool crystal. Unmanned ships steamed straight from port to port, carving white lines on the blueprint. In this land equations silently proliferated and reduced themselves on cocktail napkins and blackboards. There were candles with no wicks, lightbulbs free of filaments, shoes with eyelets but no laces. Roads led nowhere, and the pages of books were innocent of ink. It was a land so pure that only the erased could live there, and it was our job to colonize it.

"I'll draw a princess," said Blanche, convinced.

Yes, do.

Thin Air became my comfort. In school, when I went hot with shame, its blue cooled me. I bent my head over my notebook and drew, only to erase, erase, erase. Broke-necked birds took wing. Smiles acquired cheeks and eyes. The gone goat chewed a phantom can, his bent leg made straight, and extra heads grew bodies of their own and stood with empty hands on ground as white as baby powder, Ivory soap, or a blank piece of paper.

Thin Air grew like crystals in solution. I was no longer sure it was my invention. One wall implied another, was answered by a floor, a window, and a door. A sea secured a shore. One day Blanche swore she saw it, hanging over the restricted area. "A mirage," said Papa, but I knew Blanche was still mine.

R & R

I passed three days like gallstones. I held telephones. Call Louche call Audrey call home. I dialed not, neither with my left nor with my right hand. Rain rapped the glass door. Or rubber-gloved knuckles: "Would Misses be done soon?" Right hand less active but nimbler now, practicing fine motor skills on pens and pills and political buttons pinned on raincoat lapels—"Hey! Are you off your head? Fockin' mushy!" We are all twofers, indeed. Why, Blanche, could that be a sense of humor?

Then Dr. Decapitate appeared in the news once more. They had found her tracks—yes, *her*: Dr. Ozka was a woman. *Bombshell! Lady Killer Thumbs Her Nose At UK!*

She had shaken off her pursuers some time ago, but it was thought that she was still in England, though other rumors placed her in Tijuana, in Hong Kong, in Reykjavik, Amsterdam, Berlin. Someone claimed to have seen her ride into the Chunnel balancing on the backs of a team of feral dogs, screaming "Olé!" and "One bliss, One way, One head!" Dr. Ozka herself, it was rumored, had once had two heads, and had performed her first surgery close to home with a local anaesthetic, a cheese wire, and a crewel hook. Police were asking citizens to report sightings of anyone, male or female, with usually wide shoulders and an off-center neck. ("Oh *please,*" I could hear Trey say, "any decent tailor could correct that with shoulder pads.") Some said she had left a prominent stump, perhaps resembling a small peach. (Trey again: "Throw on a pashmina, and who's gonna know?") Witnesses said she was stylish, if a bit vulpine, with the long sharp canines her upper lip got caught up on now and then, the narrow jaw, but her coarse hair shone and so did

her yellow eyes. (Yellow?) She had a benefactor who had given her clinic a home in the north. The authorities were being unaccountably slow to find it and shut it down. The Togetherists had announced on national television that if the police didn't act soon, they'd shut it down themselves. I caught their second television interview in a pub. Four sheepish singletons: Link, Hitch, Bond, and Fuse. "We've formed a coalition with a conservative Christian group," said Link, a Yank, and Fuse, a Brit. They spoke with excruciating slowness, because they were following the ceremonial Togetherist practice of sharing words equally, not without occasional disagreements about portion size (Link: "coalish—" Fuse, glaring: "—alition!"). "Not our bag exactly, but they have lots of dough and strategically, that's good for us. When they try to dictate, like, policy, we have to say, like, hey! This is a mariachi of convenience, we're not going to Bedlam with your Assyrians!"

Whispered conference.

Fuse, solo: "My mistake. We are not going to *bed* with your *arses*. I mean asses."

While I watched, my right hand was in my pocket, investigating a folded brochure, its edges gone soft as felt. What was it? You remember, Mr. Nickel, the stumpy man, the gimpy man, with the prosthetic leg and the prosthetic daughter. I could not withhold a little shudder at the thought of his giggle and gush. I pulled out the brochure with the intention of throwing it away, but something prompted me to have another look at it first. It was just a brochure for the Hunterian Museum. But look, a second brochure has slid or been slid under the skin of the first, like a wolf in cow's clothing, no, I mean, like—

After I opened it I closed it again and thought, I should go back to America. I pictured the telephone, I heard the automated flight information line pick up, I felt myself authoritatively pressing the star key, or was it the pound key, pressing and pressing, until I got through to a bored angel who would change my ticket and my destiny. But even as I imagined these things I was poring over the page.

> From the minute our heavy doors seal behind you and the peace of the place cools your heart, you know. There is no place on earth quite like the Unity Centre. And when the great circular door of the shrine swings open and our founder steps through to welcome you, you know there is nobody quite like Madame O. No figure, secular or spiritual, inspires such devotion. We omit nothing . . .

Somebody's heart paused as if to listen, and then went on, like the man in the movie who thinks he is being tailed. Somebody else's heart matched it beat for beat. There was a pulse of darkness like a soft blow in the back of my brain, and I thought, I don't know why, *I'm going to die!* But then I rallied. I had a destination! It was bracing, after all my fuddling through books. I felt the tug of a plot line, and it felt like coming back to life.

As I was on my way to the train station, I thought I saw Louche standing at a bus stop, holding a Transitional Object on her hip like a baby. She had cut her hair. I ducked into a doorway.

"Excuse me!" a plump woman said in reproof, stepping around me.

"You're excused," I said.

A minute later, I stepped out and walked quickly toward Louche. I was breathing hard. I could still turn back, after all. Seeing someone I know, I thought, even if it is Louche, will keep me from—I tapped her shoulder. She turned. She was not Louche. She was not even a she. And the Transitional Object was a disassembled office chair.

So I bought a ticket.

The train strove north. Sheep with black faces, sheep with blue daubs on their backs, yobs in cold stations gaping through breath clouds. The lowering sky menaced the few trees. Isolated sunrays angled in like cop lights searching a vacant lot where something vile had been found—a bleeding brick, an entire fingernail, hair with a bit of scalp attached.

The ticket collector arrived with a chuckle and an air of faint threat. My left hand had begun crawling up the wall in the direction of the emergency pull cord. I brought it back down.

A steel tank. The reflective scars of wet furrows. An empty chip bag under a bush. These things must be imagined gliding by and turning away as they are left behind. It started to rain: countless short dirty striations on the windows.

Then the sun broke through, straight into my eyes, so the car was rubied, and fringed with eyelash-rainbows. My nose was a shining boomerang hanging over the aisle, Blanche a big blond blur, and the train was pulling into the station.

I was the only passenger to disembark, and the station was deserted. Outside, the sunlight that had seemed so welcoming proved thin and streaky, as

if still filtered through dirty glass. I could not see my shadow. I thought of vampires and mirrors and my hearts seemed to strike together in my chest, like weights in a clock disturbed by movers.

A bulbous taxi was at the curb, its driver leaning on the hood, smoking. I got in and we pulled out into traffic. "I don't have the exact address," I said after a moment, "but it's near the crossing of —— Street and —— Street." I had planned this small deception. I was going to point at another building near the clinic and wait until he drove away before walking the rest of the way.

"Say no more," said the taxi driver in a tone that could have been sardonic. I examined his long bony face in the mirror. His lips were chapped, and he licked them often with a neat, unconsciously greedy pass of the tongue. Except for this quick movement, his face was impassive.

The photograph on the brochure had showed, behind the convalescents, a slice of out-of-focus white wall that I had extrapolated into something between a modern art museum (bone-white concrete fins) and a château. When I tried to picture it more clearly it shrank, for how could something so grand go unnoticed? Still, I wasn't prepared to see a small, stained, stucco house—barely more than a cottage—on top of that peculiarly steep, almost conical hill. Poking up from among flat, densely cobbled streets and boxed gardens, the hill looked extravagant and unhealthy, like a bubo. It was closely carpeted with grass clipped to the cuticles, an almost white lawn of follicles and roots. A fence ringed the base of the hill.

The driver pulled up right outside a small wrought-iron gate in this fence. To insist upon my deception now seemed pointless. I paid him and climbed out. The taxi driver got back into the car, but did not immediately pull away. I felt him watching as I pushed open the small, heavy gate and went in.

The gate swung shut behind me and bit my heel. I limped up the stairs. They seemed wrong somehow—too steep, too narrow, as if made for people with tiny feet. At the crest of the hill, I found myself walking into the brochure. There was the chilly lawn, the little bushes. There were the patients, though today they were wrapped in blankets against the cold, a row of neat parcels propped up on flimsy aluminum-and-plastic recliners, holding up stoic off-center faces toward the thin, white sunlight.

Beheadings don't leave many survivors. Here they were, the lucky few.

The front door swung open, and a twofer stepped out. "Pleased to meet you again, join with you, come together, after our too-long separation!" said Mr. Nickel.

Cunning Collectibles' *Togetherness*

You'll love this full-lead crystal sculpture of lovely conjoined twins on the verge of passing from carefree childhood to the wonders of womanhood. Caught in a moment of stillness between restraint and abandon, these young, spirited and beautiful Siamese Twins pause at the verge of the unknown. Their delicately sculpted faces reveal their serene wonder as they contemplate the mysteries that lie ahead. A sensitive work of art, dealing with an unusual subject, and captured in the fluid forms of full-lead crystal. Cunning Collectibles hallmark and Certificate of Authenticity prove this is an authentic limited edition. May be purchased in low monthly instalments.

Box Girl

One day, our explorations took us to Dr. Goat's house, a yellow bungalow with aluminum siding and a neat square of shorn lawn. We circled it slowly, keeping low. There were some giant panties bagging on a line in the yard, and a parakeet in a cage hanging in a window with checkered curtains. Against the back of the house was a wooden shed with a tin roof. Its door was open a chink. So we went in.

It was not quite that easy. We were excited and scared. It felt as though we had to push our way in against some invisible substance that filled the shed to capacity; so, no room for us. We could feel the pressure on our chest, forcing us to breathe quick and shallow.

The air inside was hot, sluggish, material. You bit off chips of it, melted them in your nostrils. Mouth-breathing was to be recommended. The smell was a rectangular solid, more or less the dimensions of the shed, but ambitious, straining against the walls. The light was golden, and tiny needles of hay stood in it, suspended, only reluctantly swaying in the wake of our passage.

There was a stirring, creaking sound from overhead, a sound a boat or a cart might make. I pictured chickens, made a crooning sound to let them know we weren't dangerous. We weren't going to steal or wreck anything. It was enough for me just to stand in the material heat of Dr. Goat's shed, where we did not belong, and feel my own daring burning in my stomach like a lump of primary ore. I knew exactly who I was. Lay a strip of film against my skin right then, and I'd have burned my signature across it.

Something flicked past, smacked the ground beside us with a liquid sound.

We bent over it. A little brown star. Some kind of muck.

Something hot and clinging slapped me on the neck. Above us there was a hectic animal scramble. With my still light-struck eyes I peered at the cage hanging from a thick beam in the high shadows. It was rocking wildly, clashing against the beam.

We ran a long way before we stopped, each step jolting up the spine. Finally I said, "Animals don't wear dresses." A frilled dress with puffed sleeves.

"Animals don't have knees," Blanche agreed.

"Camels have knees."

"She was pretty," said Blanche.

I was unsure.

"Pretty as a princess," she nodded.

I scrubbed the shit off my neck with a handful of sand, and by the time we got home we had established that a princess was what she was. Who but a princess got treated so badly? A new character appeared in my stories. Donkey-skin, I called her, after the old fairy tale about the princess with the weirdo dad, but I was thinking of the girl Dr. Goat kept in a cage.

We did not go back to the shed for weeks, maybe months. Sometimes we saw its battered metal roof sending us sun-signs when we climbed the bluff behind Too Bad. The light leapt into my eyes as if the interval were nothing. It was hard to shut out. I'd go quiet. The beam was like a pipette, dripping some drug that excited and shamed me.

Then one day Blanche said, "Remember the girl in the shed?"

I was startled. I had nearly convinced myself that I had made her up.

"I thought you would be too chicken to go back," I lied.

We pulled open the heavy door, lifting it so it didn't scrape on the concrete and make a noise, and edged through. We squatted just inside it. A bar of sun lay across our laps like a burden, a burning stripe singeing the bottom edge of our field of vision. We couldn't see anything at first but the star-punctures in the roof and our own knees with the hairs on them standing up golden and electrified against the dark. We had made her up after all, I thought, and my face went hot with annoyance and shame. I was already thinking how I would explain this to Blanche when I heard a mumbling from the darkness

under the roof. Again I flushed. But I held my spot. A wasp swung outside the door, disappeared, came back, hoisted itself up, and soared away.

When she began to talk, it was to let out a string of swear words and others I had never heard, though I knew they were filthy from the sound of them. I started laughing, having no idea what else to do. The shed buzzed with my laughter, and afterward it was quiet for a minute before the shit started flying at us in little hot globs and we left. The sun had shifted in the sky, and it was as if someone had butted it loose and reset it farther down. The bluffs were deep red, like slabs of steak.

We scrambled over the rise and hit the road farther up, and at a distance we saw Dr. Goat coming home with a dead rabbit and his gun. So we angled off the road and hid in what was left of an old adobe hut. We were squatting in there picking through jewel-shards of glass and tufts of fur from a rabbit a hawk had nabbed when we heard his feet crunching on the stones outside, and our stomach tightened like a fist.

"Where did you come from?" boomed Dr. Goat, in the doorway. He did not look at me, only at Blanche, and I thought he was pretending to himself I wasn't there. He jounced his gun in the crook of his arm, gently, enjoying the weight of it.

"From over there," I said, promptly and vaguely, forcing his eyes to turn to me, and flapping my hand behind us.

"You weren't on my property, were you? You're not little trespassers, are you?"

"No!" said Blanche.

"I hope you're not lying," he said. "I don't like liars."

"Can I touch your gun?" I said. I took a step toward him and stretched out my fingers, brushed hot metal. He jerked it out of reach.

"Not for little girls!" he said. "Hurry on home. Does your mother know you're way out here?" He didn't move out of the door. We edged past him and hurried off.

"Hey!" he yelled after us. "Watch this!" We turned. A silver line slid up along his cheek, he tensed, and an arm jumped off a saguaro downslope of us. *Crack* answered the bluffs, and birds fell into the sky all around. We ran.

Non Compos Mentis

But it was a twofer: not Mr. Nickel after all, but the Togetherist from San Francisco. He *had* been shadowing me, I was right.

And yet it was Mr. Nickel too.

"Confused?" said the twofer. "I'll give you a hint, you've met Roosevelt here before, under different circumstances. What better disguise for a proponent of elective identity surgery than"—he pulled his collar open, and I saw the straps of a complicated harness—"a second head?"

The mount was molded closely to his collar, and even simulated in the contours of its base the different bone structure of a twofer. It was an expensive model. "Recognize me now?" He laughed merrily, bouncing a little on his toes. "Mr. Disme! Get it? Nickels and dimes? Did I surprise you? Did I? I've been looking forward to this moment so long, I pictured it happening a hundred ways, and now it's happened in just this way and no other, and it's perfect! But you're shocked. You don't know me as a double-headed Nickel, excuse the pun. You were never properly introduced to Roosevelt. Allow me to remedy that." Mr. Nickel unsnapped something and raised the prosthetic head from his shoulders like someone doffing a cap. "Pleased to meetcha, pardner-er-er-er!" said the head in a metallic chirp that ended with an abrupt click.

"American manufacture," Mr. Nickel said with a grimace. "Very sensitive to little blips and glitches." He popped a mini CD out of a slot in the base of the head and wiped it with a handkerchief, then slid it back in.

"Howdy!" said the head, in a tone of astonishment.

"Look at your face!" guffawed Mr. Nickel. "Your sister's a cool customer,

but yours is a study. I was starting to think I was too subtle with the brochure. Was I too subtle? Boy, am I glad to see you here. But I'm being selfish, I bet you can't wait to meet the others. Let's get this show on the road." He snuggled the head back into its mount, and it snapped in place. "Dr. O doesn't like me to wear old Rosie around the farm," he whispered, "says it trivializes the burden. But hey, I'm a kidder. I like to get a rise out of folks. And Rosie has his uses, she can't deny that."

The front door opened on a sour note into a small dank foyer with a peeling ceiling and the tang of mildew in the air. The big wooden door to our left was surprised by our entry, and through its gape I glimpsed a waiting room full of indistinct objects and greenish light, like an aquarium. Someone standing at the window—a twofer—spun round and through the chink, seemed to see me, then turned identically swollen faces aside, and Mr. Nickel bumped the door shut, and in the rear of the foyer beside a jumble of mops and coats what I had taken for a closet door opened and a woman in a lab coat ducked under the lintel and came through.

So this is Dr. Ozka.

"You're thinking, so this is Dr. Ozka," said Mr. Nickel. "High cheekbones. Greying strawberry blond hair, pulled back in a bun. Tomato-red lipstick bleeding into the fine lines in her thin lips. Tiny gold earrings, and a matching charm under her white coat. Shape of charm to be determined. Shape of body under white coat, to be determined. Calves bold, instep bolder. Conclusion: attractive older woman, not obviously bloodthirsty."

"Velcome," she said, and I almost laughed as I shook her cool, dry hand.

"It is *not* Dr. Ozka, however, but her invaluable 'woman Friday,' who alas, does not know I exist."

"Nurse—" She gurgled her name. I divined it from her name tag: Bolima V. Hrdle.

"Allow me to introduce Nora and Blanche Olney, who will be staying with us until . . . Who will be staying with us. Go with Nurse Gargle, girls, and settle up, and when you're done give us a yoick and I'll show you your digs." Nurse Hrdle, however, had already turned on the high heel of one red pump and was leading us back through the door she'd come out of.

"Vatch your heads," she said. "And mind the step."

The sunken room was tiny—maybe it *had* been a closet once—and crammed. I stepped down onto a stained olive carpet, far from new, but apparently newer than the writing desk at my right, and in fact all the other

furnishings, as it had been cut to fit around them, probably to save moving those ancient shelves, on which shoeboxes of floppy disks and manila folders were heaped as high as the sagging ceiling. There, at eye level, on a string taped to a low beam, a tiny straw bird spun in the wind of a fan balanced precariously on a bale of manila envelopes that almost filled the deep embrasure of a small cracked window. Below it, against the back wall, an ancient computer occupied the entire surface of a small desk with its beige outbuildings. A golden prompt throbbed on its black screen. Nurse Hrdle went to it. She spun the single desk chair that served both desks and sat, clattered briefly on the keyboard. I perched on the metal folding chair by the desk and waited. The smell of mildew was keen. After one whiff I had let Blanche breathe.

Nurse Hrdle spun her chair and scooted back to the writing desk. She got out a yellowed receipt, began totting up neat blue figures. I could not quite read them upside down, though I observed the European seven with its extra dash. It hadn't occurred to me until now that I might not have enough money. An operation of this kind—I had figured less than a bypass, more than a tit job. But that left room. She slid the receipt across the table. I looked at it—and laughed. "You do know this vould be considerably more expensive at a major hospital," she said stiffly. "But if necessary ve can vork out a payment plan. Our doctor vill not turn anyone avay for want of funds. She is committed to service, one hundred fifty percent. It is her life vork."

"No, no, it's—it's very reasonable." It was cheap, actually. I could pay in cash. "Can I use dollars?"

She enlisted a calculator and showed me a revised figure. My fingers felt foolish, counting out the bills. Not Lithobolia, just self-consciousness. I asked a question just to shift her eyes.

For a moment I thought she'd refuse to answer. "I guess I'm from the European Union," she finally answered, with a slight curl of the lips.

"I'm from Nevada," I offered, apologetically. Maybe where we called home was private here.

"I'm from Slovakia, really," she said grudgingly. "Ve were part of the Magyar Empire, part of the Hapsburg Empire, part of Czechoslovakia. Ve didn't get our own flag until Hitler made us a commonvealth. Then we were part of Czechoslovakia again. Now ve are part of the EU. Ve have a flag again," she shrugged, "but it is the Hitler flag." She squared the bills and flipped through them with amazing speed, pinching each between her lacquered fingernails.

"Thank you. You may keep this copy of the receipt, though ve vould prefer that you did not. Ve leave no stone turned. Mum is the vord. One vay!" She showed her teeth in what might have been a smile. The charm had worked its way out from under her collar. It was a single gold ring, of course.

"One way," I agreed weakly.

Mr. Nickel popped one head through the door. "Do I hear the cheerful sound of sloganeering?"

He and Dr. Hrdle seized the computer desk by its edge and, with a turn and wiggle that bespoke considerable practice, fit it into a narrow space between a file cabinet and a small refrigerator. The power cords had snagged on the fridge, and Mr. Nickel gathered them up under Nurse Hrdle's pale stare and laid them neatly on its top before he stepped back to my side. Nurse Hrdle stooped—Mr. Nickel spread his hands in wordless admiration of her hindquarters—plucked up the carpet where it met the wall, and peeled it back. The green wave rose, scraping the shelves on each side, until Nurse Hrdle had backed all the way to the front desk, holding it curled over her head. A Post-It fluttered down. Paper clips pinged. Mr. Nickel edged around the coil and sprang lightly through the gap. I wrestled my bags through and followed. In the bare concrete floor was a metal hatch with a recessed handle that Mr. Nickel was already raising to reveal a flight of narrow stairs.

"Welcome," said Mr. Nickel, "to the heart of the matter."

The hatch came down behind us with a clang and a whoosh of escaping air.

I found myself in a dank echoing hall, its pocked cement walls sealed with a thick rubbery skin of green paint. It was cheerless in an institutional way that reminded me of Cold War government facilities, like the legendary miles of tunnels deep under the surface of the Restricted Area, where hairless, phosphorescent squirrels rooted through leaky waste canisters for edibles. The floor slanted down, or maybe up—in any case it was not quite level, though very nearly, and that slight angle off true put me on edge. The water fountain set in the wall near me was pre-Boom, with a niche too narrow to admit a person with two heads, and a single bubbler on the right.

Mr. Nickel answered my unspoken question. "Former bomb shelter. The entire hill is honeycombed with tunnels, like a, well, like a honeycomb. Built by a very *very* rich, very *very* private personage, our patron, whose name I cannot tell you, not even in a whisper. Mainly because"—he giggled—"I don't know what it is."

A door opened, and a pudgy man emerged with a towel tied around his waist. My eye climbed the parallel creases in his big, hard stomach, his soft drooping breasts in their furze of blond hair, to the pink shiny stump. My skin swarmed all over. The remaining head nodded a greeting, and I pitched forward.

"Oops-a-daisy!" Mr. Nickel said, grabbing my arm.

I had tripped on a stair, that's all. "Thanks," I said, and disengaged myself. I felt again the peculiar armature I had encountered under Mr. Disme's shirt when he hustled me away from the cops. If I had given it more thought at the time, I could have saved both of us a lot of trouble. "Why did you lead me on such a treasure hunt? The brochure, the postcard . . ."

Mr. Nickel wagged his head, chuckling. "Wasn't it fun?"

"Fun!" The vile little elf was practically prancing.

Roosevelt chuckled identically, a phrase or phase behind, and agreed, in Mr. Nickel's own accents, "Wasn't it fun?" This repeated. A recording, evidently. It echoed unpleasantly in the hall. Thump something to make it stop, I thought. But the button would be in some private fold you'd have to peel back, and would have, oh, a ginger hair stuck to a gummy something on it. I swallowed back bile. Blanche's breathing roughened as if she tasted it too. We went up a short flight, not a full story, to a new level, then made a right turn and went down more stairs, then turned again and stopped. The laughter stopped mid-ha. I had to put a hand on the wall to keep from running into my guide, then wished I hadn't; the walls were slippery, and left a soapy residue on my fingertips. "It's confusing at first, with no windows to give you your bearings, but soon you'll know it like I know the palm of my hand." He winked.

He opened a door—"Whoops, sorry!"—then the door opposite. "Here you are, my dear. Home sweet home."

My room was painted the same institutional green as the halls, and contained a cot, a table, and a lamp. Faded tennis ball in one corner. There was a print of a painting of poppies tacked to the left wall at the head of the bed. The rear wall was, strictly speaking, the ceiling, an irregular curve, also green, that sloped down to meet the floor. In it was a tiny sloping window at the end of a deep recess, through which a little greenish sun shone—filtered through grass, I realized. I was inside the hill.

"The potty's right across the hall, and you saw our *Bob*"—he gave it an exaggerated French pronunciation, something between *boob* and *bub*—"coming out of the men's shower room on our way in. The women's is right

next to it, please note that it's reserved for post-ops in the peak hours of six AM to ten PM, so if you want to splash a little water on your temples before the evening session at five, please use the sink in the little girls' room. Someone will come by to escort you to Exposition at quarter to. Dinner après. Before then, could you cast a preliminary eye upon the contents of the manila envelope you'll find on your pillow? Besides required paperwork, the packet includes examples of personal statements from previous . . . clients . . . to get the juices flowing. Take all the time you need; you can drop off the paperwork with Nurse Girdle if you're eager to get things moving, but if you need more time, just ask. As a matter of course the packet contains two copies of the form, one for each of you. Normally"—he gave Blanche a fond glance—"we ask you to respect each other's privacy and look away while your twin is filling in her copy, but in this case I don't believe that applies, am I right? Please note that if you are only returning one copy, you need to check the fruitcake box, sorry, I mean the Non Compos Mentis box." He beamed at me, then shook himself all over, at which Roosevelt mumbled what sounded like "Nurse Fertile."

"Tsk! Naughty boy!" said Mr. Nickel, and bopped him lightly.

"Non compos mentis," Roosevelt said, and was quiet.

"*Brrr!* What a feeling, what a day. Dear Nora, what can I say. I'm so awfully, what is it the kids say, I'm so awfully *stoked* to see you here. I feel personally responsible for you, and, call me silly, I was beginning to worry. But in my heart I knew we'd see each other again, somewhere, somehow." He winked and backed out the door.

I sat for a long time, listening to a sullen, barely audible rumble, with intermittent gulping sounds, that was coming from somewhere below me. The traffic sounds could not be heard from here. I felt swallowed. Gradually my trembling subsided. A tiny rhomboid of sunlight moved slowly up the side of the windowsill, then slid swiftly off it onto the embrasure, where it flickered out. The minute it vanished, I missed it.

I turned on the lamp. Then I opened the manila envelope and removed a copy of the form.

Please refer now to the first page of this memoir.

I did not allow myself to hesitate. I filled out the form. I checked "Non Compos Mentis," aka the fruitcake box, and I signed my name. At the bottom of the page there was a space for a personal statement.

Statement? I would have to write a book. So I left it blank.

The Siamese Twin Reference Manual

Sample Testimonials

"I am the recto of a heterosexual twofer male in good health. It has long been a fantasy of mine to cut my own head off. My twin was reluctant but has finally consented to fulfill my deep and earnest wishes. When I was a boy we were sequestered for our protection from singleton society. Our parents felt we would be mocked and wanted to protect us as long as possible from a cruel awakening. We had a twofer nurse, Abby and Bella. Our parents pushed our meals through little windows. We saw only their reaching hands and kindly faces. When we were permitted out they wore rough handmade second heads Velcro'd onto their shoulders. My mother had sewn them from gunny sacks and my father had painted happy faces on them. We were convinced by them and found their smiles even warmer and more comforting than our parents' own smiles. In short we were happy in our country home with its deep plush lawns so green it hurt your teeth to look at them. The blades of grass squeaked together when you trod on them. We were fortunate and wanted for nothing. The tire swing hung so low it brushed the erect tips of the grass. We felt heavy and somnolent. Once I saw a snake, but it disappeared into the grass. One day a car blew a tire outside our estate and ran off the road. We looked down at it from an eminence. It was an inferior make of car. A man emerged. He had only one head on his shoulders and we believed that his second head had been cut off by the accident. We ejaculated spontaneously! The sudden emptiness of the man's shoulder carriage was electrifying. Since then I have only been able to reach orgasm by picturing in detail a surgical decapitation, a neck stump, the empty place above such a stump, or other variations on this theme. It has become an obsession. I am not sick; my brother Eugene knows I am sincere and though his religious convictions prevent his sharing this passion he is willing to make the ultimate sacrifice, or rather the penultimate

sacrifice, mine being the ultimate: my head! I do not see it as a sacrifice, however. It would fulfill my wildest dreams—and, I hope, someone else's as well, for I have confided to my twin my dream that there may be some Lady out there who is excited by the idea of decapitation and would like to see and, only with Eugene's full consent, touch my stump after I am removed. I have advised Eugene as well that while this is not my personal cup of tea, I would be very pleased if anyone would like to buy my remains to make a shrunken head or other keepsake, for a reasonable fee that would help defray the costs of surgery."

"I am healthy, sane, sober, and in anguish. I have considered suicide, but would not drag my twin into my own hell. I view this operation, in which I shall leave my sister in sole possession of our mortal frame, as the only solution. It will be a blessed release.

I think I was just three when I first realized I had a "self." I had just picked up a piece of blue beach glass that I found extraordinarily beautiful. As I turned it over in my hands, I became aware of myself looking. What was myself? It seemed to be a tiny, but extremely sensitive point, almost a wound. At the same time, I became aware that there was another self somehow adjoined to, almost inside me—a self that, at that moment, was pitching the beach glass into the sea.

I do not mean to imply that this innocent deed turned me against my twin. It was the discovery of her existence that so baffled and alarmed me. I felt very keenly that I was one, and yet my own senses informed me I was two.

As I grew older, my misery deepened. At school and on the street we drew our share of abuse for being different, but kindness hurt me just as much, since it issued from the false assumption that I was one part of a we. There was nobody who recognized my true nature. Even my twin, who feared solitude as much as I craved it, could not understand my need to be alone.

I recognize that even this self that cries "I am" was forged in a double fire. When I looked at myself, that vivid point of awareness, who was that looking? To separate I from myself is already to twin myself again. There is for me no surgical solution: without my twin, I would be a twin still. The same holds for my sister. Happy girl, she can keep herself company, while I can only split and split and split again, seeking a self so infinitesimal it cannot be divided. I believe my dream of one is an idea only two can have—a fiction. Deprived of hope, I ask only for an end to despair."

The White Snake

We kept going back to the shed. It soothed a part of us that chafed. What did school mean, compared to that universe in there? It was enough just to stand inside the door and hear the creak of the chain to feel that stories could come true, at least the terrible ones. Sometimes Blanche tried to make conversation, bringing up things I had told her about Donkey-skin, as casually as if they were fact—"That time you almost got away while your father was kidnapped by Calamity Jane and left for dead in Doom Town." Donkey-skin would seem to listen, then drown us out with cusses.

We didn't always get to see her. Sometimes the shed door was padlocked. Once Dr. Goat's car was pulled up right in front of it, instead of behind the house in the turn-around, and we were afraid to go near it. A couple of times the door was cracked open, but we heard the *baaa* of a goat inside or saw a light or even just imagined we saw one, and took off and ran to the Dead Animal Zoo that was another home to us. Donkey-skin didn't say much that we could understand, just the swear words and a rhythmic monotonous mumbling that was like a kind of singing without words. Unless it was a different language, a language nobody knew but her.

"And Dr. Goat," said Blanche. "He talks to her."

"That's true," I said. "Let's find out his secret."

We peeped in windows. Mrs. Goat puttered around, right under our noses, but she didn't notice us, she kept her eyes on her potholders.

Parakeet silently opened its beak to show the little eraser of its tongue.

One day we took a flashlight along and stayed to dinner, their dinner. Dr.

Goat sat at the table. Mrs. Goat wouldn't eat with him, we knew; we'd seen. If she even looked at him, he started up from his chair at her. He was joking, but she didn't think it was funny. There was the domed dish on the table. He lifted the lid off, frowning, and steam came out.

The white snake lay like a heavy hank of soft rope on his plate, glistening, pearly. Dr. Goat pressed the tines of his fork into the skin until they popped through. Three tiny squirts, and the snake deflated, fractionally. With a small serrated knife he sawed off the nub and pushed it aside. The cut end was a flat round of marbled pink. He unscrewed a jar of mustard. I imagined I could hear the tinny ringing of the metal lid on the glass jar. He sawed off a coin and speared it, and with the pointed tip of the knife dipped it into the jar, brought out a precise neat triangular mound of yellow, and painted the coin gold with it. He placed it in his mouth mustard side down, and as he chewed, he raised his eyes mildly toward the window.

We scrambled away, our hearts hammering.

"Did he see us?"

"He looked right at us!"

We ran in the blue almost-dark as far as the road, unmindful of rattlesnakes, but when we got to the road we clicked on the flashlight and shone it in a neat circle on the road before our feet.

"Do you know why he looked up?" I said after a minute. "The bird told him we were watching."

"How did the bird know?"

"Animals know! That's not the question, anyway."

We crunched on. A bat flashed through our beam of light, twisting inches from the ground, and following its path we saw its black shape skirl up into the indigo sky, reel, and fall away.

"What is the question, then?" she said.

"The question is, how did he understand what the bird told him?"

"OK, how?"

"I'll tell you how: he ate the white snake. Don't you remember that story? If you eat the white snake, you can understand the language of the animals. And I'll tell you something else, that's how he talks to Donkey-skin. She only speaks animal language. That's why Mrs. Goat doesn't talk to her. She wouldn't understand."

Blanche thought for a minute. "So if we ate the snake, we could talk to Donkey-skin too?"

* * *

The next day, after making sure Dr. Goat's truck was gone, we went up to the front door. Blanche was afraid to knock, and I had to force our hand against the door.

Mrs. Goat opened the door.

I said, "Ma'am, do you have an aspirin?" while at the same moment Blanche said, "Do you have a Band-Aid?"

I frowned. "She has a headache," I said, as "She hurt herself," said Blanche.

Mrs. Goat's face moved strangely, and the sheep's eyes goggled for a second behind her glasses.

"Oh, dear. Are you sure?"

We nodded. I was already looking past her at the kitchen counter, because there, unceremoniously swathed in plastic wrap, which clung to it here and there, was what was left of the white snake.

Mrs. Goat's big shirtfront shook, but without saying another thing she shuffled off. I noticed how her heels slid off the bare deflocked flats of her scuffs onto the linoleum, and it gave me an unpleasant cold shock in my own heels.

We went straight to the snake. I stuck my hand in the bag. The snake was cold, and a weird juice seeped from it and some of this ran out of a fold of the bag and onto my feet and seethed between my toes. Hurry, said Blanche. I stuck the tip of the snake in her mouth, and she nipped off the end, and we ran.

We looked back from the crest of the hill. Mrs. Goat was standing in the doorway, a glass in her hand, watching us run.

We made it to the zoo.

"Hand it over then." We were squatting next to the cow, breathing.

She didn't say anything.

"We'll split it, dummy," I said. "Give it."

"I swallowed it," she said.

"Blanche!"

"I couldn't help it!"

I glared at her.

"I'm sorry! I could—what if I translate for you? I'll be the interpreter. Nora?"

If you can't say anything nice, don't say anything at all.

The Divorce

I was awakened by a knock. It was the Major who came to fetch me. Of course I had not met him yet. He waggled his unnaturally orange mustachios at me with a practiced move of his upper lip. He wore a vaguely military cap. His other half was turbaned to below the cheekbones, so that only the tip of his nose and below could be seen, and did not speak, though the glistening red mouth (no mustachios there) was moving, mumbling something rhythmic I could not make out, mantras possibly. Readying himself, then, for the axe. Or he was gaga.

"Welcome!" said the Major, in fruitiest Brit. "Oh no, don't give that to *me,* I'm just a fellow sufferer. Those go to Head Nurse Hrdle. You can bring them along. She rarely attends the talks, but Mr. Nickel can take them to her." He held the door for me, then strode down the hall.

I hurried after him. "Is Dr. Ozka speaking?" I ventured.

"Good lord, no! You won't see much of *her* until your number comes up. Until then it's strictly Mr. Graham. Mr. Graham is her—what is it?—Expositor. He gives the evening address." He paused outside a double door, and his voice dropped to a whisper. "It's a lot of hooey, by and large. I'm aligning myself with these clowns for purely strategic reasons. Their commitment is twenty-four/seven and whole-hog. Mine's strictly on the clock, not that I'm paid for this, but I will be insofar as if I do x, they do y, namely fulfil my dream for me, which by my reckoning they will eventually if not sooner. Sure they're a screw loose, off the record of course, but I think I can use them to, as they say, 'actuate my self-potential,' and that's what matters, eh?" He winked excessively.

I followed him through the door into a large room. Twenty or thirty twofers occupied several rows of folding chairs facing a podium. In the front row were a few singletons, including French *Bob,* some of them heav-

ily bandaged. Those who were not seemed to thrust the still red and sore remainders up and out like bold new genitalia. My eyes flew to the emptied air above them, and my knees melted. I oozed onto a seat. An even number of heads swiveled to look at me. (The post-ops did not look.) Some of them nodded and smiled knowingly. I did not see Mr. Nickel. To fill space I asked the Major, "How long is it before we actually go into surgery?"

"Bite your tongue!" he hissed, glaring. "We call it the Divorce." I made a conciliatory gesture. He relented. "Well, it depends. They won't do it until they know we're ready. It happens sometimes that somebody chickens out when they get into the operating room, or the twin bound for the bin decides to make a break for it, and for this reason as well as doctrinal reasons they require the candidates to sit in assembly and suffer the exhortations of our friend up there until they're sure of them."

"Shh!" said the twofer in front of us, turning around. "It's starting."

A blond singleton in a snug turtleneck that revealed no sign of a stump or indeed any other cavil in his sleek symmetry had appeared at the podium. "Hello, old friends and new," he said, solemnly inclining his head in our direction. There was a chorus of greetings, and once again the paired heads turned and the singletons did not. I noticed, belatedly, that among the latter some were offset right, some left, and once again I felt my face burn and my bones flux and slide. "I would ask you to extend your usual warm welcome to the newest members of our community. Nora and Blanche, I think you will find that we are all ready to help and answer questions. Aren't we, friends? We are. We ask only that you do not disturb Madame Ozka, whose work understandably demands a high level of concentration and necessary downtime. Come instead to me or to one of your comrades on the journey, all of whom will be more than happy to share their wisdom. Please extend yourselves in your turn to those still newer guests who come after you." His accent was closer to mine than the Major's, but his dental consonants betrayed a different native tongue, maybe Dutch.

"Meals are at regular hours, as posted. Regrettably we cannot adjust to dietary requirements of a non-life-threatening nature. There is a lounge with some limited reading materials, also a phone and a computer, although we ask that you do not communicate with outside friends and family. In emergencies special arrangements *may* be made, but we do ask that you go through us first, since with the best intentions in the world you may inadvertently jeopardize our privacy and thereby our continued existence. For this reason you should

know that all e-mails sent from the office computer are read by myself before being forwarded to their destinations and that the phone has no outside line and is intended solely for communicating amongst yourselves. Please feel free to enjoy what we like to call our social club, where you are invited to partake of alcohol, dancing, or whatever impromptu performances gifted members of our group may be moved to stage for the enjoyment of others. Karaoke is Thursday nights, and a sign-up sheet is posted. We have a small gym and a sauna. We do ask you to be considerate, as facilities are limited. Please give priority to our post-operative patients, and you will be grateful when your turn comes, as it will, thanks to Dr. Ozka's generosity and vision and the generosity and vision, also, of the evolved persons unnamed that have made this so wonderfully possible with their sponsorship and protection.

"Let's get down to the nitty-gritty of the hard choice but, if I may, the good, necessary choice we have to make here. In a world of trying to have it all and getting more than you bargained for, isn't it great that God has given us the strength and the courage to say: Enough or rather slightly too much of a good thing?

"Ideally we like the heads to talk to each other and come to their own agreement as to which is the inferior copy and superfluous, but if one party is obviously insane, violent, or moribund we will make our own judgments. God's instrument is an extremely sharp scalpel that despite our primitive facilities here we keep sterile and in good working nick. Our spiritual sickle is of course always honed and ready. The spirit does not dull, and metal fatigue is not a problem."

The Major was looking at my lap. I looked down. I was gripping the manila envelope so tightly I had crumpled it. I smoothed it out on my knee. It would not do to let my fellow patients think I was *conflicted.*

"We try not to look at it in the light of murder or an execution. It's not healthy for our self-nurture to harbor images of the black hood and the rusty axe dribbling gore or gobbets of flesh spattering the faces of the *Mordlust*-crazed onlookers. Mengele references, for example, are the opposite of healing. We must ask you to expunge from your vocabulary those terms so overused by the gutter press, 'Nazi doctor,' 'bloodthirsty madman.' We don't look favorably on the words 'fanatic' or 'crackpot,' though we respect your right to formulate any opinions you like in the hallowed space of your own skulls. We understand that while a physical cleavage of a personal situation muddled in the extreme may not eliminate all traces of spiritual wrong-

headedness, that nonetheless the body is the matrix of the soul, maternal connotations intended, and its purification and cruel-to-be-kind downsizing or surgically mediated simplification do have repercussions in cosmic terms, not to mention the powerful symbology of the monster welcomed back into the human fold having been relieved of the burden of unrighteousness, at one whack, excuse the expression, by the benevolence of god-mandate-waving doctor and ecstatic judge empowered by heavenly ukase and accredited by human authority in the form of a respectable medical school (though the legality of our innovative approach remains, lamentably, iffy), to cut through your spiritual confusion and set you free from yin-yang dualism and creeping Manicheanism, not to mention it's easier than meditation and the Way of Poverty, plus more modern. It's very eloquent of where we are right now as a society, looking for answers, headstrong and questing and itching for this and that. We very specifically felt the need for a clinic that was a clinic, if you like, of death, rather than slavish mollycoddling to life, of permanent surgical solutions rather than tedious preventive measures and cart-before-horse, symptom-not-cause approaches. Tolerance? No thanks. One way! New friends: we'd encourage you to call yourselves pre-operative singletons or pre-ops from now on, rather than twofers or 'mushies' or what have you.

"Now, there's coffee and cakes in the club room. Let's get acquainted!"

Amid the applause and the cries of the metal chairs, the post-ops filed out. They held their heads very high. I was not the only one who watched them go.

"Why don't we go grab a cuppa, and I'll fill you in on how we do things around here?" said the Major. "Oh, here's Mr. Nickel. He'll be willing to take your forms to Nurse Hrdle, if I'm not mistaken."

"Thank you very much, my dear," said Mr. Nickel. "I would be happy to play the go-between, the Hermes, the light-footed messenger."

"Thanks a mil," croaked Roosevelt.

That night, I lay awake a long time, while the building clucked and sobbed and gobbled around me. It was very dark, and I listened to her heart beating almost in time with mine and wondered if it had always been out of synch. Once a cry rang through the pipes and rent the insubstantial webbing that had begun to spin itself around me, and I sat up from what I thought was a reverie but must have been sleep, because the room was changed, striped with violet light, and the gibbous moon goggled in the little window like a voyeur, and my hearts were pistoning in perfect synchrony.

Cunt-Ass Cock-Pig

When I told Blanche she could speak the language of the animals, she believed me. From then on she was their interpreter. When she told me what the vultures had said, I looked at her with irritated amazement. I could not tell her she was lying, as she was only lying *my* lie. I would never have admitted it, but I envied Blanche her pass-key to my imagined worlds. Although I had made them up, she was the one to whom they revealed their rich vegetable life, their profusion of curious detail. I invented the ground in front of us, but Blanche walked on it.

I was careful, still, to let her think I led the way. "Let's go talk to Donkey-skin," I said. "You can translate." We settled ourselves carefully in the stinking yellow hay, avoiding wet bits. When she did her mumbling routine, Blanche would listen with her head cocked, very serious, and then tell me what Donkey-skin had said—gnomic fragments that did not sound like anything Blanche had made up on purpose.

But Donkey-skin still didn't say much. Mostly we did the talking, at these times not even looking up at her, but at a chink in the door, so bright it seemed like a fresh-poured rod of molten steel. My stories floated up on the warm air toward the cage creaking in the rafters. Occasionally a soft polysyllable responded: "Bitchdykecuntwhore . . ." It wasn't clear how much of them she understood. Sometimes Blanche undertook to translate them into chirps and trills.

Her skinny butt poked through the bars of the cage in little rolls like pin curls, yellow-white where the bars dug in, purple in between. When she changed position, the old lines lasted long enough to make a sort of

fading, changing plaid. We watched closely, because we were hoping to catch a glimpse of her nasty bits, and we often did: a warped little mouth bunched between two crossbars. We looked at the precise line where the two lips pressed snugly together. We looked hard, as if our eyes were hungry. Unsatisfied, we kept on looking, in a sort of regretful hunt for what had made us imagine we might find satisfaction in that slit, or even for a clearer understanding of the species of hunger it was meant to satisfy, and plainly never could. You know when someone is trying to find the right word, and you think you know what it is, and you're burning to say it for them? It was like that, only without any of us knowing the word. "Cunt," said Donkey-skin, but the burning and the impatience remained.

She was pitiable, but we did not pity her. Princesses were always mistreated. We were scornful of her, even. One, she was kept like a rabbit in a hutch. Two, she peed and pooed herself. We were allowed to run free and knew enough to wipe ourselves from front to back with neatly folded squares of TP, so we were her betters. When she crossed my mind at school, my skin burned cold. Princess? Princess *Cooties,* maybe. But in the shed we called her "Your Highness," and when we looked up, the BB holes in the metal roof burned purple-green comets into our retinas, forming a darkling constellation that jigged around her, so she was something like a goddess. With an iota less civilization, we would have rolled in her poo. As it was, we pushed it with sticks and shuddered, uncovering its freight of husks and bundled fibers.

Once we saw a little stained sneaker near the door and pocketed it. When we pulled it out later, it seemed to vibrate in our fingers. It was deceptively ordinary, except that for all its obvious antiquity its soles were not scuffed even a little. It even had a brand name stamped on a little square of blue rubber at the heel. We could have bought identical ones at the Dupeworths in Grady, where we did our shopping, but we were not deceived. It was a totem. We hid it under a rock at our favorite lookout point, on the high bluffs behind Too Bad, and now and then we made a pilgrimage to look at it.

Our own real lives must have seemed as strange to her as the Maltese Ladies and Hi Jo. She sat very still when we talked about the dollhouse, the ghost keys, the Dead Animal Zoo. We learned not to mention Mama and Papa, or she would shake the cage until the beam creaked and howl imprecations, but Granny and Max were acceptable topics.

When we told her that Granny's gas station could blow half the county sky-high, she said, for the first time, something I could understand. "Even the piano?"

Blanche and I did not look at each other. "Yes," we said.

"And the Coke machine?"

"Yes."

"And the pumps?"

"Yes."

"And the sign?"

"Yes."

"And the road?"

"Yes."

"And your house?"

"I don't know. Maybe."

"Fuckin' shit. And my house?"

"Maybe."

"I know a cunt-ass cock-pig I'd like to blow to kingdom-fucking-come. Kingdom . . . fucking . . . come! Gimme a cigarette."

"What?"

"Smokes."

"We don't have any." We were breathless with incredulity.

"Get some, rim job." She started swinging her cage, and we ran, banging our hip on the door as we shot through.

We stole two cigarettes from a pack Granny had left on her dresser and rolled them into one of our socks. Greatly daring, we slid a whole book of matches into the other. When we poked these things through the bars, she made noises of animal joy and lit a cigarette at once. She smoked one, then the other. The ember made a new red star among the white ones.

"Gimme another."

"That's all we got."

"Gimme another. Gimme another. Gimme another."

"We don't have any!" Blanche cried. "Stop asking!"

A match flared and dropped burning into the straw below her cage. It fizzled and smoked. Even as we stamped it out, another match fell. "Cut it out!"

Fire dropped silently around us like falling stars, and we whirled and stamped.

Blanche burbled something: doe-talk, fox-talk, squirrel-talk.

Fire hit the back of my hand, fluttered down. "Cunt-ass bitch!" I hissed.

The fire stopped falling. I could see her dark eyes looking at me. Then the nearly empty matchbook flipped through the bars at me.

We brought more cigarettes and buried them in the straw with another book of matches. From then on when she asked for a cigarette, we put it in her mouth, and she stuck it through the bars, where we held the match to it. We performed these tasks reverently because cigarettes were another of the mysteries, like dirty words, that she understood and we did not.

It was night. Mrs. Goat's silhouette was fixed in the frame of the window. She was standing over the kitchen sink. She didn't move.

There was a light in the shed. Stars in the shed roof shone up at the stars shining down. Moths clubbed up around the bright holes and tried to force themselves in. Bats hurtled. The shed door was open in a blazing capital I.

Inside, the doctor clicked his tongue over his only patient. He was a rather ordinary man who ought to eat more root vegetables and leave the rabbits alone, who should compliment his wife more often and ask her the latest barometer readings.

"Say *ahhh,*" said Dr. Goat. See the coarse fur, the bony leg.

THE SIAMESE TWIN REFERENCE MANUAL

Person Workout with Coach Graham

What are my workout goals for today?

1.
2.
3.

10:00 AM Head Crunch

10:30 AM Pronoun Practise

11:00 AM ~~Progressive Dwindle~~ Unilats

11:15 AM “Good Balloon, Bad Balloon” Target Practise

11:30 AM Personality Reduction Exercises

12:00 PM Lunch

1:00 PM Guest Lecture: Post-op Ruiz on “Estrategias para evitar ‘y,’” “Strategies for avoiding ‘and’” (Bilingual)

2:00 PM Counting to One

2:30 PM Conversational Solipsism

3:00 PM Fortress of Solitude (advanced students only)

3:15 PM Sad Sack

3:30 PM Chanting

Today’s chant:

one way, one way, one way, one way, one way, one way, one way, one way, one way, one way, one way, one way, one way, one way, one way, one way, one way, one way,

one way, one way

Did I achieve my workout goal?

What have I learned today?

Urn or Faces?

I was disappointed. Our hill made a princely bomb shelter, but no luxury spa. It was not only frog-green but frog-cold and frog-wet. The Manual mildewed. My socks effloresced. I watched the clock for those few minutes (between 2:02 and 2:22) in which the sun entered my tiny skylight, and then raced to my room to hold my hand up to its faint, almost imaginary warmth. We had been taught a sequence of beats we could rap on the pipes below the hatch when we wanted to go out, but when I tried it, there was never any response. Theoretically, that meant Nurse Hrdle was in surgery, or in the powder room, or in consultation with one of the occasional legitimate patients, mostly tourists, who visited the clinic for pinkeye or diarrhea, but I suspected she was just ignoring me. In any case our schedule was much too full for sightseeing. Morning and afternoon we had Person Workout—solemn exercises performed mostly in silence. Sometimes we spoke into our Sad Sack. Sometimes we practiced Subject Positions. "I, I," we chanted, like seamen. "I came, I saw, I sawed." Wearing a hood over my "shortcoming," I knocked blocks off what they had been on. If I knocked the wrong block off, I had to put on the hood. On the first day of Progressive Dwindle we were each given a loaf of white bread to squeeze into the shape of a head. Every day we were to take a bite of it until it was gone, a poetic idea, but by the third day the heads were blue with mildew, and had to be thrown out. Evenings, we had Exposition. Mr. Nickel was not always present, but when he was, he generally wore his second head and sat among the twofers. Too often, next to me.

Nights, I fell asleep as if hit on the head by something soft but enor-

mously heavy. Waking was like struggling out of a pismire. Often I gave up the attempt, sank back, and slept more, slept like a fossil. I was in bed with the bog lady, that old stick-in-the-mud.

Someone pounded on my door. “Nora! Cookies in the clubroom!” I kept still. A quieter knock followed. Then footsteps, receding.

I had thought I might find like-minded people here, if anywhere, but my hopes had died the first night, when I did the rounds with the Major.

Luis and Porky, USA. Target: Luis.

“Luis, left, was his father’s golden boy. Porky, right, the pariah. Father convinced Porky wasn’t his. Couldn’t be persuaded otherwise despite scientific evidence. ‘Single egg, single schmegg. God damn Triple-A man and his God damn jumper cables.’ Left all his rhino to Luis, left Porky destitute. Luis, very oppressed by guilt over this, insisted on the Divorce. When Luis gets the chop, Porky inherits after all.” Though they were third generation and purest So-Cal, Mr. Graham always greeted them with a hearty: “Que pasa, amigos?” “Uh, no entiendo, dude.” *“Mexican-American,”* Mr. Graham scoffed. “Add the hyphen to my list of abominations.”

Evangeline and Bernadette, France. Target: God knows.

The French *jumeaux siamois* were long and narrow, with long black hair and long bony hands generally glued together in prayer. They had long eyes with long lashes, often in disarray. Evangeline: “We want the Divorce for reasons spiritual. We are taking the veil, and”—shy whisper—“we do not wish to make of Christ *un bigame*.” Bernadette: “*Mais,* we prefer not to call it The Divorce but rather a temporary *séparation,* for we will be together again in eternity. We have prayed for guidance as to which of us is let go. We believe she will sprout wings from her stump and fly directly to heaven.”

Della and Donna (familiarly, DeeDee or Double D), USA. Target: Heads or tails.

DeeDee were baccarat dealers in a Reno casino and were going to flip a coin. They wore cowboy boots and cowboy hats with the brims cut off on facing sides and a huge teal T-shirt that hung from their big breasts and spandex

leggings with turquoise and salmon geometric patterns. They had big turquoise rings and long orange fingernails and they were the only twofers I met who were there for philosophical reasons. D: "I'm my own person. I say, my money, my honey, my life. I gotta express my unique inner nature." D: "I feel exactly the same."

Jorge y Jorge, Argentina. Target: Jorge.

The Argentines, one a Poultry and Rabbit Inspector, one a librarian, often got into fights. They bore scars at the same spot on opposite cheeks, which Mr. Nickel told me were cigarette burns, self-inflicted. They seemed to be completely wrapped up in each other, though they bowed to the doctor when she walked by; they respected her as one respects a gun with a bullet in one chamber. "They have asked not to be told which one the doctor has chosen," said the Major.

Michiko and Chichiko, Japan. Target: Chichiko or Michiko.

Either Michiko or Chichiko had been disappointed in love, but nobody knew which. "Let's just hope Dr. O knows," said the Major. They spoke very little English, ate very big dinners, wore very elegant shoes. Once, in Exposition, one of them rose, keening, and skittered out of the room. Mr. Nickel unslung his prosthesis and dropped it in my lap. "Hold my ball and chain. We've got a runner!" He rushed after her. Roosevelt blinked up at me, working his rubber lips as if trying to speak. He was disgustingly warm. I shuddered and scooted him onto Jirtka's lap. She lifted him with one hand. "Alas, poor Yorick," I said. Both faces remained blank.

Jirtka and Lenka, formerly Czech, currently pursuing Canadian citizenship. Target: Lenka.

Jirtka was a bodybuilder. Her massive traps crowded little Lenka, who had fine sparse hair growing low on her forehead and a walleye. Jirtka prepared for a workout by strapping down Lenka's head with Ace bandages. ("You don't want *that* flopping around when you're deadlifting three hundred pounds.") You could almost mistake it for another muscle. "It was my wonderful trainer Deb who finally convinced me it was time to let her go. We

pursue total physical perfection, and let's face it, Lenka is a flaw, from a competitive standpoint." Mr. Graham was visibly afraid of Jirtka, who knocked off blocks with such zest she had dented Reg's athletic cup.

Reg and Cliff, USA. Target: Cliff.

Reg was a salesman from Santa Barbara with a little, stiff, fawn-colored brush of hair, a red face, and thick rounded shoulders. He was always trying to get a look under the post-ops' bandages, and had been told off for it more than once. Everyone agreed it was a shame about gentle, confused Cliff, who had the look of an animal bound for slaughter. "Della and Donna have him on heavy rotation for pity fuck. Reg is getting the old third wheel serviced regu—"

"That's enough," I said.

I thought I might have better luck with the post-ops, but the minute I got up the nerve to approach a group of them, something always happened. They simultaneously remembered a sudden errand, or Mr. Nickel chirped "Ting-a-ling-a-ling! Person class is starting!" or the Major oozed up, snuffling adenoidally, and scared them away with an almost inaudible comment: "Your stump, madam, drives me simply wild." Sometimes he let fall these utterances on purpose, I think, and then affected confusion if the addressee took offense; other times I was sure they were involuntary. Once I saw him accost an attractive older woman in the Post-Op Lounge. To prevent staining her blouse, she had augmented her bandages with an adhesive sanitary pad. Softly and clearly, he said, "Wet nappy." Then, I am sad to say, he took possession of the lady's pad and went on a tear, clutching it to his crotch with both hands and leaping with surprising agility over the communal couch and its small side tables, dodging left around M'mselles Foucault, and escaping down the hall, where a group of moist towel-kilted post-ops emerging from the steam room at the end of the hall sized up the situation and cornered him against the drinks machine. He slid to the floor and attempted to put the pad up the change slot.

When I next passed the Post-Op Lounge a sign had gone up: a silhouette of a twofer, red slash across it. It was just making explicit what I had already figured out: pre-ops and post-ops did not mix. I no longer cared. The dream of finding my own kind: wasn't that just the old herd instinct? If *my* herd would be composed of solipsists, that only made me more pathetic. Was I

a lost sheep, or a lone wolf? Wolf, I told myself. Singular or plural, I do not like my fellow man. When offered the famous optical illusion, "urn or faces," I opt for the urn, which I take to contain the ashes of a general cremation.

Mildew advanced across my wall, a slow white wave. Luis and Porky disappeared. Jirtka and Lenka disappeared. Mr. Nickel asked me to call him Oral ("It's not my name, I just like to hear you say it"), and I conceived a profound dislike for the Expositor.

Mr. Graham: "Twofers virtually control American government at this point."

Nora: "Excuse me? There isn't a single elected official in Washington who's a twofer. The constitution doesn't even acknowledge our existence."

"Listen to what you just said. Con-sti-TWO-tion."

"Yankee TWOdle!" Mr. Nickel said, whether in mockery or agreement I couldn't tell. "Yankee Doodle keep it up," Roosevelt sang.

"The self is not a toy. If you fool around with it, someone's going to get hurt," Mr. Graham said, laying a cool eye on Mr. Nickel.

My punishment for fomenting non-unity: Thirty reps of "There Ain't Room in This Town for the Both of Us."

There was something that separated pre- and post-ops besides rules, and the natural desire for the post-ops to disassociate themselves from the anatomies they had left behind. The newly single went through a certain ritual that, it was agreed, was "something else" and "more genuinely spiritual than I had really expected," and this too set them apart, since they were not supposed to talk about it, though at times it seemed like they did nothing but talk about it: the surprisingly lightweight chalice (aluminum?), the repetitious chants ("One times one divided by one to the power of one equals one"), the corny "wand" or "scepter" or "club" the doctor wielded, the fur of some nameless animal draped over the squatting initiate and then pulled off to the slow thunder effect of a big piece of sheet metal shaken by those who had undergone the ceremony before, the "rain" of red wine invoking the bloody spurts of the operating room in an exquisitely gauged ritual repetition, honoring the violence of the event but elevating it into the realm of symbol. We heard all about this ostensibly secret ceremony. Nonetheless we felt that its essence remained genuinely hidden from us no matter how much we heard, perhaps more hidden the more we heard, and that therefore the post-ops were not

wrong to ignore the prohibitions against gossip and tell all, because in fact they told us nothing at all in telling us so much about the ritual.

Dr. Ozka kept to herself. Probably if she had not, we would have shunned her anyway, like the village executioner. She ate alone, and sometimes pulled a black hood over her head. At other times she wore a lady's suit with heavy jewelry or a white coat dappled with faint stains. She was predatory and implacable, like a colossal beak. There was something of the death's-head in her wedge-shaped bony visage and something of the sickle in the staff she carried, with its crooked head. No, she was not lame. The staff was an affectation, a sign of office. Because of it we heard her before we saw her: tap, tap, tap, like a deathwatch beetle. So in the end we did not see her at all; at least, I know I dropped my eyes and edged by her as if the corridors were not wide enough for two to pass, and I had seen others do the same. So none of us knew exactly what she looked like. We were discouraged from speaking to her, but we would not have done so in any event; she was set apart by invisible plumes and epaulets. She was a totem, a kachina doll. One does not speak to a god or to the representative of a god when it is filled with the spirit. Nor does one besmirch it with representations or opinions drafted by a mortal congress; nonetheless we had our ideas about her, and we would not have liked to have them contravened by an unseemly action on her part. A girlish laugh would not have been well received. Nor would it have delighted us to see her yellow teeth bared in a grin. So we held her, secretly, to a kind of code, and in this sense she was our creation. She was right to employ an Expositor to draw our hatred and scorn.

Mr. Graham: "Personhood is an expert practice. It can be taught. Frankly it's appalling that rank amateurs are allowed to go around saying 'I' with no more idea what that means than a dog does. They ought to be laughed out of the business. Say you want a piece of art appraised. Is it authentic. Is it a forgery. What do you do, you go to a qualified professional. You want to know who you are? Come to me. *I'll* tell you who you are."

One day I skipped out of Binary Logic and went looking for another way out. I had noticed that the Post-Op Lounge was nearly empty after lunch, and the memory of seeing them cocooned in rugs on the lawn came back to me.

There was one door in the hall I'd never seen open, and I tried it. A flight of stairs led down. Though down was almost certainly the wrong direction, I went to see what I could find. A single door led to a cavernous room tra-

versed by dripping undulant pipes and lit only by the glow from the closed hatch of an enormous furnace. The air was hot and steamy and rank. As my eyes adjusted to the darkness, I saw that I was not alone. Warming himself in front of the furnace was a post-op in a wheelchair, nodding his head. He was mumbling to himself. I crept closer. “I, I, I,” he was saying. He was petting something he held in his lap.

Suddenly, his chair spun to face me. “I,” he remarked, and began wheeling slowly toward me. I backed up. What *was* that in his lap? Something I did not want to examine too closely. “I, I, I,” he said, growing agitated. “I, I!”

I turned, slipped in what I hoped was water, scrambled to my feet, and ran. The door I had come through was now locked. The wheelchair squeaked closer. I fumbled around the door, seeking some sort of catch. I am not sure, but it might have been Blanche who found the key, dangling out of wheelchair reach in the shadows beside the door. At times, we can still agree on a course of action. I dropped the key on the other side of the door and took the stairs in huge leaps, as if I were still being followed.

I considered giving up after that distasteful event, but on the way back to my room I peeked in a door labelled MECHANICAL. It was a utilities closet, but below the circuit box a louvered metal panel stood partway open, and the space behind it appeared too large for a mere air vent. As I drew close, I kicked something metal—an old dinner knife—that rang sharply against a water heater, and thought I heard something from behind the panel. I fled back to my room.

I waited until the quiet half hour before the evening assembly to go back. The panel was closed now, and flush to the wall. I stuck my fingertips in the louvers and pulled. Wished I had something flat, a coat hanger or—a dinner knife! From the scars on it, I saw it had been used that way many times before. The hinges squawked as if they might break. I stepped through into a short, sloping tunnel. After I let the panel close behind me, the only light came through the louvers, but that was enough to see me to the hatch at the other end, a round metal shield with a wheel instead of a knob. I spun it, and the door sprung open on its own, with a hiss of hydraulics—fortunate, because it was over a foot thick. Grass grew on its outside. I stepped out and gave the door an experimental nudge. It sealed behind me, and I could no longer even find any seam. The hill might have been a fairy knoll in a story: feasts and dancing on the inside, but outside, just the blue-shadowed grass shivering in the sooty evening breeze.

I was on the steep back slope of the hill, under the naked sky, tinged with salmon and apricot to the west, gibbous moon rising over the apartment buildings to the east. For the ground-floor tenants it was already night, but a cat still slept in the sun on a top-floor balcony. The hilltop too must be in sunlight. I broke into a run, slipping on the grass, Blanche knocking against my ear. For one moment at least I would have my idyll.

The sun beset me like a fever, cold and hot at once. Shivering and red-blind, I wrestled with one of the lawn chairs I had admired in the brochure, a complicated and unwelcoming construction that yielded to overtures with cries of outrage. When I had finally subdued it, as I thought, it spilled me on the lawn. Judging by the brochure, that lawn should have been a luxuriant pelt, practically purring with health, but it was shorn, scratchy, and foxed with the piss-burns of the dogs that got in through the many broken spurs of the fence. The chair lay beside me looking impossibly broken and wrong, like an umbrella turned inside out, yet smug at the same time. I closed my eyes. Still. Still.

Someone wiggled expertly into the chair on the other side of me. "How nice to share a contemplative moment!" Mr. Nickel purred. "How did you persuade Nurse Dirndle to let you out?"

"What do you mean?" I sat up.

"Mr. Graham would prefer that all pre-ops remain in their quarters."

My lip curled delicately at his name. "I've gathered that."

"How shall I put this? I'm afraid Mr. Graham insists."

"Are you saying I'm a prisoner?"

"Prisoner. That's such a strong word. But Mr. Graham does consider every pre-op a security risk. There's always the chance that the target twin will cut and run. Of course *post*-ops are allowed to leave, after a period of debriefing of course. They've shown their colors, paid their dues, kicked their bucket. You too will be allowed to come and go after surgery."

"In other words, only one of us gets out of here alive."

"You have such a dramatic way with words! I could listen to you for hours. But it's time for the Exposition. Shall we?"

THE SIAMESE TWIN REFERENCE MANUAL

Dirty Words

"Ra-di-o-ac-tive!" Circles formed around us on the playground. We ducked our heads and stared at the ground, praying for the bell.

"What are you?" someone would ask. "I'm not messing with you, I really want to know." They waited until we attempted an answer. Then they shrieked with laughter.

"Why do you have so many cooties?"

We had one secret defense: Donkey-skin's bad words. When we were being teased, I said them over to myself like a charm. What we were being called was nothing compared to the words in my mind.

Sometimes one of them slipped out. "Oooh," moaned our tormentors, as if in ecstasy, and everyone would step back as if they feared contamination. Sometimes one of the girls would run to the teacher and whisper the word into her ear. Then the teacher would tell the principal, and the principal would call Mama.

"Where on earth did you learn that word? The woman actually dared to imply that we used that kind of language at home! As if I didn't have enough trouble keeping my name clean in that town." Mama threatened to wash our mouths out with soap. "Once I figure out which of you said it. Nora?"

She always asked me first. "Not me!"

"Blanche?"

Wise Blanche kept mum.

Could you really wash away words with soap?

* * *

Gradually, something changed. The other kids decided that we were not one, but two girls. One had cooties, but the other was all right. They shared their lunch with Blanche—bartered chocolate pudding cup for fruit leather, peanut butter crackers for devil-dog—while I ate chopped olives. Once I tried to swap for a bag of raisins.

"Gross. Nobody wants to touch *your* food, Nora. Get a clue." Blanche rolled her eyes apologetically at me and took another bite of Twinkie.

The others discovered that Blanche could draw, unlike me. "Why are you erasing that? That was good! Do one for me?" they wheedled. Blanche discovered she could draw, something I had been keeping from her, and that drawing was currency. She made sketches on command. One girl wanted a kitten with huge eyes and a bow around its neck, then all the girls wanted one, and for the teacher she did sensitive watercolor landscapes that were pinned up on the burlap-covered walls.

She waxed conversant. She learned the secrets of Secret and Stri-Dex and Nair. One day she amazed me by discussing the relative merits of two TV shows we'd never watched—*Three's Company*, about a sexy twofer and her male roommate, and *Mork & Mindy*: a dark comedy, in which one half of a two-headed alien falls under the delusion that he is a simple American girl. "We don't even have a TV, Blanche," I said cruelly. Whereupon they teased me about that. Blanche, somehow, was exempt. I hadn't even known there were twofers on TV.

I grew sullen. Studied never. Cheated on tests by ignoring them: Blanche did them for me, out of pity, the sucker. I was no good at math: 5, 4, 3, 2, 1, that was counting to me. Division was confusing: does the atom split in half or in two? Grammar: plurals take an *s*, unless they don't; then they still seem like one thing, but a thing with a secret. I learned to never split the infinitive. I learned about the double negative, and that two wrongs don't make a right. At Christmas we made paper snowflakes and stencils, and I learned that things are shaped by what has been taken from them.

We went to the school play and saw a pantomime horse. It sagged in the middle, and when at last its two halves staggered apart Blanche screamed. But I was the one they teased about it afterward.

"Blanche, draw me a kitty-cat. Can you do a polka dot bow?"

"I can do any kind of bow." The bow was customized, but the cat was always the same. I knew its mad blank eyes, triangle nose, double fishhook

mouth, and six whiskers like I knew the squeak of the marker and its chemical perfume. I had unriddled the sequence of tiny tugs and tightenings in her hand. But I still couldn't draw it myself. I couldn't match its almost abstract scallops and S-curves, the thick even outlines. My cats were sketchy specters, elongated or aslant. El Greco cats, not Garfields. The outline wavered, failed to close; it looked emptied, a cat skin with no cat in it.

"What color polka dots?"

"Pink. No, red. No, pink."

Dots I understood, dots I could do. I took over. Dot. Dot. Then the pen slipped in my hand and scored a pink slash down the page.

Some mistakes you can't erase. Blanche blew a puff of air through her nose and kept her head bent for a minute. Then she turned the pages of her notebook, one, two, past the freckles of bled-through marker ink, and started over.

The girl *tsk*'d. "Nora. I know that was you," she said. "Just stay *out* of it. Nobody wants you."

I couldn't wait to get back to Donkey-skin.

The *Two Times* Editorial

"Justice Undone"

As a glance over today's headlines confirms, the problem of justice burlesqued by Mark Twain is still a problem today. (Pudd'nhead Wilson: "'Are you sure—and please remember you are on oath—are you perfectly sure you saw both of them kick him, or only one? Now be careful.' A bewildered look began to spread itself over the witness's face.") His judge's statement, "We cannot convict both, for only one is guilty. We cannot acquit both, for only one is innocent," remains the most succinct formulation of the problem. Everyone remembers the laconic testimony of the cop who fingered the Laidhole brothers for the "Miniature Golf Murders" back in the seventies, but threw up his hands at picking the culprit: "Same fingerprints, judge." Neither confessed, both were set free. What else could a just state do?

Even when the state knows whodunnit, it is difficult to come up with a punishment that targets only the guilty party. Early in the twofer boom, many states had enthusiastic recourse to the notorious MSCC or "mobile solitary confinement cell" (known to prisoners as "The Iron Mask") that locks over the guilty one of a pair, but these are not much used anymore, since the prisoner, terrified and half-deranged from suffering long deprivation of the use of those senses as have their seat in the head, often seizes control of their body, and runs amok, as in the famous case in Basket, Utah.

COMMENTS? PLEASE JOIN OUR ONLINE FORUM AT WWW.TWO-DUNNIT.COM.

Exposition

Porky reappeared, in bandages. We watched him strut up to the post-op row. "He won't be calling for the Sad Sack now," said the Major, envious. "He's won the jackpot. You watch, he won't give us the time of day."

Jirtka, too, came back, still big, but softer now. She looked more like a real singleton than any of the other post-ops, but something was wrong. She moved like a cloud, not a giant. Her eyes were often red; her hands trembled. "In the idiom of those who pump iron," Mr. Graham said, "'no pain, no gain!'"

Shortly thereafter, the Major disappeared. When he rejoined us, paler and thinner, the turbaned goiter was conspicuously absent. He now affected a succession of filmy scarves (a color for each day of the week: pistachio, raspberry, cream, blueberry, lemon, lavender, cherry) knotted over his stump, which by very particular request, as I happened to know, had not been cut flush but jutted several inches from his dashing open collars, in such a way that its contours could be faintly made out through the sheer fabric.

"Just look at that gorgeous pink *thing*. Would you squuzzle that puppy on the back of my hand, just once?" "Shh, the Expositor's coming." Louder: "Oh, darling, you're so self-identical, you're positively monadic! Way to activate your full human potential! Life sure is an extraordinary gift, and each of us has a unique and special destiny!"

One morning at breakfast Mr. Nickel was reading an English paper, several days old and grease-stained from other breakfasts. On the front page

was a prominent photo captioned, "Activist straps self to head slated for removal." The activist was an older woman, bare-shouldered under a vest covered with political buttons. She was roped to a pretty pair of blondes, their eyes hidden behind two black rectangles. Without the rope and the rectangles she would have looked like a mother with her daughters. In fact, she would have looked like . . . *Mama?*

Mr. Nickel was eyeing me over the paper. He folded it deliberately, front page in, and tucked it under his arm, smiling fondly and, I thought, reprovingly at me. Mr. Nickel wore a ring bearing a knob of amber with an insect inside it. I felt like that insect.

Mr. Graham, exhortatory: "The first person pronoun is your birthright. You've been robbed! Who robbed you?"

Dramatic pause. Some muttering.

"Nurse Hrdle!" yelled Sparky. Laughter.

Mr. Graham quelled the crowd with his cold blue eye. "You might say your parents' bad genes, or your various government's reckless tampering with the deep structures of matter, but the real culprit is bad grammar. What is a twofer but a run-on sentence? The word 'and' has destroyed more lives than VD. Actually, it *is* a venereal disease, a disease of improper sharing." Mr. Graham produced a handkerchief and dabbed his wet lips. "I . . . *hate* . . . indefinition—personal, moral, philosophical, or grammatical. The true individual is solitary, unique, and pure. *I* am solitary, unique, and pure"—he tensed his pecs before he pounded them—"and you can be too. Every day the scalpel does not flash is a day of victory for the *swarm*. My dream"—his eyes swept the assembly—"and of course Dr. O's: we line up all those mushies living in *Sin* Francisco and other hives of the puerile plural and purify them. Right down to the neck bone!"

I found myself on my feet. "That's completely inappropriate!"

"Oo-ops, I smell tolerance! Are you feeling divided, my dears?" He zuzzed the plural, and everyone laughed. "Now, let them speak." More laughter.

"I *personally* have chosen the first person, but I certainly don't think that choice should have been dictated to me. It might not be right for everyone."

"Ah, a relativist. The yin and the yang, eh? Let's all do the Venn mudra." He tilted his head in mockery as with the thumb and index fingers of both hands he formed two overlapping circles, baby fingers crooked.

"Do you really think you can make an army of monadists? Cut off the

dissident half, get the remainder to think and talk exactly alike? How is *that* solitary, unique, and pure? Isn't that 'subsuming differences in a larger whole'? I smell *Togetherist*." Donna was tugging at my shirt. I slapped her hand away, and my voice rose. "Besides, you're fucking crazy if you think this place is a monastery of your pure grammar. Monastery of *lip* service, maybe. Look around you! Half the twofers in this room are stump worshippers or extreme sadomasochists! The rest just fucking *hate* their other half and are ready to salute any flag that sanctions murder!"

"And which are you?" he said, his face ugly.

"Who *are* you anyway? Who made you Expositor? What is an Expositor? How do we know you speak for Dr. Ozka? We don't know a thing about her! Maybe she's a psychopath. Maybe some twofer hurt her feelings and she's on a personal vendetta! What difference does it make? Cut the crap and give us what we're here for!"

Donna finally yanked so hard I fell back into my chair.

After Exposition, I apologized to Mr. Graham. Then I went to my room, collected my bag, and walked straight to the utilities closet. When I approached the gate at the bottom of the knoll, I half expected to bloody my nose on a glass wall, but I passed right through. I turned two corners and wondered if I would ever find my way back to the clinic. I wondered if I would even try.

The city was uniformly grey. The air had a taint. Even the trees were dirty. There was none of the comfortable din of ribaldry, illegal commerce, and madness I knew from home. People forced into proximity to one another stared at the ground. I sat for a while in a chilly, barren park, reading a local paper I found on the bench. It didn't feel real. The paper was too thin, too smooth, too limp; the pages did not rustle when they were turned, but weakly subsided, perhaps because they were damp with some medium in the ink with which they were impregnated, and which came off in greasy engine-oil streaks on our hands and smelled like chemistry. The money too was wrong, the bills the wrong size; the coins weighed too little and shaken together made a dull rattle, not a jingle. It was toy money. It was a toy city, but not a very fun toy. Everything kept still, in a frozen, resentful way, as if trying not to breathe the blue air. Those objects that creaked into motion—a baby carriage with tiny metal wheels, an old bike, a battered metal dustpan

at the end of a stick, scraping along the cobblestones behind a broom that had lost so many straws it was more like a club—called out in pain to one another across the empty streets.

I spotted an Internet café and looked around quickly before I went in. Amid a slew of junk mail were two bona fide letters.

How's my favorite southpaw? I bet you didn't think "Relational Couture" would ever amount to anything. Guess again, sucker!!! I started out making conjoined coats for dogs and their owners, but the cleaning bills fucked me. Plus when you went into stores you had to leave your designer coat tied to a parking meter. But now, I'm knitting these sweaters with extra sleeves and necks, they accommodate two to four people. I'm selling these two-party T-shirts . . . Community Development just awarded me a grant to design a lightweight but warm windbreaker for a crowd of 15 to 35 people. Audrey actually called me a "qualified success"!!! I made her a sweater she wears even when she's by herself, the extra sleeves just hanging, which is fine. I'm calling the line NB, which everyone thinks is for Nota Bene, but it's really because, you know, it was you and Blanche who first started me wondering what it was like to have company all the time. Even under your clothes.

Later gator, Trey

No

After you left a Hysteria Harness switched on all by itself and started whizzing around the living room. I had to throw a blanket over it to stop it.

Lo

That was all? Was that supposed to have a double meaning? Did I want it to? My throat ached, and I squeaked my thanks to the man who took my couple of coins. I strode fast and pretended I was going somewhere. I had put on a bulky coat, and with the hood up I felt anonymous—an odd figure still, but not the odd figure I really was. Once I had the feeling I was being followed, and I turned and walked the other way for a block, looking closely at everyone I passed: an American boy with a beard and a backpack, a silver-haired man with an unnaturally even tan and a gold watch, and one or two others I have forgotten, but no one seemed to pay me any special attention, and the feeling did not return. Not, at least, until I looked up at the sound of a whistle and saw my taxi driver jouncing along beside me over the cobblestones, elbow poking out of the window of the cab, one hand lazily draped over the wheel.

THE SIAMESE TWIN REFERENCE MANUAL

Introducing a new line of romantic fiction for the conjoined twin:

à Deux

Romance for the two of you.

Double Dare

Bronwyn and Gennifer Thorne

Joyce and Regina were as different as night and day. Joyce was fragile as a lily, Regina a luscious cactus rose. They fought like wildcats over most things, but on one point they agreed: they both desired Jude Rainfeather, the handsome half-Apache horse-wrangler whose pride was fiercer than the Nevada sun. Jude never threw a glance in their direction, but underneath his flinty exterior raged a torrent of desire for the contrary beauties. When outlaws set fire to their uncle's ranch, he pulled the pampered pair onto his stallion and swept them away to his own rough bed. After a night of unbridled passion, he felt an unfamiliar sensation stirring in his breast. Could it be love? And with a dark secret smoldering in his past, could he risk letting a woman—or women—into his heart?

THE LIBRARIAN'S ASSISTANT

Blanche's new friends avoided Chris Marchpane, so she did too, averting her eyes with her new see-no-evil. So I sought him out to spite her. "Let's sit with Rebecca," said Blanche, so I took our lunch to the bench where Chris sat by himself, and he and I swapped cookies that looked and tasted just like cookies but were the coin of Sadness, dark and foully sweet. I bumped her into him by the lockers, forcing her forehead against his chest in front of everyone, as she went white with decency. If I could not be cured of cooties, I would spread them, suck them, soak them up.

Now I had another reason to go to the library. I would sleek in slow enough to raise Chris Marchpane's eyes. He'd push his shelving cart around after us. Around and around, until I got bored with what didn't happen and left.

One day, waiting for Max to pick us up, we wandered around the back of the library and sat down on a scalding metal step. I picked up a stubbed-out cigarette and pretended to smoke it, squinting at my hand as I knocked off a nonexistent ash. The door shrieked, the stairs shook, and we jumped up. Chris Marchpane thumped past us with a metal trashcan and shook a flurry of dancing pages into the Dumpster. On the way back he stopped, put down the trashcan, fumbled in his shorts, and brought out a pink cigarette lighter. He thumbed it a few times before it sparked. I noticed his torn cuticles.

I couldn't get the cigarette to light. I had never actually smoked one. He took it from me and lit it in his own mouth.

He held out the cigarette. "You don't smoke," said worried Blanche.

I backed up against the wall and pulled aside the crotch of my stretchy shorts, exposing the blue flowerets on my underwear. Chris Marchpane dropped the cigarette and squatted. He slid a finger under the elastic. Surprise arced through my stomach. I felt his fingernail jab me and thought about his ragged cuticles and watched his eyes. The pupil would wander slightly and then twitch back, always to the same spot: what Tiffany would call "my oyster, my shyster, my cloister, my fever blister" in an expansive mood, "my cut peach" in an arcadian, "my loophole" in a cryptic, "my hellhole" in a sacrilegious one, but most often "my cunt" or "my tight cunt," because nothing gets the job done like the direct approach. Donkey-skin had taught me that word, and that's what I thought now: Cunt, as he moved his head and the sun fell directly on it. I felt myself shrink, then loosen. I felt Chris Marchpane's finger part fold from fold and locate a passage I hadn't found for myself yet and come smoothly up it. His mouth was a little open. His hand moved, and we swayed with it. I was a finger puppet. Then the librarian called and he unplugged, breaking the vacuum with a sudden suck, and ran inside, carrying the trashcan in front of him. I found the cigarette and stubbed it out, then pocketed it for Donkey-skin.

We passed an ordinary week. Blanche and I did not talk about Chris Marchpane. Next time I walked straight to the shelf of new arrivals, grabbed one at random, and brought it up to the desk. (It was a slim book from a regional press with a droll sketch on the cover—a strangely proportioned burro cocking its head at a sunflower.) The book was stamped, smacked shut, and slid back fast enough for me to catch, from the glass box between the two sets of doors, the back of our departing car swinging out around the turn. We pushed open the front door and went out. The heat socked me in the stomach.

I walked quickly toward the rear of the building. Blanche was dragging her feet, and I tripped over the curb at the end of the parking lot and landed hard on one hand. I picked a thorn out of the base of my thumb and coaxed from the puncture a single red tear I licked up. Then I clanked up the metal stairs and pressed myself against the door, peering through the grid in the reinforced glass. The door scorched my knees, hips, elbows. I saw a shadow swimming up to the glass, turned away, and started down the stairs, trailing my hand along the rail. I heard the door open.

I led him behind the Dumpster without looking back. There I turned, backed up, stumbled on a clump of weeds, sat down. Then I lay back on the

asphalt and spread my legs, pulling my panties aside. Chris got down on his knees and grappled with his zipper.

Then he fell on top of me. His hands were fumbling between us, arranging things. I felt something dry and smooth poking against my thigh, sliding off, and poking again. Blanche made a fierce attempt to roll out from under him. I laughed spitefully and raised my knees up, against her resistance, and pulled Chris Marchpane into a better place.

His neck reddened and strained above me. Then he dropped his head between ours and collapsed. I lay under him, staring up at the sky, which was swarming everywhere with luminous specks, like pond water under a microscope, absolutely fabulous with cooties. There was a slithering and collapsing somewhere below. It felt like I had wet my pants. After a while, Chris heaved himself up on one elbow. I craned my neck to look at him, and got an unpleasant surprise: he was kissing *Blanche,* puckering his mouth like a kid. And she was letting him.

I threw him off me with a heave of my hips, and he struck the Dumpster with his head, *kaboom*. He sat up, knees bent, and hiccupped with sobs, the wet pinkie wrinkling out of his fly pulsing with his breaths. "Stop it, please stop it," said Blanche. "Nora, make him stop!"

I hissed at her. "Shut up, you stupid clut—*slut*—whore!"

"What? What did I do?" She shuddered into tears.

"What a couple of crybabies!"

"Why are you so awful?"

Because I had hoped to humiliate her, and had failed. And because humiliating her was only a front. I had wanted him—sad Chris, angel Chris—for myself.

"You made me fuck the mutant. Do you think I wanted to do that? That's . . . abuse, Blanche. That's practically rape."

Her dismay was gratifying, but when she apologized, I was angry again. What did it mean to say sorry? It meant, *I have the power to hurt you.* No!

I couldn't look at the library book we finally took home. It was a collection of cowboy songs, and Blanche got Granny to pick out the melodies on the piano so she could learn them. Every time she wailed, "Ghost riders in the sky," I felt warm asphalt against my ass, saw Chris Marchpane's face frowning down.

Pre-Op

Reader, I fucked him.

So the evidence would suggest, anyway. I was in an unfamiliar bed, naked except for something torqued around my waist that turned out to be my bra, and with an unclutched feeling between my legs. I did not know where I was. I did not remember getting out of the taxi, though I remembered getting in. I looked sideways at Blanche, who wore what appeared to be a smile.

I hit her, using her own right hand. It was clumsily done and lacked power, like a blow struck in a dream. Her head knocked against me with almost as much force as my blow. I felt the impact from both sides. My nose prickled and my eyes filled.

I swung my legs over the side of the bed and slumped there, half-enjoying the fullness and the brimming. Then I heard kitchen sounds close at hand. I got up to look for my clothes. They were strewn around the room, and I put them on one piece at a time as I found them, hopping and hunched, uncomfortably aware of my swinging breasts and the chill between my legs.

I straightened and glimpsed in the mirror the red handprint on Blanche's cheek. I felt—why not?—guilty. People are not logical, we can sprinkle poison in our garden, and still step over the snail we meet on the path. But guilt did not temper my anger. If anything, it stoked it. I went into the kitchen. When I saw him, though, I forgot what I was going to say. His shoulder blades moving under a thin T-shirt to which a few flakes of an ancient logo clung, the freckles on his bent neck, made me feel something like shyness. But then I felt myself unseal and seep.

Donkey-skin's words were still, sometimes, the only words I needed.

He whipped round and gaped.

"How dare you!" I said. "I had blacked out. I wasn't myself. How could you sleep with someone in that state? That's practically necrophilia. And you just stand there making coffee, as if—you probably only fixed one cup!"

He started to say something, but I checked him with a look. I pulled my coat on with a whirling and flapping that went on a bit too long when my hand got lost in the soft labyrinth of the sleeve, and then I backhanded the cup he now held out toward me as if to offer me precisely this opportunity. The coffee leapt like a liquid animal across the table, and I left.

Nurse Hrdle met me with a stern face, and made a phone call before raising the carpet for me. Mr. Nickel was waiting for me at the bottom of the stairs. I readied some apologetic phrases, but instead of the diatribe I expected, he handed me an envelope. I opened it, wondering greatly.

I was invited to see Dr. Ozka.

Mr. Nickel had been jiggling with excitement while I read, and now he yanked at my arm. "Come on, come on! You've just got time to get cleaned up. Put on a nice blouse, she's a little old-fashioned."

"What . . . What should I say?" I was bewildered. Why was this happening now?

"Tell her you seek spiritual unity. Say you feel ripped in half by irreconcilable urges, say you believe you were born one but your original unity has had the proverbial monkey wrench stuck in it. Say you dream of a single, pulsating sphere humming in harmony with other, nearby spheres and an inexpressible feeling of well-being fills your soul. Then a jagged stroke of lightning splits the original sphere and the universe fills with discord and the sad cheeping of birds and children and all the neighboring spheres hurtle away in all directions and everything is loss, loss, anguish and loss!"

Twenty minutes later Mr. Nickel sped me up the stairs with a gratuitous pat on the bottom and Nurse Hrdle directed me through the big wooden door off the foyer into a low-ceilinged waiting room with peeling walls and the inevitable tang of mildew on the air. I took note of an origami swan composed of hundreds of pieces of paper. Moose antlers mounted on plastic. *Terminologia Medica Polyglotta. The Merck Index,* seventh edition. *Abdominal and Genito-Urinary Injuries,* 1971. (Troubling that the reference books were all decades old.) *Ein Jagerparadis*. Titles in Cyrillic. A little geisha in a glass box. A papier-mâché model of St. Petersburg's onion-domed Church of

Our Savior on Spilled Blood. A bulletin board on which a profusion of flyers gently billowed in mysterious air currents.

The door opened, and Dr. Ozka came in, carrying a manila folder. "Am I speaking to Blanche or Nora?" she said.

"Nora," I said. Hadn't she even read my file?

The door of her office crunched shut behind me, and I stood in the waiting room beside the origami swan. I was in a state of high confusion. I scratched an itch on the saddle between our necks with the defanged tip of a ballpoint pen. Then I pulled a pink page off its pin, turned it over against the windowsill, and wrote down everything I could remember about Dr. Ozka: the out-of-date glasses, the up-to-date lipstick, the tiny rhinestone brooch in the shape of a camera that she wore in her slightly too frilly blouse. I wrote, Dr. Goat is a bony, lanky woman with a narrow forehead and strange, almost yellow eyes. There is something wrong with the pupils. She stands on her hind legs and adjusts her glasses with a weird two-fingered gesture while she holds an X-ray up to the light. Then she lets the glasses drop on their beaded string. They bounce on her narrow, protuberant chest, over which her lab coat is buttoned tight.

Then I crossed everything out, making each word unreadable by writing a succession of other words on top of it. Then, for good measure, I threw the page away.

That night I went to the club room for the first time. The post-ops strutted around, heads high, stumps jutting. I saw the Major. Today he wore a raspberry-colored scarf around his stump. He had hooked up with a vaguely attractive post-op with a limp.

I caught a glimpse of Mr. Nickel coming toward me. I ducked into the post-op ladies' room. A post-op was leaning into the mirror, platinum hair sweeping smooth sepia shoulders, applying a coat of cherry lip gloss, first to her already painted lips, then to the top of her stump.

"Want some?" she said, then saw me. "Oh." Paying no more attention to me, she took out a small compact and a brush and began to accent the rise of the stump with shading.

"Rubia?"

Her brush stopped for a moment. Then she went on daubing. "Morena. I dyed my hair."

"But I thought you were so—"

"Together?" she drawled. "Well, surprise, surprise." She drew her lips back, scraped a chip of red off a canine with a long nail. "Rubia wanted to be a scenester, I wanted the absolute. A seizure of brunette, without reference to its negative. Brunette not because blonde, but just brunette, and then, if possible, brunetter. I drew the short straw. Any suggestion that I peeked will be referred to my cousin, Chuco Charlie. Questions?"

"But you're *blond*."

An older woman came out of the stall adjusting a frilly cap over her stump. "Honey, there's a twofer bathroom down the hall. You might feel more comfortable there," she said firmly, looking at Blanche. I got out of there.

"There you are!" said the Major. "Want a drink?" He leaned toward me, his arm draped heavily over his lady's shoulders, drumming his fingers possessively on her stump.

Della and Donna had brought a book that determined what animal you were, spiritually. Confusingly, it turned out everyone was a combination. "Della is a shrew weasel zebra," Donna said enthusiastically. "What's crazy is, I'm a beaver spider antelope!"

I burrowed toward the snack table. "There's some shrimp cocktail and crudités left," Mr. Nickel said, putting his arm through mine. "Also some of these English munchables that taste like musty balls. Pardon my French. Oh for some Pringles!"

"What kind of a pickup line is 'Are you a boy or a girl or both'?" I heard.

"I don't mean to be crude, but since I came here my doody is more buoyant. Has anyone had a similar experience?"

Someone pushed past me. "I need to feed my insatiable prairie dog lizard monkey appetite."

"I listened obsessively to this Burl Ives record growing up. One song asked the question, 'What kind of an animal are you?'"

"Of course I said 'D, none of the above.'"

"It just spins around and around and won't go down."

"The Major is a hyena turtle owl."

"Can I be three cocktail shrimps and a baby carrot?"

"I mean, do we really have the option of not believing in the self?"

"And it triumphantly ends, 'I'm your shadow I'm no animal at all!' Which I think kind of dodges the issue."

"Va-va-voom!" declared Mr. Nickel. A woman with an undistinguished body had begun an above-the-neck striptease, baring an extraordinarily beautiful face, and finally, with many taunting twitches, gathered away the veil from an unusually long stump, around which a garter was fastened. There was a collective intake of breath as she slid one finger under the garter and plucked it off. The provoking ellipsoid swung for a second from her finger. Then she fired it like a rubber band into the crowd. It skimmed the dingy ceiling, shape-changing. Unconsciously I raised my hands with all the others. *Sooee!* Mr. Nickel was making pig calls to the garter to summon it to him. Little Misses Fuss and Bother behind me were already crowing victory when I reached up and took it out of the air.

"Here now, why don't you let me have that," said Mr. Nickel, and for a second we tussled, as he tried to force my fingers open, and I bumped against his chest and smelled his breath. Then the lady was there. I looked at Mr. Nickel. He winked and mimed waltzing with his arms bracketing air, then gave me the thumbs-up.

I remembered waltzing, swinging around the oil-blackened dance floor of Granny's garage in her arms, feeling the bones moving under the loose dry skin, my face pressed against, was it the real bosom or the fake one, enveloped in the good smell of sweat and birdseed. I was no good at following, I thought too hard about it, and took steps to keep my balance that nearly knocked us over. It was better to let Blanche take over; following came naturally to her, for obvious reasons. These were dreamy times, waltzed by others through the shade of the garage, dreamily felt up by the soft wind sweeping up hot off the valley. When Granny's part-time mechanic was there, she played the piano and made him waltz with us. We hung on, embedded in his stomach, soberly turning and counting. The smell of sage and gasoline was strong. Outside, every object was burning from within with the borrowed heat of the sun or turning into a small substitute sun itself, cactus sun, blue towel dispenser sun, lawn chair sun, Coke can sun, saguaro sun. Inside we were orbited by the purple ghosts of all these suns, our own dim galaxy wheeling around us, burning tracks over the sagging spark-plug boxes, the fan belts hooked on nails, the keys to the tow truck hung by the door on their dirty loop of yarn, the empty oil jugs and grey rags jammed between wall supports, the heroically battered hubcap shields, skanky air filters like soiled ruffs, the jimmied Coke machine from which the quarter that lived in the change slot would sometimes elicit a can of soda.

We kept our eyes on that Coke machine, because sometimes Granny would let us have one after waltzing. We competed for the crack of the ring and the icy fizz up the nose, the first swarming gulp, almost painful. Afterward, our heads ringing with sugar and cold, we would go and stare out at the desert as if at church, sobered by what had passed through us, like we didn't know if we could measure up to the miracle of soda. It wasn't so much a drink as an event, magical from the potent cold cylinder shuddering in our hands, feeling like it might burst, to the last painful burp forcing its way back out, bringing me back to the room, people clapping, the lady who was looking not at me but at Blanche, though that was not surprising because Blanche faced her while I faced the glossy stump, to which one of her long hairs had adhered and flexed and straightened as we moved. At the end of the dance she closed her eyes and readied her lips to be kissed, in the direction of Blanche. I leaned in and claimed the kiss instead.

That night, something came tap-tapping down the hall and stopped outside my door. There was a moment of silence. Then came a *scritch scritch* on the door. I knew who it was. I opened the door and let him in.

One and a Half kept vigil with me, fingers clattering in mine like a handful of nuts. I was reminded of Miss Hickory, who lost her nut to a greedy squirrel and became one with nature. How comforting! As bedtime reading for those to be beheaded in the morning, I recommend *Miss Hickory*.

When I woke up, he was gone. Had he ever been there?

At twenty to eleven the next morning I was in pre-op, which bore an uncomfortable resemblance to the dollhouse scullery, and by eleven I was lying down and looking up at Mr. Graham, who was saying something about oneness and brandishing a manila folder that I supposed contained my file.

It is easy to think that something had to be done, and to feel fiercely and clearly what that is, when it is impossible. It is easy to imagine impossible things. I had joked, "Spare the scalpel, spoil the child." I had said, "There is nothing more bracing than murder." Lying in my hospital nappies, I felt less sure. My heart hurt. My hearts hurt! How had I become this person? Through infinitesimal steps, unimportant decisions, each reversible. I never heard the slip of tiny latches behind me, the click of locking pins. And now I was here, on this table. Half my stock of memories were about to be subtracted from me.

Half-life: the time it takes for half the atoms in a radioactive substance

to decay. The shorter the half-life, the more radioactive the substance. The half-life of uranium-235 is four hundred and fifty million years. I figure ours at twenty-nine.

The anaesthetist approached.

Dear Mademoiselle Guillotine, choose carefully. The tiger or the lady? Good balloon, bad balloon. Eenie meenie miney mo, catch a tiger by the toe, my mother said to pick the very best one and you are not it. Woodsman, spare that tree!

There was a bucket of mean aspect by the cart I was lying on, and I wondered what it was for. Spots of rust around the rim.

It got very quiet.

Was it rust?

My Twinn

Chris Marchpane had kept us from visiting Donkey-skin for over a week. Now I wanted badly to see her again. As we were walking there, we saw storm clouds gathering over the basin. Flat-bottomed and high-crowned and dark on the underside, they skated in fast on a layer of blue that lightning turned an odd pink at intervals, making something thrill mechanically in my chest, like a pinwheel catching a wind and whirring briefly into a blur.

The sky bulked up over us. The thunder seemed incongruous in the dry air. We scrambled down to the Goats' place as the rain broke over us, ran brazenly across the already soaked lawn past a lit window, and threw ourselves into the shed.

It was like being in the bell of a trumpet. The clamor was shocking. The rain hammered on the roof, and drops squeezed through and hit us from odd angles. Donkey-skin was swearing with magnificent fluency. I felt my own voice in my throat but could not hear myself. A lightning flash made every rust- and shothole in the shed a searchlight and lit Donkey-skin, striped and grinning in her cage. The thundercrack came almost immediately, like the word *now,* the bolt had struck so close. The afterimage of stripes and teeth danced in the air before my eyes. I twirled, laughing through my own chattering teeth. I almost wanted lightning to strike and split us like an atom. "Now!" Lithobolia yelled, and I with him.

Then sunlight fell in the door like a drunk. The rain was still coming down, though in slower, fatter drops. Weirdly, it still drummed fast and hard on the roof, like a sound track out of whack. Water from the roof must be

running off the eaves onto the shed. Raindrops were falling inside as well, forming on the underside of the roof where the punctures were, making a big production of detaching themselves, then plopping into the hay.

A drop fell into the angled stripe of sun. It was blood-red.

Actually, it was blood.

I looked up. "You're bleeding!"

"Fucking dipshit whore," said Donkey-skin quietly, accepting this information. A second, almost black red, drop stood next to the first. It was so thick it stood up in the dust, a little button.

"It's like when Fritzi went in heat," said Blanche, who had seen something I had not.

Fritzi, clasped by the coyote, came into my mind, to be replaced by Donkey-skin, a thought I carefully set aside for later, in my gallery of hellish sights.

"You'll need some sanitary napkins," said Blanche, who must have been talking to her new girlfriends. "It means you can have babies. You're a *woman,*" she added, with emotion I felt was put-on.

The cacophony overhead resolved itself into a steady tin drumbeat from the eaves. The rain had stopped.

"He's making a new box," Donkey-skin said.

Lithobolia grumbled in the distance.

"For me, a new box to put me in. Dirty little slut. Raggedy-ass scum-sucking white trash asswipe. Bust me out," she added, almost inaudibly.

"What?"

"Bust me out of here. Bust me out, you shitface whore tramp cum-buckets. You weak-ass shit-sticks, bust me the fuck out of here, you fucks!" She started picking hardened bits of crap off the bars and chucking them at us. "Rancid jizz fart-licking bitch dyke rim-job! Hole! Hole! Piece of shit! *Hole!*" We ran. "What about my motherfuckin' cigarette?" she yelled after us.

We burst out of the shed and across the grass, which almost squeaked as our shoes sank into it. On the side of the house we passed Mrs. Goat, who was standing looking at the rainfall meter mounted on the fence, a sun-darkened plastic receptacle with raised graduations from which the red paint was mostly worn away.

We did not acknowledge her, just jumped the fence and ran.

I forced us up the hill toward our best lookout rock. Blanche didn't want

to go. I pulled out the shoe, which was a little damp. A pill bug rolled out of the toe, hit the heel, rolled back. The shoe was little. I hurled it over the edge. It stuck on a wait-a-bit bush a short way down. I reached over with a stick and tried to dislodge it, but it was just out of reach.

"You can see it," said Blanche on the way home.

"Shut up." I looked back. She was right. It was a little white shape like a face with no features, and yet it seemed to be looking at me.

I dreamed her cage was the walnut shell out of which Donkey-skin pulls the most beautiful dress of all, the one spun out of moonlight. It unfolds and unfolds and unfolds, its damp folds unsticking. How big is it? There is a brooch pinned to the collar. She touches it, and it becomes a black beetle, which runs up her leg and fastens itself between her thighs.

I didn't want to see her ever again. She was ruined for me.

I woke up walking. The morning sun was hot on the back of my neck, sweat cold on my forehead. Pebbles crunched underfoot. There was something heavy in my underwear, a weight that almost pulled my pants down, and banged on my thighs at every step, and I was carrying something bulky (I opened my eyes): My Twinn.

"What are we doing, Blanche?" I said. She had not taken over for years. I hadn't thought she was capable of it.

"Busting her out." She was apprehensive but determined.

"Are you crazy? A grown-up put her in there. She's supposed to be there. Do you want to get in trouble?"

She didn't answer.

"All that about the princess, you know we made it up, right? She's not a princess, she's a dirty weird little creep. We don't know why she has to be in a cage! Maybe she's dangerous. Maybe she's crazy. Maybe she bites people and gives them rabies."

"I don't care. I'm going to let her out." Blanche's jaw was set.

Where had this Blanche come from? "No, I'm not!" I said. "I mean, you're not. We're not. Why are we carrying this stupid doll?" I raised my hand to pinch her ear.

She pulled her head away. "Please let me, Nora. I'll say it was my idea. I'll tell them you told me not to."

"They won't believe you. They'll blame me. They always blame me."

"Nobody will even know it was us," she said.

"You mean *you*." We walked along in silence for a minute. "What is in my panties?" I asked.

"Wire cutters."

"Whose wire cutters?"

"Max's," she said.

"You went in Max's toolbox? Are you insane?" Blanche said nothing.

Donkey-skin had her face turned away, smashed against the bars. "Excuse me," said Blanche. There was no reaction.

"Excuse me, will you bite me if I let you out?"

Donkey-skin turned her head and sneered. "You sorry-ass cunt."

Blanche waited.

Donkey-skin sighed. "No, I won't bite you."

"OK, then I'm going to do it."

My Twinn smirked from a heap of hay, one leg jutting up. The lock was too thick to cut. Donkey-skin swore. Blanche ran her fingers over the hinges. They were curled strips of sheet metal, and I could feel them give. They were thin enough to clip easily.

The door opened and dangled, jangling, from the lock, and we took a step back. Nothing happened. "You can come out now," Blanche said.

A bone-white, bone-narrow leg slowly extended from the swinging cage. I was breathing deeply and unevenly through my nose. It was like the time Papa had called us to the shed to see a damp moth unbunch and twitch itself open from its jiggling cocoon. Unseemly, somehow. Disgusting, even.

Everything was going to be different now. But everything was already different. Donkey-skin was already retreating into the distance, like the pale backside of a bunny. "You're a woman." She had already left us behind. I saw the shuddering white meats of her butt. She wore a little girl's dress, its yoke tight under her arms. If she were not so thin, it would have split across the back where it strained and the ruffle stood up stiff and incongruous, like the fan of a lizard. She slid farther and farther out of the cage, slowly, like someone letting herself down into deep water, and hung there for a moment with her head and arms still inside the cage, by themselves nearly enough to fill it. Already it seemed impossible that she had ever fit inside it.

Double Agent

After a while, I squirmed out through one nostril and wiggled up until I was hovering just under the acoustic tiles. I turned to regard my body. I noted the dotted line like a choker around Blanche's neck. Something about this scene bothered me, but I steeled myself against feeling anything but pleasure. I wanted to enjoy my temporary ghosthood. I felt giddy, aflutter. My winding cloths would have ribbons and furbelows. I flicked my tail and slipped through the grille of an air vent, between the furry vanes of a stopped fan, up a corrugated metal pipe, and out from under the conical cap.

The hill fell away below me, dotted with bushes that I understood to be people in some complicated sense I did not need to work out in my current condition. I flicked and twirled under the polished brass knob of the sun, getting to know my new body: a little twist of egg white and spooled light, with an exhilarating tickle somewhere along the length of it. I swam toward the blue zenith, but the tickle was a nagging reminder of something like a body, so I slid back. Then for a moment I was squatting on the crest of a ridge in Nevada watching two hawks, mating or fighting, reel and tumble down the sky. I raised my hand to brush a fly off my neck.

With this I felt more strongly than before that something was wrong with the scene down there: the neck, the dotted line, the disposition of the sheets, and as, drawn by this thought, I began sliding down through the pristine air toward the pipe, I noticed with some unconcerned part of me that the human bushes had scaled the hill and ganged up on the lawn and were closing in on the clinic.

But never mind that. I had figured out what was wrong: it was my old mirror problem. What *was* that tickle?

Down the chimney came the Grinch.

I pulled on my body like a sock and opened my eyes.

Blurshine.

I thought for a moment, Oh, I see, I'm swimming! The light in my eyes was the sun swinging on the broken surface of the water, and the pinkish blur was Granny in her funny flowered swim cap. I rose, blowing bubbles. I broke the surface into the familiar smell of an indoor pool: chlorine, mildew, and decay.

"Granny?" I said, or meant to say, and blinked the water out of my eyes. The chlorine made my vision blurry, the lights were ringed by great fuzzy haloes, and there was a swinging shine that was either very large or very close. I set myself to the task of focusing on the shine, and eventually it resolved itself into a blade.

I looked over at Blanche. She was a swathed mound under sheets. Why was she draped? I should be draped. She was the one who was undergoing surgery, not me. Wasn't she? I began to scream, at least I understood myself to be screaming, except that I knew I could not be screaming, because I heard nothing and nobody moved. The scalpel divided the air above my throat, showing how she would cut there and then there and then there.

Had I screamed yet?

Then the Togetherists stormed the clinic. There was a bang that I only afterward associated with the suddenly open door. There was a face, its mouth open amusingly wide. After a minute, it was gone. The door seemed to be closed again. There was a woodpecker hammering inside the walls. I understood belatedly that this was happening somewhere else in the building.

I was alone in the room. It was time to leave.

After some time I realized I had not left yet. I tried to climb off the table. In this I was unsuccessful. I could not move my legs. I could move my arms, however. So I grabbed a leg and pushed until it slid over the side. The other followed suit, more willingly. I was a tarantula locked in a wrestling match with my own limbs.

Some time later, I was still trying to get off the table. Or I had already done so, in which case I was in the corridor.

I turned the corner. In this hallway there were a lot of people running

to and fro. Some of them had one head, some had two, some three or four. I leaned on the wall for a while. How had I failed to notice what an excellent wall it was?

The corridors were strewn with hay. I was not surprised to see the interrupting cow clopping down the hall. She would be going to my room. I followed her there. She waited outside while I got my bag. Then she led the way back to the main hall.

My animals walked with me, and together we passed unharmed through the melee. It was the Happy Kingdom. All of a sudden I understood everything. Where did the lion lie down with the lamb? In the grave. So I was dead. This made sense, and I relaxed somewhat.

A struggle was going on in the stairwell. I saw the Major, squirming his way up like a salmon. I staggered past. Mr. Graham popped up and threw his arm dramatically across the utility room door.

"I'm afraid that I can't allow you to leave in this condition," he said.

"I think I prefer to leave in this confusion. Concussion. Perdition." I saw Louche down at the other end. "Louche!" I shouted. No, I remembered, Louche's face was not blue.

"I see that you're upset. You're confused. Maybe you're angry, and it's making you behave in a way that is maybe a little childish? Maybe a little unworthy of you? Not to mention that you are reneging on your signed agreement to accept the surgeon's decision, which as you see was to remove Blanche's extraneous head."

"My head. The heads, is my head, is mine."

"Yes and no. We have papers signed by your hand that cede all rights to the disputed property—"

"Proverty!"

"—viz., your head, both before and after it parts company with the body known colloquially but not in a legally binding sense as yours."

"Is a mistake, this a mistake. There's seem to has been a mistake."

At that moment my eyes blurred and I thought I saw tufts of straw poking out of the neck of his shirt, sawdust spilling out of the corner of his beak. "Peep peep," said Mr. Graham. "Our policy is that Dr. Ozka does not make mistakes. As her representative I am here to effectuate her decisions, not to engage in fruitless banter with organs slated for removal. From our point of view I am talking to a malignant tumor."

The door burst open, felling him, and some girls in war paint stormed in.

Mr. Graham zoomed after the interlopers with a highly artificial whacking of his dead wings. I went in, crawled through the vent, and outside.

I found myself in a sort of labyrinth of odd-looking bushes. Funny, those hadn't been there before. I began twisting and turning. Finally a path opened, and I reeled out onto the lawn. There was Mr. Nickel sitting gingerly on a lawn chair, his small feet propped up side by side with an annoyingly exact symmetry. He was wincing and shaking his head, the natural one, and his face was a strange flat beige.

"I am very shaken. Very shaken," he said, seeing me. "Boy oh boy. What a blow. What kind of person would lash out at someone like Roosevelt?" I saw that his prosthetic head was much dented about the hairline, and its jaw was chewing cud. "This hits me hard. Boy do I feel this as a blow at me."

"Who did it?" I said.

There was a sound coming from Roosevelt, a mutter that would not quite resolve itself into words. I thought I made out something like "Doublebind-doublebind," but that is just the sort of thing I would hear if I were hearing things.

"That bag of odoriferous wind. That stuffed shirt. That skank in skank's clothing."

"The Major?"

"Mr. Graham."

That's strange, I thought, but my thought was scotched by a distant jingle, more insistent than that *doublebinddoublebind* that troubled the hollowness that had replaced my head.

Mr. Nickel rolled up one of his pants legs in a series of neat folds, and I saw it had been folded this way before. The last turn bared the rubber and chrome haberdashery of his knee. He seized the lower portion of the leg with one hand just above his brown silk sock, the other just below the knee, and exerted his hands in different directions around the vertical axis, or what would have been the vertical axis, had he been standing. *Doublebind-doublebind.* The lower portion of the leg seemed to squeak and then turn out on its axis beyond what a leg is ordinarily adapted to do, and a hitherto invisible seam opened enough to show the threads. At approximately 270 degrees from its original position the lower portion, foot inclusive, came off entirely. Out of its end, which was hollow, slid a red bandanna and then a cell phone, which he flipped open.

"I am so shaken," he said into it. "Now listen, I am not an action hero,

I was supposed to be protected from any direct personal attack, I am really teed off about this. Yes, the strike went off beautifully. Confusion hath fuck his masterpiece, as somebody once said. Of course I'm upset, talk to Roosevelt." He held the phone to Roosevelt's mouth, from which issued a grating noise that sounded like a blender mulling over some ice cubes.

"Now what do you think of that? Well, I should think you certainly would!"

I started to move away. He followed me with his eyes.

"Got to go, I have another call to make," he said. "Later, gator." To me: "Yes, old Mr. Nickel was a double agent. You guessed? You knew? You didn't know. What a kick, huh? Oh my cloak and dagger."

"But you were the one who gave me the clyer to the flinic," I protested.

He nodded eagerly.

"Whose side are you on?"

"Both. Neither. Either. All. I'm the instigator, the facilitator, the go-between," he said, spreading his hands. "There has to be a go-between."

"I came this close to getting my head cut off!"

"We got here just in time," he agreed. "Boy, was I on tenterhooks! The skin of my teeth got goosebumps. But the worm turns is the name of the game. Those of us who try to help the underdog"—he lowered his lashes—"if we're lucky enough to see our efforts rewarded"—and fluttered them—"have to be able to turn on a dime, get it, a *Disme,* D-i-s-m-e, to stay on the losing side. Always losing, never lost, that's my motto!"

"It's not a *game*. Blanche would have killed me!"

"You would have killed her, sweetheart, to be quite fair. Wait, don't go away mad. While I've got you, there's a certain someone who wants very badly to talk to you." As he said this, he was poking at the keys of the phone. Then, nodding energetically, with a merry-old-elf sort of giggle, he set the phone to his ear, lifting his forefinger. "Ah. It's Mr. Nickel. I have someone here for you."

He held the phone out to me, grinning. I thought, nonsensically, that it might be Blanche.

"Nora? It's your mother."

I drop the phone. Mr. Nickel *tsk*s irritably at me. I pick it up again.

"Young lady, you are busted. I've had just about enough of this. You are *not* going to cut your sister's head off. Now I want you to get on home, and no back talk. *Bzzz. Bzzz. Viss.* Sstraw in my mouse. "

"Whuz?" I say. "You're breaking up. I think."

"*Phsst. Phsst.* I tawt I tawt I taw I taw a puddy puddy *phtt phtt.*"

I disconnect. "You are a fignut. Pigment. Figment," I say to Mr. Nickel. He simpers at me.

"Quite a woman, your mother," he says.

I would like to say that he rippled and melted quite away. But it was not true. I left him there, on the bench, screwing his leg back on. I could still hear Roosevelt muttering some time later, when I was back among the topiary.

There was a couple fucking under one of the bushes. Only now I saw it was not a couple but one person with two heads, one of which was bleeding. The bush moved, and I saw it was a phony bush, and I understood that I was in a diorama. I caught up one of the abandoned bushes, which had a hollow space inside, and lowered it over my head. I felt better at once. I began creeping down the hill.

Near the foot of the hill, I looked back. The diorama had been sharply shaken up by some catastrophe, probably an earthquake or movers, because things were not quite as they should be; the dusty water had popped out of its bed and was leaning sideways (fish and all) against the leg of Mr. Nickel, who did look something like a squirrel, with his orange suntan (out of a bottle, I think, though it could also be paint) and his rust-colored hair, also out of a bottle.

Clang. I had run into the gate. Suddenly, I was sobbing. Blanche had wanted to kill me. She had tried to kill me. She had nearly succeeded!

I threw off my camouflage bush and staggered out into the street. Nobody seemed to be following. Behind me, perhaps, Dr. Ozka, that outrageous cutthroat, that fiend, was being airlifted out of the rubble, operating kit strapped to her thigh. The scalpel I had meant for Blanche was lying across an operating table, pinked with my blood instead—not that even a doctor could have told the difference between her corpuscles and mine, mine, *mine!*

I took a turn and was running down a cobblestone lane between close, stained walls. A pigeon flapped across the narrow corridor, making a shockingly loud noise. I saw the Major ahead, pink legs flashing under the towel, which fluttered up from time to time to reveal the agile, dancing genitals, like hairy spooks. They were less obscene than the shiny disc of scar tissue on his shoulders, from which a lilac scarf was trailing—a veil worn by a nymph in a baroque painting.

I passed a covered alley, a dark hole smelling of cooked cabbage, and heard shouts. At the next intersection I turned the other way, parting ways with the Major.

Something was burning somewhere in the city. The air smelled of wood smoke. In the distance fire trucks were raising their voices in ritualized distress, like paid mourners. A police car rolled slowly across a distant intersection, lights flashing, and I slowed to a walk.

Then it was quiet. I heard the rush of my breath, the rattle as a shop's grille guillotined down in its tracks, a faraway radio playing "American Woman." I passed one of the few stores that were open, and the scene inside was startlingly bright and clear and still—the ranked packages of cigarettes, sachets of tobacco and rolling papers, the greenish yellow light, the flickering blue neon sign in the window, the proprietrix at her counter, fixed in a tense watchful posture, the blue neon lighting her far side at uncertain intervals so that her face, too, blinked. I passed in the beam of light from the door like a deep-sea fish surprised by a submarine. I thought she was staring at me, and when I had gained the opposite corner and looked back from the dark under an awning, she had placed her hand on the phone beside her, so I hurried on.

A taxi turned a corner behind me, pulled up beside me, paced me. "Where are you going?" said the driver. I recognized his voice.

I didn't reply.

"You had better get in the car."

I kept walking.

"Please?" he said.

"Are you still there? Please go away," I said, looking straight ahead.

"I don't think I should. You do not look A-OK. You're not even dressed!"

I looked down, saw my white legs flashing under my hospital gown, my bare feet on the cobblestones. I had stubbed my toe, and there was a dark ring of blood around my toenail. The taxi driver stopped the car, got out, and opened the door for me. I got in.

"Can I ask a question?" he said.

"I don't want to talk about it." I leaned my head against the window. The light was making me dizzy.

"Then can I say something?"

"No."

"I know this is not exactly the time to bring this up, but at some point you might want to apologize to my brother," he said.

"What do you mean?"

"I have to be at the dispatchers by seven AM," he said. "That was my brother you met in the kitchen that day. Poor bloke!" He started laughing. I waited for him to stop. Eventually he did.

My head was spinning. "I don't understand," I said stiffly. "And if I did, I wouldn't believe you."

"Do you think you're the only person in the world with a twin?"

"It seems to me you are trying to wax symbolical, and I hate a man who waxes symbolical. Your brother, what does he do?"

"He is a postman."

"That may be," I say. "But I don't believe you."

"I don't care. Don't believe me. It doesn't matter. You're wrong, but it doesn't matter. Why are you so angry, anyway? You liked me well enough before," he said, with a wink.

"That was my sister," I took some pleasure in saying.

I woke up on his couch in the middle of the night. The two-headed chicks were staggering around on my blanket, bits of lint catching on their claws. They were dry and inanimate as tumbleweeds, but also as lively. It took a while for them to work up to speech, or for me to understand their wheeze. They cleared their throats with a shriek like a needle skidding on a record. "Hey Nora."

"Nora," the other hissed in near unison.

"Is she listening?"

"Is she?"

"She isn't very civil."

"She's quite uncivil!"

"Has she heard the sad tale—"

"You mean the one—?"

"Yes, the tale of—"

(Together) "One, two, three . . ."

And they burst into song. They sounded like field recordings come alive, all seethe and crackle. It was a weedy, thready sound at first, not much better than a wheeze, but it strengthened.

The Two-Headed Chicks Perform "The Song of the Two-Headed Lady"

Alas for the two-headed lady
and alas for the lady with one
Broken hearts, they have two parts
but the two-headed lady has none

With two heads I was born accursed
and by my mother never nursed
The midwife snatched me from the coals
and in one body saved two souls

God set this gossip next to me
to vex my ear continuously
She carped and wheedled all day long
an angel's face, a harpie's song

Then I simplified my life
with an unpremeditated knife
The parrot on my shoulder cried
"Murder!" and then "Suicide!"

HALF LIFE

With a coping saw I docked her portion
of our mother's failed abortion
No church bell ever rang so bold
as her golden silence tolled

I took her absence on my arm
and moved to town and sold the farm.
I hung her picture on the wall
and bowed my head and dressed in pall

I kept her head in a wooden box
every day I loosed the locks
I sponged her face and combed her hair
and by my art I made her fair

But then you came and I could see
you loved her picture more than me
I set her head up in my place
and with a shawl I hid my face

The beautiful head would not grow older
I was the parrot on her shoulder
I spoke for her and eased your fears
and loved you well these many years

You lit a candle by the bed
and loosed the scarf that bound her head
I woke and saw I was undone
the dawn was come, my love was gone

The blade flew down and kissed my neck
I saw the earth shrink to a speck
They held my head up to look back
at my twice repeated lack

And that is how I came to be
the only woman in history
by a judgment most precise
sentenced and beheaded twice

They buried us beneath one stone
I dreamed a mourner came alone
You placed a rose upon the mound
and paused, and laid another down

On judgment day she'll be my bride
and I will never leave her side
content to hold a middle ground
between going up and going down

Reasonable Advice

I spent my last hours in England shivering, sniffling, and half deaf on a bench in Heathrow. I was confused and defeated and, more trivially, I had the flu. There was an incessant rustling and chirping inside my head, though whether this was ghosts or phlegm I did not know and barely cared. I just wanted to go home. When I handed over my passport I remembered that I had two passports on me and did not know which one I had given him, but he handed it back to me without remark. I did not look at it before putting it away. Later I wished I had, because I became convinced that it meant I had been beheaded after all. We were over glaciers then. I could not stop shivering.

The Mooncalf greeted me with the gentle speech of her tail. I opened the door of my room, and together we considered what I had failed to leave behind. My bed was a different size, or farther away. Everything was in the wrong place without having moved. I pulled my futon onto the floor and achieved sleep.

Trey raised his eyebrows when he passed me in the hall the next morning, but did not ask questions. He was subdued. Actual success seemed to offend him, though he was warming to it, mainly because it came with money. I sneered at the grubby, warped whatsits he was teaching himself to knit. He perked up slightly at that. "They come after me," he said with gloomy pride, "in dreams, I mean. They spread their flapping sleeves."

Audrey I contrived to avoid by staying out late, then shutting myself in my room until she had left in the morning. In between, my pockets stuffed

with Kleenex, I walked. I walked to the upper Haight and from the Haight to the top of Twin Peaks and back down. I walked to Bernal Heights, to Chinatown, to North Beach. On occasion I dared to enter an international newsstand and devise some pretext to part the limp sheets of a week-old *Observer* under the unimpressed eye of the vendor. No news of Dr. Ozka. Evidently she had not been captured. "Hm," I'd say, though I knew explaining only made me odder, "I could have sworn this edition covered the civic elections in Coxwold." My mouth twitched savagely. Growing desperate, I widened my search, and did finally find—in *India Abroad*—one terse reference: "After riot, Togetherist protesters and alleged patient of 'Doctor Decapitate' are held pending trial." At least I knew the whole thing had really happened. I ate in cheap, deserted restaurants, thinking about nothing, my head thrumming with flu and MSG. Then I walked some more.

After three days of this, waking to an empty apartment, I had ventured from my room to the kitchen to make tea when I heard the thump and jingle of Audrey's boots on the stairs. I made an undignified dash for my room and ran right into her.

"Arm's length has its limits," she said. "Come talk to me while I pee." She led me into the bathroom and pointed at the side of the bathtub in a manner that brooked no opposition. I sat. The cold enamel made me feel melancholy and reminded me I needed to pee too. Audrey peeled down the linty red tights and underwear and sat heavily, bunching her woolly skirt in her lap and fixing her eyes on the floor in front of her. After a pause came the vigorous stream. She sighed and turned her eyes to me.

"So. What's going on."

"Nothing. What do you mean?" I said peevishly.

"Oh, please. Look at you."

I lowered my eyes.

"Is it a drug thing? Has Trey gotten you into some fucked-up scene? Because I will kick his skinny ass to the curb so fast—"

"No."

"Uh-huh," she said noncommittally. She finished peeing in a few hard squirts.

"It's nothing like that."

"Well, at least you acknowledge there is something going on." She took the pack of Camels she kept on the windowsill and extracted one. She had to flick the lighter a few times before it flared. She lit her cigarette, sucked

hard, snaked the hand with the cigarette out the chinked window into the airshaft.

"*Ffff*well," she said, blowing smoke. "Whatever it is, you need to stop. You've been going and going and going and you've been acting like nobody could tell you anything and you didn't need help from anybody. Now you've hit a wall. Look at you, you can hardly even stand to be a person, you wince if someone steps on your shadow. Don't look at me like that, you know I'm right. So you don't want to get help, OK, fine. Then go off by yourself, but for fuck's sake sit down for a while and figure out what's going on. This internalized freakophobia or whatever it is has gone on way too long, Nora. I mean it."

I hunched up my shoulders and scowled at the floor. "I need to pee."

"Pee in the bathtub." She let out another little trickle and brought in her hand to take another drag.

I pulled down my pants and did just that, teetering on the high, sharp edge of the tub. My feet dangled. To my dismay I was crying. I, with my refrigerated blood, my upper-lip-stiffy.

Audrey hiked herself up on one haunch and wiped awkwardly with her left hand, stubbing out the cigarette on the windowsill with the other. She stood up, pulled up her tights, and stamped her skirt down. Then she moved up against my knees and drew my head against her stomach. I buried my contorted face in the scratchy pleats of her skirt. I was still peeing, trying to do it quietly. How strange that we try not to be ridiculous even when we are in extremis.

After a minute I felt awkward. My bare butt was cold. A lanyard of shiny phlegm joined me to Audrey's skirt when I pulled away. I kept my head down and waved my hand at the toilet paper until she got me some. I blew my nose and then wiped myself with the damp wad.

While I was wondering what to do with it, Audrey said, "I have a job for you. The old lady downstairs is visiting her daughter who has some kind of thyroid thing, and she asked Trey if he would maintain the yard while she was away. He said yes because he digs old ladies, but you know Trey, he's just a big indoorsman, and he doesn't need the rent break now that he's Mister Up and Coming. And I'm too busy. I think you should do it. Free rent, and it would be good for you to take care of someone or something else for a change. You can just weed and dig holes and talk to yourself and just revamp your brain with no distractions until she gets back. OK?"

"OK," I said meekly.

"Now, I know you would rather think about practically anything else, but I really think you need to try to figure out what Blanche is trying to tell you or what you are trying to tell yourself about your relationship with Blanche." She stepped away, swiping at the wet spot on her skirt, looking at me hard. "There's obviously some heavy stuff between you that you're not going to solve by just willing it to go away."

"I know." I wondered what Trey had told her.

She propped her hands on her hips. "So what are you going to do about it?"

"I don't know."

"You won't talk to a therapist." I made the face of not listening. "Or Vyv." I shook my head. "Well, if you won't talk to anyone about it, then I think you should write about it. Even if nobody ever reads it but you. What's that story about telling your secret to a hole in the ground if you have to? The king has no clothes?"

"The king has donkey's ears."

"Ears! In other words, talk to yourself, but don't forget to listen. You might learn something. Didn't you tell me your whole childhood is a haze?" She paused. "Actually I *believe* what you told me is that Blanche is in charge of the past and you're in charge of the future, but that's NOT talking. The past is part of the future, you know, which is why you have more in common with Blanche than you want to think, and it might behoove you to get to know her. That's not charity, that's self-preservation. Cutting off your past is like cutting off, I don't know, your own *head*. What's left, for Venn's sake? The future? What's that? The future doesn't exist! You've cut yourself a pretty bad deal, Nora."

"I've actually been trying to do that," I lied. "Write, I mean."

"Really? That's great, Nora. Have you really?" She opened the door.

I felt softened, even pulpy. I shuffled after her, zipping up my pants. "Yep."

"Then keep on doing it, and I'll stop telling you what to do. Maybe you'll invent some whole new kind of language! Vyv is always talking about finding the give in our syntactical bonds and reconfiguring them. I just need you to promise that you will not psych yourself out with obsessing on yourself to the point of deciding you can live on air or turn yourself into some kind of philosopher saint. Try being a person instead, in other words not perfect.

Everyone is some kind of freak. Stop trying to turn yourself into a new kind of freak and deal with the freak you are."

"OK."

"Promise."

"I promise." It sounded like reasonable advice, but I did not think I would follow it. This made me feel so sorry for myself that my eyes filled up with tears again.

Later, I pulled the Manual out of my never-unpacked bag. A piece of paper fell out of it and performed a graceful backbend to show its other side, then slid along the floor for an improbable distance. I picked it up. It was the form I had filled out at the clinic. With my signature on it. The one I thought I had given to Mr. Nickel.

"Nicely done, Blanche," I said. I looked at it a long time.

Then I turned the page over and smoothed it out.

"Blanche," I wrote. "Dark day of my bright night." Then I crossed that out and started over.

I was writing this book.

White as a Ghost

Her feet touched the ground, but she kept falling. Blanche put out our hands, too late. Donkey-skin lay at our feet, wheezing softly.

We bent over My Twinn and started rubbing her dress and hair with handfuls of the dirty straw.

"What are we doing, Blanche?" I said.

"I'm getting My Twinn dirty so she looks more like Donkey-skin." She picked up the doll and poked her into the cage headfirst. Her legs stuck out the door.

"We have to bend her legs back," I said. We pulled My Twinn back out of the cage and bent her double and pushed her through again. Her hair caught in the door and one foot stuck outside, so we pulled her back out and turned her around and put her through butt-first, and this time it worked.

"There," said Blanche. "That will give us time to make our getaway."

The princess lay on the straw. She rocked, she flexed a knee, she was testing herself. She had to rest after every movement. To straighten her skirt could take a lifetime. The light concentrated and shone like a tiny eye in her drool. She pulled herself into a crouch. The drool got longer and whipped dizzily around, until the end stuck on the dress and it grew tense and linear and beautiful and then snapped.

This slow work seemed too fast to me. I could feel the future flipping by like pages. I could barely catch a phrase here and there. Already I was lost, new characters were introduced and then slipped away again, they sat around tables discussing other characters I didn't recognize, one of whom

shuffled to the door, a funny tucked figure like an old woman, and white as salt.

"Pale as a ghost," I said; it was a phrase from stories. Her hair was thin, clingy, pale orange, the color of locoweed. She didn't remember how to walk at first. She moved in jerks, uncoordinated, like a puppet. We led her out across the lawn.

"Stop," she said. "Get my motherfucking smokes."

"That's stupid. Come on, let's go."

"I want my smokes. Going to have a motherfucking celebration. Get me my fucking smokes!" she said, her voice rising with each word.

"All right! All right! Fuck!" I said. We ran back and scooped up the whole cache of dingy cigarettes and matchbooks along with a bunch of damp straw. She stuck the mess in her pocket.

Her stiff skirt showed dirty white lines where the caked shit, stretched, cracked and the fabric showed through. Once it had been a party dress, cheap and frilly and synthetic. It was the sort of dress that Granny called "fire-retarded"—it would kindle all at once with a *fwhomp,* set your hair on fire, then disappear and leave you naked, except for sticky black plastic boogers that would sink into your flesh as easily as needles. It was the kind of dress little girls wore at beauty pageants and Mexican weddings, the kind you found hanging in plastic bags in cheap stores in the Mission. It was fancy and toxic, like a wedding cake frosted with petroleum jelly. It had so many pleats and ruffles that its surface area was incalculably large, like a brain's. I read an interview once with an artist who made drawings about child abuse. He said the most volatile words in the English language were "little girl." When a prosecutor pronounces those words, the courtroom goes crazy. This was the dress that went with those words: a language dress, a hallucinated dress, from a grown-up's dream of little girls.

I didn't want to touch her, but she was moving too slowly. I took her by the arm and pulled her out, across the lawn, to the fence. When we reached it, I looked back. There on the other side of the lawn was Mrs. Goat. Was she always checking the barometer? I thought she must have seen us, but she didn't move. I folded Donkey-skin over the fence, lifted her legs, and over she went with a sighed, "Whore."

We slithered down the slope into the arroyo behind their house and ran into a problem. She couldn't climb out again. She sank to the ground, cursing dispassionately. She looked like a bundle of trash chucked out of a truck.

"You can't stay here," Blanche said.

"Whatever." She got out a cigarette.

"Come on!" She flinched when I grabbed her arm, but she got up and came with us. We practically had to carry her up the slope, though it wasn't steep.

At the top of the hill she shook us off and twirled slowly. "What's that," she said. "A yucca." "Fucka. What's that." "A shotgun shell, from—from a hunter." "What's that." "Teddy bear cactus. Don't touch it, the fur is . . ." "What's that." "Our lookout rock." "What's that." "Our roof. Why it's shining is 'cause the smoke pipe's catching the sun." "What's that." "The highway." "Where's the gas station." "Behind that hill." "Which way's Thin Air." "Uh . . ." "The Land of Thin Air, where *is* it?" "Out there." "What's that white crap." "That's the playa. It's white because it's gypsum. It's part of the National Penitence—" "What's that." "Your house." "No. That's not my house," she said.

We watched her go. I can't find the right word for her movement, which was scarcely walking. Nor was it staggering or limping. It was like walking in every respect except it lacked some essential engine of plausibility. It had a myriad small stages of stoppage, yet she went on, like an animated figure. We didn't even go with her, show her the way to the road. She probably knew what she was doing, is what we thought. She was practically grown up. A woman, practically.

"She walks funny," one of us said. It didn't occur to us that this was because she had lived in a cage. Against the blue-black sky, she looked phosphorescent.

PART THREE

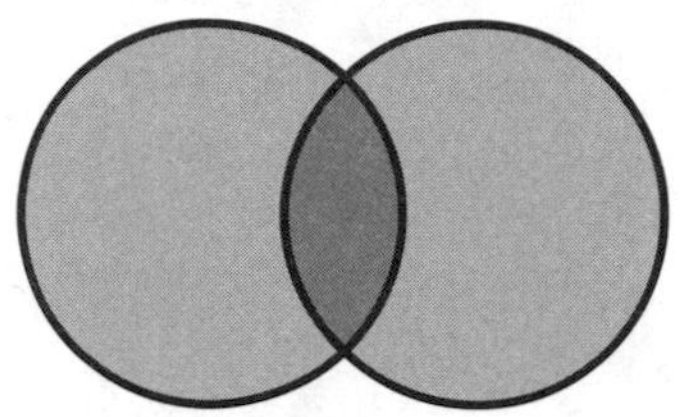

Boolean Operator: OR

Dear Diary

The reader will notice that my narrative has begun to loop the loop: 336 pages ago you read, "white night of my dark day"; 6 pages ago, I wrote, "Dark day of my bright night." (I'm still not sure which version was better.) But I still have not caught up with myself. A lot can happen in the time it takes to write 336 pages. I am writing this, now, from the desk of the Twilite Inn, in—but that can wait until I get there, some pages from now.

During the 336, while my narrative cautiously rolled forward across the backward spikes of my *ls* (*Louche* almost punctured a tire), I also kept a diary. A little pink book with a key? Alas, nothing so orderly. I jotted my thoughts on whatever came to hand—a napkin, a takeout menu, endpapers of a novel. Those I was able to find now quilt the bed behind me, trembling in the refrigerated air. I have resolved to insert them here, in their proper temporal location, giving them whatever commentary they seem to require, while allowing the forward progress of my narrative to continue.

Uncap thy glue stick, Mnemosyne.

Monday

I am writing this account for three* reasons. To find out what Blanche wants. To find out what Blanche *knows*. To supply the evidence that will exonerate

---

*I count four. Any thoughtful reader could probably add a few more.

me, should this information incriminate us. To leave a true and faithful account, in the event of my death.

Tuesday
I confided the whole story in Trey, finally. "Whoa," he said. "Bad balloon almost won."

I have looked at it from every angle, and there is no doubt that my wild first thought was right: Blanche planned to murder me. Systematically; consciously. A merely somnambulant Blanche could not have filled out her own copy of the form, let alone switched it for mine, resealed the envelope, etc. That this could be viewed as self-defense does not greatly reassure me—especially since, looking back, I see some evidence* that she conceived her plan well in advance, possibly even before† we flew to England.

When all this began, back in June, I was alone, more or less. But I burned for the pure, the integral solitude. I wanted, in mathematical terms, to round down. Now I would gladly settle for that "more or less." But it is no longer up to me, if it ever was. It's only a matter of time before she tries again.

"*Life* is a matter of time," said Trey. "Hang in there, as the executioner told the condemned man."

> A gap of some days follows. I was holed up in my room, writing at an awful pace, and had already darkened more than half of the first notebook by the date of this next entry, torn from the warped yellow legal pad we used for housemate communiques:

Saturday
Who drank my Poten-C Powersip?†
I chucked it. Was it supposed to be that color?‡

Blanche is still. My right hand is quieter than it has been in months. Sometimes on a dark night I think I am in the desert, but by day I am confident I

---

*The telephone call from Louche's bedroom was of course to Blanche's crony Mr. Nickel, who had slipped her his number earlier that day, nearly removing my pocket in the process.

†Trey's handwriting.

‡Audrey's.

was wrong. Desert peaks don't overlook such lapis and oyster expanses.

Maybe Audrey is right: maybe it is not too late to be an ordinary person, doing ordinary things. I have finally explored the yard.* Unbelievably, there are three giant carp in that pondlet. (Audrey: "Venn only knows how old they are! Think what they must have seen." Trey: "They're goldfish. They haven't seen anything.") Farther down are the barely detectable relicts of a vegetable garden, in which a few rambunctious artichokes still riot. There is a plum tree, serenaded by tipsy wasps: it crossed my mind that someday I might make jam. I won't share that wholesome thought with Audrey. Her proprietary enthusiasm for my healing process is hard to bear. The only company I can stand for long is the Mooncalf's.

Wednesday

It's good to have projects: weeds to pull, orgasms to incite. Perdita has given me back my old shifts. I take pleasure in the repetition, the constraints, the *petit mort* that does no one any harm. I have a newfound appreciation for stories in which all surprises are to be expected. On this model train track no ancestors will return,† the explosion at the end‡ is an effect repeated many times a night, the engine flies apart in numbered sections, and the boxcar crumples where the hinge is. On our way, we wave to the familiar scenery: the cow, the wishing well, the house on the hill.§

---

*The house we lived in, a shabby Victorian, slouched at the top of a crumbling knob of raw hill, sparsely furred with spiky, tawny grass. The yard dropped off more sharply than it looked, because the top leaves of the eucalyptus growing at the base of the cliff, where they caught the runoff, clattered and shone at eye level when one ventured to the bottom of the yard. Eucalyptus pods and loose pebbles and long toboggan strips of smooth bark littered the slope, making the footing precarious; in dreams sometimes I picked my way interminably along the verge, skating and sliding, on my way to some urgent appointment. Every rainy season, when houses sledded down hills all down the coast, Audrey issued gloomy predictions, but the house tilted and strained and stayed.

†The reference, I believe, is to the first Ghost Dance held by the Paiutes in Nevada in 1870, about the time the cross-continental railroad was finished. It was inspired by the prophet Wodziwob, who announced that the ancestors were coming home, and would be taking the train. When they arrived, there would be a great explosion that would annihilate the white men but spare their homes and chattel. The tribe would live the good life with their ghosts in this abandoned city.

‡See previous note, of course.

§I may have had in mind that old train set we found in Granny's garage. "Your daddy's," she said, to our silent disbelief.

Thursday

Haunted? I have a cure: poison oak. The itching concentrates the mind wonderfully. Despite Trey's yellow dishwashing gloves, my forearms are on fire. I pull up the glossy sheaves for an hour, then switch to mowing. This is what people do, I say to myself. It's a little boring, but I'll learn to like it. One day I will worry about my weight. I'll grill a burger and buy fridge magnets. Inflamed by this vision, I load the wheelbarrow much too full, then chase the teetering load down the slope, while tufts of grass lift off the levitating crest and dash me in the face. The Mooncalf canters after me, grinning. The barrow hits a rock, keels over. I leave the load where it tipped out and trundle back for more. Fantastic!

It is a relief to think about something besides my selves. Goldfish, for instance. I'm sitting on the edge of their pond right now, writing on a paper bag. They have very little water left, and what is there is black as tea, though being goldfish, maybe they don't mind. Are they provided for, happy?

Strange, in that instant of solicitude there was a small opening feeling between my legs. I poked my finger between my labia and it came out red. Now, having taken off my panties not to stain them, and squatting in the grass by the pond, I am painting my heel and wondering what the odds are that there was poison oak on that finger.*

Fly on my thigh. Do I smell *dead*? I go reaffirm civilized mores with a female sanitary product. Later, I find pollen clinging to Blanche's brows and lashes, and comb grass seeds out of her hair. I am half inclined to leave it there and see what will take root. I am my own Chia Pet!

Friday

I had been dumping my weeds and grass cuttings over the cliff, but the neighbors below have complained to Audrey, which gave me the impetus I needed to start a compost pile. Today, I was stamping down some greasewood to see if the ground underneath was flat enough to support the wood-and-chicken-wire structure I had in mind, when I saw the twinned glint of binoculars up on the hill and became convinced that someone was watching me.

Specifically, I became convinced that Mr. Nickel was watching me.

This is, of course, absurd. Still, I could not shake the feeling all day, and

* There wasn't. Thank you for your concern.

tonight I walked up the hill to the spot, taking the Mooncalf with me. Lights scribbled their reflections on the wet tennis courts. A flag clucked against its pole, an almost anatomical sound, like a throat clearing before a speech.

I showed the Mooncalf the patch of flattened grass where I thought Mr. Nickel had been standing. Too enthusiastic, she sniffed a grass seed right up her nose, then sneezed all the way home.

A gap of several days follows. The next entry reflects a falling off of the perhaps somewhat frenzied optimism evident in the "yard work" entries.

Saturday

Moony's fuzzy toy is stuck in the neighbor's juniper, where it landed after a wild throw. I bat it down with a stick, and she jumps on it, an almost natural scene. I don't hear any funny noises, there are no hobgoblins grinning from the guttering. The yard is all right. But as soon as I go inside, the house starts to change. It shifts and scrunches* like a woman wiggling into a tight dress. Beams creak, and plaster dust spills from the cracks in the ceiling. When it settles, I see that the lines of the room, even the color of the walls and certain furnishings, have changed. I recognize the dollhouse by the peculiar coarseness of the materials, the oversized knobs and hinges.

It's not just my room. Café Flore, Sunshine Market, Tacqueria Cancun: they all eventually turn into the dollhouse. When I can't see it, I can feel it: some objects are too heavy, other things too light; windows do not always work, and certain items are permanently stuck to tables. Food is hardly edible, though other people eat with plausible demonstrations of pleasure. My grande burrito looks the same as theirs, but it tastes like sawdust or clay.

There is only one possible explanation for this: Blanche's dream world is merging with my waking one.

Well, two explanations. The second is I'm going crazy.

On the bright side, I built the whole compost pile with no interference

---

*I made the mistake of asking Audrey if she had noticed the house moving. She went into a predictable panic about unstable soil and seismic tremors that culminated in a visit from an earthquake and mudslide risk analyst. Now there is a rubber tube like a catheter sticking out of the hillside below the house to drain off excess water.

from Blanche, though I used my right hand to hammer in the stakes and staple down the chicken wire. Lithobolia seems to be gone.

Sunday
Wrong.

This morning I found something in my notebook I did not remember writing.

Poltergeists are supposed to be nonverbal types. They have trouble communicating. (That's why they throw things.) They're frontier ghosts, galoots in boots, hooting, lighting their farts, doing tricks with knives and cards. That kind of spook might lasso you with a hangman's noose, or run you down with a herd of red-eyed cattle,[*] but not compose a sonnet. Or even a limerick[†]:

Some two-headed partners in crime
Went to Reno to make a quick dime[‡];
They had two poker faces,
And two sleeves full of aces,
But they lost to themselves every time.[§]

I never thought she would turn up here, on the page. In my private place.

From the last entry dates a new self-consciousness. Did Blanche wake up every night and pore over what I'd written about her? If so, I did not want her to know I knew. I began to hide those diary entries that concerned these suspicions, while leaving those I deemed more neutral in plain view, so as not to arouse her suspicions by a too-sudden change of habits. The following, scrawled on the back of an empty envelope, was tucked into a Basque phrasebook (see J for *jarraiki,* "follow").

---

*See the Stan Jones song "Ghost Riders in the Sky," a gloomy favorite of Granny's.

†Pasted below is the original page torn from the notebook, folded in half below the last line and carefully torn along the crease. Above the limerick is a line of my own, which I recopied onto the subsequent page: "We were just playing." See page 116 in the first notebook. Is it coincidental that the subsequent rhyme concerns a game?

‡Disme?

§If you did check page 116, as instructed, you will have found that what we were "playing" at was murder. Does this line suggest, then, that the game must end in a *mutual* destruction?

Thursday
I can't shake the feeling that someone's reading over my shoulder. One solution would be to write in a language she doesn't know. Lithuanian, Basque. !Kung. But first I would have to learn it myself, and do it in such an offhand manner that it escaped her notice, lest she undertake a parallel course of study, and even if I accomplished that, there is always a dictionary willing to spill its secrets. Even a secret code has a key, a key that for privacy would have to be in code, a code that would itself have a key. . . . The only private language is a language no one knows. For perfect privacy, a language even I don't know. But if nobody can read it, why write in the first place?

Like a squid, to make my escape behind a screen of ink?

Tuesday
"Come on," said Audrey, "Trey and I are taking you out on the town. I admire your writerly zeal, but you need to spend some time around human beings."

"Either of you care to join me in a relational garment?" said Trey, holding up something red, slinky, and sequined that had at least five too many arms. "Or both? No? Neither of you? Well, maybe I'll meet someone at Trannyshack who appreciates transformative couture."

Trey and Audrey's heads emerging from a sequined octopus was not an obvious balm for my troubled chakras, but it soothed me. I watched with equanimity from the back seat of the Volvo as they struggled to tuck themselves behind the wheel. Their joint body sparkled like water under the streetlights.

"Ben and Ignacio go on second, and it's already nine-thirty," said Audrey. "If we don't figure this out soon, I'm changing back into jeans."

"Heaven forfend!"

"Ben and Ignacio?" I said. "Is that who you're calling human?"

"Audrey has a boyfriend," sang the other part of the octopus. "Look, I'll just straddle the gearshift. If you stay in reverse, my manhood will be hardly compromised at all."

"Audrey! Ben? You didn't tell me." Suddenly I wished I had not come.

"You were busy," she said. "Let's rumble!"

Ben and Ignacio's subsequent lip-synched rendition, in drag ("Mary N. Haste" and "Ivana N. Ullman"), of the Carpenters' "Breaking Up Is Hard to Do" is amply documented on Trannyshack's website, to which I refer the

curious. In a photograph taken quite late that evening (No. 31 of 35) you can see a smeared Mary N. Haste and Audrey enacting a fair imitation of Hokusai's "Awabi Fisher and Octopus" (c. 1814), while Ignacio covers his eyes. Trey swears it isn't so, but I am sure at least one of Trey's limbs is implicated.

Now please direct your attention to shot No. 19. You will see Blanche's grave profile and the very tip of my nose. Behind us, in the harsh shadow of the flashbulb, is Mr. Nickel, in a babydoll dress and blond wig. I have looked at it repeatedly. I am quite sure it is he. Can a dream show up in a photograph? Or is the photograph itself part of the dream? And if he is no dream, then what is he doing here?

Friday

Sometimes, when my left hand dots an *i* or dashes off a dash, my right hand twitches, as if with an invisible pen, in invisible ink, to do the same. When I look, it stops. I look away. After a moment it starts to tap the table: Morse?

- — - - — — - — — — - - - - - — - — — -[*]

I should not look. I look. It stops.

I try entrapment. I set a pen down near it. At the little click of Bic[†] on wood it seemed to start. But now it lies quiet.

I resume writing, but I glance at my right hand from time to time. The wrist emerges from the cuff with a bony, purposeful air. I think of the sinister and inexplicable phrase, "to shoot one's cuffs." That wrist means business. But the hand is still. Sleeping? I can't escape the impression that it's, rather, lurking.

Ah!

No. For a moment just now I thought I saw my knuckles whiten. But it was just the light.

Sudden whiff of creosote, as on the desert after a rain.

Sometimes I slinked a single hair over the hiding place, so I would know if it had been disturbed. Far from calming, this multiplied my doubts.

---

*Without gaps between the letters or perhaps words, this could spell any number of things beside AUKTTHR. (Author?) Cryptographers' assistance requested.

†Which subsequently became the hiding place for this entry (tightly rolled and inserted in place of the ink cartridge).

The hairs moved even when I was awake. They seemed alive. Air currents, I told myself, but could not keep myself from changing a note's hiding place once I saw its delicate bodyguard troubled. It was not impossible, I thought, that Blanche could follow or even anticipate the steps I would take in devising hiding places. Every mind has its thruways, and she knew mine. I would have to walk jay. Hedge-jump. Get myself lost.

I knew I had succeeded when I was unable to find one of my own recent notes, locating it at last only when a stray sunbeam thrown off a passing car's mirror kindled the floating hair I had placed as a bookmark. After a few upsetting incidents of this kind, I began leaving notes for myself detailing where my diary entries were hidden.

These notes too had to be concealed. Or what would have been the point in hiding the first ones?

I soon discovered I needed further notes to remind myself where these notes were to be found. The termites of infinite regress were gnawing the floor under my feet. These—I hoped final—notes I decided to hide with only *moderate* cunning, but give them a different kind of protection in the form of a modest homophonic code generated by Trey's computer. A single example will suffice.

Fume, *astra*—I listen, Gwendolyn.*

---

* "Viewmaster, Alice in Wonderland." I had a box of assorted disks for this toy dating from my childhood, which I had found in an antique shop. The note in question ("see OED, 'hiding place'") was slipped into the paper sleeve for the Alice disk. Its address I wrote in tiny letters on one of those toothy paper strips that collect in the spiral binding of a notebook—which is where I left it. It should be noted that in this particular instance, my system failed: I didn't remember the hiding place of either note until I, quite by chance, had the sudden impulse once again to see plasticine Alice (so 3D I wanted to test her firmness between my teeth), suspended in free fall, legs together, skirt a blue parachute. When I saw the note, "Listen, Gwendolyn, the stars are angry," came unbidden to my mind. In the OED was the following entry, neatly printed in tiny letters on the back of a long receipt from Cliff's Hardware (Audrey was prop-shopping, judging by the odd melange of items: spirit gum, pipe cleaners, Goop).

Monday

Possible strategies summarized:

To write in a language she doesn't know.

To write in a language only I know.

To write in a language I don't know, either.

To write in a language nobody knows.

To not write.

To write in code.

To write in a code to which only I possess the key.

To write in a code to which I do not possess the key.

To write in a code that has no key.

To not write.

To hide what I write.

To hide what I write in a place I cannot find.

To hide what I write in a place nobody can find.

To not write.

To erase what I write, leaving only traces.

To write in invisible ink.

To write in no ink, but firmly, leaving faint impressions legible under a strong angled light.

To do any of the preceding three, then write a second text on top.

To partially erase that text, making it appear to be the concealed text.

To tear that in pieces.

To destroy certain of the pieces, leaving gaps.

To piece together what remains in a false order.

To destroy this surrogate text.

To hide all evidence that it ever existed.

To not write.

To write what I do not believe.

To write what I do not understand.

To not write.

To not write.

Maximum security strategies derived from the preceding:

1. To write what I do not understand in a language I do not know, applying a code that has no key, then erase, overwrite, again erase, tear up, selectively perforate, rearrange, and burn the result, then hide the ashes in a place I cannot find.
2. To not write.

Frankly, I am discouraged.

Every morning I wrote for several hours. When the walls seemed to come too close, I went down to the yard to work, the Mooncalf at my heels. It was Indian summer, which is traditionally warmer than foggy August. That might explain the spiny fingers of saguaro sprouts coming up all over the hill.

Thursday

It is getting hotter. Every day the goldfish have less water. I read in the paper that the jellyfish population is exploding. At breakfast (Trey had lox and bagels delivered), Audrey announced that the total mass of giant squid on earth now exceeds that of human beings. She considers this good news. "If biology supplies consciousness with its basic structures, I can't help thinking that a tentacle-based consciousness will shake things up in an interesting way. Think of the philosophy, the literature, the *films* . . ."

"Whoa Nelly," said Trey. "You told me the squid uses the same hole for breathing, eating, and fucking. I do not want to read that love sonnet."

"That was the octopus."

"Though erectile tissue on the tentacle is def."

"That was the octopus."

"I got eight hard ones for you, baby."

"I'm not sure how many tentacles a giant squid—I need to do some research." Audrey's eyes were shining. She was going to get in on the ground floor of squid porn.

Saturday
Smell of creosote quite strong at times.

Sunday
Are turkey vultures common in an urban setting?

Tuesday
The desert, the dollhouse: at least I know what Blanche is dreaming of: our past. How inconvenient that I don't remember it! One more reason to write: if the past is coming back, then the future *is* the past, and Audrey was right. Maybe I can get a hint of what's to come by reconstructing what once was.

Wednesday
Some devil made me wonder if I could write a limerick, and after much chewing of my pen, I found that I could. Why, it sounds like something *Blanche* would write, I thought, and copied it down:*

A two-headed genius did stunts
That amazed a one-headed dunce:
"What makes you so wise?"
"I think twice, I think twice,
And you one-headed think only once!"

This has led me into a hall of mirrors. If I can produce an imitation Blanche, with my right hand, then what makes me think she can't produce an imitation Nora, with her left? I will have to go over all my previous work for amendments, additions, [erasures]†—anything I don't recognize.

*On a yellow Post-It, affixed below this line, and further secured with tape.

†Conjectural. The vigorous action of a coarse eraser has flayed the page here, leaving a few blue threads strung across a scar. My joke? I don't remember.

Thursday

Is there even any point in hiding these notes? If she can wake up when I'm conscious (as a trail of broken objects shows), couldn't she read along? Sure, her eyes are closed, but with practice, couldn't she tell what words I was writing by the movements of my hands, which are also hers?

Saturday

Possible strategies, part 2:

To write what I do not believe, implying I believe the opposite.

To write what I believe, in such a context of suspicion that it appears to be what I do not believe.

To write what I believe, but leave gaps.

The former, but with extra, decoy gaps.

To mix what I believe and do not believe, so that no unilateral reading will yield a complete confession.

To write in no code, implying I am using one.

To write only the unimportant material in code, so the important material is encoded by any decoding operation.

To write in two codes simultaneously, one screening the other.

To hide only the important writing, making the unimportant seem to be all there is.

To hide only the unimportant writing, so the important seems beneath notice.

To hide nothing, so everything seems beneath notice.

Maximum security strategies:

1. To write both what I believe and what I do not believe, leaving gaps where key elements have been omitted, as well as extra decoy gaps, using two codes simultaneously, except where I use no code at all, and hide important and unimportant portions in alternation.
2. To write what I believe, in no code, hiding nothing.

Monday
Audrey urged me to think it through, let it out, write it down. "Dialogue with yourself," she said. "Get the juices flowing. Don't second-guess everything, just relax, open up, have a little faith in the process. And don't be so morbid."

My laugh was weak. "Writing *is* morbid," I said.

It is. I am raising the dead. A dead language, anyway: the dead may not walk, but boy do they talk. Blanche's zombie words are staggering among my own, passing themselves off as living.

I know, all our words are resurrected, though some are whiffier than others (*whiffy,* for example). I patch together a living language out of reanimated parts, like Frankenstein, and feel no disgust at scrabbling in the charnel house. Each of us makes her own monster, who earns a cozy co-tenancy of our tomb. We're all the last native speakers of a language that dies with us. Am I so special for tasting the rot on my tongue? For knowing whose remains I'm kitted out in?

Wednesday
Today, walking down Market Street, I remembered something I had forgotten, turned around suddenly, and thought I saw Mr. Nickel dodge into Medium Rare Music. I went back and looked in the door but did not see him. Is he just another tumbleweed, like the one I saw rolling down Market Street this morning? If he is really here, what does he want from me?

Friday
Could she *intervene*? Take advantage of a moment's distraction to slip into my skin, possess my pen, dip her words in my ink, and tell my story for me?

After every day's work, I go over my own words for fingerprints. When I don't find any, I keep writing. Sooner or later she'll slip up.

But then I wonder if I'm the one being watched, and I get out my eraser. I don't even know what I'm hiding, but in this mood everything seems damning. I rub and rub. I try writing a little. Then I take it back. I've written pages on this line alone.* See how thin the paper is. It's scuffed to felt and worn

* This entry is on a page torn from the middle of the second notebook containing pages 120–240 of the preceding. I have tried to make out the words I erased, and can see only

right through in spots. See the scars. The blank spaces aren't just empty. They're stained with words I've taken back. Sometimes the same word is reinstated, then revoked again. This book has been so much erased that its larger part, like an iceberg's, is invisible. I begin to feel that *that* is the real book. The words you are actually reading are just a sort of erased erasing, a cautiously omitted omission.

Saturday
I am forgetting what cannot be erased: the spaces. An eraser wielded against a blank page does not further whiten whiteness, but leave a mark. These too are writing utensils:

1. The marshmallow-pink rubber bar.
2. The silver wand with the hard white tip that leaves a scar, and a stiff brush at the other end to sweep away the dust.
3. The art cube, crumbly as hash.
4. The two-toned pencil/ink eraser, lean and angled.

Monday
My writing goes very slowly now.* The memories, when I draw them forth, are vivid, but so, I reflect, are Tiffany's stories, to those ears in the ether. Am I being fed a line, or feeding myself one?

I have slacked off the gardening. Probably a mistake.

Toenails skirl: here comes the Mooncalf. "Someone wants out," I say. She wags her tail. I will take her up the hill, I think. But when we get out, I think I see Mr. Nickel down the block, perched on a fire hydrant, tossing rocks into a planter made from a toilet. I go right back in. The Mooncalf is confused. I take her out back to the quondam vegetable garden. We wrestle up a huge thistle, exposing a dense porridge of round river stones and mud that looks a lot like the Grady Conglomerate, though that is not possible.

It is *very* hot. Goldfish in crisis. Dry grass the color our hair was once. I smell smoke, ozone, sage, creosote.

Is the creosote in my mind, or in the world?

---

the shadows of hooks and nooses. I have abandoned these efforts, which do not feel wholesome.

*Could it be because I kept erasing it?

For that matter, is the world in my mind, or in the world?

Tuesday

*

Friday
The yard is still safer than the house, despite my unpleasant discovery under the thistle. It is too minutely detailed to be a fraud. The scene painter does not daub the underside of the fiberglass boulder, or bring live ants to the picnic. There is a teething animal (rat or squirrel) living in the crawl space under the house that is gradually reducing a plastic bottle to chips. Nearby, untouched, is an old bucket with a dry cat turd in it, through which a red thread coils. These are the fragments I shore up against mirages. Without them, I'm a taxidermy girl in a wind-up world. The lightning-struck madrone topples down the bluff to the grind of gears. At night they winch it up to fall again tomorrow. The coyotes howl from concealed speakers, the bald eagle catches the same fiberglass rabbit twenty-four/seven, and the mushroom cloud is done with dry ice and mirrors.

The goldfish, though. I still think the goldfish are real.

Monday
Something awful has happened. Audrey has volunteered for the Symbiotic Solution.†

---

*The above represents a full paragraph from *The Confidence-Man,* Melville, in which, meticulously, only the blank spaces have been underlined.

†Experimental surgical procedure recently reported in the *San Francisco Chronicle*;

I asked Trey if he would help me set up an intervention.

"This is not a good balloon bad balloon situation," he said. "This is more like good balloon, acceptable balloon. Or maybe good balloon, balloon that's none of our beeswax. Good balloon, balloon of the impenetrable mystery of—"

"Oh, shut *up*!"

"—the human heart. She's going to need new clothes!" he realized, clapping.

Wednesday

Today I decided to save the goldfish.

First, I probed the pool with a spade. The sludge I brought up cascaded back into the pool. I thought of the bucket in the crawl space and went after it on my stomach. I tipped out the cat turd and set to work dredging up buckets full of muck and old leaves from the pond and emptying them into the wheelbarrow. After turning almost upside down to fill the first bucket, I climbed right in with the fish. My feet sank into cold, velvety squish. An invisible tail flicked my shin.

When the wheelbarrow was full, I slowly wheeled it down to the moribund vegetable garden. It was hard going; whenever I went over a bump, the black muck lunged for the edge and slopped heavily into the grass. My arms ached. "Honest work," I said to myself, planning my conversation with Audrey. I worked for hours, in the end straining the water with my fingers, feeling for leaves in water opaque with the muck I had stirred up. Then I

---

see below.

Symbiotic Solutions is researching the creation of artificial second heads for patients who believe they are twofers locked in a singleton body. "My patients are not loonies or novelty-seekers," said a spokesman. "They have all the attributes of a conjoined twin except a second head, and they are suffering in a body that feels wrong to them—that feels, in fact, amputated. Some report phantom sensations in the nonexistent body part. Most have lived for some time in the twofer community, wearing expensive, cumbersome, and unrealistic strap-on surrogate heads. This unsatisfactory solution does ease their psychic pains to some extent, but theirs is a marginal existence, neither singleton nor double. They crave the real thing. That, of course, we cannot provide; science cannot breathe a human soul into a prosthetic head. But we can do the next best thing. With a handsome, natural looking head covered with their own living skin and hair, these unfortunates can correct the error of nature and live a relatively normal life."

ran some clean water into it. The pool was now even shallower than it had been.

My fish were swimming in nervous flurries near the surface, well away from the mud-storm churned up by the hose. Maybe they couldn't breathe. So I turned off the hose to let the muck settle. My fish, I called them. I even gave them names: Molloy, Malone, and the Unnamable. I'd been reading Beckett. Then I went back upstairs and made myself a cup of coffee. I wanted to let the water clear before I went out again. I wanted to see my friends frisking in their new pool. At dusk I went out. "Let's go see my little guys," I said to Moony.

The pool was still and impenetrable. On the flocking of muck that coated the floor evenly from end to end, bugs had inscribed curly paths, slightly browner than the pulpy green of the blanket to either side. The thought that the fish must be under that blanket, dead or dying, horrified me. I splashed some water in the pool to rouse them, but there was no reply, only the slow boiling up of the muck, brown cauliflower-clouds rising and breaking against the surface. I waded from end to end, feeling for them, but they were not there.

"No," I said. I ran to the vegetable garden. Absurd thought: I had somehow scooped them up in my bucket without noticing it, and dumped them out with the mud. But they were not there either. They were just gone: absent, abducted, plucked. I ran back to the pond. The Mooncalf bounced along beside me, wagging her tail. I hated her good humor. I tried to kick her, and slipped on the still-wet grass by the pond.

I could hear myself making strange noises.

The fog flew past. The smoke flew past. The saguaros raised their arms in dismay.

There was someone on the hill, watching me.

The stars are angry, Gwendolyn.

Friday

Of course some animal caught the goldfish as they flurried too near the surface, made nervous by my dredging and the hose. A heron, a raccoon, even a cat could have done it. But I know who the real killer is.

If only, etc.

So a few goldfish died. Am I really taking it to heart? Well, well, I am an exemplary human, after all. We elect these small consolers, knowing they

don't give a damn about us, and we don't know a thing about them. We mock up an interlocutor in whatever flurry of molecules can keep a mask on. We're ventriloquists in love with our dummies. Then burying them with pomp and heartache. Who killed Cock Robin? You did, baby.

It had seemed a harmless enough delusion, though. All I wanted was somebody to say hello to. Target practice for love; or if not love, cordiality; if not cordiality, at least tolerance. AND, not OR: live and let live. What went wrong? All I wanted was to make their lives better, their mysterious, real lives. I didn't want to prop them behind a desk with an inkwell and three quills. I wanted them to be different from me.

How grotesque that I killed them with good intentions, I who have so many bad ones. I'm a mad nurse spritzing the ward with cyanide from a pair of oversized hypos; my huge dugs moisten my dress with a superabundance of maternal feelings; I sensed that the little guys needed me, I heard their pathetic bleats, goldfish don't bleat, nonetheless I came running, my still-unsuckled teats throbbing with yield. Alas, I'm badmother: I coax a black sap from my nipple and paint baby's lips with it, watch her stiffen and turn blue. The resin sizzles at my nipples, and when I touch a match to it two flames leap up. I take my teats in my hands and squirt a burning rain, little flames falling, and I burn down a forest. The dappled eggs cook in their nests, like the fawns too afraid to move.

Finally, I am crying.

Sunday

Perdita called. "What's this I hear from the customers about goldfish? Girl, I appreciate a vivid imagination, but you have definitely lost the plot. You were supposed to be doing phone sex here. Emphasis on *sex*? Nobody is going to pay three bucks a minute for Virginia-fucking-Woolf."*

"What's this I hear from Perdita about goldfish?" Audrey said, taking my arm and guiding me downstairs. "I have to shop for 'Tortoise Takes All Comers.' Walk with me."

"I killed the goldfish," I said.

She looked startled, then rallied. "Well, go easy on yourself. Goldfish are

*Perdita is not a reader, or she would not have paid me this misplaced compliment. Better comparisons might be Poe, Shelley (Mary, I mean), or the anonymous author of that classic that starts out, "Great green gobs . . ."

practically *for* dying. They exist to teach children about mortality. Have you quit writing?"

"No."

"Good. Don't." She locked the door behind us.

I turned, and saw Mr. Nickel. He was standing on the other side of the street, shading his eyes in my direction. He beamed. "Nora!" He took a few quick steps toward me. Then he saw Audrey behind me and stepped back onto the sidewalk, holding up his hands apologetically.

"Who was that?"

"I don't know."

"He seems to know *you*."

I searched for a response. "He's a Togetherist. He's trying to convert me." Mr. Nickel was mincing away, making a joke of his retreat.

"Oh, in that case . . ." Audrey started after him. She would engage any door-to-door believer in parley.

"No!" I spoke more vehemently than I had intended.

"Why not?"

"He's schadenfreudlich, he's XOR, he's—" I gaped. How could I impress upon her that she must never, ever talk to him? The very idea made me shudder. What if he said something about the clinic? But it was not just that. "He's *radioactive*."

"So you do know him."

"Ish." I started walking, hoping she would follow. "What are you going to conjure turtle pussy from?"

"Tortoise. A finger cot, a scrunchie, marzipan . . . mint jelly . . ."

"And is this a heterosexual tortoise?"

"I'm considering a bisexual four-way with a turkey, an oyster, and either a mosquito or a golden retriever."

We sailed into the safe harbor of terrapin pudenda, leaving Mr. Nickel behind.

Tuesday

I went back and compared my limerick to Blanche's. It took me two hours to find them, in adjacent books (Saramago and Soares). I do not intend to put them back. In fact I am beginning to think I should assemble *all* my writings before I have completely forgotten where I hid them.

I was hoping to detect some difference between them, however tiny. There is no difference.*

Wednesday
In fact there is: Blanche's sounds more like something I would write. "They lost to themselves every time": that has my flavor, wormwood. While the optimistic rhyme of *wise* and *twice* is something my vanilla twin might like, not I.

Have I misunderstood her? Myself? Dollhouse closed, seam showing.

Thursday
I keep thinking the goldfish must have died for a reason. But that's just gilding the cat turd. You can't use the lives of other creatures to teach yourself a lesson, however needed. By symbolic logic they should have lived. Horrors might come in twos, but it's wonders that come in threes: Atlanta's three golden balls, Saint Nicholas's three golden balls, Donkey-skin's three walnut shells. But they were not symbols, nor wonders; they were simply what I asked them to be: real. Not part of my story. Their own fish.

And as fish sometimes do, they died.

Actually, they disappeared. That's what appals me most: the blank green gaze of the pond. Where did they go? It's as if they dissolved into the air. I could tell myself their ghosts will swim in circles around my head forever, inaudibly reproaching me. Or I could tell myself that nature is a wheel of deaths and births, hopping with spiders that also kill (like me) and also die in the beaks of birds that kill and die in the teeth of cats that die and are eaten by vultures that also die. The water bugs I threw out with the mud, not looking too closely for fear I'd pity them, were stubbed out by the sun in minutes.

But these are just stories, and have nothing to do with the fish themselves, whose dying moments were doubtless not eased one bit by reflecting on the cycle of life. Nor, of course, has my guilt anything to do with them, or my pique at good intentions gone bad, or the solace it gave me to think that affording them room to swim would be one small thing to cite in my own defense, a reason it was better for me to have been living than not, or my pique at being robbed of that reason.

---

* We might entitle this phase of my inquiry, "I think 'I think twice, I think twice' twice."

Saturday
Became very upset last night upon reflecting that the open notebook in which I was drowsily scribbling "Bad dolly!" itself resembled a dollhouse—hinged at the center like mine—the two halves folding out to permit access to the interior passages—folding shut to present a seeming whole. Dollhouses within dollhouses . . .

Sunday
Audrey cornered me and demanded we have lunch. We drove to North Beach. We considered the painfully named Bite of China, billed as an "Eating Saloon with Delicacy Delights," but chose instead a gourmet organic food restaurant, open three days a week. Our talk did not go well. Audrey demanded to know what was going on. I said I was "processing things."

"What things?" she said. "It's about time you told me exactly what happened in England."

I didn't want to talk about it.

"Don't you think you should?"

"Audrey, *drop* it," I said.

"I will not! You're not yourself."

"Who am I, then?"

She shooed the question away. "I'm not even sure the writing is a good thing anymore. It's too one-sided. You're like one hand clapping. Where's the other hand?"

"Around my throat," I said or thought of saying.

"If you won't talk to me, would you consider talking to Vyv?"

I snorted. "Venn's just Togetherism lite: 'We are one, sort of.'"

"Not really," she said. "You ought to take a minute to read about it. If only to find out what you're NOT," she added cunningly. She rummaged in her bag and pulled out a folded piece of paper printed on both sides.

"Later," I said, putting it in my pocket. "Maybe."

"OK," she said, and snapped her menu shut. "I'm going to have the mahimahi." She unfurled her napkin with too much elbow, compressing her lips, and when the pony-tailed waiter came, ordered the butternut squash ravioli. I mooed.

"What?" said Audrey sharply.

"Moooo."

The waiter mooed merrily back at me. "What can I get you?"

"Moooo."

"Wow, what does that mean? Cow? *Beef?* Oh, milk!" he exclaimed. "You want milk, right?"

I nodded, tight-lipped. Audrey was looking at me hard. I did not look back at her. I was trying to form my napkin into a mushroom cloud. The waiter returned.

"One house white. And here's your moo!"

How could I tell her what was really wrong, that I had discovered a feeling I didn't know I had or could have: when Blanche tried to kill me, my feelings were hurt. I couldn't believe she would do that to me, her *sister!* And for an awful moment—you know how I hate mirrors—I saw the world reversed, and thought: I can't believe I would do that to her, my sister.

Monday

What do I fear? Myself? There's none else by;
Richard loves Richard, that is, I and I.
Is there a murderer here? No. Yes, I am!
Then fly. What, from myself? Great reason why,
Lest I revenge? What, myself upon myself?
Alack, I love myself. Wherefore? For any good
That I myself have done unto myself?
O no, alas, I rather hate myself
For hateful deeds committed by myself.
I am a villain—yet I lie, I am not!
Fool, of thyself speak well! Fool, do not flatter.
My conscience has a thousand several tongues,
And every tongue brings in a several tale,
and every tale condemns me for a villain: *

Thursday

"Tell me about your twin."

"I'm sorry, I don't have a twin. I'll reconnect you to the operator."

"No, I want to talk to you, Magoo."

---

*A (heavily underlined) page from *Richard III* (Arden edition).

"Super, but I don't have a twin."

"If you say so."

"What do you want to talk about, Mr. . . . ?"

"Mr. E."

"Mr. E, what do you want to talk about?"

"You know, the dead and other has-beens such as ear trumpets, typewriters, and our own former selves, are neither simply gone, poof, nor happily alive, forever, in an adjacent pleat of the space-time fabric over which, ant-like, we toil."

"They're not?"

"Nope! They are, rather, in a position analogous to that of, say, dolls . . . or maybe pets, for example goldfish . . . characters in a book . . . prosthetics . . . really any transitional object—you've read Winnicott, no? I.e. they require our attention to establish themselves in their natural habitat: our minds."

"Is that so? Can I ask who—"

"Between times, they wait, miniature cards clutched in their frozen paws, calabash pipe halfway to the wizened lips."

"Who *is*—"

"There is a further contention, more controversial: that this relationship is a symbiotic one. Picture a Venn diagram with two cells, the future and the past. Where the two intersect is the present, and that's where we live. Without the past, we would have no future; we would be trapped in a dimensionless present, a null set. We live because we tell stories about what has been, and dream of what will come. You tell stories, don't you, Tiffany?"

"Who is this?"

"That's a very good question, because the present-tense self has no identity of its own, it's just a bitty band of flesh between memory and anticipation, and each of us converses with many pasts, and when we're history, just ink on paper, we will converse with many future ones."

"Mr. Nickel?"

"And Disme."

"How did you get this number?"

"Isn't this a fun way to be in touch? Aren't you glad to hear from me?"

"Why are you stalking me?"

"Stalking, gracious. I've missed you, you and Blanche both, you make me feel alive. Life is strife. Louche would agree with me, wouldn't she? I was jealous of her, you know."

"You're the devil."

"Nonsense. I'm your guardian angel!"

"You've been spying on me. You've bugged my house or my suitcase or—Blanche, her mouth, her ears . . ."

"You'd be amazed at the spy-gear you can order right out of a catalog. But I wouldn't. Heavens. I'm just a good listener."

"Look, I've decided I'm not going back to the clinic."

"We'd love to have you, but we understand."

"And I'm not joining the Togetherists either."

"We'd love to have you, but we understand."

"What the fuck do you want from me?"

"Would your mother approve of that language? She asked me to keep an eye on you. That's why I'm here."

"Why doesn't she keep an eye on me herself?"

"Wow, gee. I'm sorry to be the messenger, but—well, I'll let her explain. I've recorded a message from her. It's stored in Roosevelt's memory bank, just a minute . . ." [whirring sound]

"'Hon? Are you OK? It's your mother. I'm in jail, but don't worry, I'll be out soon, but I won't be allowed to leave England until the trial's over. Now I know you've had a hard time and you aren't speaking to each other, but I want you to try and see each other's point of view. Do you hear me? You will value that relationship in the future. And I know you [crackle] my funny little beliefs, but I also think it's important for the *world* that you attempt to [crackle crackle] another [crackle] right nearby, as close as [crackle, crackle, click.]'

"Got that? Swell. Now I can tell her I've spoken to you, and you're fine—you're fine, aren't you? Are you fine? Over that goldfish thing?"

[click.]

Saturday

The yucca everywhere is just plausible, but I can no longer ignore the Joshua trees that have sprung up all over Duboce Park, sprouting even in the streetcar tracks—how will the transit system carry on? Blanche is winning. The desert is coming.

Tuesday

All morning while I was writing, I could watch a reddish ovoid separate from the lower left corner of my window, bob right, just grazing the sill, pass through a flaw that stretched and finally pulled it in two, reform, sink below the sill, then two minutes later, perform the same trip in reverse. For the last half hour, however, this has ceased. Finally I open the window and lean out. Mr. Nickel is perched on a campstool right under my window.

"Why are you still here?" I am so angry I am panting.

"Nora! I know I'm being a pest, but I just can't drag myself away, I'm so interested in you and Blanche; I feel so connected to you . . ."

"You're trying to drive us even further apart."

"Further! I wouldn't flatter myself that was possible. I just"—he spreads his hands, with what should have been a disarming grin—"really like you. I like to be near you." His eyes are moist with sincerity.

I slam the window shut.

Wednesday

I can no longer ignore the obvious: if Blanche can persuade me that skulls can talk and make me tell that story, what other lies have I dutifully written down? If my thoughts aren't safe from her, how can my words be? I don't have to imagine her popping up to scribble a bit, then diving into the gutter like a bookworm. She can lie back, close her eyes, and let me take dictation.

In college, I used to rewrite my books. I scratched out sentences and whole paragraphs, all the soft meat, and discovered their secret skeletons. I thought someday I would publish them on a small press and live in nervous anticipation of the day one of the original authors, undead, came to visit. In this book too another book is buried, and it's hers. It isn't hidden, exactly. It's there for anyone to see. The dictionary has all the words we need. It holds the answer to every question. It's just a matter of learning how to read it.

But now, everything I thought was mine begins to look like hers. I'm lip-synching my autobiography. This fake book, full of spelling terrors. I pore over it, looking for notes from underground.

Breathe lightly and never criticize her experiments.

Below lies a nobody called her enemy.

I can just make out the shape of Mr. Nickel's head in the darkness.

Thursday
Audrey has started the process of augmentation, driving up to Sausalito to leave blood and tissue samples at Symbiosis Labs, which turned out to be one skinny man on a houseboat. He strode in, buttoning his lab coat over fuchsia Speedos and shiny white thighs on which the black hairs had been all slicked down with coconut oil, as gusts of sweet reek confirmed. I can vouch for this detail because I was there, having agreed to drive Audrey home if she got woozy after giving blood. By then we were not speaking to each other.

"To be honest, Vyv objects too," she had said, handing a ten-dollar bill to the tollkeeper. "She thinks I'm trying to fix the free play of identity. She says a spiritual condition doesn't require a materialist excuse, some, like, *lump* that proves you're what you think you are. But I think she's trying to deny that the body conditions what we think and feel. I mean, we *are* lumps. Ultimately. Big lumps of gristle. Thank you, sir."

"Sir lump." We swept into the crab-colored creel of the Golden Gate Bridge. "By that logic, shouldn't you be a healthy, happy singleton?"

"Well, sometimes Mother Nature gets it wrong," she said. "I'm just a little slip of her tongue." A truck rocketed past in the opposite direction, just a yellow divider away, and we fishtailed in its wake.

"If you're a slip of the tongue, I'm a whole fucking speech defect. Buh-body. Puh-person. Could we get out of the turncoat lane?" Mornings, this lane was southbound. I found that unsettling.

"Being plurally-personned is not a defect, it's a *privilege,*" she said stiffly, snapping on her signal.

"Oh, pardon me, did I use language degrading to your brand-new minority? How fucking presumptuous. Do you really think sewing a meatball on your shoulder makes you a twofer? You're not a twofer, you're an idiot with a meatball on your shoulder. I'll tell you how I know: only a singleton would think it was a privilege to be plural."

"Oh, look who's talking! Only a twofer would think there was such a thing as *being* singular." She surged into the right lane.

I furiously rolled down my window. Blanche's hair bannered out and glued itself to the outside of the glass. To the left, as if held back by the cables, was a depthless grey bank of fog, but to the right were limpid volumes of space, mudgreen sparkle and the tiny white slivers of sails, all presently leaning the same way. Into this the five hundredth soul had lately disbursed its

endowment of misery. No jumpers today, unless Audrey was one, jumping out of her old life into a new one. Who was I to question that? I'd tried the same thing in the other direction. I ate some long breaths of the cold salty wind and calmed down.

"What does Ben think? Doesn't he prefer singletons?"

"Wow, I think that's the first time you've actually said his name."

I didn't comment.

"He's struggled with it, but he says he's almost positive it's me he likes, not my body."

"That would be the exact opposite of your lump theory."

"Look, Nora Either-or-a, if people were consistent they wouldn't be people. You happen to have a fall guy for your inconsistencies. But if Blanche magically disappeared I bet you'd find out that a lot of what you were calling Blanche was you all along. Don't look at me like that. I'm saying this is a *good* thing. It's probably on the strength of what we don't know about ourselves that we get by. We're blurry, thank Venn. Our grey area"—she took both hands off the wheel to form a sort of yoni—"is our window."

"Incidentally, how do *you* spell grey?" I said.

She didn't answer.

I looked over. I was appalled to see that she was blinking tears out of her eyes. "The problem with trying to figure out your philosophy of life is that while you're working on it, you have to keep living. I'm just trying to live, Nora."

We swept up to the double tunnel with rainbows painted over both arches, gateway to the moneyed mellow of Marin County. I rolled my window back up and leaned against it, my eyebrow crushed against the hot rim of Blanche's ear.

Under the rainbow, into the dark.

"Help yourself to a beverage," said the doctor, looking at me in a way that somehow bypassed my face, as if he were applying mental calipers to my cranium. The refrigerator was full of pinkish shreds in jars, and plastic skulls covered with a slick of goo, and troubling meatloaves. I selected an orange drink called Vitalitá, thought of death, sat down on the deck in back to write this account.

This beverage tastes strange.

Oops, is it a beverage, or some poisonous preservative?

I find I don't care.

The waves are all urging in one direction, out to sea. It is calming to think of the ocean stretching from shore to shore, rounding the earth's curve, and with ripples and swells the whole way, tirelessly generating effects, though it has no audience. I see my magnified cheek and the quivering wing of my right eyelashes reflected in my 25¢ thrift-store sunglasses.

I meant to talk to Audrey on the way home. Tell her about Mr. Nickel, that I think he is trying to drive me to some desperate act—I don't need to explain about the clinic—that the writing is not helping, that I'm not feeling at all well. But listening to the waves whisper "recede, recede, recede," I know I won't. She is over the rail, already out of reach.

Friday

I feel Blanche dragging herself toward me along every line, fastening her talons in the counters of my p's and q's, and I cannot stop her. In fact, I am helping her. This writing is not separate from her waking, it is part of it. Oh, I have good reasons for doing it (a suicide leaves a note, a murderer mails a mocking letter to the detectives after him, a poisoned dictator gasps out the names of her assassins), but she has hers as well. Blanche is remembering herself through me. The fact that I am also remembering myself through her may not suffice to save me. It may even be my downfall.

Saturday

"You can feel the stiff frill of her short dress rubbing against your hips, and there are bits of straw and muck under your nails—"

"Say what?"

"Never mind. You have her up against the rose wallpaper, and her head is banging against a mirror that has pictures of her as a little girl holding teddy bears and My Little Pony stuck in the frame, and you're hammering her—"

"Oh yeah. Yeah."

"And you're watching her head bang against the reflection of her head and just then you see the door open in the mirrored room, with its wallpaper of shepherds and shepherdesses, and something comes in . . ."

"Yes?" he said, impatiently.

Earlier I used the model train metaphor for phone sex. I did not realize at the time that a forgotten line had converged upon the circular track. Sometime in the last few weeks the pointsman had switched the points. Let's say I got off on the wrong track. I didn't notice the landscape morphing, the green

flocking fading to sand, the bogeyman mugging from behind a cactus. "He was wearing a lab coat and a name tag on the pocket . . . he was covered with coarse fur . . . his horns stuck straight up . . ."

Click.

"And he carried a stethoscope in his cloven hoof," I said to the dead receiver. Tiffany had changed genres. She was telling ghost stories.

Perdita has fired me, of course.

Today

In my personal statement, which has become a book, I have almost reached the point I started writing*—a dark time, but brighter than this. A paler shade of grey, or gray. My memories, the ones I haven't reached yet, are darker still, I can tell. Their shadows have already reached me.

I want to stop. I want to destroy my writing, every scrap.

Twoday

I finally went to Trey about Mr. Nickel. "Baby, I'm not the man of the house!" he said, astonished. "Get Audrey to give him his walking papers."

"I can't," I said. "He might say something to her. Please, Trey."

"I loathe conflict!" Pause. "You're killing me!" Pause. "OK. Tell you what, I'll ask Poppkiss to send a few friends over. He owes me. Do we have carte blanche?" he added impishly.

Eternit*á,* Infinit*á,* and Immensit*á.* "They won't kill him, will they?" I didn't want that. Or did I?

"No, no, that costs extra." I couldn't tell if he was kidding.

"Just scare him away." I went back to my room.

After a minute he appeared at my door. "Did you hear me say, do I have carte blanche?" I nodded. "I can't believe you didn't bitch-slap me," he said. "Please bitch-slap me, Nora. I miss your foul self."

So I bitch-slapped him. He shook his head. "It isn't the same," he said dolefully.

But today Mr. Nickel is gone.

---

* I.e. the beginning of this section.

Whenday
I think I have found all but a few of the writings I hid. I have put them in a bag with the first two notebooks, but I have not destroyed them yet. And see, I have not stopped writing.

What's black and white and read all over? Both the figure and the (hallowed) ground, I stitch up the page, "sewing at once, with a double thread/a Shroud as well as a Shirt."* The situation is grave. The plot quickens.

Someday
I'm in the lower Mission bent over in the pale lemon shade of a paloverde, looking at a speckled seedpod, rolling it back and forth under one sole. It seems as real as my scuffed army boot, as real as the fluted paper cuplet from which the blue syrup of a Mexican ice has dribbled, as real as the smashed Nukalert key chain and the dusty dental dam.

The problem with looking is you see things. The store window before me advertises only sky, except where my lightless reflection jigsaws a hole in it. In that hole hangs a rigid white communion dress swaddled in plastic. Faded plastic flowers hang around it, funereal rather than festive. I am a hole cut from the moving world. Inside me, the ghost of a little girl.

Turn your back on her. List evidence for the real world.

The Lucky Pork Store. Doc's Clock Cocktail Time. The _ _ _ ER THEATER (the TWO is missing, I mean the TOW, steady, just keep going). Envios de Dinero, Matrimonios Civiles, Price Slashers.

An old man with no feet is crossing the street in a wheelchair, deftly avoiding the cow pies and prickly pears, and periodically beeping like Road Runner. The cows in turn avoid him, I mean the cars, emitting long sad bovine honks.

Describe him further.

Dirty tube socks are pulled over his stumps, with plastic bags rubber-banded over them. A twofer in one blond, one black wig hurries after him,

---

* "The Song of the Shirt", Thomas Hood (1799–1845), in which a poor seamstress sews and sings,

But why do I talk of Death!
That Phantom of grisly bone,
I hardly fear his terrible shape,
It seems so like my own—
It seems so like my own

giving him an occasional shove that seems more spiteful than helpful.

Good. Describe the wigs.

The blond is a perfect, glossy dome, the black a scramble of skutched goat resembling roadkill. Her clothes, a baggy floral smock and slippers.

She slip-slaps up to me and I re*cognize Mr. Nickel.

"Go away," I say.

"*Que bueno* to see you too! We're connected. I know you feel it too. We're alike. No compromise for us. The cruel beauty of the will, the wedge driven deep into every steady state, every scale tipped. We're all about teeter, right? The edge, right?

"Oh, I almost forgot. I have a message for you. It's from Blanche." He tipped the blond wig and inserted his fingers into the back of Roosevelt, who rolled his eyes and opened his mouth.

Road Runner beeped, and I ran, ran, ran.

Unday

The solipsist errs.†

Noneday

I will resist erasure.‡

Doneday

I'm a sort of amputee-at-arms. Waving my phantom limbs, my purloined letters.§

Vennday

Consider possibility that Blanche is writing my experiences into existence.

Explain.

I observe my hand tracing the words "I saw a vulture circling over Mission Dolores," picture a vulture as any reader would, retrospectively "remember" it.

In that case what use is any of this?

---

*Ink changes from blue to black at this point in the word, suggesting the account was taken up later.

†My handwriting?

‡In the gaps between words, other words form.

§ This is certainly Blanche—though see the curious suggestion below.

Including that question?

Consider possibility that I am now anticipating Blanche's interventions so strongly I generate them myself—that I am haunting *myself.*

Consider possibility that I have been doing this all along, i.e. Blanche is my invention.

Consider possibility that I am Blanche.

Absurd. Offensive to logic and decency. Explain.

Projecting myself into Nora's experience so strongly that I experience myself as another. In which case I am being haunted by my own rejected experience.

So the current situation could be described as Blanche thinking she is Nora thinking she is Blanche thinking she is Nora?

Or Nora thinking she is Blanche thinking she is Nora thinking she is Blanche thinking she is Nora?

Stop it.

A while ago I wrote, "If I can write an imitation Blanche, what makes me think she can't write an imitation Nora?" But that's not the real question. The real question is, if I can write a fake Blanche, then what makes me think I am not writing the real Blanche? And its corollary: If she can write a fake Nora, what makes me think this one is real?

Who's writing this book,* anyway?

I am.

Not good enough.

Nora, Nora, Nora, Nora, Nora[†‡§]!

---

*One might add, who is writing these footnotes?

†This seems unequivocal.

‡And yet, "Since [†, the obelisk or dagger] also represents the Christian cross, in certain predominantly Christian regions, the mark is used in a text after the name of a deceased person or the date of death, as in Christian graves." Wikipedia.

§While this disagreeable symbol (‡) is called the double dagger. Is it important that in the reference volume *Generic Names of the Moths of the World,* this symbol indicates an unavailable name? Or that Her Majesty's Nautical Almanac Office (NAO) uses the double dagger to indicate regions that do not have a standard time, such as Greenland's ice sheet? Or that a double dagger is one of twelve areas of combat in Kali, a martial art of the Philippines, which for full mastery requires "the independent use of the hands, or hands and feet, to do two different things at the same time"?

I could go on, but I will not, for § is the section symbol, and it is time, oh, more than time for a new one.

Att'n: Two Times Editorial Department
c.c. The Siamystics Mailing List
An Open Letter to the Togetherists and The Unity Foundation

Be advised that your seeming ally Mr. Nickel, AKA Disme—who no doubt has other aliases, and can be seen wearing a prosthetic head (look closely at the corners of the mouth and eyes, listen for canned laughter and the faint grind of gears)—is a double agent. This scoundrel toys with human longing for his own entertainment, but he has provided us one service. His simultaneous membership in two supposedly rival clubs demonstrates what should have been obvious from the start: the Togetherists and the vivisectionists are two sides of the same counterfeit coin (a wooden nickel, I imagine), that has rolled out of the coffers of history and received a fresh coat of metallic paint: the spurious currency of the One. But remember, fission and fusion both have explosive consequences.

Respectfully,

N.O.

I borrowed Audrey's car and drove the Mooncalf out to Fort Funston Beach, taking with me the bag of writings and the letter. I thought I might burn one of them, maybe both.

Near Stern Grove, I pulled over and dropped the letter in a mailbox.

At the beach, I dug a small pit with my hands. I put the bag in it, and found I had no matches. I picked up the bag again, put my shoes in it, and walked barefoot along the high-water mark, among bleached bottle tops and tiny pink crab legs like the ripped-off arms of fairies. My dress whipped around. Goose bumps rose on my arms, and my legs stung in the salt air. Up ahead, the Mooncalf's tail stopped waving, and she went still and rapt.

She had found a dead deer in the surf, in a garnish of stinking broken seaweed, intermittently afloat. It was entirely white, and free of the flies that were in a frenzy over the rotting seaweed, because the surf kept washing casually over it, bubbling into the chest cavity through a hole. It was smooth except for a toupee-like flap of matted hair that still clung to one flank. The skin was stretched tight over the ribcage, which was a beautiful shape like a coracle's.

The mouth gaped. The skin was pulled smooth over the jawbone. It no longer had the sharp lines of a deer's jaw, and looked both more pathetic and more frightening, like some of Picasso's women, that smooth and predatory and anguished. The eyes were simple holes.

It is no doubt because of my erstwhile curatorship in the Dead Animal Zoo that I thrill to a corpse with urges that have no obvious outlet. I hovered over the relic like an angel with a specimen box hidden in her robes.

The deer was nothing but what it seemed, an unfortunate creature whose life had ended. It did not lift up its head and speak to me. Though the sand on which it lay shivered when the water drew back and seemed as dry as if no water had touched it since the rainy season, the deer was real. It was what I needed.

"I'm through," I said out loud. The Mooncalf looked at me, surmise in her eyes. "I've had my run. All right, Blanche, I'm all yours."

Cow

Donkey-skin was gone, and we were walking back home along the road to Too Bad when we heard someone coming and got behind a bush. It was Dr. Goat. The pickup was slithering up the road almost crabwise, spitting rocks from its tires. The driver was riding the gas too hard for the traction he had, so I knew he was not thinking straight. Blanche took off running, like an idiot. He saw us right away, or saw the bushes thrashing. Behind us we heard the car door open.

"Hey! Get back here!" We looked back and saw him jump out. He had his gun. He swung it up and fired up into the air. The sound came back from the bluff.

"Get your ass back here, you sick little monster. Come on, you freak motherfucker, I want to talk to you."

Dense thornbushes surrounded us. I heard rocks crunching under Dr. Goat's feet. We dropped to our hands and knees and crawled into the bushes. We scared up a rabbit close by, and it took off with a burst of kicked-back pebbles, running intricately with many dodging maneuvers, and left us behind. A thorn hooked our shoulder right through our T-shirt, but we kept going, and it tore free. On the other side of the bush we got to our feet and ran.

From behind came a bellow. "Ow! You shit-sucking whore!"

We slithered sideways down into an arroyo, riding a small landslide, and scurried up the smooth sand bottom under the low-hanging milky green palo verde fronds until our way was blocked by a tangle of sticks and blackened cactus limbs deposited there by a flash flood. We could hear the rocks

cascading down the slope behind us. We scrambled up the other side. Dr. Goat saw us at the crest of the hill and hollered.

On the desert if you want to go fast it helps if you know the way. It seemed as if our feet decided on their own which way to run, or maybe Blanche was leading and I did not notice, because I did not intend to take Dr. Goat to the Dead Animal Zoo. The small bodies had been rearranged by carrion eaters since the last time we had been there, but the cow was still there, though almost hairless now, and a little flatter than before. The hole torn in her belly had almost closed as her body collapsed slowly in on itself, and the dry hide shrank over her skeleton.

The rabbit is most likely to be shot as it runs. After it goes to earth only a dog's nose will find it out, and Dr. Goat did not like dogs. We hesitated for only a moment, panting, then we heard footsteps again, coming fast. We got on our belly and squirmed through the hole into the stomach of the cow as beetles fled in all directions.

We pulled in our feet and curled up where the ribcage made a little cave. The almost hairless hide was translucent, and the hollow glowed with an amber light. Up the shriveled neck passage I could see a dot of light that I thought might come from an eye socket. The cow lay on her side, one eye looking at the sky, one into the ground.

We hugged our knees and made ourselves very small. My breath sounded very loud in the close space. We sucked in two huge breaths, both together, and then we heard Dr. Goat come into the clearing. We let the air out very slowly. We were trembling. I felt like water, simmering.

The footsteps stopped.

"What the fuck? Now this is sick. Tru-ly sick," Dr. Goat said, but not to us. Through a tiny puncture in the hide I thought I could see a fleck of red, moving. I closed my eyes so that he could not see me. In the silence, I could hear Blanche's nose whistling softly every time she exhaled. What was Dr. Goat doing? Could he see our dark shape curled inside the cow like we could see the light of the sky?

Steps came toward us. My scalp prickled. I closed my eyes and silently prayed—to God, Lithobolia, Coyote, Granny, anyone—Come save us. Please, somebody, come.

There was a clank inches away, and something struck the hide right above my shoulder. Particles rained down on my arm. A narrow shadow fell across the roof. Dr. Goat had leaned his gun against the cow.

His footsteps crunched away. "Hey there kids—I'm not going to eat you! Don't be silly, I know you're there. Look, damn it, I know I scared you with that gun, but see, I've put it down. I'm holding up my hands now and you can see they're empty. I'm not going to hurt you, I just want to talk to you, like one grown-up to another."

We heard him take another couple of steps away.

Slowly, stealthily, I slid my hand out from under the fringe of skin. I felt warm metal. The barrel slid sideways, and we froze.

"You think you're hiding, but I can see you plain as day! If you don't come out, I'll have to come in and get you. My patience is running out." We heard him beating the bushes. "Say something, you little freak, or I might stop being so nice. What do you think about that, cocksuckers? OK, I'm going to count to ten. One . . . two . . . " He was getting farther away. My hand closed around the butt of the rifle.

"Five . . ."

We stuck our feet back out of the hole and dug our toes into the ground. Slowly, leaning on the rifle, we pressed ourselves back and up into a crouch. The neck of the cow creaked as it lifted off the ground. Some bones fell out of a hole somewhere and tocked dryly on the stones, and we stopped and listened. I could hear a myriad sifting sounds as sand and insects and particles of all kinds sought new paths down through the shifting carcass. I ducked my head and closed my eyes as I felt grains trickle down over my face.

"Seven . . ."

Suddenly, I could not move. My throat was so dry I probably could not have spoken and I did not dare in any case, but I thought as hard as I could: *Donkey-skin*. Maybe Blanche understood, or was thinking the same thing; in any case she was helping me suddenly, and it was a little easier. Half the ribs had stayed behind, in a heap at our feet, which lightened our load. The head hung down in front and almost unbalanced us. There was a rip in the neck we could see through. Once standing, we drew the warm length of the gun up along our body and stuck it out that hole.

"Nine . . ."

Then Dr. Goat came back out of the bushes and saw us.

"Holy Mother!" he said, and staggered back. He fell on one knee and snagged his shirt in the thorns. The bush held him fast. His fingers worked frantically to free his shirt. "What the—"

Then I saw him see the gun.

"Now I really think—" he said, and then the cow shot him.

The gun jumped back and kicked me in the side of the head and everything went dark red. We wheeled around in a confusion of creaking bone and skin and a shower of crawling particles. My teeth were vibrating and my tongue had gone numb. But someone held onto the gun and righted herself and tugged the hide straight so we could see again.

Dr. Goat was lying down. There was a red mess in his lap I did not want to look at too closely. His fingers were still working on his shirt.

The cow looked at him with her empty holes and shook her head at him. Some neck bones fell out of her mouth: one, two, three. One of her hooves clattered on the ground with a rattlesnake sort of sound.

Dr. Goat was moving his red mouth. His voice sounded wet, and it was hard to understand. All of a sudden I knew he was speaking another language, the one he used with Donkey-skin. He was talking to us in the language of the animals.

The cow walked up to him. Her other front leg, which was shriveled and hard, was stuck up by her neck as if someone wanted to be polite about coughing. The cow hung her head and smiled like Flossy in the picture book, and the gun barrel found its way back out of the hole in her neck.

Dr. Goat's hand fell onto the ground and picked among the stones, and out of them he selected a twig and as the bullet left the barrel he threw that in its path. Then he fell back hard and didn't cause us any more trouble.

The cowboy poets lie. Tumbleweeds rolling emptily in the winds of dusk, dessicated ruins, weathered crosses stuck in heaps of stone: these things aren't sad. I have survived a thousand sunsets without a tear. The melancholy of the desert is somewhere else, in the indifference of high noon.

At noon the sun stops. Birds shut up, animals hide. The huge surge of morning, when the sun rears up out of the night, is over; day is achieved. The flat round of the earth stares up at the sun. The sun stares down. Neither moves. If human beings move, they look small and misinformed and out of place.

There are no shadows at midday. They'll appear later, when the desert has acquired some manners, and lost some honesty. There is a kind of blindness of visibility. When everything is spotlit equally, distinctions disappear. Figure and ground are soldered together. You can't tell what is close from what is far, far away.

That was the light that shone on the Dead Animal Zoo when it acquired its first human specimen.

A hunched figure dragged itself into Too Bad. It appeared first at the uphill end of Too Bad's main street and teetered there. Then it started down along the row of false fronts. The head had a funny sideways cant to it as it shook, which gave it an ironic, almost flirtatious air. The skirts of this cow-gown dragged on the stones and caught at times and slowed and leaned and lurched forward again, leaving little shreds behind. A cactus pad rode along on the train. Black beetles lost their hold and seethed into shiny living pools in the ruts.

Somewhere a dog was barking, tail wagging like crazy, planting its hind feet and hopping up and down stiffly on its front feet with every bark, then bucking backward in jumps, all the way down the street, to where Mama was sitting on a bench in the shade, drinking iced tea. The cow stopped. Mama dropped her glass. She made a little sound, a little word, maybe no more than "Oh," but it didn't sound like it meant "Oh" at all, but something much longer and harder to say.

Then Mama screamed, and Papa and Max came running. After a quick exchange I could not hear, Max took off up the road the way we had come. Papa soothed Mama. We stood, swayed.

Finally Mama straightened and turned to us. She put out her hand and then took it back. "All right, girls," she said sternly, "get out of that filthy thing."

The cow staggered toward the house.

"Not in my house!"

We veered into the ruins next door.

The cow's legs already trailed on the ground, so it could hardly be said to kneel, but somehow it kneeled inside itself, crumpling in the center, admittedly in a place a live cow would never fold, but then dead cows are not as constrained as live ones, they are agile and fantastical. Also, as we have seen, quick to wroth, vengeful and proud. The cow sank down, and deflated as it sank, until it no longer looked much like a cow, or anything that had ever been alive.

I didn't want to come out. Almost all the beetles had left, and I had just about sorted out how to fit around the remaining bones, and though the

hide was heavy, the weight steadied me, and I liked its thick, sour, beery smell. There was a lot to think about in that smell.

A vulture passed overhead. The belly of the dead cow heaved, and after a mercifully brief term, she calved, unorthodoxly, through the stomach wall.

A couple of days later, we went for a walk. We struck off across country, going wherever way opened up, following the winding arroyos whenever the thornbushes stood far enough apart to leave a clear path up the soft pale sand, and found ourselves at the zoo. The exhibits were stirred around, animals were mixed up with other animals. Dr. Goat had pulverized a half-dozen specimens, including our best squirrel, the one that looked like he was snarling with one paw raised like a heraldic lion. But otherwise it was nearly complete.

But Dr. Goat was not there.

Someone who didn't know the desert like we did might not even notice that some of the rocks where he had been were dusted with yellow-ocher, not licked clean on top like the untroubled ones near it.

"The funny thing," said Blanche, "is how big he was, even after."

"Shut up!"

"You feel like people are going to get little when they die. Thinner and little. Like they're going away. But he was practically as big as ever."

"Shut up, shut up, shut up, shut up!"

PART FOUR

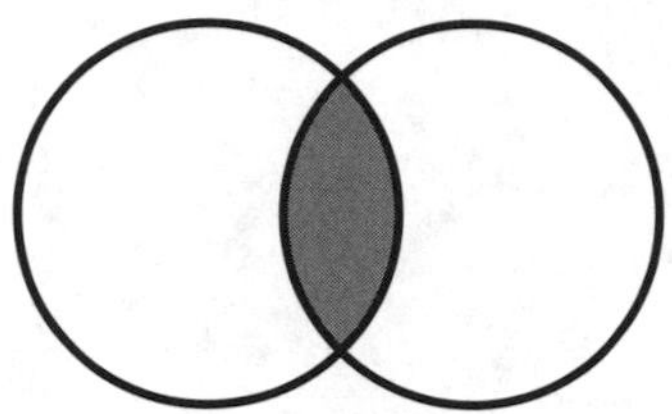

Boolean Operator: AND

THE SIAMESE TWIN REFERENCE MANUAL

Venn and You

Venn healing employs Boolean logic and the simplest form of the Venn diagram, the double cell, to counsel the marriage of self and other in the single "individual." The literalization of this model is the conjoined twin or twofer, but every singleton also contains a phantom twin. The first person *is* the second person. As we will study to understand, it is also the third, and though we have no grammar yet to give these persons voice, it is the fourth, fifth, sixth: Around our single-cell self cluster quads, quints, and other sibling selves. In time we will learn to count these petals without plucking them, and thus reducing sheer multiplicity to that all-too-familiar XOR, she loves me, she loves me not. Instead we will stick our noses into the intersection set and breathe in a heady new perfume: the AND. She loves me *and* she loves me not, I love her and I love her not, we love them and we love them not, I love me and I love me not. In time, we will all be such flowers.

The Operators

The Boolean operators NOT, XOR, OR and AND govern our relations with the other—the other in the world, and the other in ourselves. Most people will find they can identify their ascendant operator, but in the course of any given day one or more of the others may come into play. Though Western culture has been governed by NOT since the ancient Greeks, a close look at any apparent homogeneity will reveal XOR, OR, and AND at play within it. It is effectively impossible to seal out the other. The single cell splits, othering *itself*: out of this "same diff" we are born.

The process of healing is a shifting of emphasis from static NOT to dynamic AND, from the self-centered single cell to the intersection set. However, it is important to

note that NOT also has its function. As any librarian can tell you, there is a time to broaden the search, and a time to limit it.

NOT
I, not you.

I win, you lose. For me, glut. For you, famine. But a glut of light is blinding, a glut of sound deafening. In the seeming silence, the seeming dark, the other looks and listens and waits her chance. Every dog has its day, every worm will turn: NOT can never forget XOR.

XOR
"Exclusive or": Either of us, but not both.

Agon. La Lucha. War of the worlds. Black and white, night and day, Montagues and Capulets. XOR comes from NOT, strains back toward NOT. It does not acknowledge the OR that makes it possible.

OR
Either or both of us.

You could be right. I could be wrong. Let's agree to disagree: good fences make good neighbors. OR admits to AND, but schemes to inherit the earth.

AND
The intersection set.

AND is the copulative conjunction—the vaginal cock, the phallic cunt. It is the hearing mouth, the speaking ear. It is the wound that cures, and the cure that wounds. I am an other: within black, the germ of white. Within white, an inkling of black. AND is the pain that causes NOT, the flaw in NOT that permits XOR, the compassion that brokers XOR's truce in OR, the love of OR for OR that ends in AND.

Going Home

I woke up to the wallowing motion of a car with a sprung suspension. A hot wind was ruffling my hair and the backs of my knees were sweating cold, my thighs swimming together under a warm weight in my lap. My left elbow was on hot chrome and my right hand was on the wheel. Therefore, I was driving.

My eyes jumped open. Yellow dash, dash, dash: dotted line of a divided highway, curving between shallow buff cutbanks and scrub. The metal bars of a cattle guard flashed under the wheels—burst of machine gun fire—and a road sign hove up against the urgent sky. Black cow on goldenrod diamond, turning, turned, gone: no plain-Jane California cow, but a lively, wayward beast with a humped tail and a look of surprise because this was Nevada and Blanche had brought us home.

The car? Audrey's. The dress I had worn to the beach filthy now, my lap so wet it felt like I had peed myself, but no, it was just sweat and drool from the Mooncalf asleep with her head draped over my thigh, blowing raspberries through her flews. Chocolate milk turning curdy in the cup holder. My notebooks were scattered on the back seat, their pages briskly ruffled, *kerfuffle,* and a candy bar wrapper caught in a vortex was whipping around, around. My jacket and the bag of loose notes—my diary—were crammed into the right rear foot well, along with some half-empty soda bottles and my shoes.

We were rolling down the bajada from the western range. That canker sore in the middle of the basin was Grady, and the dim minatory silhouettes on the other side were the mountains over Too Bad. They were the blue-

grey of gasoline smoke, but they seemed no-colored, a little strip of nothing showing through where the sky had peeled up.

Gas? Half tank. Blanche pumping gas! And paying for it; how? Well, with my credit cards.

I braked hard for a curve where others had not, and small crooked crosses hung with garlands swam past the windows. The sun had beat the colors out of the plastic petals and turned them all the same bleached orange. Then the cutbanks melted away and I was on the flat and could speed into the quicksilver dissolve of the sky-reflecting road. A single approaching car oozed in and out of existence. Then we too rolled through a series of sandy dips, the chassis flouncing at the low points. The car flashed past with a whoop that went suddenly out of tune.

Dust was slithering and sidewinding along the road. To the right rain was falling, but not as far as the ground. The soft skeins, fine as baby hair, evaporated in midair.

The first signs of habitation were rusted pickups and refrigerators, scattered in the vast emptiness like space junk. We passed a school bus painted blue, a slide sticking out of one window, parked in a yard of stripped dirt that swirled into a cloud when the wind picked up. Then the first trailers, parked on parched lawns or squares of Astroturf. We passed two girls airborne above a trampoline stamped with two shadows into which, stopped in memory forever, they will never fall.

Operation Game Thief.

The Indian Holiness Mission.

The Red D Mart. (Only it was and had always been a blue D.)

Keep M Running Knife Sale!

Midget Motel.

Used Car Giant.

Kwik Kup. Pastrami is Back!

The old Atomic Drive-In sign, its lot full of tents and trailers appertaining to some kind of revival meeting: "Oxymoron JOIN US!"

The Hohokam Elementary School, with the same lonely tetherball poles, cords swinging free from the poles, and the same terrible jungle gym, an infernal device wrought from hot pokers.

A patrol car pulled out from behind the school and slinked after us. We rolled slowly past the drugstore where you could always get your horoscope on a slip of colored paper—yellow, pink, or pistachio—rolled up and stuck in

a plastic vial, and miniature license plates with your name on them, if your name was Jill or Walter, swung insolently from the prongs of a rotating display. Past the supermarket where four cucumbers, a cabbage, and two green peppers were repeatedly wet by incontinent nozzles. Past the pink concrete curves of Dinosaur Taco, its outdoor tables still thickly draped with fat teens in children's play clothes, thin teens in black nipple-frotting T-shirts emblazoned with band and brand names, who gawked as we passed.

We passed the old pink Fiesta Motel, which was doing good business for this time of year. Could we stop? I wanted a shower, a cold clean bed, time to think. "You brought us here," I said experimentally. "Now what?" Nothing happened, except the Mooncalf rolled one eye up at me and started panting hugely. I felt no resistance from Blanche when I turned in at the next motel, the Twilite Inn. When I opened the door, Moony started up and struggled across my lap and out the door, hurting me. She made for a patch of grass and squatted, looking back at me over her shoulder. The patrol car rolled slowly by, and then sped out of sight with a roar.

My wallet was in my jacket pocket along with a wad of receipts—for gas, but also Pixy Stix, Cheezy Dips, strawberry shakes. Kid food.

There was an old, ragged flyer taped to the lobby door announcing a petition to halt DOE plans to store nuclear waste in Grady's backyard, and I put my hand on it to quell its fluttering and saw that Max and Papa were both listed under Eminent Signatories. Mama was not. Moonie sat down outside the door and watched me through the glass as I rang the bell. It was odd to think she knew Blanche better than I did now.

There was a sign up behind the desk: "No 2 party Checks—none—0—not any." The desk clerk came out from the back. I didn't recognize her. I considered her eyebrows, which were hairless abstractions drawn in unnatural arcs not quite matching. The rest of her face belied their artfulness. She had simple dark hair and her smile was a shy pulling-away of the lips, often repeated, as if she was trying but failing to keep her mouth closed.

"Pro or con?" she said.

I puzzled over this question and could make nothing of it. "Pro or con what?"

"Oh! I thought—sorry. Most of our other guests are here for the Oxymoron. Just passing through?"

"I—we—grew up around here."

"Oh, welcome home!" she said, with such warmth I blushed. "Here's your

key. The ice machine is right outside, you can't miss it. Is there anything else you need?"

"Could I check my e-mail?"

"Of course." She took me into the back office. "Just click here. And if you need to print anything . . ."

There were three items of interest.

Where are you? Where's my dog? And my car? Please, PLEASE get in touch. If you are not dead, you will be once I get my hands on you. Kidding. I am calling the police NOW.

—Audrey

Siamystic Meanderings

Those members jailed in England last month in connection with Togetherist protests have been released and all charges dropped.

Joint actions with the Togetherists have been suspended pending investigation of the recent allegations of their secret link to the Unity Foundation.

Siamystics interested in taking part in the "Oxymoron," please contact your local group leader for directions, schedule, accommodations, etc.

Time to let go of the balloon strings? Be safe, and if you can't be safe, be sorry—

Trey

PS Check this out. Poppkiss says he had nothing to do with it.

*   *   *

Fwd: Head a Fake

Widespread speculations that the UK's notorious Dr. Decapitate had moved his operations stateside were proved hasty when close inspection of the human head found by fishermen floating beneath the Golden Gate Bridge revealed that it was a prosthetic. The head contains a sophisticated recording and playback device, and the SFPD initially harbored hopes that data retrieval specialists would be able to extract identifying information from its hard drive, but salt water had corroded the disk and all restoration attempts proved futile. Deformation of the head suggests that it fell from a great height. Nobody has come forward to claim ownership of the head, strengthening speculations that it was in use at the time of the accident; however, no body has been found. Foul play cannot be ruled out. If you have information concerning the ownership of the head, please contact Detective O'nan of the SFPD.

"Excuse me," the desk clerk said, poking her head in. She handed me a flyer. "Since you grew up here, you might be interested. If you're still here tomorrow afternoon—well, *I'm* going!"

OXYMORON!
PRO Nuke? NO Nuke? Join us!
Historic Self-Contradictory Action at the NTS

Pro-nuke and No-nuke activists join together in demanding that Nevada's National Penitence Ground be turned over to the people effective immediately.

The Nuclear Abolitionists, Parents for a Radiation-Free Tomorrow, and the Western Shoshone, long opponents of nuclear testing and

waste storage, have forged a historic agreement with pro-nuke forces including the RadioActivists, Mutatis Mutandis, and the LMV or League of Mutant Voters. The Oxymoron is supported by the Grady City Council, hitherto reluctant to take a stand on nuclear issues. "We see in the Oxymoron the opportunity to find common ground on an issue that has bitterly divided our community. Declassifying the NPG will put Grady on the map as a destination for tourists and pilgrims alike, creating abundant jobs for locals, while putting an end to the Sadness that is poisoning the state of Nevada."

Scheduled for 12 noon at the front gates of the National Penitence Ground. Local accommodations are limited; buses will transport Oxymorons from Las Vegas starting at 6 am, leaving from the Pretty Princess Casino parking lot, fourth level.

PENITENCE TO THE PEOPLE!

When I reemerged, with these documents and a stolen glue stick, I couldn't see the Mooncalf. I left the door of my room open while I washed my face and took off my shoes. Then I made tea with a bag wedged in a Styrofoam cup beside the coffeemaker, ignoring the shiny pillowlet that was the vacuum-sealed packet of coffee. There was nothing to read but the Bible and the phone book. I chose the phone book. I took it and the cup outside and let myself in to a rectangle of Astroturf with a chain-link fence around it, containing some white plastic chairs, a picnic table, a bird feeder swaying from a metal arm, a barometer, a birdbath at which some quail were doing a fussy formal dance. The wind grabbed the door and banged it into its catch behind me, and the quail ran neatly through the chain-link fence without pausing and across the parking lot into the bushes. I sat down in one of the chairs. The sky was darkening and the faded Astroturf was an impossible green, the white lawn furniture almost fluorescent. A storm was cooking up blue-black over the Moroccan orange hills.

I felt amazingly calm. I had finally had enough sleep. Ants ran over my feet. I let them. The phone book was a warm weight relaxing into my lap, like a sleeping child. I set my cup down on the Astroturf by the chair leg and flopped open the tome, which was a tome only because Grady, not big

enough to earn its own phone book, was lumped in with Reno and Sparks and half a dozen other smaller towns.

Look up the Olneys. There they were, a Too Bad listing. The wind worried the page. Turn to the business listings, look up Olney, nothing; look up Too Bad. Shouldn't a ghost town be unlisted? But there it was, full-page ad:

Too Bad the Living Ghost Town!
*Character Actors Depict Real Historical Personages
*Strike It Rich! Prospect for Silver
*Shoot-Out Every Day at Noon and Four
*Famous Time Camera Takes You Back
*Fun and Educational for Young and Old

Look up Goat. No Goat. Goard abutted Gobbel. Check the business listings. Go Away Travel. God Loves Giving Hands Thrift Emporium. No Goat. What did I expect?

Look up Chris Marchpane. March Marco Marcus. Nothing. Check the business listings, Marathon Communications, March of Dimes Birth Defects Foundation. I started to flop the book closed, it slewed, and I slapped my hand down on it. In a little boxed ad I had just spotted something. Marchpane Motor Makeovers (Expert Color Matching and Detailing, Kool Kustomizing, Mod Murals).

Well.

The wind thrashed the bushes. The ants that had been all around a moment before had disappeared, except one big sluggish ant who was carrying his oversized head around like a penance. Now he had stopped with his face to the Astroturf and was making tiny investigations. I was shielding my tea with my hand from the grit flying everywhere. Thunder broke. The roof of the bird feeder was clapping, and pinpricks of rain hit my shoulders. I retreated under the eaves.

The rain came down in white lines like hard scratches in varnish. Instantly there were mud puddles, and brown water leaped down the road and into a culvert. The lightning flashed, and an old habit sprung up out of nowhere in me and I counted off the seconds until the thunder cracked. One, two: less than a mile.

Ten minutes later the storm had passed and winged ants sucked in by its

departure were wheeling down from the clouds and staggering up again and it was dark and fragrant and the puddles in the parking lot held ridiculously beautiful blue and orange and pink fragments of the sunstruck clouds above.

I walked up the hill back of the motel to watch the light finish its changes. Some kids straddling outgrown bikes in the steaming parking lot watched me go. I knew their kind, the soft slow-moving kids, paler than you would expect, who hung around the gas station convenience store and played video games there and gabbed and ate jerky and Atomic Fireballs, chips and sodas, or silently gathered in broods around their large mothers at church socials and ate macaroni salad and hot dogs and chips and sodas and cupcakes. And the brown little boys with bleached crew cuts who rode in the back of red pickups and at five or six knew everything about guns and had tried cigarettes and performed dangerous stunts to get attention and jumped up bloody and said they didn't feel anything. I looked back from the hill, and they were tearing away pedaling like mad down the shoulder of the highway toward the setting sun, their T-shirts raised like hydrofoils behind them.

The warm wet spicy smell of sage affected me like catnip, and I had trouble not skipping. But the desert punishes spontaneity. I detached a spiny branch from my arm and went on soberly until the neon lights of the motel were over the crest of the rise from me. Around here you only had to walk fifty feet, and you were out of town.

I thought about Chris Marchpane, about all the right turns and left turns and delays and reverses it must have taken to get that painting on that car to that street in San Francisco on that day, a combination lock a genius couldn't crack. Then I thought about what it meant that he had painted me, or rather us, or rather that he had not *not* painted me, not painted me out—do you follow? After all this time thinking he wanted Blanche, not me, how odd to consider that he might have liked both of us all along.

On the far side of the valley in the shadow of the western range it was getting dark. I could see a few trailer roofs shining dull like pewter, and the thin scar of the road heading north; one pair of taillights, far away and dwindling. The sun still touched down on this side of the valley, raking sideways, throwing up long blue shadows from the smallest shrub. Blue shadows, grey-gold brush: rabbitbrush, sage, and Mormon tea. Each small tuffet had its train of blue, so they all seemed to be creeping west. The hills too, because of their back-tilt, were sweeping westward, dragging their finery behind them.

The sun went down until there were dwindling stripes of gold stretching

across the shadow area to the golden east of the basin. As the shadow moved up, the light turned red on the peaks. When all the land was dark, then for a while it seemed lighter again, and the air was balmy, and we moved with ease, in pleasure at the sweet air brushing softly past us, and the rabbits all stepped out, and the rattlesnakes crawled onto the verge of the road and lay there with their heads down in a swoon of pleasure. To the east the blue earth-shadow rose, and above it the pink and the dirty orange, and above that the still light blue, and to the west a tangerine glow behind the dark blue mountains. The basin seemed to hold a shallow lake of warm dirty water from which we looked up at the great clean untouchable sky.

Near an old dead car I found a newly dead dog. For a horrible moment I thought it might be the Mooncalf, but it was the wrong color, black and tan. Nor was it as fresh as I had thought at first glance, but already partway gone toward the lampshade, the saddle, the handbag, and blackening the stones around it with fur and particles that had been borne away by bugs or scattered by the tearing and plucking of carrion birds. But it was not much torn apart, except that one front paw had broken or been ripped off and carried away.

Where was the Mooncalf? I stepped over the paw, not after all very far away, with its pads turned up, and white bones gleaming in the sleeve of fur. "Mooncalf! Mooner," I called. I heard a far-off squeal or scream and quieted my steps and heard a coyote from the hills very clear, *yip yip yipeee,* and suddenly my heart hurt with pleasure to be home. And then the Mooncalf came dancing up over the ridge, tail low and guilty and a smirk on her face.

The last thing I remembered doing before I woke up in the desert was giving up. I imagined it as a kind of suicide. But Blanche hadn't let me go. She had driven seven hundred miles to put me where she wanted me, and then she had brought me back. You could call that a strong hint: there was something I was supposed to do. But what?

Well, there was one thing I could do: finish my story. I got the bag of diary entries out of the car and laid them out on the bed, a fragile patchwork, fluttering in the cold breath of the Genie. When they seemed in order, I began to paste them into my notebook, adding notes as needed. Outside, the night was loud with crickets I could hear even through the sound of the fan motor. When I opened the door, it was like the chant of a mob. *Cree cree cree cree.* The blue air was warm and still reeked of wood smoke from the

fires started in the hills near the mines by dry lightning earlier today, as the hotel lady had told me. The black column of smoke was leaning out over Grady as if looking for something on the other side. There could not be much to burn unless the mines themselves went up. But there was the fire, a candy-red shower and glow. A few tiny planes circled it. Their winking lights stood in the smoke. Nearby, the sprinklers were working by themselves in the dark playing field across the street, wetting the road in sudden, reckless, but quickly withdrawn gestures. In the pink light of the motel sign, I saw a praying mantis, its tiny human head turned to watch me.

I peeled off my sticky dress and took a bath in the glossy, pink, too shallow bathtub, under the heavy breathing of the fan. When I got out, my skin was hot enough to melt wax. I dried off and was wet again at once, this time with sweat. A drop of light hung from one nipple, and then I moved and it was slung off somewhere. There was a slow churning under my skin. I flopped down on my back on the bed. My heart galumphed in my stomach like some clumsy animal protesting against its incorporation. I heard something steady and secretive like sand grains trickling through invisible capillaries in the air. There were black crowdings pierced with tiny stinging lights all around me, an optical charivari that probably said damaging things about my state of health, but I liked it, and the tingling chill that now lay on my skin.

I had long slow intricate dreams like biological processes unfolding in their own time. The bed jiggled me in its palm like a coin. I let the Mooncalf out to pee sometime toward morning and fell back into bed and slept until the light woke me.

When I opened the door the Mooncalf fell in. She was sprawled comfortably on a copy of the *Grady Gazette,* in the blinding light of the sun, and lifted her paw to let me scratch her chest, her eyes rolling up at me.

I stacked my notebooks neatly, clipped a pen to the uppermost, and hung the Do Not Disturb sign from the door with a small internal click of officious pleasure. My ankles burned in the sun angling under the low awning, but the air was still cool and moist and made me feel loose-limbed and slightly drunk. Crossing the parking lot toward the office, I passed an old man with a huge speckled head who seemed to be under the impression he was walking. "Nice dog," he croaked. "Dalmation, right?" He moved his foot a centimeter and beamed.

Audrey,

Regret I am alive. Moonie is fine. I will leave her with family in Too Bad, with instructions to call you. Car is at Twilite Inn, Grady Nevada. Keys left in Room 32. Please call off the cops.

—Nora/Blanche

PS Tell Trey it's looking like sorry.

After sending the preceding I went east, uphill, walking on the shoulder of the highway. The desert had been taking me back for a long time now. It wasn't hard to guess where it was drawing me: Thin Air. But there was something I needed to get first.

The last house fell behind me. The Mooncalf trotted after me at a short distance, making short forays off the road to sniff at the bushes, and then cantering for a bit to catch up. I passed a sign for Too Bad. The sky was lifting up like a huge sail, and in the space it made the birds chased one another from bush to bush like children, clamoring happily. When a truck passed with a sucking *whoosh* they all paused, checked themselves, and then took off again.

Where my hand clasped my notebooks, they grew damp. I was sweating, but the hot wind took it off me and left my forehead improbably cold. Already my throat was dry. I should have carried water. The chill around the roots of my hair made me feel sick. I had put my dirty dress back on, I didn't have anything else, and my own smell hung around me.

The day got gradually hotter and brighter and more fretful, as if some kind of pain-killer were wearing off. The Mooncalf's tongue hung out. I toiled upward. I no longer wanted to look up at the sky, which I sensed lowering menacingly toward me. The birds quieted as the long haul of midday began.

When I finally turned off the freeway onto the road into Too Bad, which was still dirt (on the map it was marked "Improved," which it was I suppose, though barely—its ruts had been filled with gravel, the round shoulders braced with dry-laid rocks), I felt something invisible pushing against me. I moved forward anyway, and then everything was lubricated and running

and gently chuckling. How absurd it was that the jojoba bushes still confidently raised their tiny round leaves to the light, that ants truckled back and forth about their business, dying and being born and everything in between without checking in with me. How absurd, that grease-stained yellow wrapper doing a frivolous hopping dance around itself on the side of the road and then collapsing in a soft heap, as if it would have done that anyway, yesterday, or ten years ago, whether I came or stayed away. There was no trace, not even around the edges of things, of that waxy amber-colored medium that seemed to preserve the moments of my past in scenes that looked plausible but forbade entry, like the boxes in the Potter Museum. Everything looked subject to revision, temporary, without gravity.

It's the same, I thought, and I felt a strange spreading and softening all around me, as if all this time I had held myself tense against the thought of having lost it by staying away. But here it was, not different. It looked like the past and it *was* the past—that's what we mean when we say, "I'm back"—and yet nothing held me from it, not the thinnest plastic wrap. I could touch it. I bent over and scrabbled my finger in the still damp, orange dirt. I could be dirtied by it. I could—I scraped a hair-fine pricker out of the tip of my finger—be hurt by it.

Too Bad, the business concern, was just getting ready for the day. There were a few cars in the big gravel lot, and one of the saloon's swinging doors was propped open by a big greenish chunk of silver ore. That rock was as intimate evidence of my father as his footprint or the smell of Old Spice.

I saw a human silhouette through the door. I stumbled noisily and the shape turned and a pair of glasses caught the light and goggled out at me. I kept going. No one came to the door. Maybe it was not Papa; the ghost town was successful enough now to hire employees.

The house looked shoddy and small. The two halves had slid farther on their opposite paths, and the gap between was covered with a strip of plastic tarp duct-taped to the walls and roofs of each half. Someone had attempted to seed a patch of lawn beside the house, and in the center of it a hose was running into a shallow moat around a spindly tree. The Mooncalf drank noisily from the moat and then lay down in it.

I stepped onto the Astroturf landing pad, all its faded green blades now flattened one way like a dog's coat, and considered the fuzzy underthings of a moth that had applied itself to the other side of the screen door at the

level of my face. I reached out for the catch—then ducked to the left into the mesquite there. Wait, wait. I stooped there, listening. I heard nothing but my heart stammering. I had scratched my arm. You do not "dive into the underbrush" in the desert. I licked up the thin line of blood. I decided to walk around the house before trying the door, and try to figure out whether anyone was home.

I had to pick my way through the bushes that had crowded up to the walls, thriving on the runoff from the roof. I got grit in my shoes. Protected from the wind, my face grew hot and my thighs squeaked together. I could see the shine on my nose. I raised myself above the sill to look in the kitchen window and felt a weird twisting in my chest to see the familiar plastic cups of dirt and vermiculite with ailing baby cacti in them, the dusty chunks of copper ore, quartz crystals, peridot, Apache Tear, hematite, spar, pumice, obsidian. There was nobody there. Nor could I see anyone through the plastic tarp when I reached it, nor the bedroom windows in back. The pebble-glass bathroom window betrayed no shapes, and I heard nothing through the walls.

By the time I reached the other side of the tarp-covered split, I felt sure there was nobody home, and I had an idea. I could pry up the edge of the tarp where it was already loose from the patient interventions of the weather, and I believed that then, if I turned myself sideways, I could slip between the two halves of the house and in this way enter without drawing any attention. This I carried out.

Once inside, I felt like laughing. I seemed to be too tall and in danger of toppling into the cool dark spaces that kept unfolding themselves before me with a sort of silent merriment, like a magician's trick. I careened through the rooms, few as they were, giggling and coldly sweating. Maybe I already had what Granny called "a touch of sun." Everything was familiar but exaggerated, like a cartoon. Doors were angled slabs cadged from Stonehenge. A doorknob was a huge silly form, and my hand too seemed huge, turning it.

Our old bedroom door opened only partway, bumping against a stack of boxes. The room had become a storage space, heaped high with cardboard boxes and filing cabinets, and there was a metal desk wedged into one corner on what had been Blanche's side of the bed. Nothing of our room as it had been remained, except the Alice in Wonderland curtains, though the Cheshire Cat was much faded.

Where was the dollhouse?

I rummaged. It was not in the closet. It was not in my parents' room, or in their closet, or in the kitchen, or in the sitting room, neither behind the TV nor atop the wardrobe. I went back to the bedroom and looked in the closet again and found it. I had not noticed it because it was encased in a double layer of green heavy-duty trash bags fastened with twisties, and spare pillows and winter coats were heaped on top of it. But one chimney pot stuck through the plastic and gave it away.

I got a kitchen knife and sliced open its cocoon. The plastic sank back; the dollhouse gave me a knowing look.

There it was, demon of so many dreams, my first home.

Things the Dollhouse Contained

Wheeled baby walker

Playing cards

Corkscrew

Bowl of apples

Pair of spectacles resting on an open book

Bust of Sterne

Mousetrap with a mouse in it

Sash windows, most of which still moved

Salt cellar (out of scale)

Half-finished watercolor of a bucolic scene (cow in field) on an easel

Rolled napkins in napkin rings

Library with books by Burton, Johnson, Diderot, et al.

Wax boar's head on a platter

Candlestick with a flame all of blown glass

A wreath woven of hair around a funeral portrait

Monkey in a cage

Toy horse on wheels

Pictures with tiny labels "Christ Betrayed," "The Unhappy Marriage"

A wax miniature of Mother Shipton the Yorkshire witch

An ivory backscratcher in the shape of a hand

Punch and Judy theater

A serving plate with molded oysters

Was anything missing?

No.

Yes.

The dollhouse had held something else once, something important.

Donkey-Skin

The morning after we shot Dr. Goat something scrabbled at our window and showed a tiny pink claw. We crept over and saw a monkey's old face under hair white as penicillin mold. We opened the window and popped out the screen and took hold of the bony wrists she held up. She weighed no more than a cat. We had to lift her only partway, then she spilled over the sill, onto the floor.

"Is she going to get up?" said Blanche.

"Come on, get up. Don't be weird." I touched the cleanest part of her with my toe. She flinched and began to warble quietly at her knees. Odors mustered up.

"Am I hurting you? I'm not hurting you. Get up!"

She rose like a mist, as far as our waist. She could not stand up straight, and seemed afraid of the center of the room. We encouraged her as far as the bed, where she made herself scarce: a pinch of knees and elbows. "Do you think she's hungry?" Blanche said. We padded quietly to the calm, dark kitchen and put some slices of squashed bread on a plate and tried to stretch them out a little. We had to climb on the counter to reach the peanut butter. As we were climbing down again, someone screamed in our room. We got there just after Papa, still holding the greasy jar. Mama was in our room, and Donkey-skin was in the dollhouse.

She occupied the living room, dining room, and kitchen. Her hand stuck through a door into the pantry, which had preserved that dividing wall. The others were flattened. The second floor was bowed over her back. Even so, she should not have fit there. Donkey-skin was—thirteen? Fourteen? But

she was starving. Her skin, "luminous," we had fancied, "phosphorescent," we had embroidered further, was dull and flour-white between the blooms of filth. Her eyes were crusty. She watched us with a look that reminded me of a chuckwalla's when it has wedged itself in a crack and nothing short of a crowbar will pry it out. It was the sanguine eye of a lizard, unemotional. It would look just the same in the beak of a redtail. Her frock, rickrack trimmed, cack-edged, was a foul frill around her waist, and the hair between her legs was sick yellow, like grass trapped under a cow pie, and her toenails were yellow too, and curved like claws.

Mama gulped and ran outside, though she was still in her pajamas. I heard the front door slam, the crunch of footsteps, diminuendo.

"Do you know who this is?" said Papa.

"Donkey-skin," said Blanche. "*Princess* Donkey-skin."

Papa nodded. "Would she like to come out?"

She would not. She did not feel like coming out for a very long time. Papa went away, and we heard him on the phone. Mama came back, but she left us alone too. We sat next to Donkey-skin and Blanche croaked and honked at her in the language of the animals. After a while we could tell she was listening. At last, almost inaudibly, she said, "Cunt."

She slid out. Even then she crouched and held her arms tight against her body, as if she were fitting herself in a small, invisible box.

We took her down to the Time Camera to find her some clothes. We took her picture first. It's lost, but I remember that her eyes are closed, or caught in a blink. Her waistband is riding up under her arms, and the bodice puffs out emptily above it. Her bent legs are too thin, her head in its nimbus of etiolated hair, too big. She looks like Tweedle-Dee in a dress.

We didn't want to touch the shitty dress, so we cut it off her with scissors. She crouched on the floor while we ran her bath. She didn't seem to know what to do with it, so we climbed into it with her. She settled down into the steam, swearing softly. She looked like a skeleton. I did not think we could have combed her hair even if she had let us try, but we rubbed shampoo in it and dipped her skull underwater, and watched her pale hair swim. She would not let us clip her toenails.

She stood perfectly still, though her body formed the shape of a question mark while we dried her. We had to pick up her arms ourselves to poke a bunched towel at the tufts under them. We didn't attempt the patch between

her legs. After her hair fuzzed dry we put her in it: the dress, the most beautiful dress. It was blue velvet, midnight blue, with a full skirt and a bustle, and lace around the neck. She could hardly move for the weight of it, but she followed us down to the Time Camera and stood for a long time looking at herself in the mirror we keep for the tourists. She whispered something and then let us tow her in front of the camera. That picture's lost, too, but I remember she was standing up almost straight, her white shoulders rising out of the blue, like a water nymph rising from a pool, preparing to pull you in and keep you there forever— No.

Like a princess.

We took her back to our room and let her crouch in the corner while we read. We were a little bored with her. After a little while we noticed a clear puddle advancing across the floor. "She peed!" Blanche said, outraged. I didn't say anything. *I* wasn't the one who had let her out. "We aren't going to keep her, are we? She'd have to go to *school!*"

She didn't have to explain: at the mere idea, my neck and ears burned. After a while we heard a truck rattle up to the house, and the front door open and close, and Granny's voice alternating with Papa's in the kitchen. Shortly the door opened and closed again, and Max joined the conversation. Mama broke in from time to time with a sort of wail, but the low reasonable rumbling of the others soon resumed. Then Papa came and got us and led us by the hand out of the room past Granny and Max and Mama and out the door and up to the end of the road to look for a vulture he said he saw who might have a hurt wing and need some help and maybe a splint we could help him make with balsa wood and strips of an old towel. We could not find the vulture, and when we came back to the house Granny was gone, and so was Donkey-skin and the beautiful, beautiful, pee-wet dress.

"Where did Donkey—the princess go?" Blanche said.

Mama smiled. "She ran down the stairs, and all that was left was one tiny glass slipper."

"No, I mean really," said Blanche, and I was amazed. For Blanche there had never been any "really." But Mama didn't seem to hear. We sat down at the kitchen table and began to play the erasing game, drawing things and erasing them, drawing and erasing. We played industriously and with few wasted movements like workers in a factory that produced ghosts.

Blanche was worried about infrastructure. "We should draw roads for

them to walk on," said Blanche. "Water. Food. Toilets. Toilet *paper*. And—how do the erased people talk to each other?"

"Very *quietly*," I said.

She shrugged slightly, and thought. "How do you spell silence?"

Mama, automatically: "S, I, L—"

"That's not what I meant." She drew a princess with her mouth open in a big O. She drew a speech balloon with no words in it. She erased the princess, leaving just the speech balloon. Then she erased that too.

How do you spell the loudest noise you ever heard?

Papa exchanged a look with Mama, and ran out the door. Mama sat still a moment, then whirled up. "You stay here," she said fiercely, and, leaving the door ajar, ran down the street after him. I saw Papa lean out of the office door, telephone receiver at his ear, and beckon her in.

The roof started knocking and rattling. Something hit the kitchen window and a crack shot across it and glass tinkled into the sink. Something struck and then swarmed over the roof like a wheelbarrowload of marbles. Something that might have been a saguaro cartwheeled past the door. We ran into the bathroom and crouched in the empty tub, waiting for the world to end.

But the world didn't end. The rattling subsided to an almost inaudible sifting and soughing and then stopped altogether. A little embarrassed, maybe even a little disappointed, we got out of the bathtub, sat back down at the table, and started drawing again. I heard the car starting up and the sparge of rocks as it spun out. Mama came to the door and squinted in at us, monochrome with dust, nodded, and left again. Through the cracked window I saw her marching up the hill, hunched and purposeful, digging her toes into her daisy-trimmed flip-flops. A long time later I heard the car come back and Mama's voice, asking a question I could not hear. Papa said something. Mama gave a little cry. Papa spoke some more. Then he came in with a strange careful look on his face. I ducked my head.

"Girls—"

Sometimes our local drugstore displayed a wire bin full of defective toys for cheap. Lots of our toys came from this bin: plastic models with no instructions and dried-up paint pots, Pepto-Bismol-pink baby dolls that drank from their bottles but didn't pee, so they grew heavy and leaked from all their joints. Once we picked out a book of scenes with parts missing. You

were meant to fill in the blanks from the sticker page, but the sticker page was missing too. Still, it was easy to tell from the outlined shape what went there: a dog, a fire engine, a plume of smoke. The vacant outlines had the look of objects only just departed or arriving presently. That's how absence ought to behave, turning up on time to do what the missing thing would do in its place: if smoke, then billow; if fire engine, then speed keening through the streets; if puppy, then bounce around the feet of the absent onlooker. You ought to be able to recognize what's missing by the shape of everything going on around it. But "Impossible to reconstruct exactly what happened," said the paper. "All evidence was destroyed in the catastrophic explosion." A match, a cigarette, or a bolt of lightning could have started it off, or spontaneous combustion in a pile of rags left near the gas pumps, which might have been leaky, if not properly maintained. (As if Granny would permit piles of rags. Or leaky pumps.) When the underground tank caught, the gas station blew, just like Granny always said it would. Sky-high.

Ordinary Things

I had too much to carry. I unlatched the dollhouse and stuck my rolled notebook in the nursery, where it immediately expanded to fit. I had to set the dollhouse down to open the front door, then hold the door open with my foot while I picked the dollhouse up again and backed into the squeaking frame of the spring-loaded screen door, feeling with my foot for the step down. The prematurely closing door banged into the dollhouse, which hit the door frame and recoiled, driving its eaves into my clavicles and its base into my groin. The kitchen knife I had put in my pocket dug into my side. The baggy screen behind me had pulled out of the frame at one side and snagged my dress.

Extraordinary difficulties with ordinary things always make me want to laugh with joy. I heard of a man who got wound up in a piece of wallpaper he was putting up and died. When there are so many portentous struggles, how profound to wind up stuck in glue. A moth struggled up and battered softly against my neck, beat on a window of the dollhouse, then reeled down to flatten itself against the door frame.

Suddenly there was no resistance behind me, and I lurched back and turned. There was Max, holding the door for me.

I blushed to the roots of Blanche's hair. "Hi. I'm just in town for—I was getting the—" I hoisted up the dollhouse, by way of explanation.

"Oh, thank Godfrey. Your mother has been making me move that thing from one closet to another for the last fifteen years." Max's hair was completely grey now, and dashingly brushed back, and she was wearing jeans and cowboy boots and a turquoise bolo over her black western shirt. "Holy

cow, it's good to see you, Nora. And Blanche too, hi Blanche. Haven't seen you in donkey's ears. I would give you a hug, but I see your hands are full."

I chuckled dolefully.

"You've picked a fine time to visit. Your mother's down at the Mutatis Mutandis tent camp, and your father's just leaving to join the Abolitionists at HQ," Max said.

"Mama's back?"

"I've hardly seen her, but yes. She's been organizing for the Oxymoron ever since. You know, she and your father were instrumental in planning the whole agree-to-disagreement. It's the first thing they've done together in years. Quite sweet, really. If you're here for the action, you'd better get down there. It starts at twelve hundred hours. I reckon I'll be playing Shoot-Out at Noon to an audience of ghosts."

"I'll probably head down there soon."

"Well, I hope you have time to stop by later on. After the shoot-out I'm more or less free. You'll find me at the office in the Chinese laundry. Have you seen the Chinese laundry? It's new. I had to give up running the Time Camera myself after we got so much tourism, and now I'm just a damn executive, not to mention running for mayor, which takes me down to Grady more often than I'd really like."

"Max, I have a question."

"Mm?"

"You remember our neighbor, the one we called Dr. Goat?"

She looked at me strangely, I thought, but said only, "Dr. Goat? Suits him, somehow."

"What happened to him?"

She frowned. "What do you mean? He moved away. One of our employees lives in the house now, Badman Bill."

"I thought I killed him." It sounded ridiculous. "I want to know what happened to his body." I saw again the scuffed place in the desert pavement. I would always see it, because it was mine now, a tiny lesion in my memory, where something noxious had been removed. The trauma had been erased. But you can't erase the erasure itself, not without causing another trauma, and so on.

"Killed him!" she laughed. "He probably deserved it. I never liked that man, ever since he kicked poor old Fritzi. But I'm afraid your imagination has run away with you. He's alive and well in Pahrump."

"Are you sure?"

"Look, here comes your father," she said. Did she sound relieved? "Hey Lenny, look who I caught skulking around! She's digging up a little ancient history. But I say, let dead dogs lie. Though if you ever want to write a history of Too Bad, I can tell you I've learned a lot figuring out how to fake it. Techniques of adobe architecture, mining—in fact your father and I have filed a small silver claim, and we're making money from that too, not big money, but enough to bring in a little year round. Haven't we, Lenny?"

"Hi, Nora. Let me . . ." He put his arms awkwardly around me.

"Hi, Papa."

"What's this about ancient history? You showing some interest in the old homestead at last? Going to write us up?"

"Actually," I said, "I was just wondering if you remembered when Donkey-skin came to the house. The—she was the daughter of our neighbors down the road."

"*Donkey-skin?* As far as I know they didn't have a daughter. You girls always had a fantastic imagination."

"You found her. She was hiding in the dollhouse." I watched his face closely.

"You didn't often have friends over, although maybe once or—in the dollhouse? No, that's—" He stopped. "It's strange you should remember it that way," he said gently. "That was you in the dollhouse. After all the . . . when Granny died, you hid there. I mean you tried, because of course you didn't really fit. The dollhouse has never been the same, you can see where it was broken and reglued if you take a close look. You wouldn't come out."

"Until I made those hats," said Max.

"Max had a stroke of genius and made little house-shaped hats out of construction paper and balsa wood. Do you remember those? Wearing them, you were willing to come back out into the world. We let you wear them as long as you wanted. One day you just showed up for breakfast without yours, and none of us said anything, and that was that, you seemed to be fine, though you had zero interest in the dollhouse after that. But Blanche never really—well, eventually the hat just fell apart. But I guess she just never really came out of it."

Vanishing Twin Syndrome

I put down the pencil parallel to the edge of the blank piece of paper and stood up. "I think I'll go lie down in my room for a while," I said.

"Good idea," Papa said, with evident relief.

I sat cross-legged in front of the dollhouse and began rearranging the furniture. Blanche, trying to contain sobs, was making the awful strangled noises of a vomiting dog. I breathed slowly and carefully through the fracas in my chest, and eventually it quieted and I took my hand out of the fainting room and allowed her to wipe her nose on the back of it. Then I turned my head.

"Do you think it was Donkey-skin?" Blanche said. "Do you think the princess blew up the gas station?"

"Shut up."

"But do you?"

"I said, shut up." I could feel I was going to do something. Blanche would push me to. I waited for the push with what was almost a vengeful pleasure. It became as though I were not to blame for what was about to happen but she was, for not knowing what I would do if she kept talking.

The push came. "Was it because of our stories?"

"What stories?" I said lightly.

"The stories we told, about how a cloud was going to lift us all up to the Land of Thin Air, how all it took was one match." Her voice was high and strained, but she toiled on. "We even gave her the matches!"

I moved a piano from the parlor to the bedroom and back to the parlor.

"Nora? Was it our fault?"

I opened the secret attic room and picked a tiny book from the bookcase, flipped its blank pages, and put it back. I picked up the miniature dollhouse we'd carved out of soap.

"Nora?"

I sniffed the dollhouse thoughtfully. Smell of clean mothering. "*Whose* fault?" I said. "*Our* fault?"

She tensed. "You—we both—"

"*Tss!* Who let her out, Blanche?"

She dimmed.

There are brine shrimp that lie dormant in the playa for years of dry weather, and then one good rain will leave some puddles, and suddenly they are rippling everywhere like tiny albino eyelashes and breeding with exemplary enthusiasm. They are alive as can be. When the puddle dries up the brine shrimp dry with it. They're little ciphers, flakes of code. Promises, promises. They sleep, but they'll wake. At the moment Blanche had no thought of telling on us, I knew. But she would do it all the same. She would start whining about something, and Max would get it out of her. Or she would decide it was her duty to tell, this new, stubborn Blanche.

I went into the kitchen. "We're going for a walk," I told Mama.

"Yes," she said. "That's a good thing to do." She frowned, and her chin crumpled into ugly red and white creases. She thought we wanted to be alone to say our good-byes to Granny. I felt bad for fooling her, but also scornful of her for being so easily fooled.

"Do you have a canteen?" said Papa. "Don't be gone too long."

We climbed fast without talking all the way to the lookout rock. I was still clutching the dollhouse made of soap, and it grew slippery in my sweaty hand. The dry air was harsh in my throat, and Blanche's panting very loud in the closer ear. At the top we lay down on the hot stone, lungs working, thighs trembling. The sky went black around the edges and then cleared to blue.

When we sat up we saw the crater. A few cars were parked where the road ended at the Grady edge of the pit, and one cop car idled on the other side, lights flashing. We watched a car approach from the top of the range. It appeared and disappeared as it wound its way down through the switchbacks. Then it pulled up behind the cop car. The cop got out and went back and stood at the driver's window. Then the cop went back to his car and the other car backed up and turned around. We watched it appear and disappear going back the way it came.

Blanche was looking at me. She wanted me to look back so she could say something. Ignoring her, I unstuck my fingers from the smeary house and

stood it on a rock, unslung the canteen from around my neck and poured lukewarm water into my cupped hand. I bothered my hands together and summoned up a little cloud of lather. Scuds of it dropped on the sand, where it shrunk and tightened.

Finally she said, "It's not really my fault, is it?"

I sighed. I felt excited, but I spoke slowly and ticked off each point on my slick fingers. "Who kept going back, over and over? Who ate the snake, who *insisted* on eating it all herself? Who played interpreter? Who let her out, against my advice, and even went back for the smokes that dropped the fatal spark? Who killed Dr. Goat?"

At this last item she shuddered. "We did. *You* did!"

"Did I? Can you prove it?"

Her face expressed puzzlement, then comprehension, then fear. "You mean someone's going to get in trouble," she said. "You mean it's not going to be you."

"Did I say that?"

She ducked her head and fidgeted at a patch of lichen on a rock. The lichen was blood-red. The rock was fist-sized. I imagined hitting her on the side of the head with it. Then I imagined her hitting me with it. The two of us staggering back and forth on the bluff: the climax of a Western.

But there was no need for anything so *physical*. I looked at the finger that had been scratching, red now with powdered lichen. "Hmm. Your trigger finger is bloody. I wonder what that means." She said nothing. "OK," I said briskly. "We both know what happened. Now what are we going to do about it?"

"Do?"

"They'll probably give you the iron mask. It wouldn't be fair to lock me up for something that wasn't even my idea. Think. Your head. In a cage. For life. Of course, you're a juvenile. They might let you out after a few decades." A few tears dropped on my right leg. "See, now you're crying," I said, disgusted. "God, you're just a—an open book. Are you going to do that when they cross-examine you? You can't *cry*. You'd better not even open your mouth. Let me do the talking." I paused. "But why should I? Maybe I should turn you in."

"What?"

"You killed three people, including Donkey-skin. At least three. That's practically a killing *spree*. What if you can't stop now that you've tasted blood?"

"I don't want to kill anybody!"

"Well you should have thought of that a little sooner," I said. "Then I wouldn't have had to send you to the Land of Thin Air."

Her fear swept up the back of my neck, a hot wind. "What do you mean?"

I did not know whether it was possible to do what I was considering: pry Blanche so far out of her orbit that she could no longer find her way back. Archimedes reputedly said, "With a lever long enough, and a place to stand, I could move the earth." I thought I had the lever. But a place to stand, well. If I had that, I would already have won.

"We need to put you somewhere you can't hurt anyone else. Somewhere quiet."

"I know why you really want to send me there," she said. "I'm not stupid. But you don't have to. I can keep my mouth shut."

"You will," I promised. "From now on, you're going to be silent as—as the *grave*." I looked out across the bajada. Blanche looked too. The cop car's lights were tiny beside the great crater.

"I—" she said in a small voice.

"Do you want the iron mask?"

"No, but—"

"Are you Sad?"

"Yes!" she cried, mistaking this for sympathy, and burst into tears, tilting her head against mine. I shook it off.

"Then you should repent." I was confident now. I could feel the present changing into the future, and Blanche right beside me, helping.

"I do!" she choked.

"Do you really? Really, Blanche?"

"Yes!"

"Good." I unscrewed the cap of the canteen and wound the little chain it was tethered to around my forefinger, so it didn't swing forward into the stream, and directed a shining, wobbling cord of water over the tiny white house. The house started to glide down the rock. I curled a dreamy hand around it. One squeeze from Blanche, and it would scoot out over the escarpment, an architectural meteor to astonish ants and beetles. But I coaxed it safe into the hollow of my hand. It was already slightly tacky, and as it lost its shine it looked more like tooth or bone, something belonging here, or like a satellite of the playa below, that as the day dimmed was beginning to glow with its own light, as was the dollhouse, which threw a faint glow on my thumb as I rubbed it over the gables and cornices, smoothing them down to knuckles. I decanted a little more water over it, in which it bobbled around,

and lathered it up. When I parted my hands the dollhouse stood on its own cloud. "You know what this is?"

She shook her head, slinging tears.

"Penitence."

She started to speak. So I washed her mouth out with soap.

Emptiness is next to godliness. We don't really want the heavenly host to turn up for a photo op. We'd rather not see their satin skirts cinched around the thick waists, flouncing around thighs ill-accustomed to them, we'd rather not see the archangel dressed like a pantomime dame for a Christmas gala. The paintings that depict them are embarrassing: all that shine, the lacquered cheeks and powdered noses and quaint gestures, the dopily oversized wings wagging, the dopily undersized ones vibrating unconsciously, like a puppy dog's tail. You could see right up their skirts when they come stepping down the clouds, but would you really want to inspect those well-turned thighs, symmetrical as piano legs, or solve the silly problem of the crotch and whether angels wear underwear or have anything to hide in the first place? No, what's divine is disappearance, and I don't mean a running takeoff or a big flap-flap. I mean a spasm of absence, absolute. Almost atomic. Only take away the mushroom clouds and shadows, too, and the spectator's silly sunglasses. Leave nothing. Really nothing.

Vanishing twin syndrome usually occurs in the womb. In our case it came about considerably later in the developmental process.

The strangest thing I'd ever felt was my own right hand.

The second strangest thing was my left hand.

So these are fingers! I tightened them.

The soap squirted out, described a tiny parabolic arc, glanced off my knee, and hit the sand.

I was on my knees, sitting on my feet. Those are my knees, the third and fourth strangest things. That sting, a stone, under my left kneecap.

The fifth and sixth strangest things: feet. My toes jammed together in the hot hollow of my shoes, the knuckle of my big toes stubbed against the roof. Nettle-burn of the crushed baby toes.

The froth of suds on the sand had shrunk and dried to a brittle lace. The dollhouse was much smaller, and several ants were stuck to it and were waving their free appendages in unhurried complaint.

Soap removes dirt: No more filthy girls in cages. No more filthy men twitching and burbling up cellophane red words I could forget now. No fragrant, bluebottle-bothered zoo. No Chris Marchpane slobber and poke. No kinship with mutant lambs and severed breasts. No kinship, period. No ghost town, no dollhouse, no Sadness, no stories, no greasy smear of me on her, and her on me, and both of us all over the poor poisoned landscape. No we. Witness the American dream: a self-made self. I was alone.

There was a dot of cold on my cheek. Not my tear, hers.

All the apparitions that stuff diaries and occasional books, those solicitous and mute or minatory and moaning spooks and goblins, hobs and hants, were piffle compared to this. As if to exist were anything special! The world always has room for one more thing. The walls will stretch, the floor will bear the weight. In this vale of stuff it's not presence that's a mystery. If we could call down angels and aliens and make them citizens, we'd treat them like all the other immigrants! No, what we like about the things that go bump in the night is that we never stub our toes on them. We love our missing persons. A lost child milks the heart from the back of the carton, but the kid slurping her Grape-Nuts is just a brat.

I was not haunted by her. There wasn't a wisp or a whisper left. There was nothing there but the unremitting presence of everything that was not her. The world seemed intolerably full. The air ruffled my hair, tugged at my sleeve.

That was the dreadful thing: how complete the world was without her. There was no sudden shortage, no gap. Everything pressed forward as it had always done, with no commemorative diffidence. The world is too much with us, but with me especially. I had gotten used to splitting it with someone else. Funny, I had always padded my portion. I didn't know the whole shebang would be more than I could stand.

Twain, re *Those Extraordinary Twins*: "It was not one story, but two stories tangled together, and they obstructed and interrupted each other at every turn and created no end of confusion and annoyance. I could not offer the book for publication, for I was afraid it would unseat the reader's reason. I did not know what was the matter with it, for I had not noticed, as yet, that it was two stories in one . . . a farce and a tragedy. So I pulled the farce out and left the tragedy."

And then there was a long, long silence.

The Land of Thin Air

I started down the slope of the bajada with the dollhouse in my arms. The juniper thinned out and was replaced by a quantity of catclaw and mesquite and whitethorn bushes through whose tiny leaves the light poured like water through a sieve. The sun could find hardly a single point of purchase on the land from which to throw a shadow. I did pass one group of cottonwoods that must have struck their roots into an invisible spring. I thought I remembered them from my childhood, though they had been much smaller then. They were squared off below at cow height and the desert pavement beneath them was spackled with dung. One cow stood under the trees, as black and featureless as the cow on the road sign. Every other thing I saw was bleached by the almost-noonday sun to a uniform dun color like that of institutional carpeting.

The dollhouse made it hard to see where I was going, and my dress seemed to fling itself at every thorny bush and swoon there, and each time it happened I had to set down the dollhouse and disentangle myself, though after three or four such episodes I lost my patience and from then on just tore myself away, to the permanent detriment of my garment. Once, this labyrinth had no secrets from me; the honey mesquite with the oriole nest in it or the ocotillo that had grown up through a tangle of rusty barbed wire were as good as street signs, but new bushes had sprouted, and the arroyos had grubbed out other paths through the earth. For a short stretch my feet seemed to find a clear path of their own accord, and I sped up, thinking I had found my way, but then I stepped right into a sprawling prickly pear, tried to change direction while my whole weight was still leaning into the

step, and fell. Luckily I landed on top of the dollhouse, not in the cactus. As it was my ankles were pretty well chewed up, and a bit of the railing around the widow's walk made a row of tiny regularly spaced puncture wounds over my hipbone.

I had been making my way along a hogback between two deep and nearly parallel arroyos. I had been keeping to the spine, more or less, but now I veered to the right and considered the strip of red sand at the bottom of the cleft. The periodic flash floods that scoured the arroyos kept them relatively free of cactus and small scrub, though the bigger bushes that thrived on what moisture lingered there sometimes closed over them entirely and made them impassable to anything larger than a jackrabbit. Still, the sand might be easier footing for a while. I rode a slide of pebbles down, the dollhouse in my lap, my shoes filling with grit. I half-fell, half jumped down the damp cutbank at the bottom and landed on my knees in the hot sand. A caucus of quail burst out of a bush with a heart-rattling racket of wingbeats, and the late-coming pebbles disturbed by my slide clattered down and bounded off the cutbank and were silenced in the sand.

Then it was quiet. It was also much hotter, or rather the real heat of the day could now be felt; my face, chest, arms were suddenly wet with the sweat that, above, the constant wind rising up off the valley had dried. The wind was only intermittent down here. When it passed through, the snake grass on the banks sighed, just audible under the crunch of my footsteps, the rattle of insect invisibles in the mesquite bushes, and the grasshoppers that popped up clicking and careened in a short arc, making a ratcheting sound or a soft *brrr* depending on what kind they were, and then froze where they landed.

The arroyo proved a good road, broad enough for me and my burden to pass freely between the bushes on the sides of the V. A flood had preceded me not long ago; the cutbanks were raw and still damp, and there were dark sickles of moist sand in the shadowed curves of the flood bed. Out of old instinct, I turned to look at the sky behind me; Papa had taught me that rain falling miles away in the mountains could cause a flash flood here below under a sunny sky. But the eastern sky was clear and blue.

I became aware of a new sound, a hum at the lower limit of hearing, and noticed a number of bees swinging slowly around me, though without signs of excitement. I stopped, lowering the dollhouse for a better look, and saw the swarm clinging to a bent, leaf-stripped sapling, like a wad of snagged flood-cargo. The bees crawled slowly in mesmerized implosion, knitting, in-

folding, and droning steadily. Individual bees would lift off and circle lazily around and then cement themselves to the clump again. I watched for a time. The ball of bees was about the size of a head, and I had the sensation that it knew I was there. Well, of course it did know I was there, collectively. But it seemed about to speak. Slowly, so as not to alarm the bees, I toiled back up the side of the arroyo. The bee wardens kept pace with me without seeming to exert themselves until as if by agreement they all fell away.

When I gained the ridge I set down the dollhouse and bundled my skirts up and pulled down my underwear and squatted to pee. The warm wind came up-slope balmy and cool on my labia. My pee brightened the colors of the pebbles and sank steaming into the sand between them and disappeared. I stayed squatting longer than I had to, gazing out at the expanse below. The playa was blank white and lost the clarity of its edges in its shimmer. It was much bigger than it looked from my vantage point, extending to the south well beyond the point at which it was cut off from view by the lower slopes of the mountain to the left of us, which although part of the same range as the one I now descended, advanced farther into the basin. It was taller, too, and from it I had been told one could make out some sort of construction upon the playa, deep in the restricted area. But from here the playa was of an uninterrupted whiteness. It had an illusory softness that made it look like a piece of cloud set in the earth. The highway, which passed in a straight line across the valley as if to demonstrate there was nothing there worth stopping for, cut across the northern end of it. It cut across the town as well: a sparse botheration of low buildings, lawns as rectangular as accent rugs, and a clump of messy cottonwoods plundering the spring from which the town drew its water. Trailer roofs and sprinkler jets shone. A little way out of town the drive-in movie screen was showing bone-white to a host of tents, and beyond it, stranded in the middle of the basin like a cow pie, a pile of tailings from the mine bore a white G.

I bobbed a little to shake myself off and patted myself dry with quick touches of a hot clean rock that gave me little shocks of pleasure, and then I set down the rock, which was already dry, and pulled off my underwear over my shoes and left it on a rock and went on with the air blowing soft and clean up between my legs. When the slope had gentled enough that the arroyos began smoothing themselves out into wide stone washes I ceased to follow their westward trend and angled leftward, to the southwest. Soon the scrub was lower than knee high and comprised mostly of creosote and snake

grass, and I could move more quickly. My arms were sore from carrying the dollhouse in front of me and my lower back ached from leaning back to compensate. After a while I hit upon the idea of balancing the dollhouse on my head, where it seemed lighter and also provided a little shade, and I went on in this way and came at last to the first barbed wire fence.

I turned left, following it, until I found a section where erosion had enlarged the gap under the bottom wire and left one post hanging from the wires instead of supporting them, so it seemed to be standing, slightly aslant, on air, and at that point I slid the dollhouse under, and then followed it. Something sharp dug into my groin: the knife in my pocket.

When I got up, brushing pebbles off my hands, there were little lights flashing and zinging around me and the sky pursed and flared in spots like an old balloon, and so I sat on my heels in the thin shade of a mesquite and with my hands shading my eyes I took stock of a scatter of rabbit droppings among which ants moved like burros among boulders. I listened to a fly droning nearer, and when the sound cut out, I joggled my leg and heard it again and then it stopped and again I joggled my leg. I pulled out the knife and held it suspended over the ants but they took no notice and doing it gave me none of the slightly sick pleasure I had felt when I was practicing decapitations in what felt like another life.

That was you in the dollhouse.

Memory, itself a kind of dollhouse in which I replay in miniature the story of my life, swung on concealed hinges and opened a new wing. Tables twirled on tiny turned legs, chairs played musical chairs, freezing in new positions, and now I did seem to remember the quiet creaking of the papered balsa walls pressed coolly against one ear; the miniature light fixture above me, too close for focus, so it divided into two partially overlapping, diaphanous images; the feeling of safety that infused my whole body with warmth and lassitude.

I pulled the dollhouse toward me and rolled it over till it stuck in the sand at an angle. All the furniture hit the ceiling, and some small object on the ground floor found the stairs and rolled up them, which was down, until it came to a resting point under the roof.

I drove the knife into the base of the dollhouse. The thin wood split easily, and cracks radiated from the hole. I sawed two rough half-circles in each half of the house. When I closed the dollhouse and latched it, they made two complete circles.

I laid the house on its back on the ground and unlatched it and folded out the two front halves. It felt like spreading a woman's thighs. Then I slowly lowered myself down backward. When my neck and Blanche's found the sawed half-circles in the center, I reached out to the hinged wings on either side. I tried to lift them and found I wasn't strong enough.

I sat up again and propped the wings up with stones so that they were no longer flush with the ground but rose up aslant on either side of me when I again lay down with my neck in the cutaway, and with some of the lifting already done in this way I was able to pull the two sides up, Blanche's first, then mine, and lower them carefully over us so that the two halves of the holes met around our necks.

I lay for a moment staring out the front window at the sky. The blood was pounding hard in my head. Then I reached up and touched the front of the house and saw my hands climb, like pink King Kongs, past the windows. I sought and found the latch on the front of the house by feel and fastened it. Then I tried to sit up. Of course I could not. For a moment I panicked. Then I unfastened the latch, opened the dollhouse for the third time, folded open the front halves, sat up, propped up the whole dollhouse at an angle, and then performed the whole operation over again. This time when I moved to sit up the house came with me. Unsteadily, I got to my feet. The floor rested on my shoulders.

I was alone in the room. That's a sentence I could never form before and tell the truth. I was in the library, once the scullery. A toppled chair rolled from one side of the room to the other. A darkness weltered up to bemuse me and tiny lights swarmed through this domestic scene. Maybe I staggered: outside the window, the desert tilted and veered, but I was safe indoors. I waited. The dizziness passed, and I went on. I was protected. If far below me someone's legs were in difficulties with a succession of fanged monsters, it was no concern of mine. In any case there was scant danger of snakes now, in the heat of midday, and on the playa no cactus grew.

Stepping out onto the pure white I felt a moment's vertigo, as if I were performing some impossible act, walking on light itself. The sun seemed to shine from all sides at once. My shadow anywhere else would have seemed a figure made of light. My kneecaps and the underside of my arms burned with the light of the sun turned back up on itself.

Here because of the salt there was no sagebrush or creosote or even rabbit brush or snakegrass. There were no lizards or quail and almost no living

things at all, though I saw that in the crisp bright shadow of a Keep Out sign, a corpse-still grasshopper kept its council. There was no shade otherwise, except the stiff memorial band of shadow around each rock, and my own shadow with its precise contours, like a keyhole into which only I would fit. Rocks were few and looked incongruous there, as if some purpose of which they had once formed a part had moved on and left them there. They had a truculent, self-conscious air. I imagined they were a sort of untranslated message, as if they might have liked to be arranged into words like the rocks by the road, but had far too much to say.

That was you in the dollhouse. Did Donkey-skin ever exist at all? Or was Dr. Goat just an ugly man who had kicked a dog once? Something passed between me and the light, and I tilted back my house head, bracing it with my hands, and looked up through the smeared window. Overhead, a jet fell silently sideways. Late came the sound of it, which was also a feeling in my stomach like something rupturing. The plane was turning and catching the light so as to dissolve into it, momentarily, then pivoting like a pen spun in fingers, silhouetted, wings spread, and for a second seeming stopped and therefore falling, slipping sideways toward the earth, then curving up with an impression of strain that sympathetically affected the back of my neck. Trailing two dirty pipe cleaners of exhaust, it swung silently out over the mountains against a beatific cloud mass and disappeared until thunder broke again overhead and I looked up to see it close above, turning on its wing almost upside down, and so repeat.

Then it seemed to be gone. It left behind a tense expectancy, like an opening in a conversation in which something violent might be said.

Something hurtled into my legs. I inclined my house. It was the Mooncalf, who did not like loud noises. She stood trembling and panting between my legs, her head wedged into my crotch. I bent over, and she bucked up and daubed the front window with her nose. I found the hard spot between her eyes, where she liked to be rubbed. I had completely forgotten about her! "Clever Moony," I grieved. I should have tied her up, asked Max to take care of her.

Now that she had my attention, she came out from between my legs and began skipping and flouncing. She carried a shank of teddy-bear cactus aslant on her back like a hair curler, and another entoiled in her tail. She carried these extras buoyantly, however, wagging her tail with outrageous self-satisfaction. She had dust all over her muzzle and a fat lip on one side from

a bug bite. She did not seem surprised by my house-hat, as some dogs might have been. I wished I had another one to keep her safe.

"Blown to smithereens," I said. She wagged her tail. I said it again, liking the sound of it. "Blown to smithereens." What exactly were smithereens?

A sort of smithereen ran at me and crouched beside my shoe, imagining itself to be in hiding. I bent over it. I could see its blue throat quaking under the stiff raised bill. A smithereen was a lizard, in this case. One might have thought I meant a bird. What was it doing so far from shelter? Perhaps a hawk had fumbled it. It would not last long out here.

I have always felt sorriest for these incidental characters. You can persuade yourselves that people deserve what they get. It is possible to muster up a little venom for almost anybody, in my experience, including yourself. (Especially yourself.) But not for smithereens. One minute they are skittering over the hot stones, free and ferocious, in their own eyes at least. The next, *whomp*. A giant hand plucks them up—it did in this exceptional case at least—and feeds them in through the little front door of an airborne house just the right size for them. . . .

Suddenly I was in a Max Ernst collage! The eerily ordinary drawing room, slightly old-fashioned. The lizard reclining on the settee, sinuous and elongated, its tail a barbaric surprise on the accent rug. The confusion of scale: a giant ear visible through the drawing room door. Of course the lizard would not pose, but hurled itself against the window, slid down, and ran around the room, knocking the furniture awry. Its tail wound itself through the rungs of a chair, slung it around. I was poked in the nose by the miniature clawed foot of a miniature chair leg. The lizard found the stairs, ran up them. I heard it rattling things upstairs and thought of poltergeists.

I had never been so far out on the playa. Between the white planar surface below me and the sun above, I felt weightless, suspended in a thin but buoyant medium made of heat and light. The knowledge my feet had of the press of the earth beneath them seemed some kind of delusion or a petty thing unworthy of consideration. My head seemed very far away from my grounded sneakers. I was the tallest thing for miles. Given my size, I did not see how I could move forward at all because the hot sky pressed down against the hot earth pressing up with the hopeless determination of lovers who have fought and will do it again, and it did not seem as though there could be room for a third party in that clinch. The further I went, the more I seemed to be prying apart layers of some incandescent material.

A black beetle flew slowly careening and shrieking out its fluxing buzz like something grieving, and soon it was struck to earth as if by an unseen blow and its cry cut off. It continued crawling on the white with black pieces of its wings dragging behind like rags until it grew dusty with white powder and began to disappear. The sky was going paisley with little flares and detonations, and my mouth was exceedingly dry. It occurred to me that I might have some water with me. I felt for an upstairs window, pried open the casement like a housebreaker, and felt inside all around, touching in turn the rocking horse, the high chair, the crib. That the hand was in the nursery will be obvious, a dusty behemoth crouching and flouncing above the tender mite.

Except that as I recall we had lost baby years ago. I remember a pink blur disappearing into a citadel of thorns and cactus pads, in the gentle jaws of a pack rat. Now she lives there, joined at intervals by waves of cognate siblings, pink and bald. She lies among them at the sweet maternal harbor while they grow fur and sharp tooth and toe and play rough games with her and then at last they leave her behind, the changeling in the cradle, an eternal worry to her adoptive mother, but a lasting joy as well.

Back to the nursery, to these objects the hand addressed, greeted, then passed by, until it found the cistern, detachable, belonging to the bassinet. And unclipped this from the wall, ascertaining from its weight and slosh that it was still full, after all these years. Or perhaps Blanche had filled it at the kitchen sink before I left, but I think not. And so, clutching its booty, out the window flew the hand, like Peter Pan. It opened the front door and entered the foyer, where the cistern slipped out of our fingers, but that didn't matter, because by tilting my head I could roll it this way and that, and I entertained myself for a little while with the sound it made rolling, and then I caused it with appropriate tilts and countertilts to roll into my room, carrying a chair before it, and bumble against my mouth, where with judicious touches of the tongue and lips I disposed of the chair and brought the cistern around into position. You can imagine it took me some time to open the cock, but I had time, and so at last by dint of holding one bit between my teeth and rotating the rest with my lips and tongue I caused the cistern to release a thin stream of sour water into my mouth.

And so we went on. The sun was admonitory and unmoved. The wind came with a dry swipe, licking up grit. Suddenly a dust devil stood beside me, fox-colored and shifty. Within its swirl was a denser core. I could make

out four little hooves, and then two little noses. The two-headed lamb had a frayed velvet saddle strapped around its ungainly, sausage-like midriff, and One and a Half was in the saddle. *Mmm, mom, moo, moon, mummy*, he said. Sand scoured the panes of the dollhouse and seethed around the eaves. My body hid in the skirts of the devil, and no doubt from outside the house looked like it was carried on the wind, right past the sign that said:

No Trespassing
National Penitence Ground
Silence Please

Half Life

"*Security breach. Security breach. Security . . .*" droned One and a Half. The two-headed lamb he rode trotted close to me, and as the heads took turns leading, it veered left and right and left again, bumping me repeatedly, as if herding me. The Mooncalf stuck close to my other side. I could see only dust beyond my windowpanes, but between the two of them, there was only one way I could go. Blind, I went.

The dust devil seethed and whistled in my eaves, but I could hear One and a Half as clearly as if he were seated on the piano bench at my ear. "Penitence monitors identify a heavy concentration of perimeter-violating green blips exhibiting purposeful behavior vis-a-vis the front gates," he reported, "evocative of a ravening horde of Oxymorons boosting one another over the fence. Best est. 780-935, more coming, note some blips may represent two or more personages, recent studies employing twofers have revealed that old-fashioned imaging sensors count two heads twice or not at all. The computer has understandable difficulty with the concept 2=1, thinks Officer Pangborn."

Bump. "How do you even know what a computer is?" I said, irritated. "Weren't you born in 1783?" Even within the dollhouse, I could taste the salty dust.

"Twenty-seven solitary green blips in other border areas exhibit erratic behavior. Officer Pangborn's experience is that ninety-seven percent of erratically-behaving blips are bunny rabbits. The remaining three percent are other desert fauna. Request imaging? asks the computer. Request infrared scan, lite language-strafe, probability analysis, satellite photo? Request in-

terpretation? Imaging confirmed. Rabbit, rabbit, rabbit, rabbit, rabbit, rabbit, rabbit, deer, rabbit, rabbit, rabbit, rabbit, rabbit, rabbit, deer, coyote, vulture, rabbit, rabbit, rabbit, rabbit, rabbit, rabbit, rabbit, rabbit, rabbit, tiny house with legs."

"Ha, ha," I mouthed. His voice sounded different now, and I thought in a minute I might recognize it.

"Fucking great. Fucking Baba Yaga, thinks Pangborn, who is a Soviet spy. The computer is going insane. Happens to all of them sooner or later, here. Language gets to them. They start hedging: 1 plus 1 is two, *usually*. Babbling about sunflowers and such. Citing dissenting views. Fucking yeshiva students, fucking poets, these Penitence computers."

The dust devil slowed, drifted sideways, wound what remained of itself onto a spindle of sky and withdrew. I saw One and a Half's upper jaw part, letting dust spill down the lower head. "Blip #27, AKA Agent Black (disguised as a small house) creeps on a pixilated diagonal into the no-speakum zone. She is carrying the—"

What was that?

Wobbling behind the heat-warped air, the bobbing green and purple retinal bursts, the old impurities and new scratches in the glass windows of the dollhouse, was something unlike all these. I had the funny idea it was a city. The dollhouse lurched as I broke into a shuffle. A tiny book dinged me in the lip, a sofa champed against my chin, and after a while I saw there really was a city, standing upside down on a fault in the sky. Thin Air! The inverted houses flexed and flared and then steadied and stood firm, depending from a flake of land that was stuck in the sky like a sliver of mirror glass in an eye.

A mirage is no phantom, Papa had told us, but the reflection of some real thing on the ground below, glancing off the plane where two different densities of air meet. It could be miles away, though, and already my breath was tearing at my throat. I slowed.

Even at a walk, moving forward had become difficult. I had to plan each step before I took it. Sometimes I confused the intention for the deed. Then Moony would blunder into the back of my leg, and I would remember and move on. Each time I set my foot down, the thin crust crunched and gave way to powder as fine as talc and terrifically hot. One of the problems that preoccupied me was how to step so lightly I did not break through the crust into it. I did not discover a way. My shoes were ovens. The Mooncalf was now so white with dust she looked like her own ghost. Her tongue emerging

from that sameness that matched the sameness around her was a shocking color, almost lilac.

"She is carrying the Device," repeated One and a Half, whom I had almost forgotten. I looked back. "Computer retrieves an ancient phrase from the Penitence archives: Recommend Dollhouse Manouver?" His voice altered. "No, snarls Pangborn, and for good measure, Override, in case no leaves room for interpretation. We've got a situation on our hands. All men to the front gate."

"Well, that explains why nobody's shot us yet," I rasped. I could see our tracks through his ribcage: the zigzag path of the lamb, Moonie's neat line of divots, my twin trenches. But beyond them, a storm blued the southwestern range. I felt a tiny prickle of hope, not for myself, but for the Mooncalf, who would need water soon. Was it heading this way? As if in answer, a gust of wind banged the front door, carrying the warm spicy smell of wet creosote and sage. Moonie flopped down on my feet, heavily, and I took a step back to catch my balance. A patch of horizon yawed in the window frame. Something interrupted the view. I lost it, found it again.

One and a Half cleared his throat—which was strange, since he did not have one. "Explanation of the Device," he said. "Its intricate wiring, cleverly disguised as ordinary ink, has been laboriously handwritten by Agent Black, under the constant guidance of the mysterious Agent White. Actually, Agent Black *is* Agent White, but both are unaware of this fact. The deception is necessary, since the Device has been created through the exchange of coded messages between Black and White, an exchange so cunningly orchestrated by HQ that neither is aware of the larger purpose of her personal and at times, apparently pointless ramblings. Collapse the difference between Agent White and Agent Black and boom, no Device. Further explanation of the Device—"

"Shh!" I said. Whatever it was, it was coming toward us, drumming up consecutive puffs of white dust like smoke signals. These hung in the air, peculiarly shapely and cohesive, like thought clouds in a comic strip. I could trace the path of the pursuer I still could not make out in the advancement and multiplication of them. I could hear a rhythmic thumping coming from it, oddly offset from the puffs of dust. The light was schismatic and deceitful and so it took me a long time to determine, from its luminosity and the shape-describing shine glancing off it as it rose and fell, that what I saw was a glass jar full of a cloudy liquid. I had last seen it in the Potter Museum, at which time it had been sealed with a thick cord of callous-colored wax encircling the lid. The lid had been jettisoned since then. In this jar the two-

headed pig fetus that had been its quiescent inhabitant for more than a century was hopping across the gypsum like a contestant in a sock race. The fetus was splitting its sides, literally: bits of its intestines were wandering out of the crack and flailing in the splashing formaldehyde, so more and more it was swimming around in her own innards, and occasional shreds popped out of the top of the jar and sprung away across the desert. The jar came to a halt before me. The fused faces rose up from within it, their ivory snouts pointing left and right, like a cartoon of a pig shaking its head. "We we we!" they squealed, in two-part harmony.

I yanked my foot out from under The Mooncalf's heavy haunch and took a step back. The Mooncalf scrambled to her feet.

"Want to hear a poem?" said the pig. Receiving no answer, it cleared two throats, closed four eyes, and opened the pale clefts of its mouths. "After you," said the mouth to the right.

"No, after you," said he to the left.

"If you insist," said the one to the right, and cleared its throat again. "A Siamese twin had two cunts—" he said.

"Which performed some astonishing stunts!" said the other.

"What found its way in—"

"To the right-handed twin's—"

"Would come out of the left-handed one's!" they chorused.

"Isn't that *juvenile*?" crowed one. The other, in a hushed voice: "You know, I never got to grow up. I've been a baby in a bottle my whole life. Or do I mean, my whole death?"

"I'm sorry," I rasped. My voice sounded strange.

"Not your fault! Want to hear another joke? Knock knock—"

"The *Device,*" insisted One and a Half. But it was Blanche's voice. I turned and ran until my sweat darkened the carpet and my breath clouded the windows of the room. It didn't matter, there was nothing to run into here. I could hear Moonie behind me, panting raggedly.

When I slowed at last, the thumps of the pig jar slowed commensurately. In the intervals between, I heard something else.

I swung around, plucking open the front door. Through it I saw something tattered and stained sneezed out of the dust cloud that had boiled up behind us. It was a dead pigeon, flattened to a discus. I turned to keep it in view as it rolled like a plate on its rim up to and past me and right in the doorway of a low enclosure of crumbling concrete from which rusted iron

rods reached skyward, twisting. In the middle of what had once been a floor, it wobbled and spun and sang, "I saw another self behind the glass and I flew to challenge her and broke myself against her. I lie between the sky and the reflected sky, and only in my shadow can I see any depth to this world." Then it tipped over, and silence fell on the ruins.

I had arrived. Erewhon. Never-Neverland. The Erased Place, the Silent Planet; the Land of Thin Air. Doom Town.

Under shoals of dust I saw the crumbling relict of a paved road leading into the ruins. I went down it.

There was no city. Just sheer sky, white dust, and the broken remains of a fiction. The buildings, what was left of them, were pitted and gnawed, as if by a teething infant of colossal proportions. They were concrete bunkers, nothing like the Manor; most were roofless. Doors and windows were absent altogether, or clung in a few charred fragments to hinge and sash. The desert within the walls was no different from the desert without, except that the wind eddying around the corners had swept the gypsum into tent curves as regular as computer models.

I passed a steel octagon bolted to a post—a stop sign, paint-stripped. I passed a blistered, excoriated school bus and a clutch of cages whose bars had rusted thin as thread, snakeweed growing up through them. Their doors hung open, swaying slightly. Out of one strolled a turbaned mongoose, piping a sad tune. "Here's where the animals were caged, to be turned to smoke and rumors," he said.

I fumbled blindly for the Mooncalf, folding her sleek ear around my finger. "I know," I said.

"Are you Sad?" It was my voice, this time. I didn't reply. The mongoose resumed his melancholy tune, and from around the charred stump of a telephone pole appeared the scrambled kittens.

"Is there a part for a monster in this musical?" they chorused. "Can I do my audition piece?" They struck a pose.

"How comes it that thou art out of hell?" one head inquired.

"Why this is hell, nor am I out of it," said the other. Then they broke into song, cabaret-style.

I was born the same day as my body
Our folks gave us both the same name
They scolded me when she was naughty

She broke my toys,
She played with boys,
I got the blame.

My body gets all the attention
My body is everyone's pet
On my birthday, I barely rate a mention
She takes the cake,
I lie awake,
That's what I get.

She wears my clothes, she borrows my umbrella
Fishes for change in my purse
She gives away all the secrets I tell her
Sleeps with my lovers,
Hogs all the covers,
Rewrote this verse.

Other voices joined on the last verse—One and a Half, the pigs, the two-headed lamb.

I know one day my body's going to kill me
We'll be buried beneath the same stone.
She'll never know how it will fulfill me
When worms and decay
Bear her away
And I'm alone.
Finally alone.
Leave me alone.
Leave me alone.

Thus serenaded, I walked straight through Doom Town and out the other side, then turned and followed its perimeter until I met my own tracks going in, accompanied by Moonie's and other, stranger ones. Those first ruins were different from the others, I saw now. The walls were a warmer color and had worn down into softer, rounder forms, closely interlocked. They were obviously the foundations of a single large house, not many small ones. A por-

tion of the front steps still led up into the sky. They were faced with stone, lovingly laid: you didn't put that kind of effort into something you meant to destroy. I might have found the Manor after all. It wouldn't hurt to think so.

I stepped inside, and turned. If that's the front stoop then the living room would be . . . I took a few paces to my left. Now I was in the dollhouse, *and* I was in the dollhouse. Doubly home: a good place to wind up. I pulled off my dress—the wrong way, because of the dollhouse on my head—tearing the collar as I worked it down over my hips, and laid it out by feel on the ground. The animals congregated around me as I took off my shoes and socks and placed them side-by-side under the dress where feet should go. Then I unlatched the house and cracked it open. My notebooks fell out in a shambles and something slapped onto the sand: my passport, the fake one with only one name in it. I stacked the books and laid the passport on the dress, something like a memorial stone. The congregation applauded, those with paws, or rocked their jars on the gypsum. Then I closed the house again and latched it.

I sat down naked beside my flat, paper-doll self, in the shade of my house-hat. Moony flopped down between my legs. The wind was picking up. My dress fluttered on the ground and skirmishes of gypsum passed over it. Some dust remained, caught in its folds, and as these deposits grew heavier and spread out over the flimsy fabric the pattern faded, the colors paled, and my dress began to disappear. The light grew strangely yellow. A cloud-shadow raced over us, and then a shadow stayed. I waited.

And nothing happened.

The two-headed kitten nudged my hand. The two-headed chick scratched lines in the dirt, looking at me meaningly. One and a Half tapped me on the shoulder. "What?" I said.

In the pompous voice Blanche used for class presentations, One and a Half said, "Explanation of the Device: The National Penitence activity has not destroyed sadness, but split it from its source. Sadness survives but cannot be understood, except by animals, ghosts, and the body, where it takes the form of disease. What cannot be understood, cannot be cured. The Device refigures sadness by painstakingly crocheting together the knowledge that Penitence has erased and dispersed."

I sighed and picked up my notebook from the pile. What had Blanche wanted from me, all along? A story. And this one was not finished.

After that day on the mountain, Blanche shut up. She slept the rest of the day and all that night; the next morning, she was still sleeping. My parents and

Max did not seem, at first, overly concerned. "Shock," they said wisely. "Let her sleep." They did not ask me what had happened on our walk and of course I did not tell them. As for Dr. Goat, Donkey-skin, and Granny, nobody spoke of them, and their bodies were, as far as I know, never found. And so I was free to believe that Granny was not dead, but in Oaxaca. She had blown up her own gas station to dispose of Dr. Goat and prevent a witch-hunt against our kind—*Siamesas Diabolicas!* Then she'd high-tailed it across the border with her sidekick Donkey-skin. When Mama and Papa said we were going to Mexico, not long afterward, I was sure we were going to meet them, though the ostensible reason was to take Blanche away from the scene of her trauma. I sizzled all the way with secret excitement, and when we crossed the border I was bouncing on the seat. Everywhere we stopped I scanned every face, peeked into every alley. I played along, not mentioning Granny once. It wasn't until we were in the long line to reenter the States that I said, "When do we get to Oaxaca?"

Mama rumpled my hair, then, as an afterthought, Blanche's. "Our little world-traveler wants to know when we get to Oaxaca! We're not going to Oaxaca, funny, you have to take a plane to get there."

"Are we taking a plane, then?" I persisted.

"Not on this trip, hon."

I burst into tears—of rage, not of grief. I still believed Granny was waiting there, eating pastries with her feet up on a metal chair, while Donkey-skin played Shady Ladies on a xylophone.

I never shook that idea, I just forgot it, like everything else we didn't talk about. But what I did not remember remembered me. Right after the gas station exploded, there was a big rain. Talkers said the dust cloud from the explosion might have seeded the clouds. The lake had water in it for the first time in months, like a mirage taking itself really seriously, and a boy from my high school passed out face down with a bottle in his hand and drowned in an inch of salt water, brine shrimp kissing his pickled lips, while his friends played "Jesus walked on water" fifteen feet away. Drowned, in Grady! Gloria Barnes said you could hear the toads groaning in the ditches down in the basin from as far away as Ryder Peak. Then the rainy season commenced, and it too was heavier than usual. Some of the barrel cacti got so fat with water that their accordion folds smoothed out, then burst.

And another strange thing happened. Especially around the gas station (where the gas station had been, that is, not where they were bulldozing for the new road), but in Too Bad too and even in Grady, though not on the

playa because of the salt, an unfamiliar crop started coming up: two tiny, soft green leaves on a pale stem. Nobody could figure out what they were. Some said they came from outer space, that some Martian Johnny Appleseed had laid his green thumb on us. The sprouts grew uncommonly fast, and put out more leaves, then divulged a heavy spiky bud. Sunflowers! The local paper did a story about it, mentioning Charles Fort and rains of fishes. The pastor wrote a sermon around it. A Rocke Shoppe printed up postcards.

The knowledge took shape before it found words. A sunflower burst open behind my eyes, scattering seeds that sprouted and bloomed too, so that all my mind seemed brightly lit, no shadows left. In its blaze, a snapshot of Oaxaca faded, curled and blew away. Sunflowers, sunflowers, sunflowers! Granny's fake titty, scattered for miles, was blooming.

I unclipped my pen from the spiral binding and started writing. For the second time, I walked up the highway to Too Bad and slipped through the seam into my old home, where the dollhouse gave me a knowing look. Granny blew sky-high again, I washed Blanche's mouth out with soap, and Max held the door for me. For the second, third, hundredth time, I hid in the dollhouse for protection, and walked out onto a dry lakebed as blank as a page, my shadow inked beside me. "Silence Please," I wrote. "Explanation of the Device." "Are you Sad?" "Sunflowers!"

Everything happens twice, first in the fact, and then in the telling. At least twice: the telling, too, is doubled by the hearing of it. A cleft passes through the center of things, things that do not exist except in this twinship. That cleft is what we sometimes call *I*. It has no more substance than the slash between either and or.

I have spent my whole life trying to make one story out of two: my word against Blanche's. But we are only as antithetical as this ink and this page. Do these letters have meaning, or the space around them? Neither. It's their difference we read. There are two kinds of blindness, that of darkness and that of light. But in the cat's eye of our intersection I can make something out: a faint, awkward figure in a frilly dress, like a child's drawing of a princess. This is her story, which is ours.

I could have told this story better. I could have tried to invent a new grammar with room for both of us. Wedged in a second person, *you*, between the first and the third. But it is too late for that. The storm is close now. Thousands of Oxymorons are throwing blankets over the barbed wire and swarming onto the Penitence Ground. Hundreds of guards are backing up

slowly, waiting for instructions. Officer Pangborn is arguing with the computer. A lone police car, lights silently flashing, is turning off the highway onto the road to Too Bad where Marshal Max is pacing slowly away from the place where Badman Bill would be if he were not currently practicing nonviolent resistance techniques. In San Francisco, Trey pulls on a sequinned dress with 20 sleeves, and twirls, a one man Busby Berkeley routine. Seen from above, he's a spiral nebula in which new worlds are born every minute. Audrey consults a baby name book. She has just had word that her tissue has accepted the plastic form, and she should start thinking about choosing a name for her new head. Or should she take a new name too? She considers Lula and Sula, then hears my spectral voice: "My last request—don't do it!" Louche invents a Bilateral Spanky-Panky. "This hurts me as much as it hurts you," she says, and for the first time in history, this statement is true.

The two it takes to tango, tango. The sound of one hand clapping is heard by a Mr. Clive Henman of Arundell, England, who will never be the same again. Others, who did not hear it, will never be the same either. A two-hundred-and-twenty-year-old house, divided against itself, stands a little bit longer. Max fires a blank at nobody, growling, "There ain't room in this town for the both of us." And I am closing in on myself on twin tracks. I have made a Venn diagram after all: this book.

Here, I'll draw it.

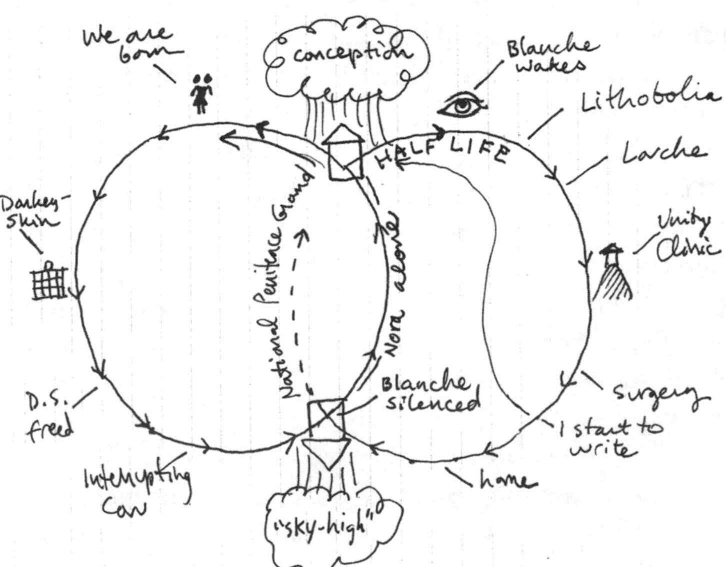

One and a Half leaned over to look and nodded approvingly. "When the two coils of its bifurcated structure are joined, and Agent White and Agent Black meet in a single point bearing every resemblance to a period or full stop, the Device will, not ex- or implode, but un- or anti- or deplode, restoring the lost sadness to our riven world."

Look at the diagram. Imagine this: each ring is a clock face. One runs clockwise, the other, counterclockwise. Now fold the left one onto the right. You will observe that they now turn the same way, clockwise. Spread them again. Fold the right one onto the left. What direction are they rotating now?

You can turn back the clock, and without even trying. Every clock runs backwards and forwards at the same time. It just depends what side you're looking from. So I hold out my arms to the dead. Come One and a Half, come all. Dead Animal Zoo, come. Even Dr. Goat, even old Nickel-and-Disme, if you're really dead. Come back, Granny. Come back, Princess Donkey-skin.

Come back, Blanche.

Five, four, three, two, one—

Contaminant lifts from throats and thyroids, milk cans and feed bins, orchards and sheepfolds.

The infant lambs receive their own hearts like valentines delayed in the post.

Fallen hair swims up to the scalp, lost teeth root themselves in the gum.

From creosote and honey mesquite and yucca and jojoba and saguaro and barrel cactus and cottontail and mule deer and rattlesnake and roadrunner and phainopepla and canyon wren and bush tit and quail, wasp and stink beetle and praying mantis and scorpion and centipede and tarantula, a silvery ash flurries up. It spools into the middle air, augmenting the pink cloud that is already withdrawing, homesick and heading home, posting southwest fast as the wind and then faster than any ordinary wind and arriving already brawling upon the scene of a colossal donnybrook, joining a collocation of spectral fists contesting with one another rampageous and unaimed at first but discovering, now, a shared disposition for downward and inward.

A towering white body sucks in its stomach, hunches. It is concentrating, concentrating.

The Hilton Twins are singing "Me, Too." I see the Biddenden Maids passing out cakes two at a time to a shuffling line of two-headed lambs. Lines

of decapitated ants march out of a crack, holding their heads like clutch purses. The ground splits and biform skulls rise up through the grit, scaring up binary bunnies (white tufts held high) and bifurcated rattlers, tails a blur (there's danger they will bite themselves in the confusion). A rabbit's tail that should have disintegrated twenty years ago hops by in the company of Mike the Headless Chicken. The Interrupting Cow sweeps up, leaving a trail of black beetles across the white. Something flame-colored crosses the window pane in triplicate. It's Molloy, Malone, and the Unnamable, swimming in air.

The mushroom cloud remembers what it had forgotten: the bomb. Things unhappen quickly now. A sphere of influence as delicate as a soap bubble detaches itself from the edges of the universe and begins to move inward, acquiring emphasis. With a declaration composed of the synchronized seizures of a myriad eardrums it shrinks to a point. A hurricane hurries home. A fireball draws itself inward, pulling trees and buildings erect behind it. Cinders become birds, shadows bulk up, fur and flesh glove the bones of a terrified dog that is calming quickly. A light as bright as a second sun shows him settling to chew his mangy tail. Then the light goes out. The split—

"Mu!" says the Interrupting Cow, and the storm arrives. The first raindrops strike the gypsum around me and come up Braille. Each bead of water landing in dust clothes itself in dust and rests on dust without wetting it. Landing on my powdered leg it makes a skin-colored circle with a frilled edge. On my page, a shiny blister plump with inky slur. Rain taps on the roof. There is an answering ruction from my upstairs inmate, waking from a reptilian reverie, alive after all. The Mooncalf plunges her muzzle into her plump haunch, then assaults her foreleg, mistaking the sting for an insect's. The storm is a towering blue-greyness with definite edges that does not resemble a passing event or a state so much as a material thing. In its upper reaches horizontal lightning joins something to something else with sudden scripture, and converts a mass of cobbles and smoke into a cathedral vault. Then thunder throats the news, and the Mooncalf bolts wide-eyed under the stairs, spraying my book with grit.

Turn the page.

I am writing without looking, watching the storm-front whelm the distance still between us.

Yards away. It gains the laggards of my recrudescent friends, slicks skulls, disarticulates scapulas and clavicles, plashes in the pigs' vessel.

,   .
.
.
,   ,   .
,
,
.   ,   ,
.
,   ,   .

?   ,   :   .
;   (
).   .   ,“
.   ,   .   ?”
“,”   .   —   —   .   ,
.
.   .
,   .

.
,   ,   ;
.   ?   .
.
:   ,   ,   …
.   ?

I look down and see that my ballpoint has been sponged clean by the wet paper. The page is blank, except for the occasional ding where I bore down on a comma or a dash. But I can read it perfectly.

I scribble until the ink comes. I want to go back and fill in the gaps. But somewhere in the house, someone is speaking.

“Nora?” I say.

Author's Note

Half Life could hardly be mistaken for nonfiction, but it brushes lightly against fact in a few places. Fallout from nuclear testing does cause genetic mutations, though conjoined twins are by no means common downwind. The National Penitence Ground is very loosely based on the Nevada Test Site, though I have freely rearranged the local geography, flora, and fauna. Neither Grady nor Too Bad exists, but Doom Town does, though not exactly as I have described it. Until a few years ago, when its collection went to auction, so did Walter Potter's museum. One and a Half was a real person, and his skull still resides in the real, and marvellous, Hunterian museum. Other historical conjoined twins who haunt this book are Mary and Elisa Chulkhurst, Millie-Christine McKoy, and Violet and Daisy Hilton. Mike the Headless Chicken also existed, demonstrating that one can learn to live without almost anything.

Thanks to Rocky "Hard Rock" Miller, who told me stories about prospecting for uranium in the '40s and '50s, and showed me some ore. Thanks also to Allucquere Rosanne Stone, whose account of a class she taught inspired Louche's Transitional Objects workshop, and to Scott Larner, a former student, for turning in a piece consisting of three electrifying pages, entirely blank except for punctuation marks. Avital Ronell and Judith Butler both helped shape my Venn theory, though they may be surprised to hear it. The unattributed quote about Millie-Christine in the Manual is by a nineteeth-century French journalist whose nom de plume was Touchatout; I found it in the excellent *Millie-Christine: Fearfully and Wonderfully Made*, by Joanne Martell. Martell, not Audrey (as Nora claims), was the translator. Countless

other books helped me, but especially Carol Gallagher's magnificent *American Ground Zero.*

Finally, most particular thanks to Jonathan Lethem, Kelly Link, Caroline Janiak, Wesley Stace, Coates Bateman, the Howard Foundation, Ira Silverberg, Jill Schwartzman, Sean Meyer, and my sister, Pamela Jackson, who is nothing like either Blanche or Nora—fortunately for both of us.